Foul *Hooked*

A Shagball and Tangles Adventure

A. C. Brooks

This book is a work of fiction (sort of). Any person, place, or thing, that bears any resemblance to someone you know, or somewhere you've been, or some thing you've seen or done, is purely coincidental (for the most part). The rest is all true. I do, of course, reserve the right to deny even knowing you, should you file a lawsuit against me claiming you were depicted as a character in this book. You may *think* you know who you are, but you *know* you know who you're not, and so do I. So quit reading this and start reading the book. You'll laugh, you'll cry, (possibly, if you're a girl), and if you like it enough, you'll buy my next book, which is tentatively titled: "*How to keep friends after you've fictionalized them in a book*"

Acknowlegements

A special "THANK YOU" goes to my wonderful wife Penny, who encouraged me to actually start writing this book, instead of just talking about it, which is easier, but not nearly as much fun. Without her guidance and feedback, there's no telling where this story might have ended up...except in the trash. Thanks for keeping me on track and letting me know when to say when.

Chapter 1

Splash! After jumping some seventy feet or so off the stern of the cruise ship, *Good Time II*, Mini-E hit the water hard. Although painful, he thought it ironic he had gone from pig-ass drunk, to stone-cold sober in record time. A feat he wished he knew how to replicate during a roadside sobriety checkpoint. *Well it sure as shit doesn't matter now, because this is the end,* he thought. He wasn't exactly sure where the hell he was, but a good guess was the middle of the ocean. More precisely, about halfway between Miami and the Bahamas. Far enough out that even if somebody saw him go overboard, there was almost no chance someone would find him before he drowned. *Works for me.* The more he pondered it, he was amazed he didn't get knocked out from the fall. He should have been sinking straight down to Davy Jones' locker by now. Then he noticed a big air bubble had formed inside his jumpsuit. It must have inflated like a parachute during the fall, and had him bobbing along the surface of the unusually flat sea.

Oh Christ! Not the jumpsuit, not the fucking jumpsuit. He hated his white sequined jumpsuit with its "Mini-E" embroidered on the sleeves and lapel, but when you're an Elvis impersonator (albeit a short one), it's part of the gig. OK, not just short, but an honest-to-God, perfectly proportioned midget. The zipper on the front of the jumpsuit had jammed from the fall, and, try as he might, he couldn't free it. *Damn it!* He tried reaching his little arms over his shoulder to push the air out, but came up short. *Of course, story of my freaking life.* He really didn't want the whole drowning thing to drag on; if he could just get out of the suit, he'd suck down some seawater and go Titanic. "Fuck Me!" he yelled, as he struggled with the zipper again, bobbing his way north in the Gulf Stream, destination unknown.

Chapter 2

"It's over, Shagball. We don't hook some fish tomorrow and the show is over. Kaput, fini, c'est la vie."

To be truthful, I wasn't entirely shocked at the words coming out of my producer's mouth, but it didn't make it any easier. *Shit!* I couldn't believe how quickly my luck changed. Only a year earlier, at the urging of a friend, I answered a classified ad looking for a fishing show host. Somewhat amazingly, I had been hired. I say somewhat, because I knew I needed more than luck to get hired—I needed a plan. I came up with one, and after getting the job, I guess you could say it worked like a charm. As luck would have it, the interview/audition was on a Friday afternoon. Friday was my day off, so my plan was to catch some dolphin, throw 'em in the cooler, and head up to the audition.

That's exactly what I did that fine March morning. I headed north out the Boynton Inlet, trolling my usual squid and ballyhoo rigs. The lines in both riggers popped out in a hundred and fifty feet of water, directly off the Ritz-Carlton. *Bingo!* Dolphin were jumping through the spread! Soon I had four nice ones in the fish box of my twenty-foot, 1982,

Robalo center console. After cracking a cold one, I powered up the twin Evinrude 88s and headed back to the dock. There I filleted all but the biggest fish, a nice twenty pounder.

When I got to the audition, there were about twenty-five other wannabe fishing show hosts in front of me, waiting their turn. Most of them seemed to be bass fisherman who kept talking about how many fish they caught the day before. *Bass fisherman?* I thought. *Shit, my odds are improving.* After seeing most of the competition quickly shuffle in and out of the audition looking dejected, my name was called and I was greeted by a towering man of about six-nine who introduced himself as a television producer. He stood behind a video camera and had me answer a bunch of background questions, finally asking why I would make a good fishing show host. I told him, look, number one, I can catch fish, and number two, I can guarantee we'll have a good time doing it. Not surprisingly, he told me that over the course of the week he auditioned about a hundred and seventy fishermen who all said the same thing. Some of them were even well-known local captains, unlike me.

"Sure," I said. "I bet every one of them told you about all the fish they caught *last week,* or how you should have been with them *yesterday,* right? That's just a pile of typical fisherman bullshit. You wanna see the dolphin I caught a couple of hours ago? 'Cause they're on ice...in the trunk of my car."

He looked out from behind the camera. "No shit?"

"Do I look like I'm shitting? Come and take a look." On the way out to my car, we passed the rest of the auditioners. They looked *just* a little bit confused as we left the building. When I got to the car and popped the trunk, there was the tail of the big dolphin sticking out of the cooler. I slowly opened the lid to reveal the nice twenty-pound bull (it was a male), in its entirety. Next to it sat a couple of gallon-sized zip locks filled with fresh fillets.

"Wow! You caught that today?"

"Like I said, just a couple of hours ago...want some fillets from the ones that *didn't* get away?"

As he walked back to the studio carrying a big sack of fillets, I drove away thinking the big bastard might turn out to be my biggest catch ever. Turns out, I was right, for a while at least. Now I was listening to him tell me my show was about to be canceled, because on our last five trips we had been skunked. We hadn't caught a single fish, none at all. I was skunked, as in not being able to catch a cold. Skunked, as in a big fat zero...nothing but goose eggs...absolutely nada. I had gone from being the envy of the dock to the laughingstock, and couldn't figure out why.

Chapter 3

The Gulf Stream was carrying Mini-E north, at about three to four miles an hour. He figured he had been in the water for about an hour, and had maybe a half hour left before the air bubble in his jumpsuit dissipated to the point where his four-foot-two, hundred-and-thirty-pound body, would start sinking like Lindsay Lohan's career. Straight to the bottom. Do not pass go, do not collect two hundred dollars. He thought he had been more than drunk enough that when he jumped off the ship, it would be over quickly. *Wrong.* Not only did he survive the fall without any serious injuries, but his damn jumpsuit acted like a flotation device. With the zipper stuck, he was trapped in the suit. As the air slowly seeped out of it, he reflected on his last night on the cruise ship.

He had finished his five o'clock show, and wasn't scheduled to perform again until nine, for the after-dinner crowd. Per usual, he was following his normal routine of going for a workout, and then heading back to the cabin he shared with his girlfriend, Darla, for a quick shower and a bite to eat. Only this time, when he got to the ship's weight room, he found it temporarily closed while maintenance workers finished cleaning the carpet. It had just been soiled by an overweight passenger who did too many squats after eating at one of the ship's buffets. *The shit you see on a cruise ship, literally.* So back to his room he went. He figured he might catch Darla before her dinner shift began, and get a little action. He needed it. Darla had been acting more than a little moody lately, and he thought it might be an opportunity to get things back on track.

He felt hopeful as he slipped the key card into the lock and stepped into the room. Now, recalling what he had walked in on, he splashed some seawater on his face to make sure he wasn't having a nightmare. He immediately spit some out. *Nope, no nightmare here, just a shitload of salt water.*

Darla had been lying on the bed, on her back, with her head toward the window, engaged in a sixty-nine position. As the unknown party's head lifted from between her legs and looked straight at him, he realized she might have been the ugliest chick he had ever seen. He staggered backward in horror, fully expecting the ugly chick to pull a Linda Blair. She was that disturbing. He then promptly dropped to his knee and threw up. Stunned, he was still retching as the ugly chick quickly dressed and headed down the hall. Darla dressed too, and stepped into the hall, saying, "We'll talk later, after my shift." Without another word, she walked away in the opposite direction of her lesbian lover, as if it were no big deal. *Yeah, right.*

The problem was, Mini-E didn't feel like talking later...or now...or ever again for that matter. He simply grabbed his emergency bottle of Cuervo, and began drinking. For some stupid reason (oh yeah, he was pig-ass drunk), he managed to suit up and head to his nine o'clock show. Once on stage, he began slurring the words to "Heartbreak Hotel." Normally a very good singer who drew plenty of applause, he was quickly heckled by the crowd. Tonight was not the night for heckling Mini-E, however, and he ended up punching a passenger and pissing on stage. *Or was it the other way around?* He couldn't recall, but when the entertainment manager stormed in, as the passengers stormed out, Mini-E told him he was just impersonating the summer-of-seventy-seven Elvis. Not amused, the manager told him he was fired when they got to Freeport. Mini-E replied, "Fluck you, I quit now." Then he staggered to the back of the boat, and without a second thought, launched himself over the rail.

Chapter 4

"What?"

"You heard me, Shagball, it's over. No fishy, no showy." Jamie, my producer, didn't mince words, I'll give him that.

"Don't worry," I told him, as he walked to his Yukon. "Tomorrow were gonna slay 'em. They're gonna be thick, just like the old days...like fleas on a dog's back." I didn't really believe it, though, and I knew that he knew I didn't believe it. *What the hell was going on? Why couldn't I catch a friggin' fish all of a sudden?*

After landing the show, I had been true to my word, and we caught nearly every saltwater fish imaginable. You name it. We caught dolphin, wahoo, cobia, snook, snapper, kingfish, and sailfish...everything but a big, blue marlin. It was just like I told Jamie, "If it has a fin, we're gonna bring it in."

Due to his freakishly tall stature, Jamie was able to get camera shots that others couldn't. Combined with my increasingly easygoing on-camera dialogue and some great fishing footage, the show became quite a success. Sponsors were fighting to be part of it, and I took full advantage by personally negotiating a deal with Viking Yachts to be the official boat of our show...

Fishing on the Edge with Shagball. Turns out the CEO was a big fan, and he invited me for cocktails on board one of their boats when I bumped into him at the Palm Beach International Boat Show. After downing a few drinks and trading a few fish tales, he offered to give, that's right, give me, a used, thirty-eight-foot convertible. The only stipulation was that I use it for the next three years on the majority of shows we shot off the Florida coast. I knew exactly which boat he was talking about, and he knew it. He probably saw me crawling all over it with unbridled lust in my eyes earlier in the day. I reflected on his offer for exactly one nanosecond before my highly seasoned negotiating skills kicked in. I looked at hit him with a big fat smile on my face, and asked, "Fred, where do I sign?"

The very next day (which was the last day of the boat show), I inked a contract with both Jamie and Viking Yachts. Then I was handed the keys to the custom 1982 Viking. A great fishing boat with classic lines, especially for free. Call it coincidence, karma, whatever...that the Viking was a1982, the same vintage as my little Robalo that helped me land the show in the first place. I was marveling at my good fortune as Jamie and I cruised south down the intracoastal. We were headed to my new slip at the Water's Edge Marina, in Boynton Beach. It was next to the local watering hole Three Jacks, and across from the Habana Boat restaurant. Jamie and I had become good friends by then, and he was happier than a pig in shit when he joined me on the bridge with a fatty in hand. I remember thinking, *"Could life get any better than this?"* Answer? No.

Now, just a few months later, I was sitting in the cockpit of the Viking I christened the *Lucky Dog,* wondering why the fishing gods had decided to cut bait on me. Wondering if I was going to lose my show, my boat, and my dignity. *Who was I kidding?* To hell with my dignity. I didn't want to lose all the perks (i.e., free drinks, food, and tackle) that my fishing show status provided. Determined not to let it all slip away, I headed down the dock to Three Jacks, seeking answers. Namely, why was I, or was it the *Lucky Dog*, seemingly jinxed?

Chapter 5

With the air in his jumpsuit just about gone, and his head barely above water, Mini-E noticed he had drifted into some type of floating grass, mixed with debris. *Great, just great...There has to be a bunch of crap in the water when I wanna take a big gulp and end it.*

That's when he saw it. That's when his blood ran cold. *Shit no! Oh shit! Shit! Shit!* In the moonlight, reflecting off the water, a large fin cut a swath through the floating debris, not twenty feet from Mini-E. Cursing his little arms, he slowly began pushing himself backward, away from the shark. A minute ago, he was ready to gulp down some seawater and pay a visit to Davy Jones's locker, but the thought of being eaten alive was something he hadn't contemplated, and it did not sit well. *Not one fucking bit.* With his legs in the act now, he propelled himself faster, in sort of a reverse breaststroke. Bump. His head hit a five-gallon bucket. *What the hell?* The shark seemed to be circling him now. Keeping his eyes locked on the ever-nearing fin, he kept swimming backward. *Christ! The debris is getting thicker!* Now he brushed up against a mini-fridge floating in the heavy flotsam. *Couldn't be a full size fridge that I could climb into, has to be a fucking mini-fridge...cute.*

Momentarily distracted, he lost sight of the fin. *Oh shit! Where'd it go?* Panicking now, he thrust backward as hard as he could, when, "Ahhhhh!" Mini-E screamed in terror as a sharp pain seared through the back of his neck. *He got me!* But why was he still conscious? In fact, why was his head still attached to his shoulders? *Let's see...my head's still attached to my neck, and my neck's attached to...*"Owwww!" he yelled, as he realized something was stuck in his neck. He reached back and felt a large piece of wood. With both hands, he gave a mighty shove, and the object dislodged with a splash. With one hand, he stroked the water, turning to see what he backed into, while the other probed the wound in his neck. *Shit! I'm bleeding like a stuck pig! This keeps getting better and better.*

As he completed his turn, however, Mini-E's hopes suddenly leapt. He saw what he had swum into. It was a nice-sized pallet, and he had been pierced by a nail sticking out the side. *A pallet. A beautiful old, barnacle-encrusted, big-enough-to climb-my-tired-ass-up-onto pallet. Hallelujah! There is a—Shit!* About thirty feet away, coming straight at him from the other side of the pallet, he saw the fin. Although the pallet was only about five feet away, the man-eater, or in his case, half-man-eater, was closing quickly. With adrenaline pumping through his veins, Mini-E did his best Michael Phelps (minus the bong), and shot toward the pallet. *Swim! Swim! Swim! His brain screamed.* As he reached the pallet and began pulling himself up, he could see the fin disappearing below the other side. *This is gonna be close.* With a last gasp, he kicked with all his might. He lost his shoes in the process, but made it up on the pallet. *Yes! I made it! Frigging shark's not having Mini-E tartare tonight, baby!*

In fact, Mini-E was absolutely correct. No shark *was* going to make a meal out of him. As he rolled over and sat up, a huge splash covered the pallet. He watched in disbelief as a large bottle-nosed porpoise surfaced, and began tail-walking around the pallet, making the same sound as Flipper. Falling flat on his back, Mini-E laughed so hard he started to cry. Looking up at the stars, he thought about Darla, the closet carpet-muncher, and about how jumping off the cruise ship maybe wasn't the best idea he ever had. Realizing he no longer wanted to die, he started laughing again... then promptly passed out.

Chapter 6

The Water's Edge Marina where I kept the *Lucky Dog* was a throwback in time, nestled among newly built high-rise condos. It was a throwback because the marina housed a flavorful mix of commercial fishing boats, dive boats, sport fish charter boats, boat and Jet Ski rentals, and a few recreational boats like mine. In marinas like this, the competition for customers can be fierce, and you don't want to get caught in the crossfire. In general, the charter boat captains and crew hate the dive boats, and vice versa. The dive boat operators hate the recreational boaters. The recreational boaters hate the commercial fisherman and the dive boats. Practically everybody hates the Jet Ski rental operators and the people who rent them. Everybody hates everybody, and there's always plenty of tension and drama on the dock. It's a perfect circle, if you will. A perfect circle that encompasses a vast and ever-changing supply of dock rats. Not furry disease-infested rodents, but humanlike creatures often one step from the gutter, nearly all with apropos nicknames. You can find them 24-7, lurking in the shadows, sometimes looking for work, sometimes just lurking. Any odd job will do...as long as it pays cash.

Cash that enables them to buy beer, booze, broads, and crack...but not necessarily in that order. While some are good people who are maybe a little down on their luck, some are just plain skeevy.

As I walked down the dock toward the bar, the heckling began. "Hey, Shagball! Heard you're still on the schnide! Heh, heh, heh." *That was from Ratdog; his name says it all.* "Hey, Shagball! Heard you ain't caught a fish since Christ was a kid." *Ah, another gem from Skeeter.* I just kept looking straight ahead, ignoring them. I knew better than to acknowledge their taunts, but had to admit it was getting to me. *This shit has got to stop.*

Of course Shagball isn't my real name, my real name is Connor Jansen. Most everybody calls me Kit, but once the show took off, it was back to Shagball. A name bestowed on me back in my junior golfing days. True, it had nothing to do with fishing, but when I proposed naming the show, "Fishing on the Edge with Shagball," Jamie loved it, and we ran with it.

As I passed the fuel dock and ship's store, I saw a friendly face sipping a can of Budweiser. "Hey, Graybeard, how goes it?" I asked.

"Better than you, I guess, heard about your troubles."

"Yeah, seems I'm stuck in a bit of a slump, but tomorrow's another day." *Keep telling yourself that Shaggy. Damn.*

I finally made it to the bar, and was glad to see my good friend Captain Ike, also nursing a Bud, the longneck variety. "Hey Tooda, how's it going?"

"Not bad, Kit, have a seat." I nicknamed him Tooda, because a bad back keeps him onshore unless the seas are two to four foot or less, hence, Tooda.

Every decent fisherman has someone who showed them how to *catch fish,* and not just *fish,* and Tooda showed me. When I first moved to Florida over twenty years ago, I began regularly chartering his boat, the *Hose Me,* with a couple of other guys. We soon became friends, and he taught me how to wire up a ballyhoo rig, as well as his own custom squid rig. It's a trolling combination that has caught me countless fish over the years.

As I took a nice long pull from an ice-cold Heineken, he said, "So I hear you're still the mayor of Skunktown."

"Good news travels fast, huh? Cap, what am I missing here? I'm using the same rigs I always do, fishing all my go-to spots, and everybody else is catching fish but me."

"Have you changed up some lures?"

"Check."

"Re-spooled your lines?"

"Check."

"Matched your GPS to your trolling speed, to make sure you're not going too fast or slow?"

"Check."

"Hmmm."

I signaled the bartender, and she brought us a couple more beers.

"Sounds like maybe you've been hexed."

"Hexed?"

"Yeah, you know, hexed, jinxed, voodoo doll kinda stuff. Hell, it could be as simple as someone putting bananas on your boat."

"Bananas? Are you serious?"

"Damn straight, you got bananas on the boat, you're not catching spit."

"Come on, I thought that was just some old fisherman's superstition."

"It is, but it's true."

According to Tooda, the legend came from Cortez, Columbus, or maybe one of the Pilgrims. For all I cared, it could have come from Noah, Moses, or Kevin Costner in *Waterworld*...I needed answers. Anyways, Tooda claimed that one of these early long-distance voyagers had a cargo full of fresh fruit, vegetables, and grains, including a large quantity of bananas. The bananas quickly rotted and spoiled all the rest of the food. The ship and crew were soon beset by scurvy and plague. Ever since then, most seagoing captains have shunned them as being bad luck. "Plus, you can slip on them," he added. *You don't say.* Well, true or not, I was grasping at straws, and willing to try anything. I thanked Tooda, bought him another beer, and then headed back to the *Lucky Dog* to look for bananas.

Chapter 7

As I cut across the parking lot, I saw another buddy of mine, Hambone, haggling with some Haitians at the back of his pickup. Hambone was a charter boat captain who also held a commercial fishing license. This enabled him to legally sell fish to restaurants and the public. He also had the most seniority of all the charter boats in the marina, and considered himself king of the dock. He had his back to me, and as I neared his truck, I saw him take some money from the Haitians. They happily walked away holding sacks full of fish.

"Hey, Hambone, moving some of those tasty blue runners?" I asked.

"Blue runners? Come on, dawg, you know that's Haitian prime rib."

We laughed and shook hands. A blue runner is a small reef fish, usually caught while trying to catch much tastier fish like snapper and grouper. They're normally used as live bait for much larger species, like kingfish, wahoo, and sailfish. Some people, however, and not just Haitians, will eat virtually anything that comes out of the ocean. That makes guys like Hambone very happy.

"How 'bout a cold one?" he asked, reaching into his cooler. "I won't toss it, so you don't have to worry about catching it."

"Very funny. Sure...why not? You can put your two cents in as to why my touch runneth cold, while my frustration runneth hot."

As he handed me an ice-cold Coors Light, I marveled at his physique. He was about three feet wide and five and a half feet tall, weighing around 260 pounds. Sort of a cross between a fire hydrant on steroids and a sumo wrestler. Hambone used to work as a bouncer in Delray, back in the day, and I heard plenty of stories about his bouncing skills. All the stories had the same theme. Hambone shouldn't have been called a bouncer because when he puts you down, there ain't no bouncing. You stay down...for a long time. Now I'm no pipsqueak at six-two and 225 pounds, but just the same, I was glad we were friends. I was pretty good at taking care of myself, but it was nice knowing he would cover my back if I needed it.

"So what do you think, Hambone? Tooda says maybe I got bananas on the boat. I was just headed there to start looking."

"Could be. I've had the occasional customer bring bananas on board, and if they do, I pitch them over. No exceptions. You don't mess with superstition."

"So I've been told. I'm outta here, thanks for the brewski."

"Hang on a sec, Kit, try this lure on your next trip. One of my customers gave it to me; maybe it'll help change your luck." With that he handed me an odd-shaped, one-ounce jig head. It was painted white, with white feathers, and a 9/0 hook.

"I'll give it a shot, Ham, thanks."

As I headed off to the *Lucky Dog*, I figured Hambone gave me the ugly jig because he would never in a million years use it. It probably had little chance of catching anything other than sea grass...But with my luck the way it was, I hung it on a lure holder in the cockpit as I stepped aboard.

Chapter 8

I tore the *Lucky Dog* apart. Starting in the cockpit, I looked everywhere. In the empty fish box, in the battery compartment, under the bait prep sink, and under the gunnels. I lifted the floor hatch and searched by the engines, but found nothing. I went up to the bridge and checked under the dash, and behind the electronics. I even looked up by the radar, but still found zilch. I went down from the bridge and into the cabin, where I opened all the cupboards. I found some sunscreen in a yellow tube, called Banana Boat. Not taking any chances, into the trash bag it went. I searched the galley and found a couple of yellow hand towels. *Say good-bye, little towels.* Finally, I went through the head, and the forward berth. The only additions to my outgoing trash were a yellow toothbrush, and a pair of pillow covers. I'm pretty sure the pillow covers started out white, but sweat and other body fluids had turned them into a swirling off-jaundice shade. They were nasty. I probably should have pitched them awhile ago. With trash bag in hand, I headed back through the cabin. I opened the cockpit door to find none other than the admiral standing on the dock.

"Admiral, what's up?"

"Nothing, man, just made the rounds. I had to drop some fish dip off at the Habana Boat, and thought I'd swing by and have a cold one if you were here."

I handed him the trash bag to dispose of on the dock, and he came aboard while I grabbed a couple of beers from the fridge. He wasn't really an admiral, of course; he was the head chef at a private club in Gulfstream. His real name was Ray, and along with two other partners, we once owned the Robalo together. Ray never grasped the group ownership concept though, and was dubbed the admiral because he wanted to call all the shots. Needless to say, the name stuck, and we remained good friends, even through the dissolution of our pseudo-corporate ownership structure. With the group ownership program not working, the admiral ended up buying out all the partners, me included. A little over a year later, when he decided to get a new boat, I bought it back from him. The admiral spent a lot of time in the marina when he wasn't working, because some of the charter captains gave him their kingfish and amberjack to smoke. He would smoke the fish and give them back half, and with the other half (his share), he made a killer fish dip. It became so popular that the Habana Boat began using him as their exclusive supplier.

It was late in the afternoon, and a balmy seventy-eight degrees, so we sat in the cockpit and shot the shit while knocking back a couple. I told him about my banana search-and-destroy mission, and he told me about the hot new waitresses at the club. His story was better. "So what do you think, Admiral?

I didn't find any actual bananas on the boat...any suggestions?"

"Yeah, get us a couple more beers."

"Come on, dude, I'm serious." *Man I really am desperate, asking the admiral for fishing tips was like asking Donald Trump if he knew a good barber.*

"Well, let me see...you going out tomorrow?"

"Yep."

"What time?"

"I told Jaime to be here at the usual time, six fifteen in the morning."

"If I were you, I'd change it up, and leave earlier."

"You think?"

"Why not?"

I thought about it for a few seconds, and couldn't come up with a single good reason why not. "You know what, Ray? You're absolutely right. I'm calling Jamie and telling him to be here at five. We can be out the inlet by quarter after, and fifteen miles off before sunup."

"Sounds like a plan to me." He stood up and stepped off the boat, adding, "Good luck, Shag, bring me something back to smoke."

"Man I sure hope to. Take it easy, Admiral."

I watched him drive away and dialed Jamie on my cell phone. He took the new departure time just like I thought he would.

"Five o'clock in the fucking morning? Are you for real?" I knew he would be thrilled at the prospect of getting up at four.

"You heard me right, big man. I'm real as rain... if tomorrow's do or die, we're gonna do it early. It's gonna be a long day, so don't forget to go to Publix and pick up some subs. Get some rest, and I'll see you at five."

"Jesus, you *are* serious."

"Five o'clock in the morning, Jamie. Not five fifteen, or five thirty, but five o'clock...comprendo?"

"All right, all right, I'll be there at five. *Shit.*" Click.

Chapter 9

Ting! Ting! Ting! The alarm on my Timex Expedition wristwatch sounded. I reached over with my right hand to turn it off, then rolled over in the forward berth of the *Lucky Dog*. I pushed the button that illuminated the face, and it read four thirty in the morning. *Yikes!* Truth be told, I wasn't real keen on heading out at five either, but my fishing show, and all that went with it, was on the line. I was bound and determined to keep the dream alive, and not go down as the reigning king of Skunkville. I splashed some water on my face, brushed my teeth, put my show clothes on, and then headed up to the cabin. It was pitch black, save for a few inadequate dock lights, as I stepped outside to stretch and have a look around. Almost immediately, I turned back around and shut the door behind me, scratching my head and rubbing my arms. I forgot how bad the damn no-see-ums were, especially at low tide. I found a can of insect repellant and sprayed some on, then poured myself a glass of juice, racking my brain trying to think if I forgot anything...I didn't think so.

Right after the admiral left the day before, I checked all the lines and re-tied some knots. Then Tooda rang me on my cell. He told me Evvy had pulled into the marina, and everybody was loading up on fresh ballyhoo. "If you want any, you better get over here quick, 'cause they're going fast," he warned.

"Hell, I'm still on the boat," I told him. "I'll be there in two minutes. Thanks, Tooda."

I grabbed a cooler, and jogged across the parking lot to find Evvy doling out ballyhoo by the dozens, at forty cents apiece. I picked up ten dozen, and brined them back on the boat. Then I set about rigging up some fresh ones for my do-or-die trip. I kept telling myself it had to be considered a good sign. Evvy came up from the Keys maybe only once every month or two, and you never knew when. *Maybe my luck was beginning to change.*

Suddenly a set of headlights cut across the parking lot, and pulled up in front of the boat. I checked my watch, and it read five minutes to five. Jamie was actually early. *I'll be damned...another good sign.* It took us ten minutes to load the camera gear, food, and ice, and another ten for us to get out of the Boynton Inlet. I checked my watch again. Five fifteen, baby! *Right on schedule.*

Chapter 10

Late spring is usually a very good time of year for fishing in south Florida. Dolphin and other pelagic species appear in numbers as the ocean temperature warms. Of course, there are several factors that can affect whether fish bite or not. They include the phase of the moon, tidal action, currents, and wind direction, just to name a few. Many east coast captains will tell you that wind direction is crucial. Most prefer a gentle southeast breeze, the typical trade wind pattern. In my experience, this is indeed the most productive, so I was glad to find a gentle five-knot wind coming out of the southeast. Wave action was only two feet or less as we headed offshore. One drawback to heading out in the dark, however, is it's hard to see what's in the water. Sometimes you can blow right by a promising area to fish, which is referred to as overshooting the runway

Typical things you look for that might hold fish are current edges, color changes, weed lines, and virtually any object floating in the water. I decided to take advantage of our early start by running as fast and as far offshore as possible before sunrise. I pushed the throttles down on the twin, three-hundred horsepower

Cats, and we were clipping along at a steady twenty knots. The conditions were rife for activity, and I couldn't help but feel good about our prospects, despite the incredible slump I'd been in.

With a nearly full moon still hanging in the predawn sky, Jamie and I watched from the bridge as a school of flying fish leapt from the water and glided away from the port side of the boat. Their scales shimmered in the moonlight as they flew en masse, before plunging back into Mother Ocean, a handful at a time. I love having nothing but water below, sky above, and the horizon ahead. *Life is simple and distractions are minimal.*

My eyes scanned from port to stern, as I searched for a sign to tell me to throttle down and put the lines out. I checked the compass and GPS, confirming we were on my preselected heading of a hundred and fifty degrees to the southeast. We were already sixteen point four miles from the inlet, and making good time. I noticed only one other boat, about four or five miles behind us, heading north at trolling speed. I briefly wondered if I had indeed overshot the runway, but quickly decided to continue running offshore. I never liked second-guessing myself anyways—*it's hard enough to get the first one right.* Golden shafts of sunlight began shooting toward the heavens from the edge of the horizon. I lifted the Ray-Bans dangling from my neck strap, and put them on in place of my regular glasses. The polarized lenses worked their magic, providing definition and depth perception to sea and sky.

Jamie pointed at the GPS, which now showed we were twenty-seven miles offshore, and he hollered over the engine noise. "WHEN ARE WE GONNA FISH?"

I heard him, but didn't reply. I was studying something about a mile or so ahead, trying to make out what it was. He nudged me in the shoulder, trying to get my attention. I throttled down and pointed due east.

"THERE! BIRDS DIVING IN THE WATER!" My words seemed to hang in the air, floating along with us like smoke on a battlefield as we coasted to idle. *Yes! This is it!*

I began directing Jamie. "Go down in the salon and bring the rods out before you get the camera ready."

Jamie hustled down the ladder and I heard a thud, followed by a "Goddamn it!" He smacked his head on the cabin doorframe for the umpteenth time, the perils of being a human beanpole.

As we drew closer to the birds, I could see they were diving on what looked like a nice weed line, running from north to south. I decided to swing south of them, cut across, and then troll north along the eastern edge. Jamie had the rods in their proper holders, and headed back into the cabin to set up the camera. *This time he ducked.* Once we cut across the weed line, I turned north, running about forty yards from the eastern edge. I then put the riggers out, turned on the autopilot, and headed down to the cockpit to start getting some lines in the water.

On a boat this size, autopilot is a godsend. It allows you to program in a course heading and not have to worry about steering. It's also nice to have a lower helm station in the cockpit like the one in my customized Viking. This allows you to be down where the action is and still be able to control the boat without having to climb up to the bridge. Normally we had other people onboard who could take the helm while I fished and Jamie filmed. Being six weeks into the slump-of-the-century, however, we were on our own. I proceeded to put the lines out, and placed a ballyhoo with an Alien lure on the port rigger, closest to the weed line. I dropped it back a good forty-five yards, then put a custom Tooda squid rig on the starboard rigger, a little closer in. On the flat lines clipped to the stern, I put out a naked ballyhoo and another squid rig. They were about twenty-five and fifteen yards back, respectively. Lastly, I put out my big Black Bart teaser, called "Xtreme Breakfast," made a few adjustments to the lines, and maneuvered the boat a little closer to the weed line.

Look at all the crap caught in this weed line. It can boggle the mind what you find floating out in the ocean sometimes. I began noting the usual suspects piled up in the thick weed. A life preserver, some empty ice bags, a tattered sardine box, a little Styrofoam, and a five-gallon bucket.

From the port side of the cockpit I saw we were less than a quarter mile from the diving birds. As I turned to look in the cabin to see what was taking Jamie so long, I noticed the odd lure hanging by the door that Hambone gave me, and realized I forgot to put out the shotgun line. A shotgun line runs right through the middle of the trolling spread, and is positioned farthest back from the boat. It's preferable to run it from a higher position, like the bridge, to help prevent it from getting tangled in the other lines. If you're going to run a shotgun line, it should be put out first, rather than to have to feed it out between your riggers and flat lines. But it was too late for that.

I quickly grabbed a rod with a TLD-50 from under the starboard gunnel. On a whim, I grabbed Hambone's lure and tied it on the line. I dropped it back through the spread past my port rigger, a good seventy to eighty yards back. I climbed up the ladder, put the reel in gear, and stuck the rod in one of the bridge-mounted rod holders. Climbing back down, I looked at the weed line again. *Was that a mini-fridge floating by? Christ, what next? A convection oven?*

"ShagggggBallllll!" I heard Jamie calling my name from inside.

I opened the cabin door and stuck my head in. "What the hell are you doing?"

"Where's the toilet paper, dude? Can't find it."

"Behind the paper towels, under the sink, there should be a couple of rolls. Hurry up, man, we're—SNAP!"

At the sound of one of the rigger clips popping, I spun around. The port side rigger rod was bent over double and burning drag. "FISH ON!" I yelled, as I grabbed the rod and saw the huge splash behind the boat. *Shit!* The weed line jutted out in front of the boat, and we were about to plow right through it. I reached for the lower helm controls with my right hand, while holding the rod in my left, and steered away from the weed line.

I heard Jamie storming through the cabin behind me when—Wham! Jamie hit the doorframe again with his head. He almost dropped the camera, yelling, "Fuuuck meeee!" I didn't give a rat's ass though. There was something big thrashing around on the line, and the drought was about to be over.

Chapter 11

In Mini-E's dream, he was a young kid back on his father's shrimp boat, in Biloxi, Mississippi. He could see his father's face, a cross between Captain Quint from the movie *Jaws*, and Lou Ferrigno *The Incredible Hulk*. *It wasn't pretty.* He was in the bottom of the ship's hold, and was shoveling ice onto a pile of shrimp. His father's gigantic face was looking down on him from the hatch above, yelling, "Faster, you lazy-ass midget! This ain't no carnival!"

The faster he shoveled, the larger the shrimp pile grew, until it was literally raining shrimp down on him. Tired, hot, and thirsty, he grabbed a handful of ice, and retreated to a corner of the hold. He sat down and started to eat it. Something was very wrong though... it didn't taste like ice. Suddenly gagging, he began spitting out spoiled raw shrimp, and watched in horror as thousands of little crabs emerged from between the ship's planks. The crabs were everywhere, and began devouring the regurgitated shrimp covering his feet. Ouch! One bit him. Ow! Another one bit him, only this time it was on his ear.

He heard the low rumble of a diesel engine. Was his despicable father gonna leave him down there on the trip back to Biloxi? "NO WAAAIT!" he cried. "Don't leave me down here you son of a" SPLASH!

The dream came crashing to a halt as Mini-E flew headfirst off the pallet and was dragged through the water backward. Birds...what were they? Seagulls? Were flying all around him. *What the hell?* Something had him by the collar of his jumpsuit! *Damn this fucking jumpsuit.* As he struggled for the surface, he swallowed a mouthful of seawater and started gagging for real, arms flailing and eyes burning.

"What is it?" Jamie asked, as he pointed the camera back at the melee on the surface.

"I don't know. I saw a flash of white, and then— *What the fuck? Did I just see a hand waving at me?*"

Reaching back to the lower helm station, I throttled down to idle, and we slowed to a drift. The thrashing in the water continued, however. "HO-LEE-SHIT!" Jamie said, while looking through the viewfinder. "There's two little arms and a head! You got some kid hooked by his collar—reel him in before he drowns!"

In total disbelief, I cranked the drag down and started reeling. Mini-E rolled over face-first before completing a 360-degree revolution while continuing to flail his little arms as he was dragged to the boat. Spitting out seawater while facing skyward again, he managed to holler, "Help! Help!"

Shaking my head, I yelled back, "HANG ON! YOU'RE ALMOST TO THE BOAT!"

Jamie kept filming as mystery boy reached the boat. I took the Penn International eighty-wide out of gear, and placed the rod in one of the holders on the stern. Then I swung open the tuna door, and stepped onto the swim platform. With one hand, I grabbed the back of his collar, and with the other removed the hook. As I hoisted him up on the transom, I heard Jamie laughing under his breath. I saw why as mystery boy stood up, and staggered through the tuna door. He was wearing a white sequined jumpsuit, with the words Mini-E embroidered on the sleeves and lapel. He wasn't a boy, though; he was a man...a man with a serious five o'clock shadow. In utter amazement, I shook my head, taking in the full package. Or should I say, half package. He was maybe four feet tall, and 130 or so pounds, but perfectly proportioned. He wasn't a dwarf...*what the hell was he?* Some kind of perfect midget? A dwidget?

Then, in an even more unlikely...dare I say normal voice...he said, "If you two are done gawking and taking pictures, maybe you can spare me some fucking water."Now I started to laugh too, and Jamie put the camera down under the stairs, on top of the tackle station. *Oh, Sweet Jesus! They are not gonna believe this back on the dock, they are not gonna fucking believe this.* As our catch of the day sat down on the stern, I rushed to the galley fridge and pulled out four, sixteen-ounce bottles of water.

Jamie followed me inside and whispered, "Dude this is classic! I can't wait to see the footage!" *No argument here.* I turned and headed back to the cockpit with water in hand.

As soon as the guy that reeled him in went to get water, Mini-E grabbed a fillet knife from the tackle station, and began cutting himself out of the jumpsuit. He vowed to never again wear a jumpsuit...ever. He tossed the shredded remains into a five-gallon bucket and smiled. He was now officially retired as an Elvis impersonator. He briefly thought about Darla, and his asshole boss, wondering if anybody reported him missing. *Doubtful.* He figured nobody would notice until the ship got to Freeport. Darla would be the only one who might be looking for him, but she was probably too busy eating demon pussy. *Fuck it.* Not only was he done with his Elvis gig, he was done with cruise ships altogether. "No mas," he mumbled to himself...*No mas.*

Chapter 12

I stepped through the cabin door to find the little guy standing at the stern in his underwear, holding one of my fillet knives. I said, "Hey, man, you're not about to go all O.J. on us...are you?" He didn't say anything. He just set the knife down and massaged the back of his neck. It was then that I noticed some blood on the back of his jumpsuit, which he apparently cut off and tossed in a bucket. "Shit!" I said. "Did the hook get you?"

"Nah, I got stuck by a nail on that pallet I was floating on."

I handed him a water and he chugged it down, so I handed him another, saying, "Better get some peroxide and a bandage on that." I pulled out the first aid kit from beneath the bait-prep sink, and set it on the countertop. When I opened it up, I was looking down at a pair of blackened, rotten bananas. They had turned to mush, and stank like hell. Tiny insects were crawling all over the contents of the kit, and some started to fly up in my face. "Goddamn it!" I yelled, then grabbed the banana muck and tossed it over the side. Next I turned on the fresh water hose and sprayed out the inside of the kit, before removing the peroxide and a waterproof Band-Aid. I wiped them off with a rag, thinking Tooda was right. *Some fucking asshole stashed bananas on my boat, and put me on the skunk train. Son of a bitch!* I turned around to tend to the injured party, who was just finishing his second bottle of water. "So, my man, gotta name?" I asked.

With his back turned to me, I cleaned and bandaged the hole in his neck, and he replied, "Dupree."

"Dupree what?"

"Langostino Dupree."

"Langostino? Are you serious? Like the shrimp?"

"Yep."

No fucking way. "Well my name's Kit, but I'm also called Shagball, the tall guy's Jamie, my producer. We were hoping you had fins, because we're trying to get some footage for our fishing show." I heard a sound behind me, and glanced back to see Jamie standing there filming.

"Jamie? For Christ's sake," I said. "You see those lines in the water, the ones that are all tangled to shit? Well how 'bout you please put down the fucking camera, and start reeling them up. It's gonna take some doing to get them straightened out...Jesus!"

I normally didn't boss the producer around, but come on, *enough's enough.* Langostino thanked me for bandaging him up, and asked for another water. "Sure, here you go," I said, handing him one. In a couple of minutes, Jamie had the lines up to the boat, and it was a total clusterfuck. Even the teaser was wrapped up in the mess. *Oh, this is gonna be fun.* I looked at Langostino, and said, "I'm guessing you're probably hungry too, and we haven't eaten either. Let me grab some sandwiches, and then you can tell us how in the hell you ended up out here."

He gave me a thumbs-up in mid-chug, and Jamie was cussing and struggling with a massive clump of tangled lines as I went in the cabin. I opened the fridge and pulled out the two twelve-inch subs Jamie brought. As I unwrapped them, I saw they weren't cut, so I picked up a knife and halved them. I grabbed a few paper plates and towels, thinking I should keep the knife handy, because I'd need one to cut out the tangles. I knew Jamie would never be able to clear the lines, and I certainly didn't feel like messing with them at the moment. Before heading back out, I went to the forward berth and stuck a pair of shorts, and a T-shirt, under my arm. My little brother Pete left them behind on a recent visit, and I thought that maybe Langostino could use them. I stepped back out to the cockpit, and set the clothes and sandwiches on top of the tackle station. Then I turned, with knife in hand, ready to cut some lines.

Chapter 13

"Huh?" I looked at Jamie, who was looking at Langostino, who was just setting the last rod into the forward port holder. All the lines were clear, and the baits were sitting on the cockpit floor, ready to be redeployed. I looked at Jamie, and muttered, "What the hell?" With a big smile on his face, he just pointed at the little guy. *I couldn't believe it. It wasn't possible... was it?* "He cleared all those lines by himself?" I asked.

Langostino turned to me and pointed at Jamie. "Well, old flagpole here sure as shit didn't do it...now how 'bout that sandwich?"

I passed the sandwiches out, still not believing my eyes. How in God's name did he untangle that clusterfuck? In what? Two minutes, tops? Clearly, there was more to shorty than meets the eye. "I believe this calls for a beer," I announced. Jamie took the cue and headed into the cabin to get his cooler, which was sure to be packed full of Heineken Light. I gave Langostino the shorts and T-shirt, and he put them on. Not surprisingly, they were a little big. "Maybe you'll grow into them," I absently thought aloud, instantly regretting it when he shot me a look that said, *very fucking funny.*

As we downed our breakfast of champions, I queried our guest. "Langostino's a real mouthful—you got a nickname?"

He pointed to the five-gallon bucket. "It used to be Mini-E, that was my getup. I was an Elvis impersonator...*was*...but no more, I just retired."

Jamie said, "How 'bout Tangles?"

Langostino and I both looked at him, and in unison, said, "Tangles?"

"Yeah, I never saw anything like it the way he cleared those lines. He was like some sorta savant playing the piano, only he was untangling lines."

Hmmm, not bad, not bad at—WAAAAAHHHH! WAAAAAHHHH! The twin blasts of a large ship's horn made me spit out some salami. We rushed to the side to see a large freighter bearing down on us, only a couple of hundred yards away. "SHIT!" I yelled, while reaching for the controls. I turned us hard to starboard, away from the weed line, and floored it. Not five seconds after accelerating away from the freighter, I thought I heard the sound of line screaming off a reel. Looking around, I saw that all the lines were still on deck, what the—"FISH ON!" I screamed, pointing up at the shotgun line. *I forgot about the shotgun line!* It had been in the water the whole time, drifting all the way to port, almost ninety degrees midship. The funny-looking jig that Hambone gave me must have sunk down, and when we accelerated, it shot toward the surface, only to get eaten by something...*something very big.* Before I could say another word, Tangles flew up the ladder like a monkey on crack. *Man, can that little dude move.*

Chapter 14

Seeing that we were clear of the freighter, I eased the throttle back to a slow troll, keeping an eye on Tangles up on the bridge. I noticed he didn't make the mistake of taking the rod out of the holder without a fighting belt ready. He correctly opted to reel from the rod holder, but the fish kept taking line at an incredible speed. "Half the lines gone!" he yelled.

I grabbed the fighting belt hanging on the bottom rung of the ladder, and put it on, while Jamie went for the camera. Then I took the motors out of gear, and climbed three-quarters of the way up the ladder. "Hand me the rod!" I urged, and Tangles eased it out of the rod holder, handing it down to me. I put the rod in the gimble of the fighting belt and shot a look back at him. *Nice work, Tangles.*

The line was almost straight off the stern, entering the water maybe fifteen feet away. *Shit! Whatever it was, was sounding!* Losing line fast, I increased the drag as much as I dared on the fifty-pound test. It didn't slow down the fish a bit, and the line began to smoke. "Holy shit! Quick, somebody—" before I could get the words out, Tangles was at my side, pouring water over the reel. *Hmmm...boys got some skills.* Now the line wasn't fifteen feet behind the boat, but more like fifty or sixty feet.

Jamie was filming, and began to pray under his breath, "Please don't lose him, please don't lose him."

The four hundred yards of line was now almost completely gone. "Damn! We're gonna have to—"Again, before I could get the words out, Tangles scampered back up to the bridge. Facing the stern, with his back to the controls, he began backing down on the mystery fish. *The little shit knows how to back down backward? Are you kidding me? Boy's got some splainin' to do when this is over.*

The *Lucky Dog* was now reversing through the water, and I slowly began to gain some line on the beast. Water was splashing over the stern, and I got drenched, but was gaining line. Now I had a good hundred and fifty yards back on the reel, and the line was directly behind the boat, maybe ten feet away. I signaled for Tangles to stop backing down, but he beat me to it, and the boat stopped taking water over the stern. I pushed the drag down a touch more, and kept cranking as I stepped backward...when whoosh! I hit the deck. My visor fell off as my left foot slipped on the salami I'd spit out a few minutes before. I cursed, almost losing the rod when I took a hand off it to push myself up from the deck. Jamie and Tangles were laughing, and the fish took advantage of my tumble by taking back a hundred yards of line. For over an hour, I fought the fish, from port, to starboard, and back.

Finally, I caught a glimpse of it. Jamie was standing next to me, looking through the viewfinder of his video cam. "What is it?" he asked.

Before I could say what I suspected it was, Tangles replied, "I think it's a big yellowfin."

We turned to look up at him on the bridge, when the fish made its final run. Tangles was right, at least I thought he was. *Little son of a bitch was just full of surprises.* The fish apparently didn't like the sight of the *Lucky Dog* though, or maybe it was just camera shy, as it peeled off another sixty yards of line. I kept cranking, and several minutes later saw the hundred-pound fluorocarbon leader come into view. The big fish was right behind it.

"Good call, Tangles," I said, as the big tuna surfaced.

With the camera rolling, Jamie shouted, "Jesus! He's huge!"

As if reading my mind, Tangles materialized next to me. He opened the tuna door and stepped onto the swim platform, holding a gaff taller than he was. I stepped forward to the opening, and with a few final cranks of the handle, had the fish at the back of the boat. I started walking backward, trying to guide the fish onto the platform and through the door. It began to thrash violently, and I feared it would spit the hook, which was dangling precariously from its lower lip. Right then, Tangles reached out with the gaff and stuck it behind the gill, dragging it through the door onto the deck.

Chapter 15

"Yeah, baby! That's what I'm talking about," I crowed, as I looked into the camera. "That's Fishing on the Edge...with Shagball." There was a lot of hootin' and hollerin' going on as I high-fived Jamie, and low-fived Tangles. The yellowfin was thrashing on the deck, and we were downright giddy, practically dancing circles around it. "That sucker's gotta be a hundred pounds," I gushed.

"I think he's bigger than that," said Tangles. As he opened the floor-mounted fish box, the tuna thrashed again, and the hook fell out of its mouth onto the deck. As I put the rod back into one of the holders, I slowly shook my head. *That was close.*

Tangles spread a bag of ice around the fish box, taking the other one out. He then pushed the tuna in, and asked me to hand him a knife. I pulled out a big Forschner from the tackle station and handed it to him, watching as he slit the tuna's throat to bleed him out.

Jamie stepped out of the cabin with three more beers. As I took one, I said, "That Tangles knows what the fuck he's doing. I hope you took notes."

We were laughing as Tangles dumped the other bag of ice over the fish. He had to bend the tail in order to close the lid. I handed him a Heiney and nodded. "Dude...you earned this one."

The three of us clinked bottles, and Tangles made a toast. "To pigs that fry on the Fourth of July."

I'm pretty sure that, like me, Jamie never heard that one either, and had no idea what it meant, but we laughed and drank anyways.

I looked at my watch and it was only quarter to nine. *Wow, what a start.* I decided to go up on the bridge and check the GPS, to see where the hell we were. According to the Raymarine unit, we were thirty-two point four miles northeast of the inlet. *Whoa!* I knew we needed more ice for the big yellowfin, so I plotted a course for home. Once I had the autopilot set, I yelled, "Hang on!" In seconds, we were heading back at a comfortable fourteen-knot clip.

Chapter 16

"What's Jamie doing?" I asked Tangles, as he joined me on the bridge.

"He's lying down on the sofa, says his head hurts."

Remembering the two hard knocks he sustained prior to hooking Tangles, I laughed out loud. "All right, now what's your deal? That was some show you put on down there, not to mention the way you backed down on that tuna." He went on to explain how he had grown up working on his father's shrimp boat in Biloxi, and spent what little spare time he had fishing the oil rigs in the Gulf of Mexico. "So...you always been this short?" I asked.

"No, I was smaller when I was born."

Stepped right into that one. "OK, that was a stupid question."

"You think?" He then said that when he was eight years old, doctors found a tumor on his pituitary gland, which controls growth. When they cut it out, they ended up having to take out much more than they planned, and that's when he stopped growing.

I said, "No shit."

He just looked at me, shaking his head. "No, no gland."

So my boy's got a sense of humor too, Guess it would help given the circumstances. "So...what are you now? About twenty—twenty-five years old?"

"Try thirty-five."

"Thirty-five? Are you kidding? Damn, you're almost as old as me, I'm thirty-seven." *Christ, little sumbitch looks in better shape than I am.* "OK, Tangles, now for the sixty-four-thousand-dollar question. How in the hell did you end up on a pallet, in the middle of the ocean, wearing that dumb-ass jumpsuit?"

When he got done telling me the story about his last night on the cruise ship...the jump...and the floating in the Gulf Stream...I said, "Seriously, dude, the other chick was that ugly?"

He confirmed she was triple bag coyote ugly, and I involuntarily shivered at the thought. "What was with the bananas in the first aid kit?" he asked.

I gave him a brief synopsis of my landing the fishing show, and the long dry spell that had now ended by catching the big tuna. I said, "Now that I think of it, Tangles, if I hadn't hooked you, I wouldn't have opened the first aid kit and found the bananas. Without getting rid of the bananas, we wouldn't have caught the tuna. I guess I should thank you—you're my new lucky charm. You saved my fishing show from being canceled."

I saw Tangles sniff his nose, and then I smelled it too. Jamie was down in the cockpit smoking a joint, and he looked up at us. "You guys wanna toot this fish whistle?" Before I could say anything, Tangles reached down and Jamie handed him the joint. *So my boy likes to burn too. Well, well, well.*

Chapter 17

We were about eight miles from the inlet, when it occurred to me it might be prudent to find out if there was some massive search going on for Tangles, despite him claiming it was highly unlikely. I turned on channel sixteen of my ship-to-shore radio, and listened for any man-overboard searches. Thankfully, the Coast Guard channel was all quiet, indicating no search was going on. I asked Tangles if Darla had a cell phone on the ship, and he said she did. I handed him my phone, and told him to call her to let her know he was OK. Reluctantly he obliged, and I listened to him leave a message, saying he went for a midnight swim, and got picked up by a fishing boat. He also said he hoped he never saw her again, and that her girlfriend should enter a Cloris Leachman look-alike contest. *Ouch.*

After a few minutes of silence, I asked Tangles what his plans were once we got back to the dock. "Are you going back to Biloxi to see your parents?"

"Nah, my asshole father passed away a few years ago, and my mom remarried and moved to New Orleans, right before Katrina hit. Last I heard, she and her new husband evacuated to Houston, and they're still living in a FEMA trailer." Houston, he said, was not an option for him.

Hmmm, looks like my boy needs a little help. I kicked an idea around in my head for a few miles, and reached a decision. As we passed through the Boynton Inlet, I told Tangles he was welcome to stay on the *Lucky Dog* until he got back on his feet.

"What?" he said. "You're kidding me...right?"

"Hell, it's the least I can do. Thanks to you, the guys on the dock won't be calling me Captain LePew anymore. The way you run a cockpit, there won't be any trouble getting you some charter work if you want. My only stipulation is that you help keep the boat clean, and when I need you for a trip, I got dibs. Also, you can't advertise that you're staying on the boat, because it's not a live-aboard marina. It shouldn't be a problem though, because the dockmaster's a friend of mine. What do you say, Tangles? We got ourselves a deal?"

For the first time since being on board, Tangles cracked a big smile, and stuck out his little hand for me to shake. As I shook it, I was thinking, *this could be interesting.* Little did I know.

Chapter 18

"All right Tangles, let's give 'em a show." With Jamie filming, and me on the bridge, I had Tangles hoist the big tuna out of the fish box. He held it up by the tail as we passed the fuel dock and restaurants. It was quite a sight, with Tangles balancing the big fish on its nose on the deck, the tail rising over his head. Customers in Three Jacks and the Habana Boat were leaving their tables to get a better look. Everybody was clapping, and the dock was buzzing, as yellowfin tuna are not a common sight in these parts. Blackfins, yes—yellowfins, no...especially not this size. I spun the boat around and glided up to the fuel dock, which was now full of people. Everybody wanted a look at the big fish. Robo, the dockmaster, came out, and I signaled to him that I needed fuel. People were snapping pictures on their cell phones as I climbed down to join Tangles and Jamie.

"Let's get this big boy weighed," I said, as one of the dock rats came out from behind the ship's store with a wheelbarrow. Jamie and I hoisted the fish onto the dock, and then into the wheelbarrow. Only the head and a little more than half the body fit in. The tail slapped me in the nuts as I wheeled it over to the hanging scale at the end of the dock. *Ow! Still putting up a fight, huh?*

Graybeard suddenly materialized in front of me with a Bud in hand. "Looks like you got the monkey off your back, Shagball, nice job."

"Thanks, G-man, it's good to be back."

I caught sight of Ratdog and Skeeter, lurking in the background. Skeeter yelled, "So the blind squirrel found himself an acorn!" Ratdog said nothing, he just gave me a funny look, and slipped back into the crowd. *Hmm, what's that all about?*

As the tuna was lifted tail first, there was a collective gasp from the crowd. The scale registered 100...110...120...122 lbs! Doing my best impression of bass fishing legend Rowland Martin, I hollered, "SON! Look at that!" I then proceeded to take a picture with my cell phone, and high-fived the world. So much attention was paid to the tuna, that no one asked about Tangles. *Just as well.* We put the fish back in the wheelbarrow, and I asked Jamie to take it down to the cleaning table, while I brought the boat around.

I winced as Robo handed me the fuel bill. "What's with diesel being more expensive than gas?" I asked.

"I know," he said. "Sign of the times."

"Sign of some messed up times." I sighed and shook my head.

"At least you got something to show for it today. Great catch, Shag."

I thanked him as Tangles and I stepped back on the boat. Two minutes later, I was backing the *Lucky Dog* into her slip, and was once again impressed by Tangles, the way he handled the dock lines. He used one of my telescoping boat hooks like a conductor, and moved from bow to stern like his tiny ass was on fire. *Little bastard was good...real good.*

Chapter 19

With the boat tied up, I locked the electronics on the bridge, and headed down to the cockpit. Realizing I forgot to get more ice for the fish, I sent Tangles back to the ship's store to grab a couple of bags. As he headed down the dock, Jamie stepped back on the boat and joined me in the cabin for a beer. We clinked bottles for the second time that day, and Jamie said, "Shagalito, you really pulled one out of your ass today."

We laughed, and he kept repeating how he couldn't wait to get back to the studio to start editing footage for the show. "This might even be a two-parter," he excitedly said.

"First catching Tangles, and then the tuna."

I told him that I had just made Tangles my new mate, and he would be staying on the boat for a while. *He about shit his pants.* "Are you serious? Oh my God, wait till this footage hits the air. People are gonna freak when they see him in action. I can't believe what I saw today myself. This is great!"

I took advantage of his elation by handing him the fuel bill. *Timing is everything.* Normally, Jamie griped about every little expense, but he was so pumped up, he just slipped it in his pocket. He said, "I gotta get back to the studio, I want this aired ASAP."

Tangles arrived with the ice, and spread it over the fish, as Jamie loaded the last of the camera gear in his Tahoe. I said to Tangles, "How 'bout I clean the fish, while you start cleaning the boat?"

"You got it, boss!" *Boss, huh? I'm liking this little cat more and more.* I told him where the cleaning supplies were, and in seconds he was scrubbing and mopping the cockpit floor. Jamie then helped me lift the tuna onto the cleaning table. I was glad I opted for an extra long one when I had it made, because I needed every inch. I filleted and bagged Jamie a few pounds of the sweet red meat, and he was smiling from ear to ear.

He said, "See you later," waved toward Tangles, and left.

I pulled a sixty-four-quart cooler out of my dock box, and spilled a bag of ice into it. Then I got to work on the rest of the fish. People were still milling around, taking pictures, and I heard some know-it-all douche bag tell his wife, "Honey, that's what a big yellow tail snapper looks like." *Some things never change.*

Chapter 20

I was just about finished cleaning the fish, when Tooda arrived. "Looks like your luck changed, Kit. That's a helluva fish."

"Thanks, Tooda, you were right...boy, do I owe you. Somebody planted a couple of bananas in my first aid kit. As soon as I got rid of them, we hooked into *this* bad boy. Can you believe it?"

"Hell yeah, I believe it. I told you that superstitious shit was nothing to sneeze at."

"Here, you want some tuna?"

"Nah, I'll take a beer though."

"I buy, you fly. Got some in the galley fridge."

As Tooda was about to step on the boat, Tangles came out of the cabin holding two Heineys. *I was beginning to think he was some sorta mind reader.* He handed the beers to Tooda, and I introduced them.

"Tooda, this is Tangles, Tangles, Tooda." I briefly thought of the famous Letterman exchange, "Oprah... Uma...Uma...Oprah." I chuckled to myself as they shook hands, and then Tangles headed up to the bridge to continue cleaning.

Handing me the other Heiney, Tooda asked, "where'd you find *that* kid?"

"Floating on a pallet, in a weed line, about thirty miles off."

Tooda's mouth opened to say something when his cell phone rang, interrupting his train of thought. *It didn't take much.* He walked a few steps down the dock, talking on the phone, while I filleted the last of the tuna. As I dropped it in the cooler, I figured it held about sixty pounds of fillets. I spread some more ice over the fish, and closed the lid, thinking about the sashimi bash that was now imminent.

"Gotta run," said Tooda, as he closed his phone. "Gotta hot date tonight."

"Go get 'em, Captain, and don't forget to wear your raincoat." I cringed as he walked over to his pickup, hoping he'd remember to "rubber up," before conducting on the skank train. Tooda was a divorced and retired firefighter in his midfifties who was known for dating a constant stream of women. Mostly, women either on their way from, or on their way to, rehab. His dates gave new meaning to the phrase, "rode hard and put away wet." *Yikes.* Me and the admiral (another good friend of Tooda's), were constantly trying to get him to upgrade his standards. Unfortunately, it seemed to be a lost cause...because he apparently had none. As far as friends went though, he was as reliable as they got. I slid the tuna carcass into the canal, hosed off the cleaning table and dock, and looked at my watch. It was only two thirty. *What a day so far...un-friggin'-believable.*

Chapter 21

The boat was spotless. Tangles was in the cabin, wiping off the fridge, when I told him to take a break, and grab us a couple more beers. He reached in, informing me that I was down to under a six-pack left, then handed me one. I asked him to reach under the sink and hand me the small cooler I kept there. Then I sat on the sofa and took three zip locks full of tuna out of the big cooler, and put them in the small one, along with some ice.

"Come on, let's go," I said. "We need to get cleaned up and find you some clothes. We got some celebrating to do."

I grabbed my car keys, and locked the cabin door as we left the boat. Tangles was ahead of me as we stepped up to the parking lot, and he stopped next to the passenger door of a Tacoma pickup. I walked past him and slipped a key into the trunk of a bright red, 1994 BMW convertible, parked next to it.

"This is *yours?*" he asked, letting out a low whistle as he walked around to the passenger side of the Beemer.

"Yep, she's a beauty, huh?" I took one of the bags out, placed the cooler in the trunk, and shut it. I drove up as near to the ship's store as I could, and asked

Tangles to deliver the tuna to Robo, compliments of Shagball. *It's always a good idea to be on friendly terms with the dockmaster.* With Tangles back in the Beemer, we headed north on US 1. It was just a few miles up the road to my apartment in Lantana. On the way, we stopped at the Winn-Dixie supermarket to pick up some beer, wasabi, and ponzu sauce.

Tangles used the shower, while I rummaged through one of the twelve large Rubbermaid containers that supported the king-size bed in my one-bedroom apartment. *Shit, wrong one.* I slid the container back under the bed and slid out another. I knew I had some decent shorts from my svelte days, stashed in one of the containers. Although I currently had a thirty-six-ish-inch waist, I held out hope that I would lose some weight, and once again wear the size thirty-fours, if not the thirty-twos, that I saved. Tangles said he wore a size twenty-nine, and I figured if I could round up a couple of thirty-twos, he could make do with a belt. *Yes!* I found the container with my old shorts, and discovered two pairs of Ocean Pacifics and a pair of O'Neils, that were thirty-twos. I didn't have any underwear though. *Hmmmm, looks like Tangles be going commando...Oh well, probably not the first time.* I looked in the closet, and pulled out a pale blue V-neck top that my upstairs neighbor Melody left behind recently. I found an old belt, and tore out the Liz Claiborne tag from the back of the V-neck, just before Tangles came out of the bathroom.

Chapter 22

I took a quick shower, and came out to find Tangles wearing a pair of the OP's with Melody's shirt. I was hoping she wouldn't be sitting out on the balcony when we left. Looking at Tangles, I realized he looked like someone I knew, but couldn't quite put my finger on it. Maybe like the hypothetical spawn of Danny DeVito and Russell Crowe if you chopped him off at the knees? Well, not exactly, but he did have quite a mop of dark curly hair once it was washed and dried. The shorts were a little big, as expected, and the shirt looked interesting. OK, maybe it was a little gay, but otherwise he looked presentable, standing there in his bare feet. *Oh shit, I just realized he had been barefoot the whole time.* I was so used to all the dock rats who worked barefooted, that I hadn't thought twice about it. Tangles thanked me for the shorts and belt, but said nothing about the shirt.

"What's the matter?" I asked. "You don't like the shirt?"

"I'm a little concerned you might try to feel me up after a few more beers."

"You wish."

"Seriously, it's got shoulder pads."

"Yeah, but they look good on you though."

"No way, no fucking way I'm—"

"Don't sweat it, dude, we're gonna swing by K-Mart to get you some shoes, you can get a shirt too...if you want."

"I want."

We were walking across the lawn to the parking lot, when I heard, "Kit? How come you didn't come and say hi?" *Shit, it was Melody, my full-time neighbor and part-time girlfriend.*

"Sorry, Mel," I said, as I opened the car door. "I'm in a bit a hurry. I'll have to catch up with you later."

"That's what you always say. Hey! Is that kid wearing my shirt? I've been looking for it."

"See you later!" I repeated, as we drove off.

I spotted Tangles twenty bucks, and he went into K-Mart, while I stayed in the car to make a couple of calls. I wanted to invite some friends down to the *Lucky Dog* to have some sashimi. Ten minutes later, out came Tangles. He was sporting a new pair of knockoff docksiders and a Kid Rock T-shirt, holding a bag. *Go figure.* He climbed in and tossed the bag with Melody's shirt in the back.

I said, "OK, T-Dog, let's roll." Two minutes later, we pulled up in front of the chikee bar, in the parking lot of the Ole House, which proclaimed to be Florida's oldest waterfront restaurant. I always thought their food was some of the oldest, but it had great intracoastal views, and they didn't gouge you on drinks, so it was hugely popular. I looked at my watch and it was two minutes after four, happy hour had just started. *Perfect timing.*

Chapter 23

I pulled a sack of tuna from the cooler and we headed into the chikee bar, which was about three-quarters full. The chikee bar was under a tiki hut that sat about thirty people, and protruded out over the water. It also had some new tables situated around it, courtesy of a recent deck expansion. From the chikee bar, you had fantastic water views, and could see the inside bar area, as well as the dining room, which sat under its own giant tiki hut. You also had a view of the Lantana Sportsman's Park and boat ramp, as well as all the boats docked along the seawall. The Ole House was an institution, and there was nothing like it anywhere. Sportsman's Park was sort of a mini version of the Water's Edge Marina, where I kept the *Lucky Dog*. It was a great spot. In fact, I was on the waiting list for a slip. Turnover was minimal though, and I wasn't on top of the list...yet.

As Tangles and I settled onto a couple of stools, one of my all-time favorite bartenders came up and set a Bud Light down in front of me. "Hey, Bubba, how's it going?" he asked, then turned to Tangles. "And what can I get for you, young man?" Rudy was a classic. He was fifty-five-ish, maybe five feet four inches tall, with a slight build, and a Southern accent. He was a fixture at the chikee bar, having worked there forever. He called all the guys "Bubba," and referred to single women as "lonesome doves." When he wasn't working, he'd spend time gambling down on the Indian reservation. One very late night, with no one around, he told me he got special perks at the casinos because he was part Indian.

"Come on, Rudy," I had said. "Your bullshitting me again."

He told me Rudy wasn't his real name, and pulled out his Florida driver's license to prove it. I looked at the picture of a younger-looking Rudy, and read the name below, which I shall never forget, Travis K. Rainbow. "Travis K. Rainbow?" I blurted out, practically falling off my stool in a fit of laughter. "Come on, that's the cheesiest fake Indian name I've ever heard. Don't tell me—the K stands for Kemosabe...right?"

"No, it stands for Killdeer. Like the bird."

"Oh, I see, so the bird is the word. That explains it. *Right.* Sure you don't mean Killbeer?" I began laughing again but he started to look miffed.

He insisted the license was genuine, and swore up and down it was his real name. Somehow though, and I never did get to the reason why everybody just called him Rudy.

I pushed the bag of tuna toward him as he set down a Bud for Tangles. "Here's some yellowfin tuna we caught this morning...enjoy."

"Wow...yellow fin? Thanks, Bubba, you didn't have to do that, next round's on me."

Tangles asked where the bathroom was, and I pointed it out, past the pool table on the right.

I looked around to see how many lonesome doves were nesting, and was disappointed to see just one. *Give it a little time, Shagdog. Come midnight there'll be plenty of wings a flapping.*

After taking care of a few customers, Rudy returned. "So, Bubba, who's your little friend?"

I told him that besides catching a big-ass yellowfin, I had rescued him at sea. It sounded better than admitting I foul-hooked him while not paying attention to the lines.

"Well I hope he knows what he's doing with that pool stick, 'cause those boys he's playing with don't play for nothing." He nodded toward the inside bar.

"What?" I turned to see Tangles on his tiptoes, leaning against the table as he struck a shot. Some people at the bar started clapping, and another guy holding a cue stick threw his Guy Harvey cap down, took his sunglasses off, and handed them to Tangles. Wearing his new shades, a pair of 1980s vintage Porsche Carreras, Tangles sat back down and finished his beer in one swallow.

Rudy warned Tangles, "Better watch yourself, Bubba, them boys don't take to losing well."

Looking back toward the table, Tangles just nodded. "Hell, the way they play, they oughta be used to it."

Rudy started laughing, and I introduced them. "Tangles this is Rudy, Rudy...Tangles."

As they shook hands, Rudy suggested, "How 'bout that round I promised?"

Tangles ordered a shot of tequila, and I shrugged. "What the hell, same here."

As Rudy poured us a couple of shots of Cuervo, he asked, "So, Tangles, where you from?"

"Biloxi," he responded.

"Biloxi? Man, that place used to be great. Back in the day, I ran around with the cutest little blackjack dealer you ever saw. A real firecracker, but let me tell you, Bubba, she could charm a hungry gator from a chicken farm."

We downed the shots, and I ordered us a couple more beers as Rudy continued his walk down memory lane. "Yes, sir" he reminisced, as he reached in the cooler. "When Marie came a calling, old Rudy came a—"

"What? What did you say her name was?" Tangles interrupted Rudy in midsentence, lifting his new shades to his forehead and eyeing him intently.

As Rudy set the beers down in front of us, he gave Tangles a funny look. "Her name? Why just the sweetest name you ever did hear...Marie...Marie Dupree."

Chapter 24

The Water's Edge Marina, where I docked my boat, was really two separate marina operations. All the slips on the canal where I kept the *Lucky Dog*, were owned by the condo association of the newly built high-rises. They stood where there once was nothing but wet scrubland. The association prohibited all commercial vessels whatsoever. They had been kicked out several years earlier when the developers bought the property. The ones who saw the writing on the wall got out early, and were able to secure slips in the canal between Three Jacks and The Habana Boat. The others were shit out of luck. The restaurants had their own dockage for boating customers, but the forty or so slips that lined the canal as it ran west, until it dead-ended, were owned by a little old lady named Milfred Lutes. It was referred to as the C-LOVE Marina.

Milfred and her family had owned the property for generations. They also owned and operated the seventy-seven-foot drift boat named *C-LOVE*, which sat at the end of the canal.

The rest of the slips were rented out to commercial fisherman, dive boat operators, a Jet Ski and boat rental outfit, and sport fish charter captains. The waiting list was extensive, because it was one of the few remaining marinas that allowed commercial boats. Marina after marina had been scooped up by deep-pocketed developers during the great real estate boom at the turn of the new millennium, and the commercial guys were left holding the bag.

Milfred had turned down countless offers over the years, and as the boom went bust, the developers finally stopped calling. That suited Sonny Slade just fine. Sonny was the middle son of Syd Slade, the owner of Three Jacks. Syd owned a dozen waterfront restaurants up the east coast, in Boston, and even the Bahamas. While Syd was no dummy, the same could not be said about Sonny. In fact, he was pretty much a total fuckup. His older and younger brothers both proved themselves competent restaurateurs, but everywhere Syd sent Sonny was a complete disaster. The only thing Sonny knew how to run was his mouth, and Syd had to hire a full-time attorney just to fend off the sexual harassment lawsuits that followed in his wake. The last thing Sonny's father told him when he sent him to Florida was, "Keep your dick in your pants, and your hands out of the till."

Sonny had no real duties at Three Jacks other than making deposits at the bank. He usually just sat at the end of the bar, with his dog at his feet, trying to pick up women. He hated being the black sheep of the family, and was determined to redeem himself. Somehow, someway, he was going to show his dad that he wasn't such a fuckup after all. So when he heard one of the waitresses say something about her aunt Millie being real sick, his ears pricked up. Sonny knew all about the old lady who wouldn't sell the adjacent

C-LOVE Marina, with its numerous boat slips, and valuable commercial zoning. His dad wanted it bad, and tried several times to get her to sell, but she never budged. He strained his ears as the waitress talked to a table of people who seemed to be friends with her family. "Yeah, she's in a real bad way...No, it doesn't look good...I don't know what's gonna happen to the marina...No, there's not much family left...Yes, she's in Bethesda, bet she'd love to see you...OK, thanks, I'll be sure to tell her you said hi."

So she's in Bethesda Hospital, right down the street. Sonny was nothing if not opportunistic, and started to seize on an idea that presented itself to his scheming little mind. *If I can pull this off, Dad will give me whichever restaurant I want, and I won't have to take shit from anyone... especially my asshole brothers.*

Chapter 25

Tangles head wasn't that far above the bar to begin with, so when I say his jaw hit the bar, it really hit the bar. Rudy stood there with his palms turned up, looking from Tangles, to me, and back. Tangles spun around and placed his hands on the bar, staring at Rudy. "Marie Dupree who used to deal blackjack at Harrah's? In Biloxi?"

Rudy didn't say anything, he just looked at me like I had set him up. So I gave him my best "I don't know what the fuck's going on" look, because I didn't. Then it suddenly it hit me, Dupree was Tangles last name. *Ho- Lee- Shit!*

"How long ago?" said Tangles.

Looking nervous now, Rudy asked, "How long ago what?"

Slamming his beer down on the bar, Tangles replied in an eerily low voice, "How long ago were you running around with her?"

"What's it matter, Bubba?"

"What matters," said Tangles, with slipping restraint, "is Marie Dupree is mymother."

Now I've never seen Rudy at a loss for words in my life, but he started stammering and stuttering something fierce. "It...It...It was a lo...long t...t...time ago, Bu...Bubba...Ha...had...had to be th...thirty, thirty-five years a...at least."

Rudy wasn't looking too good, and was glad to be called away by another customer. Tangles took a long pull from his Bud, and rubbed his hand over his eyes.

I said, "So what, so Rudy knew your mother back in the day. Don't get all worked up about it." Inside, however, I was thinking, this is *un-fucking-believable.*

"So what? So what?" Tangles said, raising his voice. "So what is my dad used to beat my ass bloody when I was a kid. He used to call me a little bastard, and my mom a whore. Whenever my mom got home late, he'd say, 'So you been out screwing that Injun again?' He didn't take it out on her, he took it out on me. I never believed she was the whore he made her out to be, but now I'm not so sure. If she was banging this bartender Rudy, hell, she may have been banging some Injun too."

I had been watching Rudy out of the corner of my eye, and could tell he was listening to Tangles as he served the other customers. When Tangles mentioned the word Injun, Rudy knocked over a beer he was setting down. As he mopped it up, he shot a glance at Tangles, and I watched the color drain from his face. *Well, this is a little awkward.* Having a great sense of when the party's over, I asked for the check.

In another first, Rudy said, "Don't worry about it, Bubba, I'll catch you next time."

As we got in the car, I could see Rudy watching Tangles. I was thinking, what's he so shaken up about? So he banged his mother back in the seventies. *Who didn't bang somebody's mother back in the seventies?*

Chapter 26

We were halfway back to the marina before I ventured to say anything to Tangles, preferring instead to listen to some Weezer on the radio. Listening to them helps me get my mind off things, and I thought it might work for Tangles too. I started singing along, "If you want to destroy my sweater, hold this thread as I walk away..."

"Come on, man," I finally said. "I want to introduce you to a few people on the dock that can give you some work, and you need to have your game on. Besides, we got some celebrating to do. I still have the fishing show, you're not shark bait anymore, and that was one sweet yellowfin we boated this morning."

For the second time that day he cracked a smile, and nodded. "That *was* one helluva fish, wasn't it?"

We fist bumped, and he shot me a quizzical look. "I've been meaning to ask, how'd you come by the name Shagball?"

"When I was a kid, I use to shag a lot of balls, hence, Shagball."

"I didn't think you swung that way."

"Very funny, I used to play a lot of golf when I wasn't working on the driving range. My job was to pick up, or shag, balls. That's what it means...smartass."

We pulled into the marina, and I parked over by the *Lucky Dog*. I figured we might be hitting it pretty hard, so I grabbed a couple of waters off the boat. We both downed a bottle as we walked across the parking lot to the commercial docks, by Three Jacks. Hambone was just finishing up with an afternoon charter, stuffing a wad of cash in his shirt pocket as we walked up.

Looking up from the cockpit of the *Ham it Up*, he asked, "What is this? Bring your kid to school day? Just kidding. Heard all about the big tuna, but not the little tuna." He nodded toward Tangles. "Whaddup? Whaddup? Whaddup?"

I calculated he was on his seventh Coors Light, figuring his charter got back about five, and it was quarter till six. *At least he's in a good mood.*

I said, "Come on down for happy hour and I'll tell you all about it."

"I'll be down as soon as I get the boat cleaned."

"You're cleaning the boat? Where's Two-Brick?"

"Two-Brick no showed, I'm looking for a new mate."

"I might be able to help you out there, see you at the bar."

As Tangles and I worked our way down the dock, I heard him shout, "If the admiral's down there, tell him I got some fish for the smoker!"

As we passed the rest of the boats, I introduced Tangles to a few more people, and we were congratulated on the big catch. First we saw Eight-Toe Earl, the shark fisherman, then Kodak, who runs the lobster boat, and then Captain Karl, who runs the charter boat *Jolly Roger*. I invited them all over to the *Lucky Dog* after happy hour, to sample the fresh tuna.

We stopped in the restroom before entering the bar, and I was lost in thought as I did some liquid recycling. Tangles seemed to have shaken off the Rudy banging his momma thing, but then again, he didn't know Rudy's real name. Was Rudy really the Injun that Tangles' dad suspected his mom was screwing all those years ago? Would he feel any better if I told him his mom wasn't screwing a bartender and an Injun, but that maybe they were one and the same? I doubted so, and figured it would be best to let Rudy break it to him if he wanted to. *When in doubt, stay the fuck out.* Good words to live by when it comes to other people's business.

Chapter 27

Happy hour was in full swing. The bar was a rockin' and we were a rolling. I had been conductor of the skunk train for so long I almost forgot how much fun it was after a good day on the water, and today had been a great day. There was a lot of backslapping, and let me buy you a beer, no, let me buy you a beer, going on. My concern over Tangles not being in the mood to party was clearly unfounded. I turned around with a beer to hand him, and he was chatting up a table of co-eds on late spring break. They were giggling at something he said as I walked up.

"Hello, ladies." I smiled, handing Tangles a beer. "I see you've met my man Tangles, the talk of the dock."

One of the girls, a smoking hot blond, replied, "We like, understand that, you two like, caught a nice fish this morning."

"Nice? Let me show you nice." I pulled out my phone and cued up the pic of the big yellowfin tuna hanging from the scale, then handed it to her.

"Wow! That's like...humongous! Ashley, look at this," she said, passing the phone.

Her friend Ashley took the phone, and went, "Wow! That's cool, that's oxy-cool!"

What the hell, if not for me, for Tangles. I had to ask, "I don't suppose you two like sushi, do you?"

"Well like...duh," the blond said. "Like, who doesn't like sushi?"

"Well it's your lucky night then, because we're serving yellowfin tuna, sashimi style, on my boat the *Lucky Dog*, in about an hour...and we'd love you to join us."

"Ewww! Sashimi? No thanks, that's like nowhere near as good as sushi."

"Well, of course, we'll have pizza too," I added, with a wink to Tangles.

The girls shrieked, "Oh my God! We like, love pizza!"

Christ, the lengths we go to sometimes. I got my phone back and told Tangles to tell the girls how to get to the boat, thinking they'll probably need to MapQuest it.

I heard Hambone yell, "Yo! Shagball," and turned to see him leaning against the corner of the bar, well on his merry way. I joined him for a beer, and recounted how I foul-hooked Tangles and then caught the big tuna using the lure he gave me. He was dying with laughter over the Tangles part, and in total disbelief over catching the yellowfin on the goofy jig he gave me.

"So you're telling me that half-pint over there really knows what he's doing, huh?"

"No doubt about it, Ham, he owns the cockpit."

"Shit! You telling me he can keep up with the Hambone? He can keep up with this?" Spotting a gap along the side of the bar, he launched himself into one of his patented cartwheels. I'd seen him do it dozens of times without incident, and always marveled at the dexterity his Buddha-like body had. This time was different though. This time as he came up out of the cartwheel, a waitress rounded the corner holding a tray of drinks, and he hip checked her into oblivion. Some of the drinks landed on the new face of Three Jacks, Sonny Slade, who was sitting on the end corner of the bar, by the waitress station. The rest were evenly distributed over the dining area, as the poor waitress crashed to the deck, four tables deep. Hambone dove after her, trying to grab her before she hit the floor. Although he failed, he did manage to snag a bottle of Coors Light out of midair. He was first to rise from the carnage, and did so beaming. "Look! Didn't spill a drop!"

He then helped the waitress up, and half carried her back to the bar, profusely apologizing to everyone along the way. I'm sure I wasn't the only one who thought she might need to be Trauma Hawked to the nearest hospital. After all, she had sustained the equivalent impact of a Mini-Cooper being T-boned by a Hummer. Amazingly, she appeared to be all right as she was escorted to the restroom.

Sonny Slade, on the other hand, went ape shit. "You fucking idiot!" he screamed. His face was crimson, and the veins in his neck were popping out. "This fucking shirt costs more than that piece of shit boat of yours!" Then his dog, some kind of poodle mix, got in the act. It started barking and twisting around in circles. Sonny held a bar towel, and was wiping his face and shirt as he continued his diatribe. "You're out of here, you fucking imbecile! I don't ever want to see your fat fucking face in my bar again!"

Hambone was genuinely embarrassed, and shrugged. "Sorry, it was an accident, I'm really sorry."

"Sorry?" Sonny screamed again. "Sorry is you thinking you're Dorothy Fucking Hamill in my bar! Sorry? You bet your ass you're gonna be sorry when I—aaagh! Shit!"

I couldn't believe it, but his dog got so excited he bit him right in the calf. It seemed the whole bar was laughing as Sonny kicked at his poor dog. He hopped around on one leg as blood oozed from the bite. Hambone handed twenty bucks to the bartender, stopping in front of me long enough to say, "Tell that little buddy of yours that if he wants to make some money, to be at my boat at twelve thirty tomorrow for an afternoon trip."

Chapter 28

Milfred Lutes sat in her hospital bed, and contemplated what the doctors had just told her. The cancer had spread, and she had maybe three months left...maybe. *Why didn't I sell the marina when I had the chance?*

Only six months earlier, after her initial diagnosis, she had it under contract for seven and a half million to a developer. Then the economy tanked, and lending dried up, killing the deal. She had passed up countless offers over the years, because running the C-LOVE Marina was her life, and she wouldn't know what else to do. Even the city of Boynton Beach had tried to buy it, but after all the hassles they'd put her through, they were the last ones she would ever sell to. The marina had been in her family for generations, and it was her lifeblood. It killed her to think about selling, but with no one prepared to take the reins, she figured it would be best to get it sold before she passed away. Unfortunately, though, she knew it would be tough to get top-dollar, given the pathetic state of the economy.

She also knew something that nobody else did. When the property was passed on to her, she had been left a hand-sketched map, drawn by her grandfather. The map showed where two large diesel tanks were buried on the property, with instructions to keep the information to herself. An attached note, left by her dad, explained that the great hurricane of 1928 wiped out the above-ground tanks. Not knowing any better, they buried them, rather than haul them away. Of course, since then, saving the environment had become a political and social hot button, and hazardous waste removal a big business. She had done some research on her own, and discovered it could cost hundreds of thousands of dollars to remove the tanks, and even more if there was significant soil contamination. She thought it prudent to leave that can of worms unopened. The numbers were particularly galling, considering her granddad paid only twenty-five thousand dollars for the whole place, back in the early twenties. She dreaded the thought of having to hire a broker to sell the property, and paying a fee of five or six percent of the purchase price. *Highway robbery, that's what it is!*

Now she pondered her own mortality, and wondered how to break the news to her nieces, especially Holly. Holly was her late brother's only child, and was particularly close to Milfred, having been raised by her after her parents' deaths. Her step-niece Sarah was pleasant, but otherwise unmotivated, and working as a waitress at Three Jacks. Milfred used to like Three Jacks. She went there all the time until Syd Slade bought the landmark restaurant, and ruined it, in *her* eyes. She hated that Sarah worked for Slade, and offered her a job selling tickets to the drift boat. Sarah had turned her down though, saying she couldn't get up that early. *Kids!*

Holly, on the other hand, had a good job. She was highly skilled with computers, and helped Milfred's bookkeeper whenever she had a problem, which was more and more often it seemed. Holly's business card described her as an IT consultant. Milfred had no idea what it meant, and frankly didn't care. She loved Holly as if she were her own daughter, and knew Holly's feelings for her were the same.

Milfred was thinking about picking up the phone and calling Holly, when the nurse came in and announced, "Miss Lutes, you have a visitor."

Milfred smiled, thinking Holly had read her mind. She had come for a visit, even though it was the middle of the morning, and she normally came after work.

"Come in, come in," she said, with a great big smile. It quickly evaporated when a slick-looking stranger entered. He was holding a bouquet of roses, and cooed, "Here's some beautiful flowers, for a beautiful woman."

Chapter 29

"Who the hell are *you*? You're not Holly."

"No, I'm not," replied Sonny Slade. "But if she's half as pretty as you are, then I can't wait to meet her too."

"Nurse! Nurse!" Between not seeing Holly, and having some snake oil salesman appear at her bedside holding roses, Milfred was upset.

"No need to get excited, I believe you know my father, Syd. He asked me to deliver these roses to you."

"Syd?"

"Syd Slade, I'm his son Sonny. I've been managing the Three Jacks for the last couple of months. Your niece Sarah mentioned you were in the hospital, and my dad asked me to drop by and wish you well."

"Well...that's very nice of him, tell him...tell him I appreciate it."

Milfred didn't believe for one second that Syd sent her roses. He hadn't spoken to her since she turned down his last offer to buy the marina, and he had been pissed. She heard about Sonny, but had never met him until now, thinking he might well be the sleaziest of the Slades. "So how's your Dad doing?"

"He's doing fine, even though the restaurants aren't doing so well, due to the economy. He sure would like to diversify if the right opportunity presented itself."

Here it comes...son of a bitch finds out I'm sick and sends in his lackey son to try to sweet-talk me into a deal. "What kind of opportunity is he thinking about?"

"Well, you know, he's wanted to acquire the C-LOVE Marina ever since buying the Three Jacks. So if you were to think about selling..."

"Well, I'll keep that in mind, but I'm afraid you're a day late."

"A day late? What do you mean? Dad's been making you offers for years." Sonny was starting to feel a little bothered.

"Well that's true, but I hadn't heard from him in a while, and just yesterday these nice gentlemen from the Ocean Group paid me a visit." Milfred liked to play a little poker back in the day, and she was bluffing hard.

"The Ocean Group?" Sonny didn't like the sound of that at all.

"You know...the Ocean Group? The ones that tried to buy that trailer park on the sea, Briny Breezes, for five hundred million? Well that deal died when the neighboring communities raised a stink, and the economy tanked, but they still have a pile of money, and just yesterday they paid me a visit."

"Oh, r...*really?*" Sonny tried to make it sound like he was just casually interested in this piece of information, but it came out all wrong, much to Milfred's delight.

She was really enjoying tightening the screws on old Sonny. "Yes, sir, we agreed to terms...and they're coming back on Wednesday, with a deposit check and a contract to sign. So you see, you're a day late."

Sonny walked to the window while extracting a monogrammed hanky from his back pocket, then wiped his sweaty brow. When he turned back to face Milfred, she thought he looked a little like that famous actor. *Who was it? James Caan?*

"How much are you selling the marina for?"

"Not that it's any of your business, but eight million."

"SHIT!" Sonny slammed his hand down on a metal cart, and some medical instruments clattered to the floor. Milfred flinched a little, but was loving it. "Didn't you turn down eight million from my father a few years ago?"

"Well yes, but that was then and this is now."

Sonny started to lose it, and turned to face the window again, trying to keep his cool. He furiously mopped his forehead while muttering under his breath, "That was then and this is now." *Are you fucking kidding me? One day late? I don't think so.* He gathered himself as best he could, and turned to face Milfred again. "You're absolutely right, Miss Lutes, that was then, and this is now, and now I am telling you that my dad will match that offer."

"Oh dear, I don't know. They promised me it would be a quick close and they don't need financing, it's a cash deal. I just don't see how you would be able to do better than that these days."

"How quick are they willing to close?"

"Sixty days."

"We can close in forty-five days. How much of a deposit are they putting down?"

"Two hundred and fifty thousand dollars."

"We'll put down three hundred."

"Oh, I don't know, it just wouldn't be right. I told them we had a deal."

"But you didn't sign anything...right?" Sonny was getting hot again.

"Well no, but—"

"But nothing," insisted Sonny. "How 'bout we put up three hundred and fifty thousand...Nonrefundable."

"Nonrefundable?" asked Milfred.

Sonny couldn't believe he'd just said it either, but he knew how bad his dad wanted the property, and how bad he wanted to prove his worth.

"Make it four hundred thousand and you got yourself a deal, Sonny boy."

Did she just call me Sonny boy? Why I'm gonna squeeze her wrinkly little throat until her head pops off. Shit! He hadn't even asked his Dad yet. Would he be willing to put up a nonrefundable, four hundred grand deposit? Who was he kidding? Of course he would, he wanted the marina so bad he could taste it. With his temple throbbing, he put on his best toothy smile and squeezed out the words. "OK, it's a deal."

Milfred raised her hand to her ear, pretending she didn't hear him. "Say what? You like veal?"

"A deal! I said we have a deal...it's a deal." Sonny really wanted to pop her, but somehow managed to restrain himself as he reached down to shake her wiry old hand.

Milfred gave him her lawyer's number, and then openly wiped her hand on the bed sheet. As she watched him leave, she thought, no, it's not James Caan he looks like, but that squirrelly looking guy with the bulging eyes from the movie *Fargo*. What was his name? She couldn't recall, but smiled anyways. *Gotcha, Sonny boy, gotcha!*

Chapter 30

I woke up for the second morning in a row on the *Lucky Dog*...what a night. We partied till the wee hours, and I was certain to hear from the dockmaster Robo about noise complaints from some of the condo owners. Oh well, sometimes you just have to say "what the fuck," and last night was one of those times. It seemed like everybody on the dock showed up, along with most of the Three Jacks and Habana Boat staff. I had such a good time I forgot to call Melody and invite her down. *Or did I?* Maybe my subconscious was telling me I needed a little elbow room. Regardless, the tuna didn't stand a chance. Looking at my watch, I couldn't believe it was already eleven thirty. I yelled to Tangles, who was still snoozing on the couch. "Wake up, party boy! You got a charter in one hour."

I could hear him stirring as I brushed the last twelve hours out of my mouth. *Yuck!* At least I didn't have a hangover, thanks to the Extra Strength Excedrin I religiously take after imbibing large quantities of alcohol.

"Which boat is it again?" he asked, as I splashed water on my face.

"It's the *Ham it Up.* You start cleaning up this mess, and I'll run out and get us some breakfast sandwiches from Mickey D's."

"OK, boss."

I jumped in the Beemer, and as I was pulling into McDonald's, I saw Sonny Slade drive by, with a big shit-eating grin on his face. *What's that all about? Maybe he got laid? Nah, guys a douche bag. Hmmm, what then?*

As I stepped back into the cabin of the *Lucky Dog*, I was pleased to see Tangles did a pretty good job cleaning up. I took the sandwiches out and put them on paper plates, as Tangles came out of the bathroom toweling his hair. "I thought you were getting us some Egg McSomething's?"

"We missed breakfast, but they had a Big Mac special, second one for a penny, that one's mine."

As we scarfed down a couple of Big Macs and fries, Tangles grinned. "Those girls really liked the pizza." We shared a laugh, and Tangles asked if I had any advice for his charter with Hambone.

"Yeah, steer clear of the cartwheels."

As he headed over to the *Ham it Up*, I thought about how close the previous night had come to ending badly.

The co-eds had been so enthused after the pizza arrived, that they performed a little girl-on-girl dirty dancing in the cockpit. There were at least twenty-five to thirty people on and around the boat, and I had been standing on the dock smoking a cigar, taking it all in. When the girls finished their dance to a loud round of applause, I saw the blond set her beer down. She talked in her friend's ear over the music, and stepped off the boat, presumably to head over to Three Jacks to use the bathroom. My one cardinal rule for parties on the boat was that everybody had to use the Three Jacks bathroom so as not to overload the holding tank.

The city had recently purchased the fuel dock and the plot of land it sat on for an exorbitant price, and had a couple of construction trailers and dumpsters there. It was poorly lit, and as the blond Ashley walked past them, I thought I saw movement in the shadows, to the side of one of the dumpsters. Even though I was standing with a group of people and engaged in conversation, alarm bells were going off in my head. You see, I have an uncanny knack for spotting trouble. Over the years, it's saved me and my friends countless times from bad situations getting worse, and it gave me an edge on those unavoidable occasions when I needed to dole out some hurt. Everybody seemed oblivious to what was going on as I tracked the girl in my peripheral vision. She was about sixty yards away, when I noticed her come to a halt between the dumpsters.

I excused myself from the group and flicked my cigar butt in the water. Then I looped around behind the trailers and made my way through the dark, toward the dumpsters next to the parking lot.

As I got closer, I could hear Ashley's voice beginning to crack a little. "I...I said I don't want any, p...please. I'm just heading to the bathroom, l...let me pass."

I was coming up behind whoever had stopped her, and heard the voice say, "Why don't you just drop your shorts and go right here? I promise I won't look... much."

That was all I needed to hear. I stepped up behind him, and said, "Hey, dirt bag." Startled, he turned

toward me as I delivered a hard right uppercut to his
solar plexus, right in the old breadbasket. The crack
pipe he was holding clattered to the ground as he
keeled over. I followed up with a heavy right elbow to
the back of the head, putting him down and out, but
not in Beverly Hills.

Realizing it was me, Ashley grabbed my arm, and
cried, "Oh, my God! Oh, my God, thank you!"

I rolled the guy over with my foot, and didn't
recognize him. More importantly, I figured he would
never recognize me. It was too dark and happened
too quickly. I gave him a swift kick in the ribs for
good measure, *the dirt bag*, and then turned to Ashley.
"Come on, I'll walk you to the bathroom."

After she did her thing, we headed back to the boat.
I suggested that since it was late, she get her friend and
I'd walk them to their condo. Now I'm no saint, but
being the oldest of four kids, I had two little sisters,
and didn't want anything bad happening as a result of
one of my parties. Still, when Ashley planted a big kiss
on my cheek and thanked me again at the condo door,
I thought, *Christ! Why'd she have to be so hot?*

Walking back to the boat alone, I was thankful
for having had someone mentor me at a young age
in the art of self-defense, or offense, as it should be
called. At sixteen, I landed a summer job working in a
paper factory. I was small for my class because I was a
year younger than everybody else, being born in late
September. Consequently, I was a target for bullies.
Most of the guys at the factory were blue-collar stiffs
who didn't give me the time of day, except for one guy
in his late twenties named Scott. He wasn't very big
either, but he was an ex-marine, and after seeing me

in a confrontation, he took me aside on coffee break and explained the art of successful fighting.

"Look," he said, "don't try to be a hero, or impress anyone. It's always better to avoid a fight, than get into one in the first place. Keep your wits about you, and if you smell trouble coming, head the other way. However, if, *and only if,* you're in a position where a fight is inevitable, and there's no way around it, throw the first punch, and keep throwing them as hard and as fast as you can. Nine times out of ten the guy who throws the first punch wins, because someone jumps in and breaks up the fight, *or*...you'll have pounded the other guy into submission. Always use the element of surprise and nail 'em first, especially if they're bigger than you. There's no such thing as a sucker punch, there's only suckers who get punched." *It was probably the single best piece of advice I ever got.*

Chapter 31

Sonny was so excited he nearly ran the red light at Woolbright and Federal on his way back from the hospital. As he screeched to a stop, he reached for his cell phone and dialed his father, who answered, "Hello?"

"Hey, Pops, I did it."

"Pops?"

"I mean, um, sir."

Realizing it was Sonny calling, Syd took a deep breath, and wearily asked, "Exactly what did you do, Sonny?"

"I made a deal to buy the C-LOVE Marina, you know, next to the restaurant."

"*What?*"

"You heard me right, I just left the old lady in the hospital and she's agreed to sell it to us."

"Milfred's in the hospital?"

"Yeah."

"What's the matter with her?"

"Hell if I know, probably got hemorrhoids or something, who gives a shit, no pun intended."

"Very funny, how much does she want?"

"Eight million."

*"Eight million?*You agreed to pay *eight million dollars?* Are you fucking crazy?"

"I think you mean crazy like a fox. The developers who tried to buy Briny Breezes are set to sign a contract Wednesday, but thanks to me, we have a chance to man up on Tuesday, and ace them out."

"Man up? Who the *fuck* you think you're talking to, Sonny boy? I'll man up your ass, you don't watch your mouth...eight millions a lot of coin."

"Sorry, sir, I just got a little excited. I know how much you want the marina. Besides, you offered her that much a couple of years ago."

"Yeah, but that was then and this is now."

Say what? First he calls me Sonny boy, and now it's the "that was then and this is now" bullshit. Maybe the old man and Milfred should hook up. "What are you telling me? You gonna let these developers buy it out from under you?"

"Will you *shut up* for a second? I know you're not one for reading the papers, but newsflash, the economy is in a deep recession, and the stock market took a dive. You think I got eight million clams just lying around?"

"Can't you just borrow it?"

"Oh sure, why didn't I think of that? I'll just stroll in the bank and ask for eight million bucks, and they'll fill up a suitcase full of cash and say, 'Have a nice day, Mr. Slade.' Are you kidding me? I swear to God your mom must have been banging somebody else when you were conceived. Jesus!"

"You telling me you can't swing it?"

"Did I say I couldn't swing it? No. But it'll take some serious finagling to pull it off. What else is Milfred asking for?" This was the part where Sonny thought he may have gone too far, and he was now more than a little nervous to tell his dad about the big deposit, and quick closing. He decided to tweak the truth a little.

"You still there Sonny? What else did she say?"

"Well, we had to better the offer on the table. We gotta put up three hundred thousand, nonrefundable, and close in forty-five days."

"*WE?* What's this *we* shit? Unless you got skin in the game there's no *we*, Sonny, it's *me.*"

"I meant it like we're a team, sir, that's all...I know you're the man."

"No shit, Sherlock, just remember, there's no u in team."

"What?"

"Forget it, I'll make some calls and we'll talk tomorrow. I don't like nonrefundable deposits and it's a lot of money, but I'll be damned if I want somebody else controlling the C-LOVE Marina...and, Sonny?"

"Yes, sir."

"See what can happen when you and that fucking poodle get out of the bar once in a while?"

"It's not a poodle, Dad, it's a Labradoodle."

"Whatever, you did a good thing getting her to sell, even if the terms are a little rough. I never had any luck persuading her, maybe there's hope for you yet."

"Thanks dad, talk to you tomorrow."

Sitting in his car in the parking lot of the Manatee Bay Apartments, Sonny was so happy he started to get hard. He couldn't remember the last time his father had given him a compliment, albeit a backhanded one. So why'd he have to call his dog a poodle and ruin the moment? If there were two things in the world he hated, it was being called Sonny boy, and having his dog referred to as a poodle. He was thirty-eight, for Christ's sake, and his dog was half Labrador, and half poodle. Still, almost everybody called it a poodle... *assholes*. Sure, it looked kind of funny and would never have been his first choice, but an ex-girlfriend left it behind and he had grown attached to it.

Actually, he thought, there were three things in this world he really hated. He also hated having to climb up and down three flights of stairs to his apartment every day. Didn't the damn builder ever hear of an elevator? The only benefit to being three stories up was the great view of the Boynton Inlet from his bedroom and balcony. Still, it was up and down, up and down, every friggin day. Entering the apartment, he called out, "Mr. Jenks, I'm home." On his first step inside, he planted squarely in a pile of dog shit. Mr. Jenks came bounding up to him, stepping right through the same pile as he jumped up on his leg, tail wagging. "Goddamn it, Mr. Jenks! Not on my Tommy Bahamas!" Sonny rushed to the sink and wetted a paper towel, cursing as he tried to wipe the crap off his expensive shorts. He grabbed a plastic grocery bag and picked up the pile of shit, then headed back down to the outside dumpster. God he hated the stairs, and swore for the umpteenth time his next apartment or condo would be on the ground floor if it didn't have an elevator.

As he walked back up the stairs for the second time in two minutes, he thought about the hundred thousand dollar difference in the deposit money, between what he told his dad, and what he had agreed to with Milfred. He figured he would just take it out of the Three Jacks operating account and replace it after closing. It shouldn't be a big deal, but he wished he hadn't lied to the old man, knowing how pissed he was gonna be when he found out. On the other hand, at the end of the day, old Sonny would be the big hero for putting the deal together, right? *You bet your sweet ass I will.* He stripped out of his shorts and sprayed some Shout on the nasty stain, then tossed them in the wash.

While putting some new shorts on, he looked out the window toward the Inlet and saw the old scow, *Ham it Up*, heading out. He watched as it spewed black smoke from its midship smokestack, the one they call Hambone up on the bridge. The same guy who cartwheeled through the restaurant, spilling drinks on everyone. *Well, have a nice day you slobapotamus, because as soon as the deal closes, you'll be the first to get thrown out.* He started laughing out loud, and the dog started barking. "That's right, Mr. Jenks," he said, patting him on the head. "There's gonna be a new sheriff in town. Sonny's his name, and ass kickin's his game."

Chapter 32

After Tangles headed off on the charter with Hambone, I cleaned up the boat a little and grabbed the laundry bag in the closet of the forward berth. I headed back to the apartment to get a load going, and left Melody's shirt hanging from the doorknob to her place. I was glad she wasn't home, because I didn't feel like explaining why I didn't make it for our semi-regular, Friday night hookup. I shouldn't have to explain anyway; isn't that why it's called hooking up and not dating?

Once I had the laundry going, I tackled the three S's, a shit, shower, and shave. It was Saturday afternoon and I was running late for meeting up with the boys at the Surly Snapper. Just about every Saturday afternoon a group of us got together to drink a few beers and shoot the shit. The group expanded during football season, and petered out a little in the spring and summer. The smoking ban almost wiped us out entirely, but the owner fought back with a new chef, and the food was pretty darn good, so we continued to patronize it. Plus, for me, it was right around the corner, just like the Ole House.

As I walked in I saw Tooda and the admiral nursing coldies at the bar, and I sat down on a stool next to the admiral. The admiral always seemed to have an empty stool next to him. His loud (some say obnoxious) demeanor tended to have a repelling effect on strangers. "Hey, dawg," he greeted me. "Where's your sidekick?"

"Tangles? He's on a charter with Hambone."

"You must not like him very much," chimed in Tooda. "One charter with the Hamasaurus and he's liable to hit the road."

"I don't think so. He's a tough little shit, and knows his way around a cockpit. The way Hambone goes through help, he'll probably try to chain him to the boat."

I bought a round of beers, and as the bartender set down a Bud Light in front of me, my phone rang. I took a long swig, then answered, "Hello?"

"Shagbawl, how yew dune?"

"Kingfish Stew, how the hell are you?" I stood up and excused myself, stepping outside the bar so I could hear better. The caller's real name was Stewart, but I dubbed him Kingfish. He and his brother fished the SKA tour (Southern Kingfish Association), from their home base in North Carolina, and I fished a tour stop with them in Miami a few months earlier. We did pretty well in the tournament, made a good show, and became friends.

"I'm dune awlright, but my crew done gone AWOL, and I'm looking to fish the Key West tournament next week. Yew interested?"

"What days are we talking about?"

"Tournaments Friday and Sadderday, with check-in Thursday night."

"Sounds good, let me give Jamie a call and see if he can cut loose, if he can, then we're good to go."

"Get back to me sune as yew can, kay?"

"You got it, Kingfish, I'm gonna call Jamie right now, talk to you later."

I gave Jamie a call and he was totally psyched to go to Key West. "Dude that's awesome, no prob for me to blow out of here Thursday at noon. Wait till you see this Tangles and Tuna footage, it's gonna blow your mind."

"Jamie, I was there, remember?" Knowing Jamie, he was probably smoking a bone in the editing room right now, sometimes he spaced out a little.

"I know, dude, but I'm telling you it's killer. I'm gonna try to get it aired starting Thursday. I'll have it on the Web site by Wednesday, at the latest."

"Great, I know a reasonable place just off the strip, so I'll make the hotel reservations if you want."

"Thanks, Shag, talk at you later." I called Kingfish back and told him it was a go. The plan was for him to trailer the boat down to my apartment sometime Wednesday evening, and he would crash on my couch.

"All right, Kingfish," I said. "Give me a call when you're about an hour away."

"Yew got it, Shagbawl. See yew Wednesday."

Chapter 33

After having a couple more beers with the guys, I headed back to the apartment and finished up the laundry. *Still no Melody.* Looking out at the intracoastal from my bedroom window, I dreamt of the day I could buy a house on the water. I had been saving up for several years, but had written off the idea of a home on the water until the real estate market crashed, and made it not so farfetched. There were deals to be had, but you still needed cash, lots of it. I was still a ways off from what I needed, and hoped the deals were still there when I was ready. Unfortunately, or not, if you were a buyer, I was pretty sure that housing prices would remain in the shitter for years to come. Funny how hundreds of billions of dollars in taxpayer bailout money went to the big banks to keep them afloat, so they could continue to pay their fat-cat bankers billions more in bonuses, for helping 'cause the housing crisis, and near financial Armageddon. Nice work if you can get it. *Thanks, Congress.*

Before I got too pissed off thinking about it, I picked up the phone and called the office, to let them know I was going to be out on Thursday, as well as my usual Friday. My real job was as a commercial real estate broker. I handled leasing for a group of Palm Beach investors who owned shopping centers throughout Florida. I generally spent about twenty to twenty-five hours a week in the office, and they paid me hourly, plus commissions on leases. The fewer hours I spent in the office, the fewer hours I billed. Nobody had a problem with my taking time off, as long as the work got done.

I hopped back in the Beemer and popped some Weezer in for the drive back to the marina. Spending three or four days a week in Palm Beach was a major factor in my buying the convertible Beemer, a brand of car I never thought I'd own. One good reason was that there was much less likelihood of being pulled over. In Palm Beach, nobody looked twice at a nice Beemer, but if you were in a five-year-old pickup, you stood out like a sore thumb. You'd be pegged as a landscaper, or a granite and marble guy, or maybe a pool maintenance worker— definitely not a local. Still, I wasn't sold on it until I discovered that it had a pass-through from the trunk to the backseat. The Germans designed it for carrying snow skis, but it worked perfect for fishing rods too. I ended up getting a good deal on it, and have had it for ten years now. I thought about getting rid of it recently, but after checking comparative car prices, I decided to have it painted, and replaced the convertible top. Now it looks like new, and still runs great, getting almost thirty miles per gallon on the highway, and about twenty-one around town. Plus, I had put a bad-ass stereo system in it when I first bought it, and it's just plain fun to drive.

I was singing along as I pulled up to the *Lucky Dog*. "On an island in the sun, we'll be playing and having fun..." *You gotta love Weezer.*

I headed across the parking lot and could see Hambone filleting some fish on his cleaning table, with a Coors Light standing by. Tangles was cleaning up the boat, and when I got close, I could see a half dozen nice-size dolphin, and a few kingfish, waiting to go under the knife. "Looks like you had a pretty good trip, Hambone."

"Hell, I been cleaning for a half hour already, my customers just left with three sacks of fillets. When they're happy, I'm happy." He patted the wad of bills stuffed in his shirt pocket.

"Tangles worked out all right, I take it."

"I'm telling you straight up, dawg, that little dude's got some serious mojo working. It was like he was reading my mind, which ain't exactly easy to do. You know what I'm saying? Whaddup, whaddup, whaddup?"

Tangles got off the boat, and as he stepped up to the dock, Hambone peeled off four twenties. He handed them to him, saying, "Nice work, grab us a beer."

Hambone finished cleaning the fish as we drank our beer, and he told Tangles to take a sack of dolphin fillets for himself. *What? Hambone giving fish to a mate? He must have really impressed him.* Hambone said, "I got an 8:00 a.m. charter tomorrow, Tangles, think you can handle it?"

"Cat got an ass?"

We laughed, and Tangles agreed to be at the boat by seven thirty the next morning. As we headed back to the *Lucky Dog*, I asked Tangles what he thought about Hambone.

"I think he's got himself one hell of a new mate."

I just shook my head and laughed. *Cocky little shit.*

Chapter 34

Tangles was understandably beat, so I left him on the boat with my spare key and told him he could use the bed.

"Thanks, but the couch works just fine. Here's forty bucks for what I owe you, for clothes and beer." He held out a pair of twenties, but I told him to keep it until he had a little more bank. "Well...take the fish then," he insisted. "I'm gonna grab something from the restaurant later."

"You don't have to twist my arm," I told him, as he handed me the bag of fillets. "See you tomorrow after your charter."

As I turned to get in the Beemer, he said, "Shagball?"

"Yeah?"

"Thanks for helping me out, I really appreciate it."

"Forget about it, but if I hear you had more co-eds on the boat and didn't call me, you're done."

"Not tonight, boss." He laughed..."Not tonight."

I headed back to my place and found Melody sitting on the balcony, talking on the phone. She hung up and peered over the railing as I walked across the lawn to my door.

"Well, look what the cat dragged in."

I looked up and smiled, holding up the fish. "This cat's got some fresh dolphin fillets, how 'bout dinner? I buy, you fry."

"Such a sweet talker, how could I say no?"

Melody did a great job sautéing the fish in white wine and butter, serving it with some broccoli and rice. I pulled out a nice Pinot Grigio from the fridge, and five minutes after clearing the dishes, we were doing the horizontal cha-cha. *She was quite the dancer.*

After we caught our breath, I rolled out of bed and put my shorts on, saying, "I'm going downstairs to take a quick shower—wanna go see Rudy? It's only nine and they probably have some entertainment."

"Fortunately for you, I don't have any better offers. Give me fifteen minutes and I'll be ready."

Approximately eighteen minutes later we pulled up in front of the chikee hut, and secured the last two open bar seats. A minute later, Rudy sat a Bud Light down in front of me, shooting Melody a quick glance. "Hey, Bubba, what can I get for this pretty young filly your with?"

"Rudy, this is Melody. You've met her before—what would you like, Mel?

"Rudy shook her hand, and was grinning ear to ear like it was the first time he ever laid eyes on a good-looking gal. She asked for a white wine.

"How come he never remembers my name?" she complained, as he turned to pour her a glass.

"He doesn't remember anybody's name, that's why he calls all the guys Bubba, and all the women fillies, or lonesome doves, or whatever."

"If he wasn't such a cutie, I'd be pissed."

"Rudy a cutie?"

"Yeah he's sorta cute, and he does have that Southern charm."

"Hmmm," I said, as Rudy set a glass of wine down in front of Melody.

"So where's your little buddy at?" he asked.

"He worked a charter this afternoon and he's all tuckered out, so he's taking it easy on the boat tonight."

"The boat?"

"Yeah, he's staying on my boat till he gets his bearings."

"So he's gonna be staying around for a while then...I suppose."

"I suppose."

I told Melody all about the Tangles and tuna story over dinner, but I hadn't gotten as far as telling her about Rudy and Tangles' mom.

She asked, "Rudy seems awfully interested in your new friend Tangles—what's up with that?"

"Oh, I forgot to mention, Rudy use to date Tangles' mom back in the day."

"WHAT?"

"Yeah, small world, huh?"

"No, not that small...you're putting me on."

"Go ahead, ask him yourself."

"You're serious?"

"Be my guest," I said. I gestured with an open hand toward Rudy as he finished up with a couple of customers, and he asked if we wanted another round.

I nodded yes, and as he set us up, Melody struck. "So, Rudy, I don't mean to pry, but Mr. Wonderful here is telling me that you used to date the mother of the little guy he plucked out of the ocean yesterday. I don't believe him...as usual."

"Well, darling, looks like old Bubba here wasn't steering you wrong, at least this time. The young man in question did indeed claim that my sweet Marie *was, in fact,* his momma. A fact that I have yet to substantiate, however."

"Wait a minute, Rudy," I cut in. "He told me his last name was Dupree before you said her name, and he also said she was a blackjack dealer at Harrah's, which you didn't dispute."

"I'm not saying it's not possible, Bubba, but the young lady I knew couldn't have children. She told me her husband was shooting blanks, so if it *was* her, she must have remarried later on to someone else, that boy's what...maybe twenty-five years old? Now that I think of it, I probably should have carded him."

"Try thirty-five," I countered, before realizing the implications.

"Shoot...now you're pulling my chain, no way that boy's a day older than twenty-five."

"That's what I thought too, but he told me he was thirty-five." I looked at Mel who had these big bug eyes going on, and it dawned on me. Rudy was seeing Tangles' mom around the time he was born, and, according to Rudy, Tangles' dad was impotent.

"Ho-Lee-Shit!" I said, as I turned to Rudy. It all seemed to fit...Tangles' dad accusing his mom of screwing around with an Injun, and calling him a little bastard. Rudy claiming to be part Indian...the timeline...*Good God!*

"Bu...bu...bubba, that can't be right. He's prob... probably tired of getting c...carded. He must have a fake I.D...He can't, he can't, he c...can't be thirty-five."

I was floored, and the look on my face must have scared the shit out of Rudy, because he turned white as a ghost, like he was about to pass out.

"RUDY!" one of the waitresses shouted to get his attention. It momentarily snapped him out of his petrified state, and he went to the end of the bar to pour drinks. I saw him take a wet rag and wipe his face several times, glancing back at me.

The band reappeared after a short break, and as the opening notes to CCR's "Born on the Bayou," started to play, Melody squeezed my knee with a smile. "Wanna dance?"

Chapter 35

Sonny watched the last page of the fax disappear into the machine and took a deep breath. His father would be receiving it up in Boston in a few moments. *No turning back now.* First thing Monday morning, Sonny visited Milfred's attorney Bob Boone. He had an office on Ocean Avenue, just a stone's throw from the restaurant. At his dad's instruction, he told the attorney they were willing to close in forty-five days for eight million. The only stipulation was they needed fifteen days' due diligence to review rental agreements, and do a property inspection, before agreeing to the nonrefundable deposit.

The attorney placed a call to Milfred, and after a brief discussion, hung up. He said, "Give me ten minutes and I'll have the contract ready."

Sonny had never heard the words due diligence in his life, and was somewhat surprised that the old lady agreed so quickly. *Hot Damn! Pops really knows what he's doing.* Sure enough, ten minutes later he had the contract in his hands.

He went back to his apartment and made a copy. Then he changed the deposit to read three hundred thousand dollars instead of four hundred, and faxed it to his dad. Feeling nervous about the sleight of hand, Sonny suddenly had the urge for a smoke, and dug out his emergency pack. As he stood on the balcony and lit up, his dog started to bark at him. "Shut up, Mr. Jenks, I'm just having one." *One at a time that is...Quitting's a bitch.* As he watched the boats come in and out of the inlet, the phone rang. *Shit, that was quick.* He waited two more rings to gather himself before answering, "Hello?"

"Sonny, it's me, everything looks good, we're putting the marina under contract. On Tuesday morning I'm gonna wire two hundred thousand from up here, and another hundred from the Three Jacks operating account, to this Bob Boone."

"What?" Sonny's knees started to weaken as he snuffed out his smoke, and flicked it off the balcony.

"You going deaf? I just said we're doing the deal."

"No, I mean...you're taking a hundred grand from Three Jacks?"

"Yeah, that's right. That a *problem?*"

Oh shit, shit, shit. "No, no problem, it just leaves us a little thin with the big fishing tournament coming up and all."

"What are you talking about thin? I was just online and there's a hundred and forty-four grand in the operating account. Besides, those tournaments are moneymakers, not the other way around. I need all the cash I can get my hands on to make this happen. Fucking banks will only finance five million. I'm out of pocket for the rest. "

"Oh, OK."

"I'll talk to you later." Click.

Sonny plopped down in the chair on the balcony, mentally calculating how he could come up with a hundred grand. He had only about ten thousand in his personal checking account, and had no savings. He had fifty or sixty thousand in a 401K, but it was managed by a friend of his dad's, and he wouldn't be able to touch it without his dad catching wind. *Shit! What the hell am I gonna do?* Calling his dad back and explaining the artistic license he took with the contract was not an option.

Racking his brain, he suddenly remembered a line from a song by one of his all-time favorite groups, Hall & Oates..."I need a drink and a quick decision..." Yes, he certainly did. Glancing at his watch, he saw it was nearly lunchtime. *Hmmm. Why not head up to Rachelle's for a couple of drinks and maybe a sandwich? Nothing like naked women with Nip'n' Tuck titties to help clear the mind.* Sonny grabbed the keys to his leased Mercedes and headed out the door, nodding toward the dog. "See you later, Mr. Jenks."

Chapter 36

Rachelle's was a so called "upscale" strip club in West Palm Beach that had a surprisingly good lunch buffet, and a self-proclaimed, "best steak in town." It had been built in the late nineties for a rumored seven million dollars, and quickly sported a roster of the hottest strippers around. Only the cream of the stripping crop worked there, because this was the place where serious Palm Beach money came to have fun. Competition among dancers for stage time and the right to fleece, and maybe hook up with a trust fund baby, was fierce. Only the hottest of the hot survived, and Rachelle's had more survivors than the "Miracle on the Hudson." Located off I-95, close to the airport, and just ten minutes from Palm Beach, it became an instant success.

Although Sonny was new to town, he was already considered a regular, having dropped thousands of dollars on lap dances and "private dates." He loved the atmosphere, and considered it a "classy" place. He particularly liked that the dancers knew nothing at all about the sexual harassment suits he racked up trying to score with waitresses at his family owned restaurants. To them, he thought he was considered something of a "player," and wanted to keep it that way. Of course, to the dancers, being a "player," just meant you were a moron who threw lots of money at naked women who teased you. Nevertheless, Sonny was feeling a little better as he handed his keys to the valet, who nodded *good afternoon* as he opened the front door.

Sonny inhaled the sickly sweet smell of faux French perfume and roast beef, as he passed the buffet on his way to the back bar. A few years earlier, the place would have had a fairly decent crowd, even for noon on Monday. Now, with unemployment up, and the economy and housing market down, he found himself all but alone. Alone, that is, except for a few topless waitresses, and a couple of tables of lunch goers.

"Hey, honey, what I can get you?" asked the aging blond bartender, with the store-bought boobs. Clearly, the afternoon talent was a step below the evening shift.

"How about a Bloody Mary?"

"You got it, big boy—mild or spicy?"

"I don't care, just make it strong."

"You want a double?"

"Is the pope Polish?"

"No, you're thinking of the last pope. The new one's German."

"Polish, German, whatever...How 'bout a little less talky and a little more poury."

After shooting him a look, she whipped up a double and set the drink in front of him. "You running a tab?"

Sonny pulled out his gold card and laid it on the bar. She looked at the name on the card and it rang a bell...Sonny Slade. "Sonny...Sonny Slade...you're a regular, *aren't you?*"

"Yeah, but I don't normally come during the day... Jordan, is it?" He reached out his hand, noting her name tag.

"The one and only," she replied, as they shook. "Nice to meet you, Sonny. So what's got you here at noon on Monday?...Not that I'm complaining."

"You don't wanna know."

Actually, he was right, she didn't want to know, but six months ago the club managers called a staff meeting. The staff didn't need to be told that business was way down, but they were told anyway. They were also told to keep their eyes and ears open for any opportunity that could make money. They were encouraging prostitution, drugs, gambling, identity theft...anything that could bring in a buck. It was a matter of survival, they were told. If business stayed in the dumps, the place was going to close and they would all be out of a job.

Jordan had strong survival instincts, and smelled a hint of desperation coming from her only customer. She would know, being a bit desperate herself. Every chance she had she tried to learn obscure facts and trivia, having applied online to be a contestant on the television show, *Who Wants to Be a Millionaire?*

"Try me," she offered. "As you can see, it's not too busy."

Sonny took a huge swig of his drink, knocking back half of it. "I got myself in a jam."

"What kind of jam?"

"Financial." Sonny downed the rest of the Bloody Mary in another large gulp.

"Your gold card isn't bad, is it?"

"No, not yet at least."

"Another?"

"Do bears shit in the woods?"

"You would think so, but according to a *NatGeo* special I just saw, they predominantly defecate on and around riverbanks and lake beds. So technically, the answer would be no."

Sonny squinted at her, annoyed. "Thanks for that little factoid. I'll keep it in mind next time I'm kayaking in Saskatchewan...now pour."

As Jordan poured another bomb, she pressed on. "What? You got like a lot of credit card debt, or your house is about to be foreclosed or something?"

"I wish. I got a big real estate deal in the works, and I need to come up with a lot of money fast, or the shits gonna hit the fan."

She handed him his second Bloody Mary with a skeptical eye. "Real estate? In this market?" Even Jordan knew how shitty the real estate market had become. Hell, you had to live in a cave not to.

"It's actually a marina." Jordan's interest suddenly perked up like her fake boobs, because she had heard the club's owner had a nice boat he kept in a marina somewhere. She also knew that marinas were highly sought after, and more importantly, that her boss Gino was known to arrange short-term loans. She pressed the silent manager's button under the bar as she watched Sonny pound his second Bloody. "Well, Sonny, believe it or not, I just may be able to help you with your problem."

"Really?" Now the rough-looking blond had his attention. He heard a door being opened, and watched as a wide-bodied guy in a black suit approached from one of the doors in the back, marked, "Manager's Office."

Mr. Wide Body walked up next to Sonny, and looked at the bartender. "What's up J? This guy giving you a hard time?"

"Not at all...In fact, I think you might be able to help this gentleman with a problem he's having."

"That so."

"Maybe. Gino this is Sonny, he's an evening regular. Sonny this is Gino, the club manager." They shook hands and Gino sat down next to Sonny, vaguely recognizing him from one of his previous visits. Jordan pulled out a Red Bull and set it in front of Gino.

He nodded, then looked at Sonny. "So, Sonny, what's your problem?"

Chapter 37

I was at the office on Monday when Tangles called. I spent all day Sunday trying to get my head around the idea that Rudy could be his real dad, but was having trouble believing it. I decided more proof was needed before anybody said anything to anyone.

I picked up the phone. "What's up, T-Dog?"

"I got hold of Darla this morning and she's gonna mail me my stuff, I'm wondering where I should have her send it."

"What kind of stuff?"

"My wallet, toilet kit, last paycheck, some clothes... Why?"

"Well, if she's mailing your wallet and paycheck, you should have it sent here to the office. If it gets sent to my apartment and nobody's there, it might get left at the door, and something could happen to it."

"OK, what's the address?"

I gave him the address of the First National Bank Building, which was taken over by Wachovia, and now Wells Fargo. The investor group I worked for had a small upstairs office that was discreet, and more importantly to them, oozed prestige.

"I'll tell Jan, my secretary, to keep an eye peeled for it; she hits the mailroom twice a day. So what else is shaking?"

"Not much. No charters today, so I cleaned up the boat. I'm here at the ship's store using your buddy Tooda's phone, he thinks I should go to the V with him for a few beers."

"Unfortunately for you, that's probably the best offer you're gonna get all day. Go easy on him on the pool table though, better yet, partner up with him, and you'll have a friend for life. I'll catch up with you later."

"OK, boss, see you later."

"Tangles?"

"Yeah?"

"Enough with the boss stuff."

"OK, boss."

"Prick." I wished I could see the looks on their faces at the VFW when Tooda strolled in with Tangles. The VFW became a popular daytime drinking spot for some of us when the Three Jacks, and everybody else, raised their beer and drink prices too high. Granted it wasn't on the water, but it was air conditioned and you could get a cold Bud for a dollar seventy-five, and a mixed drink for two bucks. Of course, you had to be a veteran to be a member, but members could bring guests. For the most part, it kept the riffraff out, and it was a nice quiet place to relax and have a few. It was also halfway between my apartment and the marina. I stopped in every now and then when I knew Tooda or the admiral was there.

"Who was that?" asked Jan. I proceeded to tell her the whole story, and at the end, told her about the package coming in the mail.

"This is unbelievable."

"What part?"

"The whole thing. Catching a midget thirty miles off, catching a giant tuna...Oh yeah, and finding out the midget's *real* father could be the local bartender Rudy. Oh my God! Even I know Rudy!"

"Everybody knows Rudy. He's been tending bar at the Ole House for at least twenty-five years."

"I thought he was a lifelong bachelor."

"So did he, but that may be changing in a big way."

"I can't wait to meet this Tangles."

"Well, you won't have to wait long to see him, because the show will be online by Wednesday. It'll start airing Thursday on the boob tube."

"I'm calling everybody I know, this is *crazy.*"

"One thing though, not a word about Rudy possibly being Tangles' father. We need concrete proof, and if it is Rudy, he needs to break it to him. It shouldn't come through the grapevine.

"My lips are sealed."

I cocked my head to the side, and looked at her with a raised eyebrow. "Jan?"

She held up her hand, and pinched her forefinger and thumb together, before zipping them across her lips. Then she turned them like they were locking, and handed me an imaginary key.

"OK, OK...I believe you. Now let's get down to business, break out the rent rolls. Let's see who's got a lease expiring in the next three months."

Chapter 38

Gino watched Sonny leave the club and then turned to Jordan. "How much he tip you?"

"Exactly fifteen percent."

"Fifteen percent? What does he think this is? Fuckin' Applebee's?"

"Everybody's skimping nowadays."

"Well he ain't gonna be skimping if we float him a hundred big ones, that's for sure. I'm gonna fill the boss in, and see what he thinks."

Gino left the bar and headed back to his office. Then he placed a call on a secure line to the real owner of Rachelle's, his boss, Donatello DeNutzio, aka, Donny Nutz. Donny Nutz, or "Double D," as he was once called, was head of the Carpoza crime family's south Florida region. It was a region he managed to extend over the years, into Puerto Rico and the Caribbean. The call was routed from a bagel shop in Boca, to a used car dealership in Macon, and eventually to the back room office of a delicatessen in Jersey City, called the Rye Smile. As usual, Donny Nutz picked up the phone but said nothing, waiting for the other party to identify himself or herself first. He thought it made whoever was on the other end a little nervous, and therefore gave him an edge...He was usually right.

"It's Gino."

"Yeah?" It took only one word for Gino to know it was indeed Donny Nutz on the line. He sounded like he smoked three packs of Camels a day and gargled with gravel.

"I got a customer down here by the name of Sonny Slade who needs a hundred grand tomorrow. Says he can pay it back in forty-five days. Says his family owns a string of restaurants up the coast, including one down here. Says there's some marina they're buying in Boynton, next to his restaurant, the Three Jacks, and he needs the cash for a deposit."

"So he says."

"Yeah."

"Well, here's what I say. Take a drive down to his restaurant and check it out. Ask a few questions, and make sure this guy is who he says he is."

"Aren't you gonna ask why he needs to borrow a hundred grand if his family's so rich?"

"I ain't in the asking business, I'm in the telling business, and right now I'm telling you to get your ass down there and check him out. Capiche?"

"Capiche."

"I'll call you after I get the skinny on his family's business. Keep your phone on." Click.

Chapter 39

Donny Nutz picked the phone back up. *Boynton, huh?* He called information and got the number for the Boynton Beach City Hall. He asked for the mayor's office, and was put through to a secretary.

"I'd like to speak to the mayor."

In a well-rehearsed, clipped voice, the secretary responded as usual. "I'm sorry, but the mayor's busy right now. If you leave your name and number he'll get back to you as soon as possible."

Sure he will, probably sitting right there reading the newspaper, with his thumb up his ass. "How 'bout I stay on the line while you pop your pretty head in his office? Tell him it's Donny...from JC."

"Donny? From JC? I'm sorry, like I said, he's tied up right now, but if you—"

"Irene? Did I hear you just say Donny from JC?" The mayor set down the *Palm Beach Post* and stepped out from behind his desk on his way to the door.

"Umm, ah, excuse me for a moment, sir." Irene cupped her hand over the receiver and loudly whispered to the mayor, "Donny from JC?"

"Put him through." The mayor closed his office door and went back to his desk.

"Umm, the mayor just finished his meeting and will take your call now, hang on while I transfer you."

"Well how's about that."

Feeling more than a little embarrassed, Irene patched the call through. She couldn't help but wonder who the heck Donny was, and where on earth was JC. The mayor rarely took unscheduled calls, but this time he seemed eager to talk to this Donny character. The mystery man with the deathbed voice.

"Donny?"

"Vincent, how's the mayoring business?" The voice was unmistakable, as rough and gruff as they come. It was indeed Donatello DeNutzio on the other end.

"Very political. To what do I owe the pleasure of today's call? It's been a long time."

"What can you tell me about a guy named Sonny Slade and the Three Jacks?"

"Sonny? From what I hear, he couldn't manage his way out of a paper bag. His father, Syd, is a pretty shrewd operator though. He's been a pain in my ass ever since he bought the restaurant. The city's been sued several times over easements, right-of-ways, property line disputes, you name it. Guy's a real son of a bitch. The city tried to buy him out a couple of years ago as part of a community redevelopment program, but he had none of it. Why the interest?"

"This guy Sonny's looking to borrow some money he says he needs for a deposit on the marina next door."

"The C-LOVE Marina? No way would old Milfred sell to him. She knows the city would pay more for it than he would. My guess is Sonny's got a gambling debt he needs to pay off. Word is he spends a fair amount of time at the dog track."

"Whatever, I figure since he's in your backyard you might know a little about him, and whether he's the type who might rabbit on me."

"Skip out on you? I wouldn't worry about it. Even if he *was* crazy enough to stiff you, you could squeeze the old man."

"That's what I figure too—the restaurant does pretty good business, no?"

"Are you kidding me? It's a friggin gold mine, even with that idiot Sonny messing around. The food sucks, but it's an institution down here, been around forever."

"OK, Vince, that's all I need for now."

"Whatever you want, Donny. If I can help, you know I will."

"I know." Click.

Mayor Vincent Mandula hung up, and stared at the phone for a second. It had been what? Twenty-five years since he had last talked to Donny Nutz? He thought about the unlikely way he had become indebted to the renowned mobster.

Back in the early eighties, he had been an assistant DA in Jersey City, New Jersey, and had been assigned to the anti-racketeering task force. An up-and-coming wise guy by the name of Donatello DeNutzio had begun to monopolize organized criminal activities in the city. For two years, he had been building a case against him, using informants, wiretaps, and the like.

Just as he was preparing to issue a grand jury indictment, the unthinkable happened. His little sister was forced into her car at gunpoint after leaving a local nightspot early one morning. She was found the next day on the side of a county road, clinging to life after being brutally raped and beaten.

After weeks in the hospital, she was barely able to give a description of the attacker to police. It turned out to be a recent parolee who Vince had prosecuted some years earlier for another rape. A jailhouse snitch relayed to the cops that she had been targeted for being Vince's sister. It was payback, plain and simple.

The DA himself took the case, recusing Vince despite his pleas to be the lead attorney. At trial, it came out that the accused had not been read his Miranda rights in a timely fashion, and there were a number of prosecutorial screwups, including not releasing pertinent information to the defense team. What had initially looked like a slam-dunk case unraveled and the guy walked.

Vince was beside himself with anger and guilt, knowing that she had been targeted because she was his sister. Worse yet, the perp stuck around town as if to taunt him. Vince was young and hotheaded, and couldn't take it. It was driving him crazy, so he decided to pay a visit to Donatello at one of his known hangouts. Against his better judgment, he struck a deal with the mobster. He would lose the case file against him and look the other way concerning mob business, if Donny would make the scumbag who raped and beat his sister go away.

Although Vince had only meant for Donny to make him go away as in leave town, Donny took it literally. Two days later, the guy's body was found in the parking lot of Giants stadium on game day. He had been tortured and executed, with one shot through the heart, his balls cut off and stapled to his lower lip. Because it looked like the gangland slaying that it was, Donatello DeNutzio had been the prime suspect, but there was no evidence to indict him with. Ever since then, the law enforcement community, and subsequently the press, referred to him as Donny Nutz. Vince quit the DA's office a couple of months later, after his sister died from her injuries. Looking for a new start, he packed up and moved to south Florida. It was there he opened a private practice, and eventually became mayor of Boynton Beach.

Chapter 40

Gino pulled into the Three Jacks parking lot in his big black Hummer. He powered down the window, saying, "I'll park it myself," to the valet. He pulled into a spot that the valet pointed to and parked diagonally, taking up two spots. He locked his Glock in the glove box, and activated the car alarm as he walked toward the bar.

The valet approached him again. "Sir, I'll need your keys, please."

Gino tilted his head down, and peered over the top of his mirrored sunglasses. "I don't fucking think so. I won't be long."

The young valet was more than a little intimidated, and replied, "Uh, sure, uh no...no problem, sir."

Gino walked down the dock looking at the boats, and stepped into the outside bar, thinking he should have left his jacket in the Hummer. He asked the bartender if there was any air conditioning in the place. She laughed, and pointed to the inside bar. "It's a little cooler in there." He made his way to the inside bar and sat down, ordering a Red Bull and Stoli. He removed his jacket, and placed it on the chair next to him. *Cooler, my ass.* As the bartender set his drink down, she asked if he would like to run a tab.

"No thanks, I'll pay as I go." He set a twenty on the bar, and when she returned with his change, he asked, "Is Sonny around?"

"He should be here any minute—he's usually in by four. He'll be sitting at the end of the outside bar with his dog, you can't miss him."

Just then his phone rang. He saw that it was from a "private caller," and answered, "Hello?"

"OK, here's the deal." It was Donny Nutz. "First, I want you to check his driver's license to make sure he is who he says he is. Then tell him we'll deliver a hundred K tomorrow morning, if he agrees to repay a hundred and thirty-five, in forty-five days. That's twenty percent juice a month, plus five grand for the effort. Call it a processing fee if you want."

"Got it."

"Call me if it's a go, and I'll have the cash delivered to the club tomorrow morning. You can take it from there." Click.

Gino was putting his phone back in his pocket when he saw Sonny and his dog take a seat at the end of the outside bar. He picked up his jacket and left some money on the bar, then walked over to Sonny and put a hand on his shoulder. "Nice place you got here."

Sonny turned, and was startled to see the strip club manager standing there.

"Gino, I uh, wasn't expecting you so...so soon. I um...take it you have some news?"

"Matter of fact, I do, but first let me see your driver's license."

"My license?"

"Yeah, most guys keep it in their wallet." He glanced down at the funny-looking dog at his feet, then added, "but with you I'm not so sure."

Sonny ate the insult and pulled out his wallet. Then took out his license and handed it to Gino.

He looked back and forth a few times, from the license, to Sonny. Once satisfied it was him, he nodded. "OK, let's talk somewhere private."

Sonny put the license back in his wallet and led Gino upstairs to the second-floor bar, which was kept closed unless booked for a private party. After looking around and feeling confident they weren't being listened to, Gino cut right to it. "According to the boss, you qualify for a loan at twenty percent interest, plus a small processing fee."

Sonny mulled the number around and was relieved, he figured the rate would be much higher. "How much is the processing fee?"

"Only five grand."

Hmmm, not bad at all. "Sounds great, Gino, I really appreciate it...you can get it to me by tomorrow afternoon?"

"Not a problem. But understand one thing, Sonny. Forty-five days from tomorrow you need to pay back a hundred and thirty-five grand, or you're not gonna like the consequences."

"A hundred and thirty-five grand? Holy shit! I thought you said I qualified for twenty percent interest?"

"That's right, twenty percent interest per month, starting tomorrow...do the math. Like I said, you don't wanna know what the late fee's all about."

Sonny thought he was gonna puke over the side rail, right on some happy hour customers. Mr. Jenks noticed, and started barking at Gino. *Wonderful.* "Quiet, boy, no barkee, no barkee...that's a good boy."

Once Mr. Jenks calmed down, Gino said, "Hey, no skin off my back, you don't want the money, just say so."

"No, no, wait a sec...just give me a second to think." Sonny had his hands on the railing and was looking south down the intracoastal, trying to decide if he should just call his dad and level with him.

"What's the big deal?" Gino asked. "A place like this probably does thirty-five K every weekend, but like I said..."

Mr. Wide Body's right, thought Sonny, and with the fishing tournament coming up, he might even be able to cover the entire interest payment from the proceeds. His decision was made, and he nodded. "OK."

"OK, what?"

"OK, I'll take the money."

Gino smiled as he pulled his phone out and dialed. Ten seconds later he spoke into the mouthpiece, "It's a go." He was quiet for a few more seconds, nodded, and hung up. "I'll be back around eleven tomorrow morning with the dough." As he headed down the stairs, the dog lunged toward him and started barking. Sonny pulled him back by his leash, admonishing the dog like he somehow understood what he was saying. "Barky Von Schnauzer! No Barky Von Schnauzer!"

Gino turned and shook his head, looking up at Sonny. "You know, you really oughta teach you're poodle some manners."

"He's a Labradoodle."

"Sure he is...and I'm the fucking tooth fairy. See you tomorrow."

Chapter 41

The next morning was slow on the dock. It was blowing about fifteen knots out of the southeast, so most of the boats stayed in. One of the drawbacks at the Water's Edge Marina was that the ship's store, where customers paid for fuel and bought supplies, had no bathroom. Consequently, everybody walked over to Three Jacks and used their restrooms, which were located on the outside of the building next to the parking lot. At a little after eleven o'clock, Robo needed to relieve himself. At sixty-seven years old, his prostate wasn't what is used to be. As he walked across the parking lot, he saw a black Hummer come to a stop in the turnaround circle, and a guy in a black suit and sunglasses stepped out, holding a briefcase. It was the same guy he had seen in the bar at happy hour the day before. He had been having a scotch after work, and saw the guy approach Sonny and ask for his driver's license. At the time, Robo thought he looked familiar, and might be a cop or something. Perhaps old Sonny's got himself in a little trouble. *Wouldn't be the first time.*

Robo was the dockmaster, and as such, it was his duty to know everything happening on and around the docks. Three Jacks was an unavoidable and integral part of his domain. The mystery guy headed into the near-empty bar as Robo went into the bathroom to take care of business. His curiosity was weighing on him almost as much as his prostate. *Do cops drive Hummers?* Nah, probably not on official business at least. *But who the hell wears a suit to a waterfront bar?* Robo decided to investigate a little more, figuring he'd go into the bar and get a cup of coffee, even though it was the last thing he needed. As he entered the bar, he didn't see Sonny or the mystery guy, so he walked past the coffee station. When he got to the inside bar, he was surprised to see they weren't there either. Confused, he turned around and walked back to the outside bar, suddenly hearing footsteps from above. The mystery man was coming down the stairs first, with Sonny behind him. Robo turned to the coffee machine and poured himself a to-go cup, hearing the mystery man say he'd be in touch. As he started walking back down the dock, he noticed the mystery man in front of him wasn't carrying the briefcase. *Huh.* He stopped at the parking lot cut through where the restrooms were, and glanced back to see Sonny heading his way with the briefcase tucked under his arm like a football. *What the heck's going on here?* He stepped into the turnaround heading toward the ship's store, just as the mystery man in the Hummer drove by.

Now he knew why he looked familiar. He looked like that guy Baretta from the seventies cop show if somebody dropped an anvil on his head and squashed his face. *Note to self,* he thought, as he walked across the grass to the ship's store. *There's definitely something rotten in Denmark.* Robo vowed to keep an even closer eye on things; after all, it was his job.

Chapter 42

I was on my way to pick up Tangles at the VFW, when Jamie called.

"Dude, I just got the show done, my Web guy put it up on the site about half an hour ago. We've already got fifty e-mails all saying the same thing...*it's fucking awesome!*"

"That was quick. I thought you said it wouldn't be up until Wednesday."

"Shag, I've been living in the studio for the last four days to make this happen, you don't know the half of it, hang on a sec..." I could hear him talking to someone else, maybe on another phone, and then he came back on the line even more excited than before. "That was my Web guy. He posted the show on YouTube. We're going viral, baby!"

I was laughing—when he got excited, it was contagious. "That's a good thing, I guess."

"Good thing? Wait till John Q. Public gets a load of you and Tangles in action. It's a friggin masterpiece of incredibility!"

"Keep me posted, I'm pulling into the V to pick up Tangles right now."

"Buy him a beer for me. In fact, buy one for yourself as well, this could be big."

I had never heard him so excited. "Count on it, I'll talk to you later." Click.

It was about four thirty when I walked into the VFW. Tooda and Tangles were sitting in the corner, laughing with a handful of other customers including the admiral. They each had a stack of drink chips in front of them. The golden rule at the V was no gambling for cash, but you could play for drinks, hence all the chips. Figuring they had been there for at least three or four hours, I knew they would be tuned up.

Tooda saw me first. "Hey, Shag, commere, lemme buy you a beer."

I took a seat to the left of Tooda, with Tangles on his right. Tooda signaled the bartender, and she set me up with a Bud Light, taking one of Tooda's chips. "Looks like you two had a good day at the pool table," I commented.

Tangles said, "She-it, evrybody wans to break up the dynasty of the two Ts, nobody wans to play us anymo."

They laughed and clinked cans, and Tooda slurred, "Thas righ, me and Mini-Soda Flats here been unbeatable, wanna rack 'em up? Whaz the matta? Chicken say chicken."

They laughed and clinked cans again.

I thought to myself that some people just shouldn't be allowed to hang together for the greater good, like Paris Hilton and Nicole Ritchie. When you put them together, they're way worse than apart. They feed off each other's worst traits, making them unbearable to be around, hot or not. Tangles and Tooda were about to reach that point, until I decided to play Yoko and break up the band.

I looked at Tangles. "Time to drink up, unless you wanna walk back to the boat...I got some errands to run." I didn't really have any errands, but they were two sheets to the wind and I wanted the breeze at my back.

"OK, boss, r...ready when you are."

I downed my beer, and replied, "Let's do it."

Tooda looked at me. "Right here? You two oughta get a room." Everybody chuckled.

"Very funny, you want a ride too, Tooda?"

"Nah, I'm gonna jus scoot on home, gotta hot date."

Fortunately, he lived only a mile away from the V and could take the back way home. But still, he shouldn't be driving, let alone riding a scooter.

"Don't worry," said the admiral. "If I see him stumble on his way to the scooter, I'll take him home myself."

"Hell, he might be safer on the scooter."

Everybody at the bar laughed again. Tuesday's were the admiral's day off because the club was closed, and he was known to start knocking them back early. Per usual, he was feeling no pain by late afternoon.

"Alrighty, then, let's roll, Tangles."

Eight minutes later, we were back on the *Lucky Dog*. Tangles stretched out on the couch, announcing his plans for a nap. I told him I was heading back to the ranch and that I'd see him later. He was snoring by the time I left the boat.

Chapter 43

Milfred was back at home on her waterfront point lot on Sabal Island. It was in Ocean Ridge, maybe five minutes from the marina. Despite her doctor's objections, she decided to discharge herself from the hospital. She made it abundantly clear she was not continuing with chemotherapy. She was going to live out her final days at home, and hire a private nurse when the time came. *Why the hell shouldn't she?* She hated hospitals, and missed sitting on the deck watching the boats go by.

Her lawyer had just left, right after she signed the contract to sell the marina to Syd Slade. She couldn't believe he went for the nonrefundable deposit and purchase price of eight million, despite her conceding a fifteen-day inspection period. She hated the fact that Slade would end up with the marina, but fortunately for Slade, she hated the city more. She knew the mayor would flip when he found out about the deal, and wished she could be there in person when it happened.

Just then the doorbell rang. She was expecting her niece Holly, and couldn't wait to see her, even though she dreaded having to tell her about her condition.

She used her cane to make her way to the door, and opened it to see Holly's beautiful face. She was smiling and holding flowers in her hand.

"Aunt Millie, I've missed you so much!" Holly gave her a big hug, then took Milfred by the arm and led her into the kitchen.

"My dear, you just get prettier and prettier every time I see you. How are things going with you and Mark?" Holly had confided in her aunt months earlier that she and her husband were having marital problems, but she wasn't ready to tell her everything just yet.

"Come on, Millie, let's not talk about my marriage." She had told her aunt she was in town because she was a bridesmaid in a friend's wedding, when in reality she had moved back to her Jupiter condo for good. In fact, she was officially divorced, and the only thing she ended up with was the condo. Her husband of four years had not only cheated on her, but had cheated his investment clients as well. Mark had been convicted of fraud and was heading to prison for at least five years. Holly was trying to rebuild her life, and figure out what to do with the rest of it. The only thing she was thankful for was that they didn't have any kids involved.

"All right, dear, I won't press you on it for now, but that husband of yours is an *idiot* if he lets you go. Come now, would you like something to drink?"

"I'll take a water, please."

"Well help yourself, you know where everything is. I'm heading back out to the deck, we can chat out there."

Holly was shocked to see there was hardly anything at all in the fridge except for bottled water and some prune juice. She grabbed a bottle and followed Millie out to the deck.

"How come there's no food in the fridge?"

"Um, I uh, just got back from the hospital."

"What? You didn't tell me you were back in the hospital, is everything OK?"

This was the part that Milfred dreaded. "Not exactly."

Holly grew alarmed and grabbed her hand as she sat next to her on the couch under the awning. "Millie, what's going on?"

"Oh dear, I'm afraid the cancer's back, and I haven't much time left. I'm not going back to the hospital for any more chemo, I'm staying home. I'm sorry."

Holly's eyes welled up, and she threw her arms around her in a bear hug, crying, "No, no, no, oh, Millie!"

"Now, dear, it's all right, I've had a good life, and you're the best part of it."

"Millie, you can't leave me, you just can't, it's not fair!"

She was crying hard, and Millie was stroking her long blond hair, even as her own eyes welled up. She cooed, "Now, now, it'll be all right, honey, it's OK, it's OK."

After a solid minute of holding her, Holly pulled away and looked into her eyes. "How much longer do you have?"

"The doctor said maybe three months."

Holly wiped away her tears, trying to act strong for her aunt. "Well, all right then, I'll just pack up my stuff and move in with you, you're going to need some help."

"Oh, dear, don't be silly. I'll hire a nurse when I need to, besides, what about Mark?"

"Forget about Mark."

"Well, what about your work?"

"I'm a computer consultant, Millie. I can work from here if I need to. All I need is high-speed Internet access.

"High-speed what?"

"Don't worry, I'm sure it's available here, no arguing about it...I'm staying with you. In fact, I'm heading back to Jupiter right now to get my things. Wait, I need to go to the store first and get some food before you starve."

"Food? Don't be silly, I'll have the deli down the street deliver me something, I have an account."

"OK, then, it's settled." Holly kissed her aunt on the cheek, and rose from the couch.

"Is there anything else you need before I go?"

"Yes, one more kiss." Holly bent down and gave her another kiss and a hug.

Milfred said, "Holly, my dear, thank you, I'm so glad you'll be keeping me company."

"Me too, Millie, me too."

Chapter 44

Mayor Vincent Mandula couldn't believe what his CRA director had just said, that Slade had the C-LOVE Marina under contract.

"WHAT? You've got to be kidding me...right?"

"I'm afraid not."

"When did this happen?"

"I just found out, but apparently the contract was signed late Tuesday."

The mayor slammed his fist down on the desk, startling the shapely woman he hired a few years earlier to spearhead the Community Redevelopment Association. Donny Nutz had tipped him off on Monday, but he had dismissed it out of hand. *No frigging way.* "How much are they paying?"

"I haven't seen a copy of the actual contract, but the rumor is eight million."

"Eight million? Christ, she turned down that much from us, what, two years ago?"

"Yes, two and a half years, to be exact."

The mayor was drumming his fingers on the desk as he weighed his options, not finding any he liked. He couldn't believe that Milfred Lutes had snubbed him and agreed to sell to Slade. It would totally stymie the city's redevelopment plans for the waterfront. It would leave them with nothing but the fuel dock and a small parcel of land they overpaid for in *anticipation* of buying the marina.

"Kristy, I don't have to tell you how bad this is. If Slade purchases the marina, the waterfront development plan is dead. If the waterfront development plan is dead, then the CRA is dead, and if the CRA is dead, then guess what? You're out of a job and I'll be voted out of office in November. *Shit!*"

He was right. Kristy Kane didn't need to be told how disastrous it was. She spent the better part of three years and hundreds of thousands of dollars of city money on architects, engineers, and designers, who brought her vision to life. There was even a scale model of the new waterfront sitting downstairs in the lobby of City Hall. The waterfront development project was to be her crowning achievement, launching her career to new heights. Perhaps even to the chair that her overbearing boss was sitting in right now. She wasn't about to just sit by and watch it go down the drain without a fight. "We've got to stop the deal from going through somehow," she agreed.

"Wow! Now I know why you get paid the big bucks. Thanks for pointing out the obvious, Miss Einstein. Why don't you go work on the somehow, and get back to me. I need to think...close the door on your way out." He gave her a little wave of hand, dismissing her as he gazed out the window. She was infuriated and opened her mouth to say something, but spun on her heel instead, her face turning red. She didn't want to let the prick know he'd gotten to her, but couldn't help slamming the door a little harder than necessary on the way out.

Chapter 45

We were on our way to Key West. Jamie and I were in his GMC Yukon. Kingfish Stew and Tangles rode in Kingfish's F250, which towed his red twenty-seven-foot Contender, the *Kingdom Come.* Jamie called me the night before, saying our YouTube video had something like a hundred and fifty thousand hits, and we were an Internet sensation. He thought Tangles should come with us, and I agreed. I called Kingfish, who was fine with it, and then asked Tangles, who was stoked, because he had never been to the Keys. He started doing a Hawaiian-style, ukulele sway, and sang a Beach Boys song in a surprisingly pleasant baritone. "Key Largo, Montego, baby why don't we go? Bermuda, Bahama, come on pretty mama..." I laughed my ass off. *Shorty was a real piece of work.* I had brought along my Motorola handheld walkie-talkie's so we could communicate between vehicles without having to rely on the sometimes spotty cell service on the way. As we approached Florida City, I radioed Tangles.

"Hey Tangles, tell Kingfish to get off at the Florida City exit and go to the Super Wal-Mart."

"Roger that, Skipper, that's a big ten four."

"This is a walkie-talkie, dude, not a CB radio, you can cut the trucker lingo."

"No can do, mon frere. Kingfish says Wal-Mart's a go, over."

"See you there."

"That's affirmative, Eagle One."

Jamie and I laughed, and I said, "Eagle One? Jesus, it's like he thinks he's on an Apollo mission."

At Wal-Mart we loaded up with beer, water, food, ice and some munchies. Four days in the Keys requires plenty of supplies, and we weren't about to be lacking the essentials. Sure, you can buy groceries down in Key West, but you'll pay a fair share more than you will on the mainland. Florida City is the last stop before the Keys, and is therefore a natural place to stock up.

As we continued our journey south on U.S.1, we passed through Key Largo, Islamorada, and then Lower Matecumbe. We left Lantana about twelve thirty, and it was now almost three thirty, on an absolutely gorgeous day. The scenery never fails to impress, even after all the times I've been to the Keys. There's sparkling blue water and white sandy beaches on both sides of the road, accented by swaying palms and pastel-colored stilt houses with metal roofs. The scenery is so stunning you look right past the crappy trailers and run-down commercial buildings.

When we hit the seven-mile bridge, I decided to radio Tangles for his initial impression. "How do you like the Keys so far, my little tyke with the mic?"

Jamie laughed in my ear as Tangles replied, "Wow! This is unbelievable...it's nothing like Biloxi, that's for sure."

"It's nothing like anywhere else in the world, my man. See that old bridge below us on the right? That's the one they blew up filming *True Lies*, with Schwarzenegger and Jamie Lee Curtis."

"*True Lies?*"

"You've never seen *True Lies?* It's probably the best film Arnold ever made, and the ladies absolutely love it, you really need to get out more."

Jamie said, "He's never seen *True Lies?* What, they don't have cable in Biloxi?"

About an hour and a half later we checked in with the SKA at the host marina, on the southeast side (the Atlantic side) of Key West. Once we dropped the boat in the water and put it in our designated slip, we headed to the motel to unpack. I made us reservations at a twelve-unit place just off Duval Street that I stayed at before, called the Sleepin' Inn. It was owned by a nice couple from Illinois, and had adequate parking and accommodations. Namely, each room had a couple of beds, a TV with cable, and a mini-fridge. It was affordable, and perfect for our limited needs.

As we unpacked, Jamie presented Tangles and Kingfish with their "show" shirts. They were embroidered and monogrammed fishing shirts identical to mine, and they were thrilled. We had Jamie and Tangles go get some food, while Kingfish and I went through our pre-tournament routine of checking the gear and making rigs.

We sat in the room that Kingfish was sharing with Tangles, and made a bunch of live bait rigs on light wire with stinger hooks, the preferred rig of SKA competitors. I was pleasantly surprised to find out at the tournament check-in that the Contender boat company supplied all competing Contender boats with live bait. *Nice perk.* Whenever there was a tournament in Palm Beach County, if you wanted live bait, you either had to catch them yourself, or you paid through the nose. A dozen goggle eyes or blue runners could easily cost you a hundred and twenty bucks. Contender took the cost and worry out of getting live bait by hiring locals to catch them in the days leading up to the tournament. Tournament winners usually ended up in some form of print ad, so providing live bait was considered part of their advertising budget. I guess it was a good strategy because some of the other boat companies did the same thing. Once we had an ample amount of rigs made, we checked the lines, re-tied some knots, and replaced a few swivels. *We were as ready as we were gonna get.*

I stretched out on the bed and clicked on the weather channel to get an idea of what kind of conditions to expect. Carl Parker, aka, Carl "The Nose" Parker, was on the tube, explaining that Friday would be nice, but a front was expected to move through early Saturday creating some unfavorable conditions. *Hmmm, not good.* One night when Melody and I had been watching the weather channel, she commented that Carl Parker had the most perfect nose she had ever seen. After taking a good hard look, I had to agree. It appeared to be perfectly straight and undeniably smooth. My own schnozz had never looked that good, even before I broke it in a skiing accident as a kid. From that point on, we referred to him simply as The Nose. Now, The Nose was saying it could be blowing twenty to twenty-five knots out of the south by Saturday afternoon. *Not good, not good at all.*

The door to the room swung open as Jamie and Tangles returned from a place they found off the strip, carrying greasy sacks of barbecued bliss. We scarfed down the food, then took showers and hit the rack, so we'd be ready in the morning.

Chapter 46

Kristy Kane was hot, literally and figuratively. She didn't rise to her position as CRA director of Boynton Beach without utilizing some of her God-given assets. If she needed to dust off the old playbook to queer the marina deal, then so be it. It wouldn't be the first time she relied on her BOD instead of her PhD, to get what she wanted. She was still fuming at the mayor as she pulled into the parking garage of Marina Place, one of the new condo towers that overshadowed the Three Jacks and the C-LOVE Marina. She decided a change of clothes was called for on the elevator ride up to her twelfth-story condo. Rifling through her closet, she admired herself in one of the full-length mirrors. At forty-five, she still had quite a figure, thanks to aerobics class and yoga four times a week. If her face was as nice as her body, she would have been a solid nine, but in a cruel twist of genetics, she had a "butter face." Everything about her looked good but her face. It was pretty ugly, and the one thing no amount of working out would ever change. She was smart enough to know it, and like smugly chicks do, she fought back by whipping her body in to tip-top shape. She planned on using it to hook up with a plastic surgeon, so she could get some facial work for free. Well, free that is if you don't count whoring yourself out to surgeons... which she didn't.

She stood five foot eight, with flaming red shoulder-length hair that stopped just above her ample cleavage, so she pulled out a deep cut, V-neck blouse, that accentuated it. To show off her long legs, she went with a crème colored skirt she hadn't worn in years that was cut just a little too high. Satisfied with the effect, she slipped on her coveted Jimmy Choos, and spritzed on some perfume. Posing one last time in front of the mirror, she realized she was more appropriately dressed for the swanky restaurant Taboo up in Palm Beach, rather than the waterfront dive Three Jacks.

It was almost five o'clock when she strutted into the outside bar, heads turning with every swing of her hip. She spotted Sonny Slade at his usual perch at the end of the bar, and made her way there. Sonny's eyes were glued to her as she sat down only one seat away. Normally, she would order a glass of nice white wine, but she knew there was no such thing at Three Jacks, so she ordered a Johnny Walker and water. Sonny caught the bartender's eye and pointed a finger at himself, his standard signal that the drink was on him. The bartender set the drink down on a napkin, and nodded toward the end of the bar. "This is courtesy of Mr. Slade."

Kristy feigned surprise, and flashed her brightest smile at Sonny. "Why, thank you very much." Sonny thought he recognized her as being the head of the CRA, but had never seen her dolled up like this. Regardless, he wasn't about to pass up taking a shot at the so-so looking broad with the smoking-hot bod.

"Aren't you...?"

"Kristy Kane from the Boynton CRA, yes, that's right." She extended her hand across the open seat to shake Sonny's hand.

"Of course, I'm Sonny Slade. I thought I recognized you. Didn't you have a CRA meeting upstairs a month or so ago?"

"That's right, we were briefly introduced, but it was a busy night, I doubt you remember."

"Are you kidding? Please, why don't you slide over and fill me in on the latest CRA plans?" He reached over and pulled out the chair next to him.

"Why, I'd be delighted."

Sonny was practically licking his lips as he watched the short skirt ride up even higher when she changed seats, crossing one long leg over the other.

Kristy couldn't help noticing him all but drool on her, and decided to cut to the chase. "Well, Sonny, I guess the CRA plans are going to be changing a lot, now that *you're* buying the C-LOVE Marina. When's the closing?"

"Word travels fast, huh? We're closing in forty-five days, I struck the deal myself."

"Wow, I'm impressed, a lot of parties have been interested in that property for a long time...the city included." Actually impressed wasn't too far off the mark; frankly, she was amazed, given Sonny's reputation.

"Yeah? Well, surprise surprise, there's a new sheriff in town, and his name's Sonny Slade...be sure to tell the mayor."

She stifled a laugh. *Don't worry, I can't wait to tell him.* "Speaking of the mayor, I bet you could flip the property to the city for a nice profit. They've already spent a small fortune on plans to develop the waterfront."

"Sure we could. We could also develop it ourselves, make a fortune, and tell the city to piss off. They haven't exactly been helpful to us. In fact, there's at least one lawsuit going on right now that I know of. Nah, the city couldn't afford to pay what we'd want, not gonna happen."

"Is that so?" Kristy wasn't smiling anymore.

Sonny wasn't exactly *Jeopardy* material, but he could tell Miss Kristy wanted him to sell to the city, probably worried about her job with the CRA. Taking another quick peek down her top, he thought of a way he might get an even closer look.

"You know, once we close, we're going to need someone to oversee development, design, and permitting. Someone with contacts who knows how to get things done with the city, county, and state. Someone who has the qualifications that you probably have."

"Exactly what are you telling me, Sonny?" Fifteen seconds earlier she was about to leave, but now he had her full attention. *Maybe I underestimated old Sonny.*

Sonny leaned his head in close to hers and whispered, "I'm telling you that if things don't pan out with the CRA, maybe you might want to work for us. How 'bout another drink?"

He was so close he could smell the perfume wafting up from her chest. He couldn't help taking a deep whiff, before reluctantly leaning back in his chair. Part of her was slightly repulsed. *Did he just sniff me?* The other part was in self-preservation mode. If they did buy the marina, her CRA days were numbered and they *definitely* would need someone like her. If the deal somehow died, she was safe...*best to play both sides.* She brushed back her hair and smoothed her skirt, flashing another smile at Sonny. "Why yes, I'd love one."

Chapter 47

Just like The Nose predicted, Friday was nice. In fact, it turned out to be another gorgeous day altogether. We greeted the sunrise on board the *Kingdom Come*, alongside the other fifty-two boats in the tournament, eagerly awaiting the air horn blast that would signal the start. It came just before seven, and the boats headed out the channel, peeling off in different directions once hitting open sea.

Kingfish Stew raised his voice over the roaring engines, and announced, "I got some coordinates my bruther texted me last night, and we're gunna hit them first. Hang on! Next stop is Kingalopolis, thirty miles ahead!" He then proceeded to open up the throttles on the twin, 250 horsepower Yamahas, which had us zipping toward our first fishing spot of the day. After an hour or so of unproductive fishing, except for a single eight-pound king, I was the first to speak. "Kingalopolis, huh?"

"I don't unnerstand, we should be up to our asses in kingfish—we're smack dab on those coordinates my bruther sent me."

"Maybe he should have texted the fish too," piped in Tangles.

"Tangles is right," I said. "The fish didn't get the message, so let's send them one right now." I reached in the cooler and pulled out a beer, then poured it over the side.

"Good idea," agreed Jamie. "That worked for us in Mazatlan, right?"

"Sure did, we have now presented the fishing Gods with a sacrificial Bud. What do you say we pull up those runners and put down a couple of ribbonfish rigs, Stew?"

"Aw hell, Shagbawl...why not?" Jamie wanted to get some footage, so he filmed while I explained that besides slow trolling live blue runners on downriggers, another preferred kingfishing method was to slow troll ribbonfish with colorful skirts. Ribbonfish look like their name implies—they're long and skinny— and kingfish seem to love them.

Tangles reeled up the portside downrigger, and Stew got the starboard one. We switched rigs and sent the ribbonfish down, fishing the blue runners on the surface. We had one close to the boat, and the other back a ways, on a shotgun line.

The plan was for me to take any fish that hit on the starboard side. Kingfish Stew would take the port side, while Tangles worked the deck, and Jamie filmed.

Jamie was taking a leak off the bow when Stewart's downrigger line popped free and the drag on the Shimano sang as line peeled off. "Fish On!" he yelled. I heard Jamie cussing himself as he zipped up and scrambled for the camera, which was sitting on the jump seat in front of the center console.

"Tangles, bring up the—" before Stewart could finish telling Tangles to bring up the short line,

Tangles already had it in the boat and was putting the blue runner back in the live well. The surprised look on Stew's face lingered as he started reeling in the fish. Jamie charged around the console with the camera on his shoulder when— Clang! He nailed the t-top with his head.

"FUUUCK!" he cried, and I grabbed him as he nearly fell over the side. He continued cussing with one hand on the camera, and the other rubbing his head. Ever the producer, Jamie had the film rolling and started to direct Kingfish Stew.

"Tell me what you're doing, Kingfish, talk to me."

"This is what it's all about folks, this is...Gawddamn it!" The line went slack as the fish somehow got off. Jamie lifted the camera off his shoulder and rubbed his head some more, just as the shotgun line with the live blue runner started singing.

I reached up and snatched the rod out of the holder, as Jamie hoisted the camera and started filming again. The line was really peeling off the reel, and I started narrating to the camera as Tangles and Kingfish reeled up the other lines. In my calmest voice, I said, "Since the line we are using is only twenty pound test, and the drag is set to a mere eight pounds, it's not so easy to tell how big the fish is."

I looked down and was shocked to see three-quarters of the line gone. Kingfish saw it too, and shouted, "Don't tighten the drag! Go to the bow! We're gunna chase this mutha down."

As he spun the wheel, I slowly worked my way to the bow, keeping the rod pointed toward where I thought the fish was. Jamie kept filming, and I kept talking to the camera. "We have elected to chase the fish because it's too risky to tighten the drag, not knowing how big our scaly friend might be."

The light on the camera went off, and Jamie laughed as he peered out from behind it. "You sound just like that guy from Mutual of Omaha's *Wild Kingdom*. Man, that was funny, keep going."

He started filming again, and Tangles was laughing in the background as Kingfish shouted, "Keep reeling, Shagbawl! Come on, faster, reel faster now, we need this one."

"Oh really? I thought that eight pounder put us in the mon—Stop! Stop the boat!"

Kingfish was so excited he almost drove over my line. As he throttled down I grabbed the rail for balance, and Jamie grabbed the t-top. I resumed reeling furiously, and finally caught a glimpse of silver rising from the depths.

Tangles was by my side and he saw it too. "That's a big king, Shagball! I'm on the gaff!"

As soon as Tangles reached under the gunnel for the gaff, the big king took off again, this time toward the stern. I walked my way back and shot Stew a quick look. "Let's try to land him off the stern. It'll be too hard to stick him over the bow rail."

"Yew got it, Shagbawl."

Kingfish Stew did a nice job of jockeying the boat into position, while I fought the fish for another five minutes. At last, he rose to the surface, and I dragged him the last few feet to the boat. *He was big.* Jamie mumbled, "Holy Shit," as Tangles reached over the side with both hands on the gaff and jerked up. The point imbedded deep into the fish, just beneath the gills. He slid his hands down the shaft of the gaff and heaved backward, pulling the fish in the boat. As he did so he slipped, and the fish landed on top of him, thrashing from side to side before spitting the hook. As Tangles rolled away, he yelled, "Shit!" We didn't realize at the time, but the kingfish had bit him in the wrist. Stewart grabbed the fish tamer (or Billy club, if you will), and whacked it a few times in the head until it stopped moving. There was a fair amount of blood on the deck, and Tangles stood up with his right hand clamped on his left wrist.

Jamie finally stopped filming and looked out from behind the camera. "That was awesome, right up till Stew beat its brains in. Look at the size of that thing!" We all stood over the fish and gave our best guesses. I predicted forty-five pounds, Jamie said fifty, and Kingfish declared, "I'm telling yew strade up, that there is a fifty-two-pound smoker."

"Try fifty-five." We all looked at Tangles who was still holding his wrist tight. "I lifted that slob, trust me, it's gonna go fifty-five."

Kingfish let out a big whoop and started to dance a little jig. "I toll you this was Kingalopolis, hot diggity dawg!"

We started high-fiving each other, and as Tangles pulled his hand off his wrist to high-five Kingfish, a stream of blood shot out across the deck.

"Jesus Christ!" I said. "Why didn't you say you got bit? Kingfish, where's the first aid kit?" Tangles quickly clamped his hand down on the wound, while Kingfish reached up and pulled a first aid kit down from the t-top storage. I had Tangles sit down on the jump seat, and tied a tourniquet just above his elbow, using a piece of nylon rope that Kingfish produced. Grabbing a bottle of water out of the cooler, I sat on the deck in front of him. "OK, Tangles, when you take your hand off I'm gonna clean the wound with water and then dump some peroxide on it, it might sting a little."

"You think?" Jamie laughed, and I looked up to see him filming again.

He saw the disconcerted look on my face. "What? It might make a great first aid segment, keep up the narration, Shagball. You don't mind, do you, Tangles?"

"Not as long as you get me a bottle of water first." Jamie handed him a bottle, and he chugged most of it down.

"OK, take your hand off," I told him. He did, and the blood squirted out again. I poured water over the wound and got a good look. It was nasty, about four inches long and maybe an inch deep in the middle. I poured on some more water, and then switched to the peroxide without further warning. Tangles flinched in pain and kicked his right foot out, squarely into Jamie's shin. The filming stopped as Jamie hobbled around the console biting his tongue, then letting out a "Shit! Shit! Shit!"

I wrapped the wound in gauze and then taped it up. "That should tide you over till we get back to the mainland, but you definitely need stitches, it's a nasty gash."

"Thanks, Marcus Welby's got nothing on you."

"Marcus Welby? How old did you say you were?"

Kingfish finished washing all the blood off the deck, and I looked around, seeing nothing but blue water and sky in all directions. "Where the hell are we, Kingfish?"

"Let me check the GPS...Dang!"

"What?"

"We're forty-two miles from weigh-in." We had obviously caught a fast part of the Gulf Stream, and had drifted quite a ways while fighting the fish.

"OK then, let's head back, it's gonna take awhile."

"Shoot...it's only ten, we need to put some more fish in the box."

"Sorry, Kingfish, that big king is gonna have do it for us today. Tangles needs stitches and probably some shots—you know how much bacteria are in those teeth—we gotta head back."

Tangles started to protest, but I shut him up quick. I had seen what happens when you don't get a fish bite treated properly, and I didn't want to see it again.

"Let's break out the sandwiches and have a beer while we hightail it back to the dock...sound like a plan?"

Jamie was already in the cooler, pulling out sandwiches and beer, when Kingfish spoke. "Yer right, Shagbawl, we better get the little feller back. Hey, Jamie, can yew dig me out one a them wine coolers I packed? I just love them things, they're so light and refreshing...anybody else want one?"

I looked at Tangles, and we busted out laughing at the same time.

"Whatter y'all laughing 'bout? Yew never heard a Bartles & Jaymes before?"

Chapter 48

We were the first boat to weigh in, and everybody was oohing and aahing over our fish. As the digital scale stopped digitizing, Kingfish let out another whoop of delight. Tangles was right, the big king did go fifty-five pounds, in fact, the official weight was fifty-six and a half pounds.

After taking a number of pictures and doing a brief video wrap, Jamie and I hustled Tangles to a walk-in clinic to get stitched up. Kingfish stayed behind to clean up the boat and fishing gear, and relish in the glory of the big catch.

The walk-in clinic made a stink about Tangles not having any ID, until Jamie stepped up to the plate and whipped out his plastic. Once they knew payment wasn't an issue, they probably would have treated Bin Laden if we dragged him in.

Thirty-four stitches, two hypodermics, a lot of bandaging, and six hundred and eighty-nine dollars and forty-five cents later, we were out of there. Jamie was not happy about the bill, and questioned the cashier. "Six hundred and eighty-nine dollars and forty-five cents? Seriously? For that kind of money he should have been treated by House."

"Look at the bright side," I said. "It's a small price to pay for a gory first aid segment."

"You know, I haven't checked the tape yet, but there better be a lot of blood on it. I'm talking Freddy Krueger kinda blood."

"I think you'll be happy...freak."

Tangles chimed in from the backseat of the Yukon. "For the right price, I'll bury a 9/0 hook through the palm of my hand."

After a good laugh, Jamie tried to show some compassion for a change, and looked in the rearview mirror at Tangles. "I was just kidding, Tangles, I'm glad it's not worse. Like the doc said, a quarter inch either way and it would have been your artery, feeling any better?"

"Those pain meds he gave me are good...Hell, I feel five feet tall."

Jamie and I glanced at each other for a millisecond before erupting in laughter. No question about it, the little guy was a real ballbuster. I looked back at Tangles and he was quite a sight. He was wearing one of my visors upside down and backward on his head, and his shades were flecked with droplets of blood. His brand-new show shirt, with his name embroidered on the sleeve and chest, didn't fare quite as well. It had blood schmeared all over it like he had been wrestling with Edward Scissorhands. With his arm all bandaged up and in a sling, it was apparent he lost.

We got back to the tournament weigh-in just as the scales closed at three. We had the biggest fish weighed in, as well as the smallest. It was good enough to put the *Kingdom Come* in third place at the end of day one, based on total weight. Kingfish Stew was a happy camper.

We loaded up the truck with all the gear from the boat, and headed back to the hotel. Everybody was pooped, so we decided to sack out for a couple of hours and then figure out something for dinner. I was the first up at about six thirty and took a quick shower. As I toweled off, Jamie started to stir, and I clicked on the weather channel. The Nose was at it again. "You folks down in the Keys can expect some squally weather tomorrow as this front pushes north from Puerto Rico. It's driven by this midlevel low that's moving through the Lesser Antilles." He was pointing at a bunch of squiggly lines with arrows, all diverging toward South Florida. He could have just said the weather was going to be "generally crappy in the Keys," but this was the Weather Channel. They complicate it so you keep tuning in to try to figure out what the heck they're saying. The only thing straightforward was Carl Parker's nose.

When Jamie stepped out of the shower, I filled him in. "Looks like it's going to be iffy tomorrow."

"What do you mean?"

Maybe The Nose couldn't say it, but I could. "It's gonna suck. It'll probably be blowing twenty knots out of the south by noon, with squalls. They're calling for five- to seven-foot seas minimum, that kind of iffy."

"That's pretty iffy—will the tournament still be on?"

"More than likely. It shouldn't be *too* bad early, but it'll get progressively worse. It'll end up being the captain's call when to head back in."

"Shit, you know I can't film if it's too rough. If I get the camera wet, its twenty-five grand down the drain. What do you think?"

"I know Kingfish wants to go, he's never won one of these things, and we're in third. I can't see bringing

Tangles though, not in the shape he's in. If it's too rough, there's no sense in you coming either. Let's play it by ear and see how bad it is in the morning, then we'll decide."

There was a knock on the door and Kingfish came in. "Yew boys ready to tear it up?"

"Actually, we were just discussing the weather."

"Shewt, yer not worried 'bout that little ol' front, are yew? If the *Kingdome Come* can handle the Carolina Outer Banks in November, it can handle a little ol' front down here in May. Besides, my bruther texted me and said it probly won't get here till midafternoon. We'll be back at the dock with the winning catch by then."

"Unless you're brother's name is Jim Cantore, I'm more inclined to believe The Nose. He said the front will be here by late morning."

"The who?"

"Forget it, let's just see what it's like in the morning. What's Tangles doing?"

"Little feller's still zawnked out. I thank he's all doped up. What do yew say we go get us some grub, then check out a few night spawts?" Kingfish was rubbing his hands together in anticipation like a horny teenager on prom night. I couldn't see us bailing on Tangles though, and didn't want to be out too late with the prospect of heavy seas first thing in the morning.

"Why don't you and Jamie go out and have a little fun. I'll stay here and go get something to eat with Tangles when he wakes up. Besides, I want to make a few more rigs for tomorrow."

"Sewt yerself, whadda yew say, Jamie?"

"Let's do it." Ten minutes after they left, Tangles showed up, looking a little groggy. I was finishing up the last of my custom four-hook sardine rigs I call K4s.

"What's that thing?" he asked.

"I thought I'd make a few sardine rigs for tomorrow. If it's as nasty as I think it's gonna be, I might float a few dead ones out there. You want to grab something to eat?"

"Yeah, I'm starving."

"All right, let's go." Ten minutes later we walked into a Tex-Mex joint called the Big Iguana. We plopped down in a booth and ordered a couple of Negra Modelos.When the waitress brought the beers back, she stared at Tangles, then me, then Tangles again. "Oh my God, it *is* you two!" She signaled to another waitress, and the bartender, to come to the booth. "I told you it's the two guys on the TV, look for yourself." We couldn't see the television over the bar from where we were, but as they looked back and forth, the bartender said, "Damn, you're right, Carol...boys, the beers are on me. We watch the show all the time, that yellowfin you caught was awesome. Name's Dewey, but everyone calls me Dip. I own this joint, pleased to meet you." He stuck out his hand and we made introductions all around.

By the time we finished dinner, we'd met everyone in the place including the cooks. They really love their fishing shows in the Keys. We thanked Dip for the complimentary drinks, tipped the waitress hard on our deeply discounted check, and finally headed out the door feeling thoroughly sated. As we exited, Dip hollered, "Good luck tomorrow, try to win one for the Dipper!"

Chapter 49

As Holly pulled into Millie's driveway, she decided she had to tell her about the divorce. After she unpacked her things in one of the spare bedrooms, she joined Millie out on the deck. Walking outside, she took a deep breath. "I forgot how much I love the smell of the ocean, it brings back memories."

"I bet it does, dear. You used to fish off the point all the time growing up. Your grandfather always said you were the best fisherman in the family...all those snook and snapper you caught." It was true. Her grandfather had taught her how to tie a knot, bait a shrimp on a hook, and time the tides for maximum productivity. The times they spent together produced wonderful memories she would always cherish.

"Where does the time go, Millie? It seems like just yesterday we were having one of our family fish fries, but it's been so long."

"You're right, sweetie, it has been a long time...too long. That's why I'm so glad you're here. Now tell me about how things are with your husband. Has he come to his senses and patched things up with you yet?"

"I'm sorry, Millie, I should have told you last week when it became official, but I just wasn't ready to talk about it yet. It's over, we're divorced...I'm not going back."

"What? Oh dear...honey, I'm so sorry to hear that, are you OK?"

"I'm all right, and don't be sorry, we've been separated for almost six months. It's me who's sorry for not telling you. He turned out to be a jerk in more ways than one. I should have seen it, but didn't...it's more embarrassing than anything else."

"What do you mean?"

"Mark not only cheated on me, he cheated his clients, stealing a bunch of money that he spent on gambling and girls. He's on his way to jail...the jerk."

"You know I always thought there was something shady about him, but I never said anything. So...you've been separated for a while...have you been seeing anybody new?"

Holly decided to spare Millie her recent dating disasters. A friend pushed her into online dating and she met one married guy, one stalker, and one creep who wanted her to swing.

"No, not really, but the good news is I'm back home and ready for a fresh start. Plus, we get to spend time together, which means more than anything to me."

"Me too."

Holly put her arm around Millie, and they just sat there for a few minutes, watching the boats pass by. "Look," pointed Holly. "It's the *C-LOVE* coming back from their morning trip. Talk about memories, I used to love going out on that boat."

Millie saw the look on her face and had an idea. "Do you have a phone on you, sweetie?"

"I don't leave home without it...here you go."

Holly handed over her BlackBerry, but Millie quickly handed it back. "I can't read the numbers on that darned thing, can you dial for me?"

"Of course, go ahead."

"OK, the number is eight-six-seven-five-three-o-nine." Holly dialed, and handed the phone back to her. After a few moments, Millie spoke. "Hi, Bart, its Millie... Oh I'm feeling as good as can be expected, thanks. So how'd you do this morning? Uh-huh, uh-huh...good, sounds like they're really biting. Me? No, not today, but I might be sending over a guest...OK, I'll let you know." Millie handed the phone back. "I just talked to Captain Bart on the *C-LOVE*. He said the yellowtails are really biting. They caught some mutton and a few grouper as well. Why don't you go out on the afternoon trip?"

"You think? Nah, I would rather spend time catching up with you."

"Don't be silly, you're living here now...remember? We have all the time we need to catch up. Besides, it sure would be nice having some panfried snapper for dinner. Go on, honey, it'll be good for you, nothing like a few hours on the water to help clear your mind. What do you say?

"You sure? I haven't fished in so long, the only thing I might catch is my heel."

"All the more reason to go, you're home now and you need get back to the basics, like enjoying a beautiful afternoon fishing. I'll call Bart and let him know you're coming."

"OK, I'm sold...fishing it is. They still leave at one, right?"

"On the dot, so we better fix you a sandwich or something...come on let's go in the kitchen."

Holly held her arm as they went inside, and as she made a ham sandwich, Millie spoke. "There is another reason I want you to go out on the *C-LOVE*, dear... there's not much time left you'll be able to do so as my guest."

"What do you mean?"

Milfred dreaded breaking the news, especially since just learning Holly had divorced and moved back home. She never considered the possibility, and was now wondering whether she made the right decision to sell the marina.

"I um, signed a contract to sell the marina."

"What? You're kidding me! The marina's your life!"

"It *was* my life, Holly, and it was a good one. But with the cancer coming back, I thought it would be best to get my estate in order...and that meant selling the marina."

"I don't know what to say...I-I never thought I'd see the day."

"Me neither, but I had the chance to sell at a good price and took it. You know how the real estate market is—it hasn't been this bad since I was a child."

"I know, I'm just a little surprised is all...who's buying it?"

"Syd Slade, the man who owns the Three Jacks."

"I thought you didn't like him."

"I don't, so I squeezed him for so much it's gonna hurt. The only other likely buyer was the city, and they can kiss my tired ass, all the problems they've caused me over the years. I don't trust that mayor either, something's not right about him...like most politicians."

Milfred noticed Holly turn away and go silent as she chewed on her sandwich.

"Holly? Honey, look at me." As Holly turned, she could see the tears welling up in her eyes. Holly put her sandwich down and Millie gave her a big hug, her face pressing against Holly's.

"I'm sorry," Holly choked out. "Once you're gone and the marina gets sold, there'll be nothing left for me down here. You're all I've got, and I'm not ready, I'm just not ready."

"Now, dear, please...no more crying...I want you to go on the boat and have some fun. I'm ready for a fish fry, just like we used to have."

Holly wiped the tears away and straightened up. "You're right," she sniffled. "I'll catch 'em up like Granddad taught me, poor fish don't stand a chance." She made her best attempt at a smile, then kissed Millie on the cheek and headed out the door. Watching her drive away, Millie had a sinking feeling that she shouldn't have been so quick to sell.

Chapter 50

Syd Slade was a busy man, fifteen days from contract was very little time to conduct thorough due diligence. The only reason he agreed to the quick close was that he had done plenty of research on the C-LOVE Marina a few years earlier, when he last made an offer to buy it. He was confident there was nothing he didn't know that would cause the bank to back out of the loan. Still, the bank had a checklist of items he needed to provide before they would approve the loan. Some of the information they required were his personal tax records, as well as those of his restaurant holding company. He had his accountant handle it, who had just called to say the information had been forwarded to the bank. He didn't have to worry about clear title, because that was to be provided by the seller. He had been told by Milfred's attorney that it was in the works. He had already been supplied with the rental agreements for the boats in the marina, as well as the service contracts in place. All the slip renters had yearly rental agreements that rolled over annually in November unless they were terminated by the Marina owner, by giving thirty days' notice.

The bank also required an environmental survey of the property to make sure there were no hazardous materials leeching into, or from it. They gave Syd a list of three approved environmental companies, and he needed to hire one. *No problem.* He had already been through the city records for the C-LOVE Marina, and according to them, there had never been any type of contaminants kept there. The problem came when he contacted the first company on the list. He told them he needed an environmental survey, and they quoted him twenty thousand dollars. He about shit his pants. When they asked him when he needed it by, and he said in thirteen days, they just laughed. No way could they get one done that quickly, and even if they did, it would be upward of twenty-five grand. *Say what?*

The second company he called gave him the same load of crap, and as he dialed the number to the last outfit, a company out of West Palm called Endviropro, he took a deep breath. A receptionist answered in a cheery voice. "Hello, welcome to Endviropro, the last environmental services company you'll ever need. How may I direct your call?"

"I'd like to speak to whoever's in charge."

"In regards to what, sir?"

Syd was running out of time and patience. "Take a wild guess. Could it have to do with me needing an environmental survey? Bingo! You got it. Now please patch me through to the president, or owner, or whoever it is that gets to make a lot of money for a little work."

"I'm sorry sir, but I don't like the tone of your voice. I'll put you through to one of our estimators who can..."

As it happened, the owner of Endviropro, Harvey Miller, was pouring himself a cup of coffee when he heard and saw the young temp get flustered. He signaled to her that he wanted to take the call, and headed back to his desk to see what the caller was so pissy about. He heard the temp say, "Mr. Miller will be taking your call, I'm putting you through now." The phone rang on his desk and he picked it up.

"This is Harvey Miller, what can I do for you?"

"Harvey, I asked to speak with the president or owner, someone who can make a prudent business decision. Does that apply to you?"

"Yes, I run this company, and right now I'm tempted to make the decision to hang up. Please get to the point before I do so."

"Beautiful, my name's Syd Slade, and I own the Three Jacks waterfront restaurant in Boynton Beach. I'm buying the adjacent C-LOVE Marina, and I need a Phase I and Phase II environmental survey completed in thirteen days. I'm willing to pay what it takes to get it done, what do you say, Harvey? You wanna make some fast money?"

Harvey didn't like the way Syd talked, but he had to face reality. His business was down, and he was struggling to make his seventy-five hundred-dollar-a-month mortgage payment. Like countless others, he overextended himself and purchased a five-thousand-square-foot house in Wellington at the top of the market.

"A Phase I and Phase II typically take anywhere from thirty to sixty days to complete, Mr. Slade. Remember, we have to do the testing, compile all the information, and put it in a report. You're asking me to cut that time in less than half. I would have to double up the manpower, and get started immediately, pushing everything else aside. Even then, I'm not sure we can get it done in time." Of course, he had only one small job he was about finished with, but still.

"Listen, Harvey, I don't need you to reinvent the wheel here. I know this property very well and have all the records on it, there's nothing there. I don't care if you cut a few corners, I just need it done in thirteen days. Whadda you say?"

Harvey knew he wasn't supposed to cut any corners, this was environmental business, for crying out loud. Then he thought of his kids' private school tuition, which was due in a couple of months, and bit. "It'll be twenty-five thousand, payable half now, and half on completion."

Syd cringed at the number, thinking the feds ought to investigate these environmental firms for price fixing, but he had no choice. "In thirteen days, right?"

Harvey got up and shut the door to his office before speaking. "We can get it done, but if I need to cut a few corners to meet the deadline, you're going to sign a release stating you won't sue me if something crops up later. That's the only way I'm doing it."

Syd didn't like it, but he wanted all his ducks in a row before the three-hundred-thousand-dollar deposit became nonrefundable. Plus, the bank needed time to go over the reports. A few years earlier, they were rubber-stamping everything, making loans to anyone with a pulse. Now they were looking for reasons *not* to make a loan, and he needed the environmental survey done yesterday.

"OK, I'll sign a release if necessary, but it better be a flawless report. The banks are really scrutinizing things these days...we gotta deal?"

"I'll get started on it today, you won't be disappointed. Let me put you back on with my secretary and you can give her the property address and the seller's attorney's information. She'll also tell you where to mail the deposit. We appreciate the business."

"You should."

Harvey transferred the call back to the temp, thinking what a prick his new customer was. *Well, better suck it up, twenty-five grand would come in handy right now. Very handy indeed.* He knew there wasn't a chance in hell he could complete the Phase II portion in thirteen days, but he had an ace in the hole. Only two years prior, he had been hired to do the environmental work by the City of Boynton when they purchased the fuel docks from the condo developer. Like Syd, he also knew the property well, and knew that the C-LOVE Marina was adjacent to it. He would simply use the data from his old report, and tweak it for this one, problem solved. *Ka-ching!*

Chapter 51

At 5:00 a.m. I walked outside the hotel door and looked up at the palm trees swaying in the streetlights. It was already blowing ten to fifteen knots. *Not good.* I went back inside and turned on the weather channel while Jamie continued snoring. The occasional late-night and weekend anchor, Dave Schwartz, was doing his thing. "That's right friends, it's gonna be blowing like Humpty Dumpty down in the Keys today. Keep your eyes open for a small craft advisory likely to be issued later this morning. Remember, friends, if it can float, it can sink, stay out of the drink." Thank God for Dave Schwartz. *He's bringing goofy back.*

Unfortunately, there was nothing amusing about the prospect of going out in deteriorating conditions. When Jamie got up, I told him Tangles was definitely not going, and I thought he should stay on the dock too. For once, Jamie didn't put up much of a fight.

"You think it's gonna be that bad, huh?"

"If we were in a thirty-five-footer, it would be more doable, but by no means any fun. In Kingfish's twenty-seven, it'll be wet and nasty. I'm thinking maybe, just *maybe*, he and I will go out for an hour or two, and then come back. We're certainly not going very far offshore, if we go at all."

"If you say so, Kit, we have some great footage from yesterday anyways."

"I say so, no sense in pushing our luck. Let's get going and see what the tournament committee has to say. I know how these deals work though, unless there's a small craft warning already issued, they'll say it's the captain's call."

There was a knock on the door and Tangles walked in wearing just his underwear.

"What's going on?"

"We're heading down to the boat in about a half hour, you and Jamie are going to stay on the dock. Kingfish and I might go out for a little while and see how bad it is."

"You sure, boss?"

"Unless there's some sort of meteorological miracle and this front dissipates in the next hour, yeah I'm sure. Where's Kingfish?"

"He's getting dressed."

"Let's do the same and head out."

It was about quarter after six when we got to the boat, and as expected, it was blowing even harder at the marina. What wasn't expected was the local news team awaiting our arrival. Somebody had tipped them off that we were filming, and had caught the biggest kingfish on the first day. The fact that we were a current Internet and television sensation, thanks to the Tangles and tuna episode, had them licking their chops for an interview. Jamie whispered in my ear as I approached. "Dude, I'm going back to the truck to get the camera, this is great!"

As Jamie trotted off, the local news guy came up to me and said, "Shagball, I'm Brick Slackwell from channel five. I'd like to do a quick interview with you before you head out, got a minute?"

As much as I didn't particularly care for interviews, I was thankful to still have a fishing show at all, and flashed my best smile. "Brick? For the good people of the Conch Republic, I have all the time in the world... roll the tape."

He turned to his cameraman who handed him a mic, and I saw the red light blinking on the side of the camera, indicating it was recording. "Is it true you really caught this...this person here while filming your show? None of it was staged?" He was pointing at Tangles. Jamie was back now, filming him, filming me.

"First of all, that person has a name, and its Tangles. Second, you've seen the show, right?"

"Of course, everybody has, it's incredible. That's why there's been speculation some of it may have been staged. I'm sorry if I've offended you and er...a... Mr. Tangles."

"No offense taken, Brick, but let me just say this for the record. This is a fishing show, not some overproduced reality show with wannabe actors. What you see is what you get. However, if I *was* to stage foul-hooking somebody thirty miles offshore, it would have been somebody much bigger, like Shaquille O'Neal."

Everybody laughed and I continued talking. "Why don't you talk to the man who filmed it, and the man who helped me land the tuna and the big kingfish yesterday? They're right here." I formally introduced Jamie and Tangles, and began wrapping it up.

"I've got to get moving, Brick, we have a tournament to fish."

"Thanks for your time, Shagball, maybe we can talk after weigh-in?"

"Sure thing, but first I'd like to give a special shout-out to Dip and the rest of the staff at the Big Iguana for their hospitality...thanks, guys." I saluted the camera, then lowered my hand and gave the "cut" sign, by sweeping it across my throat. *Interview over.*

Kingfish was loading up on live blue runners as I walked down to the tournament committee to see if there were any special instructions. Like I figured, the tournament was still a go. It was fish at your own risk, and we did.

The air horn went off, signaling the start, and I looked back at Jamie and Tangles on the dock, talking to the reporter. A squall suddenly dumped some rain on us and I secretly wished I had stayed behind too, but I wasn't gonna let Kingfish down...up to a point.

Once we left the protection of the bay, we started getting hammered by four- to six-foot waves. For twenty-five minutes we pounded our way out, and despite wearing rain gear, we were totally soaked. I began asking myself what the hell I was doing, tournament or not. Kingfish throttled down, and as we rolled with the waves, he asked, "What dew yew thank, Shagbawl?"

"I think this blows...that's what I think. If it doesn't start laying down in a little while, let's go back to the dock and have a Margarita."

"Awlright then, let's put out some live bait and see what happens."

Kingfish opened the live well, and cried, "Gawd dammit! They're all dead! The live well ain't working...

she-it!" Upon further inspection, he discovered that one of the wires to the circulating pump had apparently jarred loose during the rough ride out."What the hell are we gonna dew now?"

What I felt like saying was, *Let's go back*. What I said was, "I brought some sardines and a few rigs, we can try drift fishing for a while, but we'll have to leave the boat in gear to keep the bow pointed into the waves. If it gets any worse though, we're heading in...OK?"

"Sardines? Drift fishing? Yew gotta be kidding me. This is a pro-fessional SKA tournament, Shagbawl, not amateur hour, this is serious bidness."

"You got a better idea? What? You're gonna try to run those ribbonfish on the downriggers? In this slop? Have fun...I'll watch."

I could see Kingfish weighing the options in his mind. He really didn't have much choice...without my help that is.

"Awlright, let's give it a try...but I sure am glad Jamie ain't filming, wouldn't want anybody seeing me drifting sardines."

"Quit bitching and start fishing." I threw some sardines in a bucket of water to thaw them out, and we both started re-rigging a couple of rods with my K4 rigs.

"I'm gonna flatline mine on top," I said. "Why don't you put on a sinker to get yours down, you'll probably need at least an ounce in these conditions." The weather was not getting any better, and we were rocking and rolling as I kept an eye peeled for rogue waves. I hooked up a sardine and cast it as far as I could off the starboard side, using a Shimano 4500 spinning reel and rod combo.

As I placed the rod in a holder and engaged the gear, Kingfish said, "What the heller yew dune? Not even gunna hold on to the rod?" Between the conditions, and Kingfish talking trash about drift fishing, I'd had enough.

"Jesus, Kingfish! Give it a rest! I know what the fuck I'm doing. When it's this rough and the boat is rolling, notice the nice jigging action at the rod tip when we come out of a trough. Trust me, just put your rod in a holder and let the boat do the work."

"OK, OK, sorry, I never fish this way."

"No shit." Just as Kingfish was letting his line out with a three-quarter ounce sinker above the sardine, my reel started burning drag. I snatched the rod and leaned back as I started to reel. Five minutes later, we had a fifteen-pound king in the box. It was tricky fishing, because one of us always had to have one hand on the wheel in order to keep the bow into the waves. *Nothing could ass up your day quicker than getting broadsided miles from shore.*

I was putting another sardine on my K4 rig when Kingfish's line got hit. His rod bent over double, and he struggled to pull it out of the holder. It was clearly a bigger fish than the one I caught, and he fought it hard for ten minutes. I had the gaff in one hand and the wheel in the other, as I maneuvered the boat between waves that seemed to be getting bigger.

Kingfish yelled, "I'm getting him, son! He's a biggun!"

Just then, the ship-to-shore radio crackled to life, and the tournament committee chairman started to speak. "All SKA tournament anglers! A small craft advisory has just been issued from Key West to Jupiter Inlet, with conditions expected to significantly worsen. The committee has voted to move up the official weigh-in from three o'clock to twelve noon. I repeat..." *Well, what do you know, The Nose was right.*

Kingfish was fishing with heavier tackle than I was, and I was glad he was able to muscle the fish to the boat relatively quickly. It surfaced near the port stern, and I made a swipe with the gaff, but missed. Kingfish hollered, "Stick 'em again, Shagbawl, stick that fat boy!"

The fish came around again, and this time I nailed him right on top of the head. As I heaved it over the gunnel and into the boat, I turned in time to see a big wave come crashing over the opposite side. "Hang on!" I yelled, diving for the base of the helm seat. The wave smashed into, and over us, nearly capsizing the boat. I scrambled to my feet and grabbed the wheel, turning the bow back into the oncoming waves. I looked back and saw the fish flopping around the deck, and Kingfish clinging to the port side stern. He was half in the water, and had a look of shock on his face. I scanned the horizon, and after determining there wasn't another monster wave about to hit us, quickly stepped back and grabbed Kingfish under his armpits. Then I lifted him backward as hard as I could. As soon as he hit the deck, I turned around to grab the wheel, asking, "You all right?"

"Awlright? Yew better believe it, Shag Dawggy Dawg. Look at that beauty, I bet he goes thirty-five pounds! Thanks for the lift, by the way—that was close. If my rain jacket hadn't a caught on the cleat, I'd be up shit's creek." Kingfish staggered to his feet, put the fish in the box, and the rod in a holder. I relinquished the wheel to him, only after he assured me we were heading in. "Yew know what? It *does* seem to be getting a little sloppy out here. How 'bout a Bartles & Jaymes for the ride? I buy, yew fly."

Chapter 52

Holly was having a wonderful time on the *C-LOVE*. Millie called ahead to Captain Bart, who invited her up on the bridge for the ride out. The old boat chugged down the intracoastal toward the inlet, and Holly took in the sights. Mangroves filled with egrets, a manatee splashing, fish jumping, and a beautiful blue sky to boot. She asked Captain Bart, "Do you ever get tired of your job?"

"Except for the occasional obnoxious customer, no...not ever. Every day is different, and most are picturesque, just like today. When the fish are biting like they are now, it's fun to see the happiness it brings people, especially the youngsters. I'm gonna miss it."

"Miss it? Why? You're too young to retire."

Captain Bart gave Holly a funny look. "Didn't Milfred tell you that she sold the marina?"

"Well yes, I just found out about an hour ago. She told me she signed a contract, but what are you saying, the new owners are going to stop running the *C- LOVE*?"

"She told you who's buying it...right?"

"Yeah, the same guy who owns Three Jacks, Syd Slade."

"Well pardon my French, but his asshole son Sonny has been going up and down the dock letting everybody know that they're getting the boot...the *C-LOVE* included."

"WHAT?"

"I'm afraid you heard me right, he even made a crack about sinking the *C-LOVE* for an artificial reef. I almost punched his greasy face in."

"Oh my God, that's horrible! Does Millie know about this?"

"I doubt it, I sure didn't tell her...and she hasn't been around lately with her health and all. It's too late to do anything anyways, like you said, she signed a contract." The *C-LOVE* passed through the Boynton Inlet and was tracking south toward a spot off the Boynton water tower, or "champagne glass," as it was called by the locals for its appearance.

"I can't believe it, why would they want to throw everybody out? Surely not to build more condos, not in this market."

"Who knows? It's the Slades, they don't give a crap about anyone but themselves. We're coming up on our first drop, better get down there. I told Anthony to set you up with a guppy rig, we caught quite a few yellowtails this morning. If the muttons start to bite, you might want to switch to a sardine rig."

"Thanks, Captain."

"Please, just call me Bart...and it's my pleasure."

"Thanks, Bart."

Holly climbed down to the deck, and took her place off the stern. There were maybe thirty anglers onboard, and most dangled their baits over the side as the boat made its final turn to set up the drift. As soon as the engines died, lines went in the water and baits sank down. As Holly leaned over the side and watched them slowly drift toward the bottom, she felt a tap on her shoulder.

"My name's Anthony. If you need anything just give me a shout. Captain told me you know what you're doing, so I won't give you the ABCs of snapper fishing."

"Thanks, I'm Holly...how deep are we?"

"Eighty feet."

Holly tried to push the sale of the marina from her mind as she dropped the guppy rig to the bottom. She felt the sinker hit and the line go slack, then put the reel in gear and lifted the rod, turning the handle *just* a little. She dropped the rod back down and then gently lifted it again, suddenly feeling a tug. She reeled twice and dropped the line down again, feeling yet another tug, before reeling in earnest. The guy next to her yelled, "Got a fish on down here!"

The mate Anthony reappeared next to her. "Actually, it looks like she's got two. Nice job, ma'am, just lift them over the rail. All right, everybody, step back a little."

Holly hoisted a pair of yellowtails onto the deck, and the mate removed them from the hooks on the line. He took out his knife and slit each one on top. "Your mark is one on the head." He reached into the bait bucket and put a piece of squid on each of the hooks. They were evenly spaced about a foot apart from the sinker, which was attached to the bottom of the line. "OK, you're good to go, let's see if you can do it again."

"Thanks, probably just lucky though."

A few other anglers also pulled in some yellowtail, and one caught a nice mutton.

Five minutes later, Anthony was back to take two more yellowtail off Holly's line. "Just lucky, huh?"

"What's the old saying? I'd rather be lucky than good?"

"Please, I think you got plenty of both."

The guy standing next to her with a solid beer belly and wearing a Cleveland Browns T-shirt said, "Luck shmuck, save some for the rest of us amateurs."

They laughed, and one of the other mates yelled, "Lines up! We're making a move!"

Holly was having herself a ball, thoroughly enjoying the sights, sounds, and even smells of the drift boat. She forgot how much she missed it, and how important it had once been to her. She had to admit, she had been in a rut with her marriage, and a job that kept her behind a computer eight hours a day.

When Anthony came by, she asked, "Can you set me up with a sardine rig? I'd do it myself, but I don't have any pliers with me."

"No problem...yellowtails' not enough of a challenge?"

"I just like to keep my options open."

The next couple of drops were pretty unproductive for the whole boat. It seemed like the bite had turned off, and only a couple of small kings and a remora were brought up. It was a little after four, and as the engines stopped. One of the mates was heard saying, "This is probably the last drop, make it count."

Holly put a large sardine on her triple-hook rig, and sent it down to the bottom. As she played the line out, she saw that a couple of anglers on the bow had pulled up decent-sized muttons. Patiently, she kept letting more and more line out, her thumb gently feeling for any sign of a bite.

Five minutes later she felt a slight bump, and then WHAM! She got slammed. Her rod bent to the rail, and she struggled to reel in the fish. The guy with the Browns T-shirt yelled, "Miss Hemingway's got another fish on!"

Holly was sweating now, and was pissed that she broke one of her nails when her rod hit the railing. She was determined to land the fish, and directed her anger toward it as she reeled. Anthony was next to her providing encouragement. "Keep the tip up, you're gaining on him, that's it...keep reeling."

One of the other mates yelled, "OK, that's it, folks, reel your lines up, we're heading in!"

Captain Bart was watching Holly fight the fish from the bridge, and was smiling to himself. *She's a stubborn one, just like Milfred.*

Holly was cursing under her breath as she fought the fish, which was now taking her toward the bow.

Anthony was in front of her, clearing a path and shouting. "Everybody out of the way, we got a fish on!" Holly went halfway to the bow, then the fish changed direction and she ended up back at the stern. Finally, she felt the fish's head turn, and she cranked the reel with everything she had. Suddenly a red blur appeared at the surface, and there was a collective, "Wow!" from the other anglers. Anthony reached over the side with the long gaff and stuck the big mutton snapper.

He lifted it on to the deck and shook it off the gaff. "Now that's a nice mutton!" he proclaimed, as he turned to high-five Holly. Holly's arms were shaking so much from the exertion that she could barely high-five him back. Despite her trembling arms, she was thrilled and beaming from ear to ear as congratulations flowed her way. One of the mates put the mutton on a scale and announced, "Sixteen pounds, biggest mutton of the year so far on the *C-LOVE*. Way to go, ma'am."

On the ride back to the dock, the guy in the Browns T-shirt sat down next to her and complained about his luck. "I come all the way down here on vacation and catch a...what'd they call it? A remora? A damn suckerfish? Geez, what's your secret, lady? I'm tired of the wife telling me it's cheaper to go to the fish market."

"My secret?" Holly thought about it for a second. "Tip the mate at the beginning of the trip, not the end. You'll get some extra attention and advice."

He furrowed his substantial brow. "Hmmm...makes sense...yeah...yeah, I'm gonna try that tomorrow, thanks. Oh, and congrats on that big, red, what'd they call it? A muddin? Yeah, that was a real lunker. Hell, I would've been happy with one of those little yellow ones—anything but a remora, never even heard a one before."

Everybody streamed off the boat, most tipping the mates as they went. Those that caught fish, and those that wanted to maybe buy some fish, waited, while a crewmember tossed the catch into the holding area. The fish were then identified by their markings and claimed.

Holly gave Anthony a twenty-dollar bill and asked him to fillet up the mutton and two of the yellowtail. She had him put the other two in a plastic bag and walked after the big guy from Cleveland, who was heading to the parking lot. She yelled, "Hey...big guy!" She was somewhat embarrassed that she hadn't introduced herself on the boat. He turned around and looked confused as she walked up to him holding a pair of yellowtail snapper. She handed the sack to him and smiled. "Here, tell your wife this is why you like to come to Florida to fish."

He appeared dumbfounded as he took the fish. "Are...are you serious? Are you sure?"

"Absolutely, I live down here and can go anytime I want. Besides, I caught more than my share today... enjoy."

As she turned to leave, he grabbed her in a bear hug and lifted her off the ground, spinning around once before setting her back down. "Thank you, thank you, miss...?"

Pausing a moment to catch her breath, she wheezed, "I'm Holly...good thing I didn't give you the mutton or I might need medical assistance...Mr...?"

"Bruno...the name's Bruno Doltz. If you ever come to Cleveland, I'd be honored to take you perch fishing, that's my specialty."

"OK, Bruno, thanks, hope you have better luck tomorrow."

"Pretty lady, my luck's already changed thanks to you. Wait'll the missus sees what I caught—she might let me do two trips tomorrow." He gave her a big wink and she laughed as they headed their separate ways.

Holly had just picked up her large sack of fillets from Anthony, when Bruno drove by and leaned out the window of his rental car. He yelled, "Remember... Cleveland...Perch..." and was gone.

Captain Bart saw the whole exchange, and as Holly walked by on the way back to her own car, he said, "Looks like you made a new friend today. That was a nice thing you did."

Blushing a little, she answered, "Come on, Bart, you know eating too much fish might give you mercury poisoning."

Chapter 53

We were back at the dock before ten, but we weren't the first boat in. It was nice to know there was at least one captain in the tournament with some common sense. By the time we headed back, the seas were five to seven feet high, sprinkled with larger ones like the one that nearly swept Kingfish off the stern. Thankfully, we were going with the waves on the way back, so it wasn't nearly as jarring as the ride out. Nevertheless, we were both glad when our feet hit the dock.

I didn't see Jamie, so I phoned to let him know we were back. He and Tangles were just finishing breakfast at a diner, and he asked if we would hold off weighing in the fish until they got back, so he could film the weigh-in. Kingfish wasn't real happy, but relented. "He wants us to *WAIT*? Well... Awlright...I guess...but tell him ten minutes, no more. Them fish skinny up once they start drying out...better go get some more ice."

We walked up to the ship's store and got a twenty-pound bag of ice. As Kingfish forked over three dollars and fifty cents, the cashier asked, "How bad is it out there?"

Kingfish looked up at him. "Well, it ain't exactly like the Outer Banks in November, but it ain't too far off neither."

I paid for some Beer Nuts as Kingfish headed back down to the boat, and told the cashier, "What he *didn't* tell you is he got knocked half out the boat by an eight-footer that blindsided us. His rain jacket caught on a cleat, or he would've been overboard. So if you ask me, I'd say it's downright nasty. You got any friends out there, you should radio them and make sure they're all right."

I picked up the change, and as I walked out the door, I heard the cashier say, "*Smokehouse, Smokehouse,* come back...you out there *Smokehouse?*"

Kingfish iced the fish down, and we shared the Beer Nuts waiting for Jamie and Tangles to show up. He kept opening the fish box, and asking, "What dew yew thank? Thank the big one will go thirdy-five?"

"I think you're gonna dry that big boy out you keep opening the lid. Hold your horses, Kingfish, they'll be here any minute and we'll find out for sure."

"Dang, I sure wish we woulda stayed out a little longer and put one more biggun in the box. It might be the difference between first and second...or third."

"Do I need to remind you how close you were to being in *seriously deep shit?* If you had gone over, I'm not sure I could have got you back in the boat by myself in those conditions." I held my index finger up to the side of my temple. "Are you sure you're not a member of the steel plate club?"

Before he could respond, Jamie yelled, "All right, boys, let's get a little recap of the fishing before we head down to the weigh-in." He came walking down the dock with the camera on his shoulder. Tangles trailed behind sporting his Kid-Rock T-shirt and *Mod Squad* shades, even though the sun hadn't been out all day. *Somehow it worked for him.*

I recounted the fishing action on tape for Jamie, with some amusing interjections by Kingfish. When we were done, Jamie said, "Damn! Sounds like you two had fun, wish I could have filmed it."

I just shook my head. "Come on, let's go weigh these fish in before Kingfish has a coronary." Kingfish pulled out his insulated fish carrying bag, loaded the two kings in it, and we headed down to the weigh-in. Three more boats came in right after we did, and only one boat had any fish to weigh. The other boat had a nice forty-pounder, but they were so far back after day one it didn't threaten our position. We weighed the one I caught first, and it topped out at fourteen pounds. Kingfish pulled out the big boy, and we held our breath as the scale registered...thirty-four...thirty-five...thirty-six...thirty-six pounds! Kingfish let out one of his patented whoops, and the tournament director announced we were now in first place. Kingfish was hootin' and hollering, and Jamie filmed as he danced like an idiot all over the dock.

He was chanting, "The kingdome has come! The kingdome has come! Long live the kingdom come!" Jamie was laughing so hard the camera was bouncing on his shoulder, and when Kingfish grabbed Tangles by his good arm and swung him in a do-si-do, everybody on the dock lost it. I had tears in my eyes from laughing so hard. I figured he knew the odds of us still being in first after the rest of the boats weighed in weren't great, but you never know. For now, he was leading an

SKA tournament for the first time in his life, and he was going to enjoy it while it lasted. *God bless.*

Once the dancing stopped, I conferred with Jamie. We decided to check out of the hotel and head back home, since the tournament ended early. I asked Kingfish if he wanted to check out with us, and then come back for the rest of the weigh-in results, but he would have none of it. "Are yew kidding me? Ole Kingfish ain't goin' nowhere. He's staying right here and watching every *dang* fish get weighed. We're in first place, boys, yew ain't gonna leave me now, are yew? We win this thang or not, we got some Carolina-style partying to do. Come on, guys, why don't y'all stay another night?"

It was Jamie's call because he was flipping the tab, so I deferred to him. Jamie said, "Sorry, Kingfish, we have to roll. I'm over budget due to the medical expenses, but I can lessen the damage if we don't stay another night. Blame it on Obama."

We helped him off-load the gear from the *Kingdom Come*, put it on the trailer, and then headed back to the hotel. Kingfish said he'd call as soon all the boats weighed in, and the results were official.

We were just north of Marathon when I got the call from Kingfish. I had Jamie turn down the radio, and flipped open my cell phone. "Well, how'd we do?"

"Some damn thirty-five-footer called the *Smokehouse*, edged us out by two stinking pounds. Can yew believe it? *Two stinkin' pounds?* We got second place though, not too bad considering we only fished half a day yesterday on account a Tangles, and just a couple of hours today 'cause a the weathur."

"Sorry we couldn't bring home the gold for you, Kingfish. We tried...maybe next time we'll take first."

"Y'all can count on it, and tell that little dude Tangles he's one helluva mate."

"You can tell him yourself—aren't you staying over tomorrow on your way home?"

"I thank so, unless I happen upon a young gal in need of some Southern charm." "Like I said, I'll see you tomorrow."

"What? Yew don't think I can parlay my second place finish into a hot night of animal passion?"

"I'm afraid you're more likely to end up in the Monroe County jail. Stay out of trouble tonight, Stew, I'm serious...it's too far to go to bail you out. "

"Dang, yew sound just like my old lady." Click.

Chapter 54

When Holly got to her car, she gave Millie a call to tell her she was stopping at the store to pick up some things for dinner. Millie asked, "Well, how was the fishing?"

"It was great...absolutely wonderful, I'll tell you about it when I get back."

"OK, dear, see you in a little while."

Holly went to the new Winn-Dixie on Woolbright (by the intracoastal) that the mate Anthony told her about. She picked up some wild rice, broccoli, butter, lemon, tartar sauce, and a couple of bottles of white wine. Satisfied she had all she needed for a proper dinner, she headed back to Millie's.

On the way, it occurred to her that she had laughed and had more fun in one afternoon than she had in the last couple of years. *Had her life been that drab?* Divorce was certainly no picnic, but she was an attractive and financially independent thirty-two-year-old. What happened to her? Whatever it was, she was determined to reverse its course. Millie was right...naturally, an afternoon of fishing was just what she needed to clear her mind and see what she was missing.

When she returned with the groceries, Millie greeted her at the door. Despite having terminal cancer, she still got around pretty well with just a cane. "Why don't you unload the groceries, and then join me for a cocktail on the deck. I can't wait to hear about the fishing trip."

"I'll do just that. What would you like to drink? I'm going to have a glass of white wine."

"I'll make my own while you take care of the groceries." Millie followed her into the kitchen and poured herself a Dewar's and water from a bottle she kept above the sink. Holly noted that the bottle was only half full, and wondered how long ago she'd bought it. She knew better than to question her though, Millie had made up her mind to go out on her own terms, and Holly didn't want to start acting like one of her doctors.

A few minutes later, Holly had a glass of Pinot Grigio in hand, and settled in next to her aunt on the deck sofa. She recounted her delightful afternoon, and Millie replied, "Four yellowtail and a sixteen-pound mutton snapper? You must have left quite an impression on Captain Bart."

"Actually he left quite an impression on me...the crew did too...they're so nice and enjoy the work so much, it'll be sad to see it end."

"See it end? Now, dear, just because the marina gets sold, doesn't mean that the drift boat will stop running. It's quite a moneymaker, in fact the whole marina does very well. I can't imagine the new owners would change much in this economy, at least not for a good while."

"You would think, but Captain Bart invited me up on the bridge for the ride out, and he told me Sonny Slade said everybody's getting kicked out as soon as the deal closes. The *C-LOVE* included."

"WHAT? No...no, they wouldn't do that...would they? Why would they do that? Oh dear, oh dear, I never would have sold knowing that. What have I done?" Millie took a big sip of her drink, and her hand was shaking. Holly was worried that she might have a stroke or something, and immediately regretted telling her.

"Maybe this Sonny guy was just putting a scare into everybody, so when he asks for more rent, they're relieved instead of upset. That's probably it."

"You think? No, I should have known...Damn! It's exactly the kind of thing those Slades would do. What about all the commercial boats? Where will they go? They must hate me and I can't blame them...I hate me too!"

"Millie, stop it, nobody hates you, they're just naturally concerned. Come on, let's go inside and I'll whip up some fresh yellowtail with all the fixins."

The dinner turned out fabulous, and Holly wolfed her plate down. Fishing always made her hungry, and sautéed yellowtail was her favorite. She thanked Millie for suggesting she go on the afternoon trip, and told her that she had more fun than she's had in a long time.

She could tell Millie was still upset, because she was picking at her food and was unusually quiet. Finally she spoke. "Honey...You know the main reason I decided to sell the marina was because your cousin Sarah is incapable of running it, and it never occurred to me you would get divorced, and move back from Atlanta. I thought you loved your job and would patch things up with Mark. I figured selling the marina before I died would make things easier for the both of you. What I didn't figure on is Slade throwing everybody out first chance he got, but I should have. Now I'm thinking I made a big mistake by not calling you first, so let me just ask. If I found a way to get out of the deal, would you be willing to move back for good and run the marina? Of course the whole thing would be yours once I'm gone."

Holly sure didn't see that one coming, and put her glass of wine down. "Me? Run the marina? I...I never really thought about it, I'm not sure if I...If I would know how."

"Don't be silly, it's not some big fancy operation. All the slips are rented, so you just have to maintain the docks, the building, and the *C-LOVE*. The *C-LOVE* requires the most attention, but I have some good people in place like Captain Bart who could show you the ropes."

"What about Sarah?"

"Sarah's got the ambition of a loaded snail. I tried to get her involved with the marina a number of times, but she prefers to wait tables at Three Jacks because it allows her to sleep in. I'll still provide for her, but that's my responsibility, not yours."

"How would you get out of the deal?"

"There may be a way, but first I need to know if you're willing to take over. You said yourself what a wonderful time you had today. It would get you out from behind the computer and put some color back in that beautiful face. Most of the people in the

224

marina are honest, hardworking folk, who would give you the shirt off their back if you needed it. They would be thrilled if the marina stayed just the way it was, but with you in charge. I'd be thrilled too, not only because I feel horrible about the thought of all those good people being put out of work, but because I think you would love it. No, I take that back, I know you would love it. You grew up on the *C-LOVE*...It's in your blood, just look at how today went. Heck, you might even meet somebody...not that it's a concern of mine with your personality and looks. What do you say, honey? Would you be willing to give it a try if I can undo this mess I made?"

Holly thought about what Millie said, and she was spot on. She was at a turning point in her life...divorced, alone, and searching for direction. She loved being on the water, and had a special attachment to the *C-LOVE*. Plus, she knew from experience that Millie's intuition was almost always right. She told herself earlier in the day that she was determined to reverse the funk she had been in, and now the opportunity was presenting itself. That is...if Millie could get out of the deal.

She took a deep breath and exhaled. "How could I say no? You always know what's best for me...of course I'd do it. Now, how do you propose getting out of the deal?"

Millie smiled for the first time since being told about Slade's plan to throw everybody out of the marina. She reached her hand across the table and squeezed Holly's. "Well, dear, I have this old map..."

Chapter 55

We stopped at the Fish House in Key Largo for a late lunch. It set us back about an hour, but we still made pretty good time, getting back to Boynton by six. I had Jamie drive to the marina first, and we dropped Tangles off at the *Lucky Dog*. He had taken some more pain meds and wanted to take it easy, which was fine with me. We hadn't planned on coming back until Sunday, and it was early Saturday night, so I figured I'd surprise Melody and take her out for dinner.

When we got to my apartment, I saw that Melody's car was parked in the lot. Jamie helped me carry some of my gear in, like the rods and a cooler. As he set the rods down in the corner of the living room, he asked, "Feel like burning one? It's been a long trip."

"Could I stop you if I wanted to?"

"Good point, got an ashtray?"

"You know I don't smoke...here, use this empty Heineken bottle."

"Got any full ones?"

"I think there's still some in the cooler."

As Jamie fished around for a cold one, I splashed some water on my face and took a leak. When I walked back in the living room, Jamie was settling into the couch, sporting a freshly lit doob.

"I'll be right back," I said. "I'm gonna run upstairs and see if Melody wants to go to dinner." I bounded up to her second-story apartment, which was one over from mine on the corner, and knocked on the door. I could sense her looking at me through the peephole, and thought I heard her say something just before opening the door.

As it swung open, I said, "Hey, Mel, you wanna go grab—" I stopped in midsentence when I saw the alarmed look on her face. She stepped out into the walkway, shutting the door behind her. *What the hell?*

She was all dolled up and none too happy. "Kit, what're you doing here?"

"What? What am I *doing?* I thought I'd see if you wanted to go to dinner. What are *you* doing?"

"I uh, I have company."

"Company? What, your sister's in town or something?"

"No, no...company like I'm, uh, like I'm on a date. We're about to leave for dinner."

"What?"

"We can talk about it later. I just can't go on being your part-time girlfriend, with you showing up whenever you feel like it. I'm twenty-nine, Kit, I need something more...and I...I met a nice guy."

"What? I'm *not* a nice guy?"

"Forget it...we'll talk about it later, I have to go."

I stood there on the walkway for a couple of seconds, just staring at the door as it shut in my face.

As I walked back down to my apartment, I noticed a brand-new Mercedes 500SL parked in one of the guest spots. *Well, well, well...*

I walked in to my apartment and Jamie was still on the couch, enveloped in a sweet cloud of cannabis. "So where are you going to dinner?" he asked, handing me what was left of the joint. *Perfect, just what the doctor ordered.*

I took a big drag and pulled out a Heiney from the cooler. Then I cracked it open and took a giant swig, exhaling as I plopped down in the recliner. "I'm going to this new place called the Stabbed in the Back Cafe."

"What? Stabbed in the Back? Never heard of it... where is it?"

"It's right on the corner of Shoulda Seen it Coming Boulevard and Fuck Street. Care to join me?"

Chapter 56

Kristy Kane was really looking forward to updating the mayor after her visit with Sonny Slade...She couldn't *wait* to see his reaction. As she walked through City Hall she smoothed her skirt and thought about how badly Sonny wanted to get in her panties. He'd certainly given it the old college try, *not that he even knew how to spell college.* After plying her with several drinks, he said he had to go home to feed his dog, and invited her along to keep him company. OK, not so much invited, as begged. She shuddered to think how quickly he would have been pawing her if she had agreed, and resigned herself to the fact that she probably *would* have to roll in the hay with him at least once. That is if they bought the marina and she wanted a job. *Oh well, that's why I keep these legs in shape.* She knocked on the mayor's door, which was slightly ajar.

"Come in," he answered.

Kristy strode in the room and the mayor got right to it. "So, Miss Kane, have any bright ideas on how we can derail this thing?"

"Well, I did have an interesting conversation with Sonny Slade down at the Three Jacks."

The mayor set his paper down and looked at her intently. "And?"

"And I suggested to him that he could flip the marina to the city for a nice profit."

"And?"

"He basically said that the city has been nothing but a pain in the ass to Three Jacks, and there's no way the city could afford to pay what they would want."

"Super...anything else?"

This was the part that Kristy was waiting for, ever since he last dismissed her with a casual wave of the hand. "Oh yeah, he said to tell the mayor there's a new sheriff in town, and his name's Sonny Slade."

Mayor Vincent Mandula slammed his fist down on the desk, making everything on it jump and then settle down in a slightly different position. "He said that? That weaselly prick actually said to tell me that?" He slammed his fist down again and a paper clip holder fell on the floor, sending paper clips everywhere. Kristy made no move to pick any of them up. "That's it! I'm sending code enforcement down to that rathole of a restaurant to write them up for every offense possible. Who in the hell does he think he is?"

"Are you sure you want to do that, Mr. Mayor? It will seem kind of obvious that we're coming down on them because they won't sell to the city."

"That's exactly the message I want to send. Not only will we be breathing down their necks at the Three Jacks, but we'll fight whatever development plans they have for the marina. He says he's the new sheriff? Well he better get ready for a street war."

The mayor got out from behind his desk and started picking up the mass of clips on the floor. He looked up at Kristy who was getting out of her chair. "Could you give me a hand for a second?"

"I'd love to, mayor, but I've got a CRA meeting and can't be late. Don't miss that one under the sofa." She spun on her heel and was out the door in a flash, mentally high-fiving herself as the mayor called for his secretary.

Chapter 57

When I left the apartment about ten the next morning, I noticed the blinds were still closed on Melody's apartment windows, and her car sat in the same place as the day before. I had the distinct impression she never made it home from her date. I should have suspected as much when she said she "met someone," implying that it wasn't a first date. As I drove down to the *Lucky Dog*, I came to grips with the fact that I had been dumped. It wasn't that I was heartbroken or anything, but it still kind of sucked. I thought we had a mutual, no pressure, enjoy each other's company kind of relationship...one that worked for both of us...*I thought wrong.*

Hadn't she said something about being twenty-nine too? *What's that all about?* Hell, I'm thirty-seven and not panicked about meeting Mrs. Right. What's she got to worry about at twenty-nine? Should I be worried? *Christ, what the hell did I know?* I popped in some Weezer and found myself singing along as usual. "On an island in the sun...we'll be playing and having fun...and it makes me feel so fine I can't control my brain..."

That's it. I need a holiday or vacation. Only now I didn't have anybody to take one with...*shit.*

I pulled up to the *Lucky Dog* and found it empty, so I walked down to the fuel dock to see what was going on. Robo was there per usual, telling Hambone, "There's nothing I can do about it, the condo board won't let us rent to any commercial vessels...it's in their bylaws. I've told everybody else the same thing too, nothing's changed. I'm sorry, Ham...my hands are tied." Hambone looked worried.

I asked, "What's up? Why are you looking to change docks?"

Hambone turned to me. "You haven't heard?"

"I just got back from the Keys...haven't heard what?" Tangles came walking around the corner drinking a bottle of water.

"Milfred's sold the marina, Slade's buying it and throwing everybody out."

"WHAT? She sold the marina to Slade? I don't believe it."

"Believe it," said Robo. "It's the talk of the dock, as you can imagine. Especially since good old Sonny went around telling everybody that their days are numbered. All the commercial guys are freaked out. There's nowhere for them to go, least not anywhere around here. I feel bad that I can't accommodate any of them, but like I told Hambone, there's nothing I can do."

"Holy shit!"

Tangles gave me sort of a half salute with his good arm, and sat down in a chair. I nodded at him and continued on in disbelief. "This is crazy...I...I can't believe it."

"Tell me about it," agreed Hambone. "You're not the one whose livelihood is about to get flushed down the toilet. What the hell am I gonna do?"

I had never seen Hambone so flustered, and could only imagine what the other commercial guys were feeling as well. This was seriously bad news for them.

"I don't know…I need to talk to Millie and find out the whole scoop. I can't believe she would do this. " I had known Millie for a number of years, and had helped her update the rental agreements for her commercial slips. She was a sweet and stubborn lady, who I always thought was shrewder than she let on, but she was nothing, if not considerate. I knew she wouldn't knowingly sell the marina if it meant all the slips had to be vacated…no way. "I'm going to head over to her office and see if she's there, I'll be back."

"She's not there. Last I heard she was in the hospital, but I called earlier and she's definitely not at Bethesda…maybe she's at JFK."

"What? She's in the *hospital?* Since when?"

"Since…I don't know…maybe a week, week and a half ago. I heard the cancer's back…and it's not good."

I was shocked. I must have seen her just before she went in, and thought she looked pretty good for being eighty-ish. "Shit, this is unbelievable, I bet Slade coerced her in to selling while she was in the hospital. What a lowlife…that has to be it." I thought about it a second more before deciding. "I'm gonna head over to the *C-LOVE* anyways, and try to find somebody who knows where she is. Tangles…you coming?"

Tangles and I were cutting across the parking lot, when I noticed someone on the *Lucky Dog*. I changed course, and as I got closer, could see it was an attractive blond-haired woman. She was sticking something on my cabin door, and was just stepping off the boat when

Tangles and I got there. She was a real looker...I'd never seen her before.

I said, "Excuse me, can I help you with something?"

"Yes...maybe, I'm looking for the owner of this boat, a Mr. Connor "Kit" Jansen. That wouldn't happen to be you...would it?"

Oh shit, police business? I quickly glanced at my cabin door to try to make out what she stuck there. It looked like a business card. *Was she a Boynton detective maybe? Did that guy I laid out by the dumpsters somehow ID me? How could he?*

"Um...uh...please, listen, ma'am, that guy I supposedly assaulted was harassing a young lady. I'm sure she'll back me up on it if you can track her down. I believe her name was..."

"What are you talking about? Who do you think I am?"

"Uh, I'm not sure...I guess...you're not a police officer? I could hear Tangles chuckling behind me.

"What? No, no my name's Holly. I was just leaving a note for Kit that my aunt really needs to talk to him. I take it that's you? It's important."

"Yes...I'm Kit...but who's your aunt?"

"Of course, I forgot, its Milfred...Milfred Lutes...I'm her niece."

"*You're* Holly? You're the niece that lives up in... where did she say?"

"Atlanta...yep, that's me." Relief washed over me, and as we shook hands, I introduced Tangles. Tangles excused himself and went inside the boat so we could talk in private.

"I'm sorry if I offended you, I'm a little rattled. I just found out your aunt sold the marina and was in the hospital. In fact, I was just headed to find out where she is, so I can see her."

"No offense taken." Holly was smiling to herself. She particularly liked that he thought she was a cop or something. *A cop? Really?* And what about the "supposed assault." *What the heck was that all about?*

"Good, what hospital's she in? I'll head over right now."

"Actually, she's at home."

"At home? That's good…right? She must be doing better then."

"Um, not exactly, but she can tell you herself what's going on. She sleeps most afternoons, but was hoping you could join us for dinner. She said you're someone she trusts. She wants you to look at the contract for the sale of the marina, and some other documents. She needs some advice."

"I wished she would have asked me before she signed it."

"I wish she would have asked me too, so does she."

"What do you mean?"

"You'll see—can you make it tonight? About six thirty?"

"Six thirty? You got it, I'll be there."

"We'll see you later then, thanks." I watched her walk away for a few seconds, and then my phone rang as I jumped on the boat. It was Kingfish Stew, who told me he was heading up to his parents' place in Vero, rather than staying over at my apartment. I didn't bother to tell him I forgot all about him, and had just made dinner plans.

When I stepped into the cabin, I found Tangles stretched out on the sofa, nursing a coldie and laughing. "You thought she was a *cop?*" he asked. "Man, if cops were that good looking, I'd be robbing banks every day. *A cop?* Seriously...you must have had some sort of *Charlie's Angels* flashback going on there."

I couldn't help laughing with him. *What was I thinking?* "It was the way she said my full name that threw me—sounded like I was in trouble."

"Well if she's trouble, then let me be in it."

"Sorry to be a dream crusher, dude, but I'm having dinner with her tonight."

"You're shitting me, you worked a date out of that?"

"Well not exactly, I'm having dinner with her at her aunt's house, the one who owns the C-LOVE Marina. Her aunt wants me to look at the marina contract and some other stuff. I'm not sure why, she must have a lawyer, but I guess I'll find out."

"Good, then I still might have a shot at her."

"You? What about me?"

"You already have a girlfriend, what's her name? Melanie?"

"It's Melody, or was Melody, she dumped me last night."

"Seriously?"

"Yep, she dumped me like a truck."

"Wow, I feel for you, bro...but can I have her number?"

Chapter 58

Since I didn't know what we were having for dinner, I decided to bring a bottle of white wine *and* a bottle of red. For the white I went with Conundrum, a terrific proprietary blend, and for the red, a Beringer Knights Valley Cabernet. They were both a little pricey, but I didn't have to spring for dinner, so I figured why not. Plus, the first impression I made on Millie's niece Holly was a little shaky. I figured it might be a good idea to show her I had some social skills, if not good taste. I had to agree with Tangles that she was a tall drink of water...no doubt about it. She also had a way about her that I liked. OK, maybe it was her looks that I liked, but that doesn't make me a bad person, does it? I kept playing mental Hacky Sack as I picked up flowers at Winn-Dixie for Millie.

At precisely six thirty, I was knocking on Millie's door. If there was one thing I hated, it was tardiness. If I was asked to be somewhere at a certain time and agreed...I was there...on time...*Period.* Fashionably late is bullshit, it's just an excuse for the inconsiderate and inept. Holly answered the door, and I took a second to admire her before entering. She was barefoot, wearing a pair of faded jeans and a simple white blouse. Her hair was the kind of blond that lightened the more sun it got, and her face had nice color from recent time in the sun. She looked great, and we said our hellos as I held out the flowers. "I brought some flowers for Millie, and some wine for dinner."

"Oh wonderful, please come on in." She took the flowers, and I followed her into the kitchen as she inhaled the bouquet. After pulling the wine out of the gift bag, she looked at me. "Well how do you like that? A red *and* a white."

"I know Millie usually has fish, but better safe than sorry."

"Forget about the sorry, this Beringer is one of my favorites. I'm not familiar with the Conundrum, but if the Beringer is any indicator, I'm sure I'll like it. Why don't you say hi to Millie while I put these flowers in a vase? She's out on the deck. Can I bring you something to drink? A beer maybe? I'll be out in a minute."

"That would be great, I'll have whatever you're having." I headed out on the deck and found Millie in a chair, watching the boats pass by.

She heard my footsteps and turned to me. "Kit! I'm so glad you could come." I bent down to give her a hug, and she held on a little longer than usual. As I pulled away, I got a good look at her. I was shocked to see she was not looking as good as she was just a couple of weeks earlier.

She was pale and frail, not a good combo for anyone...so I lied. "You're looking good, Millie. What's this nonsense I heard about you being back in the hospital?"

"Come now, you're just being nice, I know I look horrible. Hell, I can't even bear to look in the mirror anymore. Thanks for trying to cheer up an old lady though." There was no bullshitting Milfred Lutes. That was for sure.

"Well, I'm glad to see you're out of the hospital, I didn't even know you were back in, is everything OK?" I could tell from the look on her face that it wasn't. I could also tell she was struggling with whether to tell me or not. "It's OK, you don't have to tell me, but if there's anything you need, or anything I can do, just ask. ...fair enough?" It was true, I would do just about anything for her. Back when I rewrote the slip rental agreements for her I had been having some financial problems, and she let me keep the Robalo at the marina for free. I spent a lot of time there and we became friends. It amazed me that her niece Sarah wasn't there to help out. Millie was sweet and tough, but always fair.

"Kit, I would never burden you with my problems, but to understand why I did what I did, and why I asked you here, you must know the truth. The doctors told me I have maybe three months to live. The cancer came back...it spread to my liver and brain."

This I had not expected, and it took me by surprise. I rose from the sofa, looking at her. "What? I...I thought you just had a little melanoma?" I started to choke up a little, and looked away toward the water.

"It started that way, but it wasn't detected early enough. It was my fault for not keeping up with the dermatologist appointments. Promise me you'll always wear sunscreen."

"Jesus."

Holly came out on the deck and walked up next to me. She put one hand in the middle of my back and handed me a Heineken Light with the other. She sensed the moment and said nothing as she turned and sat on the couch.

I took a long pull from the bottle and kept watching the boats, thinking about the changes coming...and not liking it. "So that's why you sold the marina. I figured there had to be a good reason, but not this."

"That was the main reason, but also because I thought I had nobody to leave it to who could take over and continue running it. Then, after I signed the contract, I found out Holly got divorced and moved back from Atlanta. We talked last night, and she's willing to take over the marina if I can get out of the contract. That's what I wanted to talk to you about."

"You don't want to sell the marina after all?"

"That's right."

"Great! What did your lawyer say?"

"I haven't talked to him yet. I want you to look at the contract first."

"Well...OK...but why?"

"I'll get to that in a minute. Holly, dear, will you get the contract?" Holly went inside and came out with a folder that she handed to me. I sat down on the sofa and took a look at the contract, which was only five pages long. With most contracts, the critical information usually appears on the first and the last pages. Since this one was so short, I read the whole thing. I finished my beer, and Holly got me another.

I didn't like what I read. "Millie, this contract is very straightforward. Slade put up a hefty nonrefundable deposit, which goes hard about a week from now. After that, he has thirty days to close. There's nothing in the contract that gives you a unilateral right to terminate. He would have to agree to tear it up, so to speak, and my guess is he wouldn't do that based on the fact that he put up a four-hundred-thousand-dollar nonrefundable deposit. Plus, everyone knows how bad old Syd wants your property. The only way I see you keeping the marina is if he fails to close for some reason, and I can't see that because it would cost him four hundred grand."

"That's my take on it too, but what if something were discovered on the property that they didn't know about? Something that raised a big stink...so to speak."

Raised a big stink? "What are you talking about?" Now *I* smelled something fishy as Holly and Millie shot each other furtive looks.

"Come now, let's go inside...Holly can start dinner while I show you the map."

"The map? *What map?*" I took Millie's left arm and Holly took her right. We walked her inside, despite her protesting she could walk with her cane just fine.

"Over here," said Holly, as she guided us into the living room. We sat Millie in a loveseat, and she motioned me to sit down next to her.

Holly excused herself to start making dinner, and Millie squeezed my arm. "Open the envelope on the table, and pull out the map." On the coffee table was an old oversized envelope, and I slid a large, tattered, piece of paper out of it. On it was a pretty crude sketch, but I could make out the borders of the C-LOVE Marina, and in one corner there was an arrow pointing down with a drawing of two containers above it.

"This is the marina, obviously...but what are these?" I asked, pointing to the two containers.

"Those are a pair of twenty-five-hundred-gallon, diesel fuel tanks. My grandfather buried them about eighty years ago after a hurricane destroyed the marina and everything else around here. He didn't know any better. Hell, everybody did whatever they wanted on their own property back then, it was different times."

"So they're still there."

"Sure there still there. My daddy passed the map on to me and told me to keep it under my hat, because he found out it would cost a lot of money to remove them properly."

"Of course Slade doesn't know about this...he hasn't seen this map...*right?*"

"Hell no...You, me, and Holly are the only ones who've seen it."

"What about the city?"

"Those idiots? They don't have a clue. Their records don't go back that far. So tell me, Kit, is there any way I can use this information to stop the sale somehow?"

My mind was racing through the options...and they were all borderline fraudulent in nature. Scratch that, they were blatantly fraudulent, and probably criminal. "Wow Millie, let me think about this for a minute."

Holly overheard us from the kitchen. "Dinner's just about ready. Kit, can you open a bottle of wine? We can talk about it over dinner."

I walked into the kitchen and saw some beautiful fillets sizzling in a skillet.

"Smells great, those fillets are good size, are they snapper?"

"You bet...mutton...caught one yesterday on the *C-LOVE.*"

"Must have been a pretty nice fish."

"Sixteen pound to be exact." Holly was smiling to herself.

"Sixteen Pounds? You caught a *sixteen-pound mutton yesterday?* Are you pulling my leg?"

"Along with four nice yellowtails too...after all, I did grow up on that boat." She saw the skeptical look on my face. "Don't tell me you're one of those caveman guys who think women can only sew and cook."

I was laughing. "No, no I didn't mean it that way. It's just that you and your aunt are full of surprises today. I'm wondering what's next."

"Well, next we sit down to dinner and figure out this fuel tank thing. Could you please pour some wine?"

Dinner was fantastic. Holly sautéed the snapper in white wine and butter with some capers on top. She served it over mashed potatoes, with asparagus on the side. The Conundrum was outstanding, as usual.

We were halfway through dinner, when Millie brought up the tanks. "So what do you think, Kit? What can we do?"

I had been mulling over the options, and had some questions of my own. "The contract isn't contingent upon financing, but this is a lot of money...do you know if Slade is getting a loan? He's not paying cash, is he?"

"I think Bank of America is loaning him the money. My attorney mentioned that he had to send copies of everything to them...why?"

"Well, it's crucial. The bank will require that an environmental survey be conducted to make sure there's nothing like...well...buried fuel tanks on the property. If they find something like that, they'll insist it be removed and the site cleaned, prior to closing.

Per the contract, Slade has fifteen days before the deposit becomes nonrefundable, so I'm sure he's trying to get the environmental work done before then. If the company that does the environmental survey discovers the tanks, and they should, Slade will likely ask that you remove them and pay for it. That would require an extension of the contract. If you denied it and returned the deposit, it would kill the deal, but you'd be stuck paying for the cleanup."

"I'd gladly pay for the cleanup if it gets me out of the deal. So that's it then, we'll just have to make sure they find the tanks when they do their testing."

"Not so fast. You can't let them know that *you know* the location of the tanks. That could open you up to a whole slew of problems. Namely, that you were withholding information and not dealing in good faith. The court might make you clean up the mess, and still sell to Slade. You'd probably be fined too. No, you can't steer them to the tanks."

Holly jumped in, "Well what should we do then? If the sale goes through, Slade is going to throw everybody out and shut down the *C-LOVE*."

Millie started talking to herself. "Oh dear, what have I done, what have I done?"

"All right all right, just hold on a second," I said. "I don't want that to happen any more than you do. Those are all friends of mine you're talking about... let me just think a second." I stepped into the kitchen and opened the Beringer, then brought it back to the table. I poured a glass for Holly, saying, "Here's what we do, we do nothing. We let the bank send in their environmental company to do the testing, which will probably be next week. They'll find the tanks, and then Millie's lawyer can play hardball with Slade and kill the deal. It'll probably cost an arm and a leg, but you should be able to keep the marina."

"What if they don't find the tanks, what then?" asked Millie.

"What then? Then we go to plan B."

"What's plan B?" asked Holly.

"No sense going there until we need to, let's see what happens next week. If they don't find the tanks, and Slade lets the deposit become nonrefundable, then we'll talk about Plan B. Don't worry though, I'm sure they'll find the tanks. That's what those companies get paid the big bucks for."

Millie looked skeptical. "If you say so, Kit, but nobody's found them in the last eighty years."

"True, but nobody's poked around looking either... right? One other thing, nobody can find out about this map, or that I've advised you what to do regarding the tanks. If that were to come out, I'd lose my broker's license, you'd lose the marina, and we'd all be in deep doo-doo." I raised my glass. "Here's to keeping the marina out of Slade's hands." Holly and Millie raised their glasses, and we clinked them together before drinking.

As we set them down, Millie said, "Thanks for coming, Kit, I knew I could count on you to help figure this out. You'll have to excuse me though. I'm a tired old lady who needs to get to bed."

Holly and I walked her to her bedroom. She gave us a hug and a kiss, and thanked me for the flowers, before lying down. We walked back into the kitchen and I helped clear the dishes, a sure sign that I was trying to get on Holly's good side. Afterward, she suggested we finish our wine on the deck. I followed her outside, complimenting the dinner. "So I would say you definitely know how to cook fish, as well as catch them. That was great."

"It wouldn't have been nearly as good without the wine you brought. That Conundrum was something else, I've always been more of a red wine drinker, but I may have to reconsider."

I could hear snook popping, and followed her out to the point where a light overhung the edge of the seawall, shining down on the water. Sure enough, I could see the shadows of fish lurking just out of light's range, waiting to ambush unwary creatures attracted to it. "This is a special place your aunt has. I use to fish here on my little Robalo...caught my first tarpon right over there." I pointed toward the docks across the channel.

Holly nodded. "Whenever my father and I visited, we'd bring some live shrimp, and float them off the point with bobbers."

"Live shrimp? That's like taking candy from a baby."

"I *was* a baby back then. My best memories are from time spent here, or on the *C-LOVE*, after visiting with Millie. Now I'm going to lose her, and I'm afraid it's all going to disappear, I just can't bear the thought."

Her voice was cracking and I wanted to hug her, but I thought it might be awkward. I just said, "Look Holly, I've seen plenty of deals crash, even when both sides are doing all they can to *make* it happen. Now that Millie has decided she wants out, the odds of us killing the deal have greatly increased. Keep your head up. It's what Millie would want."

"You're right, I've got to keep it together for both our sakes." She was shaking off the demons, showing the same sort of resolve that Millie had. She straightened up, and said, "That's enough of my boohooing. If I start feeling sorry for myself again, please tell me to can it." I chuckled a little, and she asked, "What's so funny?"

"Are you sure you're not Millie's daughter? I've seen that attitude before, and it's pure Milfred Lutes."

"Well, it's probably because she raised me like a daughter after my parents died when I was fifteen... that's why we're so close."

"Oh, I'm sorry, that's terrible, what happened to your parents?"

"They were on their way here to pick me up after I spent a weekend with Millie and Gramps. They were coming from Naples across old Alligator Alley, and had a head on with a tractor-trailer driver who dozed off and crossed the center line. It was instantaneous for them, but I still feel the pain today."

"Man, that's tough. Thank God you had Millie."

"I know, it was hard for her too though, my father was her brother. They were close, we leaned on each other a lot...still do." Holly noticed that Kit wasn't wearing a ring, and saw an opportunity to satisfy her curiosity. "What about you and your family?"

"My family? Well I'm the oldest of four, with a brother and two sisters. My parents are doing fine, knock on wood, and coincidentally, they spend winters in Naples too."

"No family of your own?"

"Who me? Nah, I spend too much time on the water. Being out on the ocean brings me peace of mind that I just can't find anywhere else. Haven't found the right girl who understands what that's all about. As a matter of fact, I just got dumped last night."

"You? Come on...I don't believe it."

"Believe it, unceremoniously kicked to the curb. I wasn't around enough and some other guy stepped in. It's not the first time, probably won't be the last."

"You don't sound too heartbroken about it."

"Like I said, been there, done that, shoulda seen it coming...but didn't. It still stings though."

"Well, I'm glad."

"What?"

Holly didn't realize what she said until it was too late. "I mean um, I'm um, I'm glad that I'm not the only one who's been on the stinging end recently." Please buy it, she thought. Please, please buy it.

"Oh, that's right, Millie mentioned you just got divorced. This has got to be a tough time for you, especially with everything else that's going on."

"It is, I'm just thankful there were no kids involved. It would have been God awful if we'd put children through it." Holly wasn't sure if he had bought her faux pas, because he seemed to be looking at her a little funny now. Not good. She decided to wrap it up before totally humiliating herself, and faked a yawn, saying, "I'm pooped. Can I get you some coffee or something before you go?"

"A bottle of water would be great, thanks." As we walked inside, I was trying to figure out what she really meant by saying, "I'm glad." It was a semi- awkward moment and seemed to fluster her a little. Was she glad that I was single? Could she be interested in me too? *Only one way to find out.* She handed me a water from the fridge, and I drank half of it before reaching the front door.

She opened the door. "Thanks for coming, Kit, I appreciate all your help. Thanks for listening too. It helps to talk to someone other than my aunt, she's got enough on her plate."

"It's been my pleasure, seriously, and I'll do whatever I can to help queer the deal. You can take that to the bank, just remember...mum's the word."

She laughed. "OK, I got it, mum, mum, mum... good night."

She began to close the door before I was ready. *Shit!* "Um, one more thing."

She opened the door back up and looked at me curiously. "Yes?"

"It's important you keep a close eye on what's going on at the marina. I'm sure there'll be some testing there this week, and we should probably get together to discuss what's going on."

"Really?"

I thought I detected the faintest of smiles emerging on her face, but couldn't be sure in the light.

"Yes, definitely. Fridays are my day off, maybe I could swing by on the boat and pick you up in the morning. We could do a little fishing, and you could fill me in on what happened at the marina."

"I could probably juggle my work schedule to take Friday off, if you think it's important." She was definitely starting to smile a little.

"It could be critical, I really think you should."

"Like a weekly update, huh?"

"Exactly, how 'bout I call you middle of the week to confirm, in case of bad weather or something."

"Sounds good, I'll talk to you later then, good night...and drive safe."

* * *

Holly shut the door again, and as she walked in the kitchen, had a fluttering feeling in her tummy. A feeling she hadn't had in a long time. She giggled to herself as she picked up her wine glass and headed into the living room. "It could be critical," he said... *Puh-leez.* She curled up on the sofa, and used the remote to turn on the television.

As she finished her wine, she scrolled through the channels and stopped on a fishing show. A man with a visor on his head had his back to the camera as he reeled. Suddenly an extremely short person...a kid?...stepped past the host with a large gaff, and hauled a big tuna through the transom door. They high-fived each other and the man who reeled it in turned to the camera, proudly announcing, "That's fishing on the edge...with Shagball." She almost dropped her glass as she stared into the face of the man who had just asked her out. It was Kit! *What the heck?* He has a fishing show? And what did he call himself? *Shagball?* She was going to go out with a guy named *Shagball? Oh my God!* Why didn't Millie tell her any of this? She laughed so hard some wine went up her nose, and she covered her mouth so as not to wake Millie as she instinctively coughed. At the first commercial, she took her wine glass into the kitchen, and set the dishwasher to run during the night. She hurriedly brushed her teeth and washed her face, before climbing into bed. She fell asleep watching the rest of the fishing show, thinking, *this is crazy!*

Chapter 59

The first city inspector came to Three Jacks on Monday morning as the kitchen staff prepared for the lunch crowd. Without even breaking a sweat, he quickly identified some rat droppings, as well as evidence of cockroaches. He left a citation that required the kitchen to be spotless within twenty-four hours, or risk being shut down. When Sonny showed up at lunchtime, one of his assistant managers gave him the news...and the citation.

"The city showed up and busted our balls for a few rodent droppings and the like. Here's the official report."

"Again? I thought I told you to make sure the kitchen crew is keeping the place clean."

"They try, but we're an open-air restaurant on the water. It's impossible to keep the critters out, everybody knows that."

"Everybody but the inspector, *jackass,* just call the pest control company again! You know, the ones we have a service contract with? The ones with that funny-looking elephant on their trucks."

"It's an aardvark."

"Whatever, get them out here pronto, and get the kitchen staff to clean the place tonight. Nobody goes home until I can eat off the floor."

"Seriously?"

"Yeah seriously, I want the place cleaned, spic and span, chop-chop."

"No, I mean you're gonna eat off the floor?"

"Tell me why I hired you again?"

"I'm your cousin?"

"Shit, don't say that too loud, I forgot what a dumbfuck you are."

The next day, Sonny was there to personally show the city inspector what a great job they had done cleaning the kitchen. The inspector seemed genuinely impressed, and gave them the OK to keep making deep-fried crap. As Sonny watched the inspector drive away, another city vehicle pulled in to the valet circle and double-parked in the fire lane. It was the fire inspector. *What the fuck?* He walked up to the fire inspector as he got out of his car. "Hello there, what can I do for you?"

"Nothing, I'm just here for a routine inspection. Make sure the fire extinguishers are charged and the exit lights are lit, that kind of thing."

"Well I'll be at the outside bar if you need me."

"Thanks, but I shouldn't."

Twenty minutes later the inspector handed him a citation for an unlit exit sign, a missing extinguisher, and a locked fire door. "You have twenty-four hours to correct the problem, see you tomorrow."

Sonny was pissed, and called over his dumb-ass cousin Danny for another reaming. "Don't we have a contract with a fire equipment company to make sure we don't have any issues like the ones in this citation?"

"Probably."

"*Probably?* How 'bout I probably *fire* your stupid ass you don't get with the program. You got five minutes to dig up the name and number of the fire prevention company we use, or I'm sending you back to Margate. Got it?"

"OK, OK, I heard you."

Five minutes later Sonny was on the phone with Don't Get Burned Fire Advisors. He was in the process of ripping them a new one when they informed him that the Three Jacks contract had lapsed due to nonpayment.

"What? What do you mean nonpayment?" he asked.

"You know, like when you get a bill and don't pay it? That's called nonpayment."

Sonny begged them to come the next day, and promised he'd write a check on the spot. After he hung up, he yelled, "Danny? Danny get your *ass* over here!" A few early lunch customers looked up from their chowder to see Danny hustle across the floor to the perturbed man with the poodle at his feet. "One more screwup, just *one* more screwup and you're done, cuz. You didn't pay the fire company, you moron! I want you to go in the office and pore over all the service contracts to make sure every *Goddamned one* is paid and current! There better not be a single porno mag in the file cabinet when you're done either...not a one...You hear me, shit-for-brains?"

"Yeah I hear you, and so does the whole frigging bar. Don't have a cow, man, I'm on it." He took two steps toward the office, then stopped and turned. "Sonny?"

"What now?"

"Even the *Hustler* scratch and sniff thirty-fifth anniversary edition?"

On Wednesday, the fire company came to fix the problems and Sonny gave them a check for the repairs, as well as for a year's worth of servicing. He was thankful no more inspectors showed up, but Thursday afternoon code enforcement got in the act. Sonny had just left the bar, and was heading to his car to drive to the bank, when he nearly tripped over a guy with a City of Boynton Beach Code Enforcement ID tag on his shirt. The guy was on his hands and knees, holding a level in one hand, and some type of triangle thing in the other. He appeared to be taking measurements of some sort on the wheelchair ramp. *What the hell?*

"Ahem, ah, excuse me...can I help you?" he grumbled.

"Don't mind me, sir, I'll be out of here in a few minutes, just taking some final measurements."

"What seems to be the problem?"

"A customer filed a complaint saying he thought the ramp was too steep. He had trouble getting up it."

"I guess that's better than having trouble getting it up."

"What?"

"Just a little erectile dysfunction humor."

"Sir, there's nothing funny about being disabled."

"Sorry, that's not what I meant, but I happen to know that ramp's up to code. We put it in when we bought the restaurant over ten years ago. The city was all over us about the handicap stuff...*trust me,* it's right."

"Ten years ago, huh? Well, that explains it."

"Explains what?"

"Explains why you're out of compliance now. The handicap codes were updated and revised last year, courtesy of the ACLU. Sure enough, your ramp's too steep. You're gonna have to get somebody down here with a concrete saw who can take the grade down. Of course, you'll need to lower the railing as well."

"You gotta be kidding me."

"Afraid not."

"Shit...Who in the hell does *that* kind of work?"

The city guy with the ID reached into his wallet, and handed Sonny a business card. It read Sam's Sawin' N Weldin'. "Just so happens my brother-in law does. You don't have to use him, of course, but I guarantee you won't have any further problems if you do." He winked at Sonny and continued his spiel. "Take your time and shop around if you want, you got thirty days to fix it. Well, guess I better check the bathrooms now, they changed those codes too. Have a nice day."

Later that afternoon, Sonny was sitting in his usual happy hour spot at the end of the bar, with Mr. Jenks at his feet. He was still fuming about the inspections. Practically every day of the week, some city inspector had been there busting balls. He was certain it had to do with the city wanting to buy out their contract for the marina. *Well, fat fucking chance of that.* Just then, Kristy Kane came swinging it down the dock, making a beeline straight to Sonny. She pulled out the chair next to him and sat down. *Damn, she looked good... especially from the neck down.*

She smiled at him. "How's it going, Sonny?"

"Not too good right now, the city's been crawling up our ass all week. They've written us up for every violation known to man, but you probably know all about that...don't you, Kristy?"

"Why don't you buy me a drink, and maybe I'll tell you."

Sonny signaled the bartender, and Kristy ordered her usual Dewar's and water. After she had her first sip, she looked at him. "This is off the record, of course."

"Naturally, now start talking."

"Well, I met with the mayor and told him you weren't interested in flipping the marina once you close, that the city wouldn't be able to afford it."

"And?"

"And he basically freaked. He said he was gonna send a message that you were not only going to be under a microscope here at Three Jacks, but you could expect the same treatment when you try to develop the marina."

Sonny slammed his fist on the bar, knocking over a container of lemons. "Son of a bitch said that?" He was trying to keep his voice down, but it still came out louder than he wanted. A few heads turned, but quickly looked away.

"That's pretty much exactly what he said, but you didn't hear that from me...right?"

"Of course not. I figured it was something like that, but it's nice to know for sure."

"So what are you gonna do?"

"What am I gonna do?" Sonny started laughing under his breath, trying to sound as sinister as possible. "Why I'm gonna sic my old man on him, that's what I'm gonna do. By the time old Syd's done reaming the mayor a new asshole, he'll probably present us with a key to the city. Fucker won't know what hit him...what do you think about that?"

It was actually just what she hoped for. She knew the mayor was a little intimidated by Syd Slade from previous encounters, and she would pay to hear the coming conversation.

"I think I like the way you think, Sonny."

"Me too...wanna know what I'm thinking now?"

She already knew—he was like a kid with his face pressed against the candy store glass. Time to give him just a little taste...maybe. "You're thinking about taking me out to dinner."

"I am? I mean, uh, right, I wanna take you out to dinner. *Damn* you're good."

She set her drink down on the bar, and swirled her finger around the edge slowly. Speaking in a low voice, she turned, looking directly into his eyes. "You have no idea how right you are Sonny...no idea."

Chapter 60

Holly took Kit seriously as far as keeping an eye on things at the marina. Every day she was on the dock, and had even met with Millie's accountant per her request. She met the girls who sold tickets to the *C-LOVE*, Regina and Pam. She had even talked to Kit's sidekick Tangles. He had been hired by Captain Bart to fill in on the *C-LOVE* when Hambone didn't have any charters. She was disappointed that she hadn't heard from Kit all week, despite Tangles telling her that he was in Sebring on business. She had been hoping he would call, it was already Thursday, and she was starting to wonder about their plans for Friday. Then she realized she had never given him her cell number...*shit.*

There wasn't a whole lot to report on the environmental tests though. Every day she saw the same guy walking around the marina. He kept sticking a long rod in the ground, taking pictures and making notes. She casually asked him the day before how it was going, and he said everything looked fine so far, but he had to wait for the test results to know for sure. She watched him probe everywhere but where the tanks were buried, which was at the end of the canal where the Jet Ski rental place was. By her estimation, the tanks were buried almost directly under the tiki hut kiosk that the Jet Ski rental guy used. Unless the environmental guy probed right next to it, she didn't see how he would ever discover the tanks. It started to worry her a little...OK, it was worrying her a lot.

She decided to go over to Kit's boat and leave a note with her number, figuring he might come down to the marina if he didn't get back too late. She stepped on the *Lucky Dog*, and was about to stick a note in the cabin door, when it slid open, startling her. It was Tangles, wearing his trademark Kid Rock T-shirt and a pair of shorts.

"What? What are you doing here?" she asked.

"I live here...and you?"

"You live here? On Kit's boat? You're kidding me."

"Nope, he's letting me stay here for a while until I save up enough to get my own place. Don't tell anybody though, it's against condo rules."

"My lips are sealed. You must be a pretty good friend if he lets you stay on his boat."

"Yeah, we're pretty tight, but I've only known him a couple of weeks."

"Now I *know* you're kidding me. Come on, what's really going on here? I saw you together on the fishing show the other night. Obviously you've known him longer than that."

"The show with the big yellowfin tuna?"

"Yeah, that was impressive."

"Actually, that's the first time we met. That was the morning he foul-hooked me."

"Foul-hooked you? Time out, Tangles, what are you talking about?"

"I thought you said you watched the show?"

"Well I did...I mean, I came across it channel surfing. I tuned in right when you boated the tuna."

"Well that explains it—you missed the beginning of the show. It's quite a story. Come on in and I'll tell you the whole thing. I even have cold beer."

Holly looked at her watch and saw it was four thirty. She still had a little time before Millie expected her for their evening cocktail. *Oh who's kidding who...I gotta hear this.* "How could I say no? I have a feeling I need to be sitting down for this story anyways."

She followed Tangles into the cabin and was glad the air conditioner was on. He pulled out a couple of Bud Lights, and they sat down facing each other at the dinette. Wasting no time, Tangles recounted the story. "Well, I was performing on a cruise ship one night, just a couple of weeks ago..."

Holly interrupted him several times with a "No way!" A few more times with an "Oh my God!" More than once with laughter, and when he finished, she declared, "That's the most unbelievable story I ever heard in my entire life."

"That's what they all say." They were laughing when Tangles' prepaid phone that he bought when he got back from the Keys started ringing. He answered, and Holly watched him say, "Hello? Hey, man...uh-huh, I'm chillin' on the LD, when you getting back? Cool... Holly's number? How would I know that? Yeah, I could probably go over there and get it, or I could just hand the phone to her...No, I'm not bullshitting you, she and I were just getting to know each other, *so to speak.*" Tangles gave Holly a big wink and Holly stifled a laugh. She had to admit he was kind of charming.

"Holly, here, talk to the big guy, he doesn't believe you and I are doing some bonding."

Tangles passed the phone to her and she said, "Kit?"

"Holly? What uh, what's going on?"

"I realized I never gave you my number and came over to your boat to leave you a note. Tangles was here and he was just telling me how you two met, it's quite a story. I also saw you on television the other night, what else don't I know about you?"

"Trust me, until recently it wasn't that interesting. Sorry I haven't called. Like you said, I forgot to get your number, and had to go out of town on business. I hope you're still up for tomorrow, it looks to be nice. I've been looking forward to it all week."

"You mean the weekly update?" She felt like ribbing him a little.

"Uh...yeah, of course, anything happen on that end?"

"I'll tell you about it tomorrow, what time are you coming by?"

"Is seven too early for you?"

"Please, the earlier the better...if you're serious about fishing that is. Seven's fine, anything I can bring?"

"You could bring some bottled water, and don't forget the sunscreen."

"OK, see you tomorrow." Click.

Chapter 61

Sonny was still suffering from a severe case of blue balls on the morning after his dinner date with Kristy Kane. At her suggestion, he had taken her to a fancy place in Delray, dropping two-hundred and fifty bucks in the process. He hadn't minded too much at the time though, because he thought he was finally going to get some. She flirted all through dinner, and afterward invited him up to her condo overlooking the Three Jacks. Before leaving the restaurant, he went to the bathroom and popped two Viagra. He wanted to impress Kristy the *hard* way. As soon as they were inside her condo, he immediately went for the gold, Sonny Slade style. Basically, that meant rubbing himself up against her from behind, while she was enjoying the view out her floor-to-ceiling living room window. She pushed him away, warning, "Not so fast big boy," but he kept charging her like a bull on steroids. After an all too brief make out session that involved as much groping as he could get away with, she suddenly got up and announced he had to leave because she had to get up early for work. He was none too happy, and briefly thought about forcing himself on her. Then he remembered all the lawsuits he'd finally settled, and reluctantly left holding his dick in his hand...literally.

When he woke up the next morning he was still high and hard, and his balls felt like they were in a vice coated with Icy Hot. He never felt so much pain in his entire life. He finally got his erection to subside thanks to a cold shower and an ice pack, but the pain still lingered. He picked up the phone and called his father, who answered on the second ring. "Hello?"

"Hey, Dad, it's me, Sonny."

Syd Slade always worried whenever Sonny called, because it usually cost him time and money. "What's going on, Sonny? Everything OK at the restaurant?"

"Not exactly, the city sent inspectors in every day this week to bust our balls about one thing or another. The mayor's pissed because we got the marina under contract, and the city wants it for their own redevelopment plans. He said we can expect the same kind of treatment every step of the way when we try to develop the marina."

"What? How do you know this? The mayor just happened to stop in for happy hour and threaten you?"

"No, nothing like that. He sent one of his lackeys to suggest we flip the marina to them for a small profit. I basically said it wasn't gonna happen. That's when he sent in the code violation cavalry. You name it, the fire marshal, the guys checking the handicap stuff, health inspectors, they've all been here. Needless to say, it ain't good for business."

"You're sure it's not some kind of annual inspection thing by all the departments?"

"I have it from a solid source inside City Hall who said the mayor is trying to harass us into selling the marina to the city."

"That piece of shit thinks he's gonna push Syd Slade around? Are you kidding me? By the time I'm through with him he's gonna have a statue of me on Boynton Beach Boulevard. Who the *fuck* does he think he is?"

"He thinks he's hot shit, that's what he thinks, want his number?"

"Goddamn right I do. You did a smart thing calling me, Sonny. Don't worry about those city schmucks getting up in your business anymore. I'll take care of it right now."

Sonny gave his dad the mayor's direct number that he got from Kristy. He was as happy as any man with blue balls could be when he hung up.

From his home up in Boston, Syd picked up the phone and dialed the mayor of Boynton Beach.

The phone rang twice, and was answered, "This is the mayor's office, how may I help you?"

"I'd like to speak with the mayor. Tell him it's Syd Slade."

"Hold on one moment, please." She hit the intercom and leaned forward. "Sir, there's a Mr. Syd Slade on the line."

"Tell him I'm in a meeting or something, take his number."

The call wasn't unexpected, but he dreaded talking to the man. He was a physically imposing, six foot four, two-hundred-and-eighty-pound, old-school restaurateur, who frankly scared him a little. They recently clashed over some property easement issues that were still tied up in court, and Slade had given him a look that said, *One of these days*...He thought it best to put off talking to him as long as possible.

"I'm sorry, sir, he's in a meeting right now. If you'd like—"

The rough voice with the slight New England accent interrupted her. "He's not in a meeting; otherwise, you would have said so to begin with. You tell him that if he doesn't pick up the phone right now, I'm jumping on the next plane to come down for a face-to-face."

"I'm sorry sir but—"

"But nothing! Tell him!"

The mayor's secretary Irene was use to dealing with somewhat hostile constituents, but the man on the other end of the line sounded like he was ready to reach through the phone and strangle her if she didn't comply.

She hit the intercom again. "Sir? Mr. Slade says that if you don't talk to him, he's coming in for a face-to-face meeting."

"Shit...all right...patch him through." The phone on his desk rang once and he picked it up.

"Syd, how are you doing? Congratulations on the marina deal."

"Cut the crap, Vince, you know I'm not doing well when I get a call from Sonny saying the city's all over us for bullshit code violations."

"Really? That's news to me."

"Oh, it is? *That's* funny, because I'm hearing that *you're* the one that sent them over. In fact, it's all because *we're* buying the C-LOVE Marina, and *you're* not. So let's cut to the chase, Vince. I'm a businessman first and foremost—how much are you willing to pay?"

"You're saying you would consider selling it to us?"

"For the right price? Sure...but it better be worth my while. I've been after that marina for years, never thought the old lady would sell."

"Me neither."

"So how much?"

"I could probably get you a million dollars more than you're paying. We could sign a contract the day you close on it."

"A million dollars?" Syd let out a derisive snorting laugh. "Are you fucking *serious?* That doesn't even pay the maintenance on my yacht for a year. You missed your calling, Vince, you should be doing stand-up."

"How much do you want?"

"From you and you're fine town? Thirteen million, and not a penny less."

"*What?* You want *five million* to flip it to the city? I could never get the commissioners to approve that."

"Well, guess what, Vince? Then you're shit out of luck. In the meantime, you better call off the inspectors, or I'll slap you and the city with harassment suits. That ought to look real good to the voters come election time this fall."

"Now calm down, Syd, I'm sure we can work something out."

"My end's already worked out. I'm closing on the marina in a little over thirty days from now. You want your end to work out? Then get approval to buy it from me for thirteen million. Once I close and start the development work, the price goes up."

"But—"

"But nothing...And if one more inspector sets foot in my restaurant for any other reason than to have some conch fritters, I'm lawyering up and taking you down. I will personally finance a campaign to have you thrown out of office. Forget about reelection. Vince, you'll never last that long. Have a nice fucking day." Click.

The mayor sat there holding the phone to his ear for about two seconds, before slamming it down so hard the paper clip holder fell on the floor again. *Shit.* He hated the way Slade talked to him like he was some kind of fucking peon. He was an *attorney*, for Christ's sake. Granted he hadn't practiced in a few years, but still. As he got down on his hands and knees to start picking up paper clips, he wondered what the hell he was going to do. He needed the marina, but Slade was out of his mind at thirteen million.

Just then, Kristy Kane came walking into the mayor's office. She saw him picking up paper clips and promptly spun around, heading back the way she had come. He never saw her and she smiled as she heard him call out to his secretary. "Irene! Will you give me a hand here for a second?"

Chapter 62

I slid the *Lucky Dog* right up to Millie's dock at precisely 7:00 a.m. Holly was standing there in shorts and a sleeveless top, wearing a visor, and holding a grocery bag of supplies. She stepped on the boat and I greeted her. "Good morning, why don't you put your stuff in the cabin and then join me up on the bridge?"

"Be right there." Two minutes later, she was climbing the ladder, and as she stepped on the bridge, she asked, "No Tangles?"

"Nah, he's working the morning and afternoon trips on the *C-LOVE* today, apparently Captain Bart took a shine to him."

"Seems like he has that effect on people."

"What do you mean?"

"Well, he's only known you a couple of weeks, and you're letting him live on your boat. I'd say you must have taken a shine to him as well."

"Oh, *that?* That's the least I could do for the poor guy. Hell, if it weren't for him, my show would have been canceled. The ratings have gone through the roof since I hooked him. The Tangles and tuna episode has been an Internet sensation by all accounts. Jamie my producer called me last night and said the show we shot in the Keys last week came out great too. We discussed it, and I'm going to ask Tangles to be a permanent part of the show. I'll probably spring that on him tonight."

"Wow, that's great. I can't wait to see the new show you just shot. In fact, I'd like to see the Tuna show again, because I missed the part where you reeled Tangles in."

"Well, you missed the best part. Don't worry though, you can go on our Web site and watch it anytime." We headed out the inlet, and the ocean was almost flat as a pancake. The sun had just risen, and bait fish were boiling near the jetties. Several boats had guys standing on their bows holding cast nets as they stalked live bait. It was a scene that repeated itself day in and day out, at virtually every inlet on the coast.

I announced my game plan for the day. "So...I was thinking we would do some bottom fishing for a couple of hours, and then troll our way north up to the Palm Beach Inlet. We can have lunch at Sailfish Marina, and then come back down the Intracoastal. What do you think?"

"Sounds like a good plan to me, Captain."

"Captain? Come on, I hope you don't expect me to put you on top of another monster mutton snapper."

"Not hardly, that was the biggest one I ever caught. Heck, I'm happy just to be on the water, it's so beautiful out here." She was right, of course, it was picture-postcard perfect. I liked her attitude too, and felt the same way about being on the water. Catching fish should always be considered a bonus.

"Where *did* you catch that big mutton by the way? We might as well start fishing there first."

"We were off the Boynton water tower, the champagne glass, in about eighty feet."

I turned the boat, and as we chugged the three or so miles south, I had her fill me in on what was going on at the marina.

"Well, there was a guy there pretty much every day," she said. "He had this long rod, plus a notebook and camera, and he just walked around doing his thing. I never saw him there for more than two or three hours a day though, and I didn't see him take any samples by the Jet Ski place. According to the map, those tanks are either directly under, or very close to, the tiki hut that the Jet Ski guy uses. I'm worried he's going to miss them."

"Well the fifteen-day due diligence period ends on Wednesday, so if he doesn't find them today, it's on to Plan B. He's probably trying to get the samples to the lab this afternoon, so Monday and Tuesday he can put together the findings."

"Speaking of Plan B, what is it?"

"I'm working on it. No sense straining my brain until we know for sure the tanks went undetected. Like I said before, I'll be surprised if they don't find them, I'm sure Slade is paying those guys a pretty penny. You ready to do some fishing?"

"You bet."

"All right, we're just about there, why don't you go down and get set up? I'll be there in a minute."

"Aye-aye, skipper."

We ended up catching three yellowtail snapper, and a queen triggerfish. Actually, Holly caught the yellowtail, and I caught the trigger, once again proving my bottom fishing skills are so-so. On the troll up to Palm Beach, we picked up a lone ten-pound dolphin off the Lake Worth pier, in about one hundred and forty feet of water. Other than that, the fishing was secondary to the sights, and we were taking it all in. First came the oceanfront mansions and the Ritz-Carlton in Manalapan. Next were the condos of South Palm Beach and the newly redesigned par three course, followed by the mansions of Palm Beach, the Bath and Tennis Club, and of course, Mar-A-Lago, Donald Trump's crown jewel.

A little ways past Mar-A-Lago, just before we hit the town of Palm Beach, I pointed toward shore. "See that big place on the bend? The one with the skywalk sort of thing between the buildings? I just read in the paper that the author James Patterson bought it and is doing a massive renovation. That house to the south of it was once owned by John Lennon. Who knows? Maybe Patterson's going to buy that one too."

"So money can't buy you love, but if you have enough of it you can buy a nice chunk of Palm Beach real estate. Holy Spimoli, that place looks humongous! I didn't know authors were paid that well."

"I don't think they are, unless you put out a book a week like he does. Guy's a freaking machine, he must write in his sleep."

"Either that or he keeps a staff of writers holed up in there, cranking out books for him. God knows it's big enough."

Just then, my cell rang and it was Jan from the office. I told Holly I needed to take the call, and she decided to go below to get some water. As she headed down the stairs, I asked her to bring me one too. I picked up the phone, and Jan said, "So, how's the fishing?"

"Not bad, picked up a few yellowtails and a dolphin, now we're just enjoying the sights. I'm up in your neck of the woods, by the way, heading to Sailfish Marina for lunch."

"*We're* enjoying the sights? *We're* going to lunch? And just who would "*we*" be, if you don't mind me asking? Melody?"

"No, she's history."

"What? Since when?"

"Since last week."

"And you're already wooing somebody new? Well, well, well...what do I make of that?"

"Don't make anything of it, just tell me why you called."

"Oh-ho, being a little *touchy*, aren't we? You must really like her."

"Come on, we just met, now what's up?"

"That package for your sidekick Tangles just came in, you want me to bring it over to Sailfish?"

"You'd do that?"

She chuckled. "Are you kidding me? I can't wait to meet your new flame. She must be something else."

"She's not my new flame. I told you we just met. I'm only helping her out with some stuff."

"Oh, I bet you are, you're just a regular old handyman."

Holly started climbing back up to the bridge with a couple of bottles of water.

"Ha-ha-ha, anyways, that would be great if you brought his stuff over. We'll be there in about a half hour."

"Oh I'll be there, you can count on it." Click.

Jan was easily the best secretary I ever had, and she had a nose like a bloodhound. If she got a whiff of something, there was no letting go until she got to the bottom of it. Best to let her satisfy her curiosity or she could drive you crazy.

Holly sat next to me and handed me a bottle. "Here you go. Is everything all right?"

"Yeah, that was just my secretary Jan, we had a box of Tangles stuff sent to the office, and it just came in. She's going to bring it over to Sailfish for me."

"That's nice of her."

"Yeah, she's great. It's a little slow in the office right now, and she was itching to get out."

We cruised past Bethesda by the Sea, the stunning Episcopal church that many of Palm Beach's bluest of bloods attend, and then the world-renowned Breakers of Palm Beach, the resort of choice for the rich and famous. We finally passed the grand estates on the north end of the island, and went in the Palm Beach Inlet. As I docked the boat at Sailfish Marina, I said, "I don't know about you, but I'm starved. I didn't have much of a dinner last night."

"I'll take that as a warning to keep my hands away from your plate. Well, don't worry...my tummy's growling too."

The hostess sat us at a four top. Right after we ordered, Jan showed up and plopped down in one of the seats, dropping Tangles' package in the other. I introduced her to Holly, and before I could say anything, Holly said, "We just ordered, why don't you join us for lunch?" Jan looked at me for some sort of signal, but I had on my best poker face.

She hesitated a second, and then said, "Thanks, but I'm really not hungry. I will have a water though, it's Africa hot out there."

It was too, probably eighty-nine degrees, which is hot for May. The waiter brought her a bottle of water, and I could see her sizing up Holly as they made small talk. The waiter came back with a conch chowder for me, and a small salad for Holly. Jan said, "You know what? I *could* go for a bowl of that conch chowder. That looks good." By the time the waiter brought her back a bowl, she and Holly were chatting and laughing like they were old friends. I was just sitting there spooning up my chowder like the invisible man. *Oh well, at least they're getting along.*

We finished the appetizers, and when the rest of our lunch came, Jan stood up. "I have to get back to the office. Well, it was nice meeting you, Holly."

"Nice meeting you too."

As Jan reached into her purse for some money, I spoke for the first time in fifteen minutes. "I got it, Jan, thanks for bringing the package."

"Thanks, I'll see you....?"

"I'm not sure. I'll give you a call Monday morning."

"OK, well, enjoy the rest of the afternoon you two...bye." As she turned to leave, she gave me a big wink that it seemed like everybody in the restaurant saw except Holly.

Holly said, "I really like her, she's nice."

"Yeah, she's great."

When the waiter brought the bill, Holly snatched it out of his hand.

"Wait a second, give me that thing," I protested.

"No way. You're treating me to a wonderful day on the water. The least I can do is buy lunch. I *am* a working girl you know."

"Oh, *really?* You're just full of surprises."

She shot me a *You know what I mean* kind of look, and smiled. "Watch it, mister."

We got back on the boat and put-putted our way around Peanut Island, heading south down the intracoastal toward Boynton. We sat on the bridge and traded stories about growing up and settling down. Something I had yet to do, and something she had just undone. We drank a couple of beers and marveled at the size of a manatee that surfaced right in front of the boat. I had to change course to avoid running it over, something that unfortunately happens too often when boaters go too fast.

"Look at that." She pointed. "Look at the size of that manatee! I forgot how big they were." The big sea mammal had to be seven or eight feet long, and eight or nine-hundred pounds.

I couldn't help myself, and said, "Holy cow, I almost ran over Kirstie Alley."

"Oh you're *bad*...that's *awful.*"

"Sorry, I can't resist a cheap shot. It's one of life's most affordable pleasures." We laughed, and when we got past the Southern bridge I opened it up a little, bringing us up to about fifteen knots. The breeze felt great, and I looked over at Holly. She had her visor off and was letting her golden hair blow in the wind, smiling out loud. She looked like she was really enjoying herself, and she looked great. *Hot fudge sundae kind of great.*

She caught me staring. "What?"

"Nothing, I uh, I'm glad you were able to take today off...it's been fun."

"It sure has. I'm so glad to be back in south Florida. I can't believe I gave this up for Atlanta, what was I thinking?"

"Hey, live and learn...right?"

We got back to Millie's dock about four fifteen, and as Holly tied us off, Millie came hobbling out on to the deck with her cane.

"So how'd the fishing go?" she asked Holly.

"Oh, Millie, it was wonderful. We caught some more yellowtail and a nice dolphin. Kit took me to Sailfish Marina for lunch, and we cruised the intracoastal back. I wish you could have come."

"My boating days are over, honey. This is as close as I come. It's too hard getting on and off."

I came down from the bridge and pulled the fish out of the fish box, then tossed them on the dock. "Here's the catch of the day, thanks to Holly."

"You're leaving them here?" she asked.

"My freezer's full. I couldn't take 'em if I wanted to. Do you need me to clean them?"

Millie laughed as Holly shot me another one of her looks and pointed. "Please, see that cleaning table there? I've worn out more fillet knives on it than you can imagine. I'll manage fine. You're not in a hurry to go though...*are you?*"

My mind was saying *Hell no*, but my mouth was saying, "Actually, I do need to be getting back to the marina. I've got that package with all of Tangles' stuff, including his wallet, and he'll probably want to use the shower when he gets back from the afternoon trip."

"Oh, oh OK. But it's not right that you're leaving us all the fish. Will you come back and join us for dinner? This weekend maybe? I mean...if you don't have any plans, that is."

She seemed a little disappointed that I was leaving, and I was *loving it*. I wanted nothing more than to spend more time with her, but didn't want to overdo it. "Sounds great, how 'bout I call you tomorrow and we'll figure out when."

"Perfect, let me grab the rest of my stuff out of the cabin, and I'll cast you off."

I followed her into the cabin and she grabbed her bag with the sunscreen and some snacks that we never got to. She turned and gave me a kiss on the lips that lasted a second longer than it needed to, but not as long as I would have liked.

She slowly pulled away, looking up at me. "Thanks for such a great day, too bad you have to go. Promise to come back and help us eat some fish?"

I put my hand over my heart. "Scout's honor."

"You were a Boy Scout?"

"You saw me helping your aunt around—where do you think I learned how to do that?"

She laughed as she untied the lines and stepped off the boat. Then she gave the *Lucky Dog* a push away from the dock, using her foot. "See you later. Thanks again, Kit."

As I pulled away, I decided to rib her a little. "Be sure to use a sharp knife. Don't butcher the fish."

"Ha-ha-ha, you need me to drive over to the marina and help you dock?"

I waved good-bye to her, and she waved back with a big smile. *What a smile it was.* Jan was right, I was definitely in full woo mode. *Here we go again.*

Chapter 63

Right before the close of business the following Monday, Harvey Miller picked up the phone and dialed Syd Slade's number. Moments later, he heard the hard-edged voice answer.

"Hello?"

"Mr. Slade? This is Harvey Miller, from Endviropro."

"You got my report done?"

"Well, that's what I wanted to talk to you about. We finished up the sample work Friday, and just got the results back from the lab. I called in a favor to get it turned around so quick, normally it takes—"

"Yeah, I know it normally takes longer, what did you find out?"

"Everything's normal, there were no surprises in the findings. Only problem is we didn't have enough time to get a Phase II done. Like I told you, that requires deeper sampling and more elaborate testing, we just didn't have enough time."

"That's not gonna cut it, Harvey. I have to have it for the bank. The deposit goes hard on Wednesday. I need the full report."

"Well, like I mentioned before, I'll produce one for you...but not without a release. Normally I would never do such a thing, but I'm familiar with the property and I'm confident the site is clean."

"Me too, but you're not so confident that you still want a release, huh?"

"Hey, you're the one in the big hurry, not me. If you want to be one hundred percent sure, then give me time to do it. I can probably get it done in another three weeks, otherwise you need to sign a release."

"All right, all right, fax me the damn release, but the report better be pristine. I want a loan commitment from the bank before my deposit goes nonrefundable."

"It will be, but this needs to remain confidential, or it's big trouble for both of us."

"No shit." Click.

Two days later, Sonny was at his usual spot at the end of the outside bar, plying Kristy Kane with drinks. He was hoping to finally seal the deal with the shifty cougar when his phone rang. His dog Mr. Jenks sat quietly at his feet as he answered. "Hello?"

"Sonny, it's me."

It was his dad on the other end. He had been hoping for his call. "Hey, Dad, what's the good news?"

"I just wanted to let you know that the bank has approved the loan. The deposit went hard and we're set to close in thirty days." Sonny shot a glance at a Kristy, who had let her hand drift down to rest on his upper thigh. She smiled back at him. *The deposit's not the only thing going hard.*

"That's great! I can't believe it! We're finally gonna control the marina. Hot damn!"

"Don't get so worked up. It ain't a done deal till we close."

"It's just a matter of time now, Pops, there's a new day coming."

"What'd you call me?"

"Uh, sorry, sir. It's just, um, I can't believe it's really gonna happen."

"It's OK, Sonny, you *should* be excited. You took the initiative, and struck the deal all on your own. Your brothers can't believe it either. Looks like some of my smarts rubbed off on you after all. You did good, boy, and you're gonna have a big part in this once we get started, you earned it."

"Thank you, sir, is there anything else I can do in the meantime?"

"Yeah, stay out of trouble...and don't stir the pot too much on the docks. I don't want the slip holders to know what's coming till it's too late. Talk to you later." Click.

Shit! It's a little late for that. No matter, what could a rag tag group of slip holders do anyways? *Not a damn thing, that's what.*

Kristy pulled her hand off his leg. "Sounds like big news."

"You better believe it, sweet cheeks. The old man says the bank approved the loan to buy the C-LOVE Marina. We're closing in thirty days, and he's gonna let me call some of the shots. How you like them bananas?"

Kristy liked them, she liked them a lot. Now she knew which side she was going to be playing for. It was time to ratchet up the stroke-o-meter. "Wow that was fast, you're quite the operator, Sonny. I'm impressed. I think a lot of people have underestimated you, congratulations." She raised her scotch for a toast, and he clinked her glass with his.

Sonny decided to play it as cool as he possibly could, just like his old man had told him. "Yeah, well it ain't over till the fat lady says it's over."

Kristy didn't bother correcting his botched delivery of the old saying. She got the point, and didn't want to bring him down. In fact, just the opposite, it was time to bring him up, time to secure her position on the Slade redevelopment team. She put her hand back on Sonny's thigh, only this time a little closer to his crotch. "Well, I think this calls for some sort of celebration, why don't you come up to my condo? We'll order some delivery for dinner and take it from there...I'm feeling a little tipsy."

It was true. She had eaten hardly anything all day and was really feeling the three scotches. She figured she'd need a couple more before letting Sonny bed her, but hey, *business is business.* She gave his upper thigh a gentle squeeze before letting her fingers slowly tickle their way down to his knee. "So what do you say, big boy?"

Sonny lowered his head and leaned in close. "I say I'm hornier than a two-dick dog, so no more games Kristy, that's what I say. Still want me to come?" Once again he surprised her. He didn't realize it yet, but she found the whole power trip, alpha male thing, a turn on. Maybe she'd only need one more drink, instead of two.

She got off the bar chair and straightened her skirt. "Do I still want you to come? The more the merrier. Lose the poodle and hurry up before I change my mind."

She spun and headed out the bar, hearing his voice over the crowd noise. "It's not a poodle! It's a Labradoodle!"

Chapter 64

The mayor sat at his desk with his head in his hands, wondering how in the hell Slade convinced old Milfred Lutes to sell. He was irate she didn't give the city a chance to make an offer. The head of the CRA, Kristy Kane, just advised him the bank approved Slade's loan, and they were closing in thirty days. He could have convinced the commissioners to pay nine or ten million, but no way the thirteen that Syd wanted. Oddly, Kristy didn't seem that upset when she left his office, saying, "You win some, you lose some...nothing we can do now." *Bullshit!* There was too much riding on the waterfront redevelopment program just to sit by idly while some snowbird restaurateur takes over. The public would be calling for his head when they realized all the money spent on plans, and acquiring adjacent properties, was for naught.

The worst part was that his old acquaintance Donny Nutz had tipped him off about the deal, and he did nothing. He wrongly figured Donny loaned Sonny some money to pay off a gambling debt. Now he realized it probably *was* tied to the deal, and wondered how much Donny floated him. *Was there a way Donny could call in the loan early, and somehow queer the deal?* He knew he would have to make it worth his while, but what other choice did he have? His political future was at stake. He decided it was time to have another talk with Donny. He didn't have his phone number, but figured he could get a hold of him through Rachelle's. He looked the number up on his computer, and headed out to find somewhere safe to call from. It was the worst kept secret in Palm Beach County that the upscale strip club was mob owned, but not everybody knew by which mobster. The mayor still had some friends in the DAs office back in Jersey City, however, friends that kept him up to speed regarding the goings on of one Donatello DeNutzio.

He needed to find a pay phone where he could make a discreet phone call. Hell, he needed to find a pay phone period. With the onset of the cell phone revolution came the demise of the pay phone industry. It was a business in its last throes of existence, and it was harder and harder to find one. *Where can I go?* He thought the CVS drugstore across from City Hall might have one, but the likelihood of someone recognizing him there was too great. It might look a little strange to see the mayor of Boynton Beach talking from a pay phone so close to his office. Maybe he was being a little paranoid, but over the last few years, a string of county politicians had been sent to jail on corruption charges, and the feds were still lurking around. He knew he could go to the airport and find a pay phone, but he didn't want to drive that far if he didn't have to. *The mall maybe?* Yes, the mall. He was fairly certain the Boynton Beach Mall had some pay phones.

As he made the short drive to the mall, he weighed his options and saw no way around getting Donny Nutz involved if he wanted the city to obtain the C-LOVE Marina. He parked the car and made his way to the food court, where he found a pair of unoccupied pay phones next to the restrooms. He took out his day planner and tore out a page, writing, "Out of Order," on it. He looked around before wedging the corner of the note into the coin slot of one of the phones, then put a quarter in the other and dialed.

He was surprised that a friendly female voice answered, rather than being kicked immediately to some automated system. "Good afternoon, this is Rachelle's, how may I help you?"

"I'd like to speak to the manager, please."

"Hold one moment, please, let me see if I can track him down." The hostess had been told to make it seem like they were busy, even when they weren't, like right now, in the middle of a Thursday afternoon. She didn't have to look far, because Gino was standing right in front of her. She said, "Some guy wants to talk to the manager, line two."

"What's he want?"

"He wants to talk to the manager, that's all he said."

Annoyed, Gino picked up the phone. "This is Gino, what can I do for you?"

The mayor measured his words carefully before speaking. "Gino? My name is Vince from Boynton, and I'm a friend of Double D's. He called me the other day and I need to get back in touch with him, its important." Double D was another nickname of Donatello DeNutzio, but not as well known as Donny Nutz.

"I'm sure it is, Vince from Boynton, but I don't know no Double D, sorry. We got some real classy dancers though, if you ever make it up this way. Have a nice—"

"Wait a second, just wait. I'm talking about Double D from Jersey City. You sure you don't know him? From *Jersey City?*"

Gino hadn't immediately put two and two together. Double D was an old nickname that hadn't been used in years. Not since his boss became known as Donny Nutz for cutting some schmo's balls off with a jigsaw. When the guy said Jersey City though, well...not too many people knew about that connection. Gino decided to check it out. "Call back in five minutes, I need to check something." Click. He told the hostess to patch the call through to the secure line when the guy called back, then he headed to his office.

He picked up the phone and dialed the boss's number, which was rerouted per usual to several places before ending up in Jersey City, at deli headquarters, the Rye Smile. As always, he heard the phone being picked up, but not answered, so he identified himself.

"This is Gino, you there?"

"Yeah, Gino, what's up?" It was him, no doubt about the voice. It sort of sounded like Clint Eastwood with bronchitis, after smoking a blunt.

"Some guy by the name of Vince from Boynton just called here. He wants to get in touch with you, says it's important."

"Anybody ever want to talk to me say it wasn't?"

"That's what I figured. I'll tell him he's out of luck."

"Not so fast. I wanna hear what he has to say, you tell him to call back?"

"Yeah."

"OK, you know how to patch him through, do it."
Click.

Two minutes later Vince called back, and Gino
picked up, saying, "You're not calling from someplace
stupid, are you?"

"No, no...I'm on a pay phone."

"All right, I'm patching you through, you're gonna
hear a bunch of clicks and sounds, and think you're
being disconnected, but you're not. Just hang on, it'll
take about a minute, and then you'll hear someone
pick up the phone. Identify yourself when you hear it
being picked up...got it?"

"Yeah, thanks." Just like Gino said, the phone made
a bunch of weird sounds and then finally he thought
he heard it being picked up.

"Hello? Hello this is Vince, is anyone there?"

"Yeah, I'm here, so what's so important?" It was
Donny Nutz, no doubt about it.

"Uh, it's OK to talk, right?"

"If Gino patched you through, we're good. I got
more scramblers on the line than Denny's on Sunday
morning, so talk."

"You were right about Sonny Slade. They got the
marina under contract. I thought he was borrowing
money to cover gambling debts."

"So?"

"So it creates a big problem for me if they buy
the marina. The city has invested millions acquiring
adjacent properties and designing plans to redevelop
the waterfront. The C-LOVE Marina is critical to the
whole thing."

"And that affects me *how?*"

"Well, how much did you lend him?"

"None of your business, why's it matter?"

"You're right. I was thinking about asking you to call in the loan early, but it makes no difference because their deposit went hard, they're closing in thirty days. Even if you called it in, he could pay it back and still close. Shit."

"I wouldn't want to call it in early anyways, guy's paying about a grand a day interest...its good business. Besides, we're all square, or did you forget that?"

"No, not at all. I was gonna make it worth your while. I just can't let them close on that property...I'll be voted out of office...Unless..."

"Unless what?"

The mayor was considering another option, but it was dicey. Still, he thought it was worth a shot. "Think you could convince Slade to sell you the marina?"

"Now, Vince, you know I can convince just about anybody to do anything, but why in hell would I want to do that?"

"I can think of a million reasons. Slade has it under contract for eight million. You convince him to sell it to a shell company you form for nine, and then sell it to me, er, the city, that is, for ten."

"I don't know. I don't like having to tie up that much scratch, why don't I just have him sell it to you for ten, and then you kick me back a million?"

"No can do, Donny. The feds are watching everything down here real close, how would I pay you out of the city coffers anyways? No, the only way it could work is like I said, from Slade, to you, to the city. No one would be the wiser."

"Except for Slade, but I ain't worried about him talking if we have a meeting of the minds. Let me think about it, I need to make a few calls. Gimme a call tomorrow afternoon, from a different phone of course." Click.

Chapter 65

I was at the office looking over some insurance documents for the shopping centers in Sebring that I leased and helped manage, when Holly called. I couldn't believe we had to have sinkhole insurance as a separate rider on top of hurricane insurance. What a racket, the odds of having a sinkhole on your property were like getting hit by lightning while holding a winning Powerball ticket. Jan took the call and put her on hold, then looked at me. "It's your new flame."

"I told you, she's not my new flame."

As I walked into the adjoining office to take the call, I heard, "Sure she's not."

I had to admit though, things were definitely headed in that direction. We had a second dinner the Sunday after our fishing trip, dining on the dolphin (also known as mahi-mahi) we caught. I was hoping to spend some quality alone time with Holly, but Millie wasn't feeling well and she wanted to bed-sit her after dinner, so I had left. But not before she gave me a warm-lipped send-off that had my blood boiling.

I picked up the phone. "Hey, you, what's going on?"

"Millie's lawyer just called and said the due-diligence period passed without objection, and the deposit money went hard. Kit, what are we going to do? They must have missed the tanks."

"Shit, I can't believe it...they missed them? Christ."

"What are we gonna do?"

"We need to get together to work on Plan B. You think Millie can handle another dinner?" Actually, it wasn't critical we got together, but I wanted to see Holly.

"She's doing well today, and you know how much she likes you. I'm sure it would be fine. We're out of fish though, finished it off last night."

"That's OK, I'm fished out. I was thinking of bringing some steaks, why don't you ask her if she's OK with that."

"All right, hold on a sec." Moments later she was back on the line. "She said she's fine with it as long as the steaks aren't from Publix. What's with that?"

Your aunt knows meat, and fortunately so do I. Publix meat quality is questionable and overpriced. They do seafood much better. Tell her she's in good hands. Also, I'd like to bring Tangles. Whatever plan we come up with will likely require assistance, and I trust him. Plus, with him staying on the boat, it would be difficult to pull something off at the marina without him knowing anyways."

"Oh, Millie would love that. We watched your show in Key West, and she thought he was the cutest thing. She was really upset when he got bit—is he doing OK?"

"Tangles wasn't too thrilled either, but he's fine, he's already back doing charters. What do you think... six? ...six thirty?"

"Six thirty's fine, we'll see you then."

"OK, bye." Click.

As soon as I walked back into the main office, Jan said, "Did I hear you say something about steaks at six thirty tonight? Well, well, well...She's not your flame, huh? Keep telling yourself that." Knowing Jan, she probably listened in on the entire conversation. Hard to get something by her, that's for sure.

"It's not a date, I'm bringing Tangles...and her aunt will be there. I'm just trying to help them with a little real estate issue."

"Sure you are, that's why you'll be bringing wine and roses."

"Give it a rest, will you? I'll be on my cell if you need me, I'm taking off."

She gave me a big smirk. "Need to get ready for your big date?"

"I said give it a rest."

"Oh I'll give it a rest all right, as soon as you admit you're smitten with her."

I just stared at her with a *give me a break* look, before caving. "OK, maybe I like her. Nothing wrong with that, right? I *am* single." I immediately regretted fessing up.

"Hah! I knew it! I can read you like a book. For what it's worth, I really like her. She's nothing like most of the women you date."

"What? What are you saying? I date skanks or something? I thought you liked Melody. She's not a skank."

"No, but she's not much better—she's your fuck-buddy."

"Wash your mouth out, young lady...fuck- buddy?"

"You know...friends with benefits? Well, it's true. Ever wonder how many other buddies she has? Ever go on her Facebook page?"

Ouch. I hadn't really thought about that, didn't want to think about it either. I grabbed my briefcase. "Well, it doesn't matter. Like I told you before, I'm not seeing her anymore."

"Well thank you're lucky stars. If I were you I'd stay away from her. You don't want to mess things up with Holly."

"Thanks, Mom, I'll keep that in mind." I headed out the door and down the stairs, but not before her voice carried down the hall.

"Don't forget the roses...go with yellow!"

Chapter 66

I called Tangles on the way home and he was ecstatic about having dinner with Holly and her aunt, maybe a little *too* ecstatic. He said, "Shit, I don't have anything to wear."

Are you freaking kidding me? "It's not prom night, for crying out loud. We're just going over to Millie's for dinner, anything but the Kid Rock T-shirt will be fine... Jesus."

"I don't know...I really need to go to the mall and pick up some new threads. All I have are some shorts and T-shirts...and a couple of pairs of jeans."

"What about that box of stuff you had sent, nothing in there?"

"Nothing presentable."

"Shit. All right, I'll pick you up and take you to the mall, be ready by four thirty."

"I'm ready now, my afternoon charter canceled."

"OK, I'll be there by four then." Click.

I stopped by Winn-Dickme and picked up some nice T-bones that were on sale. I also got some green beans, baked potatoes, and sour cream. When I got to the apartment, I was relieved to see Melody's car wasn't there. She called me a couple of times during

301

the week, and I hadn't called back. I just didn't feel like having a serious discussion. As far as I was concerned, it was over...history. I had my sights set on Holly, and that was that.

I normally didn't give a lot of thought to what I wore to dinner, but didn't want to be upstaged by Tangles. I looked through my closet and changed into a nice pair of khaki dress shorts and a Tommy Hilfiger shirt, also swapping my loafers for a pair of docksiders. Satisfied that the little munchkin wouldn't be making me look bad, I put the food in a cooler with an ice pack, and headed down to the marina. I made one more stop at a florist, and picked up a dozen yellow roses per Jan's suggestion. On the way, I heard a Howie Day song playing on the radio, a rarity. "If you're gonna be there be there, if you're gonna stay... stay tonight..." Why is it considered alternative music and given so little airplay? Alternative to what? All the other crap they play like Lady GaGa? Please, more like Lady GagMe.

When I picked Tangles up, I noticed his hair was wet and he was freshly clean shaven. I dropped him off at the mall with specific orders. "You got twenty minutes, Romeo. I'm gonna run over to Total Wine and pick up something to go with dinner."

"Twenty minutes? I'm getting some clothes, dude... not a haircut."

He stepped out of the Beemer, and I powered my window down as he walked around the front of the car toward Macy's. As I slowly motored away, I repeated, "Twenty minutes, Tangles, don't keep me waiting or you'll be thumbing you're way to dinner." He gave me a dismissive look and waved me off. *Huh.*

I picked up a couple of bottles of Liberty School cabernet this time. They were on sale and I knew from experience it was a solid choice. On a whim, I bought a bottle of Cruzan Rum Cream, an excellent substitute for Bailey's for a few dollars less. Plus, it was a little lighter and easier on the system after a big dinner. Exactly twenty minutes later I was back in front of Macy's, and pulled out my cell to call Tangles when he came walking out the door. I couldn't believe my eyes and blinked, doing a double take. He was wearing a pair of ultra-white, knee length Bermuda shorts, with a baby blue polo shirt, and a yellow V-neck sweater, draped across his shoulders. He topped it off with a new pair of black, open toe, euro style sandals. *Oh, sweet Jesus!* I had to look away from him before I busted out laughing.

He climbed in, and as we drove away, he asked, "So...what do you think?" He slid his sunglasses up on his head and pulled down the visor. He was looking at himself in the mirror while adjusting his collar with both hands. *Crazy little shit thought he looked good,* so I decided to play along. "Wow, you really clean up nice, Tangles. It's certainly a different look for you, that's for sure." *No doubt about it, he looked like he just walked off the set of Queer Eye for the Short Guy.*

"Nice duds, huh? It was on sale as a combo outfit too...can you believe it? They really have some nice salesmen in there. Hey, and what about these sandals? Only twenty bucks." He was wiggling his toes like an infant, only they were hairy...really hairy. I never realized how hairy he was until I saw his legs and feet contrasted against the bright white shorts. He definitely had a little *Planet of the Apes* thing going on there. *Holy shit!* I stifled a laugh, trying to turn it into a cough.

He looked at me. "What? You don't like it?"

"No, no, you look fine. I just had a little something stuck in my throat." I looked at my watch and had an idea. "We have a little time to kill, why don't we stop over at this new place called Bar Huey? It's right across the street."

"Sounds good to me."

I had never been to Bar Huey before, but it had a nice outdoor bar area and was supposedly a hot spot for the younger crowd. I wanted to see how Tangles would be received by the happy hour patrons.

The outside bar looked to be about three-quarters full, and we spotted a couple of seats and sat down. The bartender was a young skinny guy, with that wet, tousled hair look, and he came over to take our order. I went for a Heineken Light and Tangles ordered the same. The bartender carded Tangles, eyeing his driver's license suspiciously. After looking back and forth from the ID to Tangles about five times, he said, "Sorry, Langostino, can't serve you." Then he handed back his license.

"What? Why not? I'm thirty-five."

"The guy on the ID is thirty-five, but that ain't you, amigo...sorry."

"The hell it isn't...this is bullshit!"

I said, "Let me see that license," and Tangles handed it to me. *Son of a bitch, he is thirty-five.* I started laughing as I looked at the picture, and then the "new look" Tangles. In his driver's license photo, he looked hung over, with a week's worth of stubble, scraggly hair, and his usual Kid-Rock sleeveless T-shirt on. Now he looked like a groupie for the Back Street Boys. No way would anyone believe they were one and the same.

The bartender set my beer down and said to Tangles, "Can I get you something nonalcoholic? Maybe a virgin banana colada or something?" I involuntarily began to chuckle.

Tangles scowled and put his hands on the bar, raising himself up so he looked bigger. "Piss off, pretty boy, I want my Heineken."

"Pretty boy? That's pretty funny...*you* calling *me* pretty boy. Looked in the mirror lately, Liberace?" The bartender then put his hand up to his ear with his pinky and index finger extended like he was talking on the phone. "What's that? Oh here, it's for you, it's George Michael. He wants his outfit back."

Oh shit...here we go.

"That's it, asshole!" Tangles leapt on to the bar knocking over the drinks of the couple sitting next to us, sending his seat crashing to the ground. I reached over and grabbed him by the belt, just as he grabbed the bartender by the front of his shirt. I jumped out of my chair directly behind him, and got my other hand around his waist, yanking him back. As I did so, Tangles' hands ripped straight down the guy's shirt, popping every button off. The bartender's midriff was exposed, and he had some kind of a bellyring thing protruding from his navel. *Yuck.* He quickly pulled the sides of his torn shirt together, and as I pulled Tangles back down, Tangles yelled, "Let me go, I'm gonna kill him!"

"Shut up, dude," I whispered. "You're gonna get us in trouble."

The hostess came running up to the stunned bartender. "What happened? Should I call the cops?"

"What happened? What happened is I got attacked by Bi-Curious George here." He pointed at Tangles, who I had in a baby-bear hug.

"Look," I pleaded, "this is just a big misunderstanding, no need to call the police." I reached into my wallet and pulled out a fifty-dollar bill, laying it on the bar. "This ought to buy you a new shirt and make up for the spilled drinks. We'll leave right now, sorry for the trouble."

Tangles was still fuming as I escorted him to the Beemer. "You should have let me go. I woulda kicked his scrawny ass all the way to Daytona."

"What...and end up ruining my night by having to bail you out of the slammer?"

I backed the car up, and as we passed in front of the bar, Tangles leaned out the window and yelled, "Nice bellyring, Elton!" Then flipped him the bird.

I punched the gas and we were gone before anybody could get my license plate number...I hoped. I glanced at him and said, "You owe me fifty bucks now, monkey boy. I think you need to take an anger management class to work on that short fuse...no pun intended." I expected one of his wise-ass comebacks but he just kept looking out the window. I didn't push it any further.

Finally he cooled down enough to say, "So...do these clothes really look that gay?"

I had to break it to him—the jig was up—so I lied... sort of. "Sorry, dude...I didn't have the heart to break it to you. I figured you should hear it from someone else, but I didn't expect you to go all Chucky on him. The good news is, we have enough time for you to return those clothes and pick up something a little more...shall we say...hetero?"

"Damn...they're that bad? Really?"

"Are you kidding me? Let me put it this way...
If you had dressed like this on the cruise ship,
Darla would never have gone lesbo; you'd have it
covered."

"Shit, I *knew* that salesman was too nice."

We were still laughing when we pulled up in front
of Macy's again. I said, "Find a woman to help you this
time...you got fifteen minutes...go." Tangles grabbed
the Macy's bag with his old clothes in it, and speed
walked into the store. *Unbelievable.* I sat in the car
and started laughing again. Thirteen minutes later,
I was relieved to see him come out wearing a pair
of khaki Dockers shorts, and a navy blue Izod short-
sleeve button-down. He still had on the flaky sandals
though.

As we headed down Boynton Beach Boulevard, he
said, "So?"

"So it's a major improvement. You don't have to
worry about getting jumped by the Jonas Brothers.
What about the sandals though?"

"They wouldn't let me return them, I stepped in
some gum. What's so bad about them, anyways?"

"Nothing...if you're trying to bang an orangutan."

"What? What are you saying?"

"I'm saying you got some serious follicle issues
going on down there. I wouldn't be advertising it."

"What the hell are you talking about? Follicle
issues?"

"Hair...you got lots of hair on your toes and feet."

"You think?" He looked down and wiggled his toes
again.

"Jesus, don't do that! It creeps me out."

"What? This?" He pulled his feet out of the sandals and swung them up on the dash, wiggling his hairy little toes at me while he laughed.

I reached over and pushed his legs down with my right hand. "Good God, quit doing that or you're gonna make me wreck. I'm gonna start calling you Little Big Foot. What are you? Half Yeti? They do make a thing called a disposable razor, you know."

Chapter 67

On the rest of the ride over to Millie's I gave Tangles a quick rundown of the marina contract, the buried fuel tanks, and how I was trying to help her get out of having to sell the place.

We pulled up to her house at exactly six twenty-nine. I got the cooler with all the food out of the trunk, pulled the roses out, and handed the wine to Tangles. "Roses?" he said, letting out a low whistle. "Wow, you're really laying it on thick."

"Shut up Siegfried, her aunt has terminal cancer."

"Oh man, I'm sorry."

We walked to the door, and Holly opened it up after a couple of knocks. "Hi, you two!"

We said our hellos and I handed her a single yellow rose. "This is for you, and these are for Millie."

I handed her the other roses and she put her hand to her chest. "That is so sweet, how did you know yellow roses are her favorite? Mine too." She kissed me on the cheek, and looked at Tangles. "Wow, look at you, I hardly recognized you."

Tangles blushed a little. "You look nice too."

As usual, it was quite the understatement. She was in her bare feet wearing a pair of faded cut-off jeans, and a semi-revealing ,white V-neck top. Causal, classic, and oh so sexy. "Well thank you, now come on in and let's get this stuff put away so we can have a cocktail on the deck. It's going to be a beautiful sunset."

Holly got us drinks and I introduced Tangles to Millie. The first thing she said was, "is your arm all right? We watched the show the other night. That was quite a bite you got."

He held up his arm. "No big deal. I'm getting the stitches out next week. You should see the other guy." Millie laughed, and you could tell she was warming up to him.

I mentioned to Holly that she should put the potatoes in the oven. I wanted to season the steaks too, so we left Tangles and Millie on the deck, and went inside.

As she washed the potatoes, she said, "I'm glad you came over, Millie's worried sick about the marina deal and it's only making her condition worse. Plus, I...um...I..."

"What?" I turned away from the steaks to face her.

She set the last potato down next to the sink, and quietly said, "I'm glad you came over too. I missed you all week—last weekend was wonderful."

I moved in to her, and kissed her hard on the lips. She kissed me back, as I pushed her against the kitchen counter. My arms went around her waist, and hers reached up around my neck. When I felt her tongue hit mine I thought I was dreaming. I slid my left hand up her back, and moved my right to the countertop for leverage. In doing so, my hand came down on the corner of a plate, which promptly flipped and smashed to pieces on the floor. *Dream over.* We separated, and I saw Holly was flush in the face, and a little flustered. *Oh shit.* I stammered, "I'm, I'm sorry...Jesus, I didn't mean to do that, it...it just happened."

She recovered a lot quicker than I did, and laughed. "Sorry for kissing me? Or sorry about breaking the plate? Be careful how you answer that."

We heard Millie yell, "Is everything all right in there?"

Holly stuck her head around the corner and yelled back, "Everything's fine...I just dropped a plate... we'll be out in a second." She grabbed a dustpan and broom out of the closet and slipped on some sandals. "I'll clean this up, you go back out and—Oh my God!" She was staring at my crotch.

I looked down and saw I had an erection that created a pup tent in my shorts. It looked like it wanted to say, *Free Willie! Free Willie!* I quickly turned away in embarrassment, mumbling, "Oh shit, Oh boy, I, uh, I..."

She started laughing again. "I think you better go to the bathroom or something before heading back out. I'll take that as meaning you weren't sorry about the kiss. Don't worry, neither was I." I could hear her laughing as I hurried to the bathroom, and splashed some cold water on little Orca.

A couple of minutes later, after drying myself off, I rejoined everybody on the deck. Tangles and Millie were getting along beautifully. He had her eating out of his little hand, and she was loving it. After a while, I fired up the grill and cooked the steaks, while we watched the sun set. Tangles opened the wine, and Holly prepared the potatoes and green beans.

Halfway through dinner, Millie broached the subject that I had been giving some thought to. "OK, Kit, what do you think we should do now?"

"Well, we obviously need to expose the tanks, but we have to time it right."

"What do you mean about timing it right?" asked Holly.

"Well, we don't want them, and when I say "them," I mean the bank, to find out too soon. For instance, if they were discovered next week, it may be possible to remove them and get the site cleaned up before closing. At the very least, something could probably be worked out with the bank to allow Slade to close. We don't want that. We want the tanks to be discovered as close to the closing date as possible, so there's not enough time to clean it up or work something out with the bank without an extension. An extension that Millie will turn down, effectively killing the deal. The beauty of it is, if it works out right, you'll get to keep the deposit. It's nonrefundable now. They did their environmental inspection and nobody here knows about the tanks' existence...right?"

Everybody said "right," and then Millie added, "OK, but how do we expose the tanks without it being obvious we knew they were there?"

"How 'bout we dig them up in the middle of the night?" Everybody looked at Tangles and he continued on. "Why not? What other option is there?"

"It's not a bad idea," I agreed. "But we have to make it look like an accidental discovery. We can't just dig the tanks up two days before closing and have them sitting there in plain sight. It'll look too fishy."

Holly spoke up. "What we need is a hurricane, or flood, or something that could lift them out. It was a hurricane that caused my grandfather to bury them there in the first place. It would be nice if another one uncovered them."

I thought about it for a second. Something was forcing its way to the front of my brain and down to the tip of my tongue.

Millie replied, "That would be nice, honey, but we can't plan on Mother Nature bailing us out at just the right time—that would be a miracle."

Suddenly it hit me. "Wait, wait a second...she's on to something. With just a little assistance from the rain gods, we can dig up the tanks and make it look like they were uncovered by a sinkhole."

Everybody said it at the same time. *"Sinkhole?"*

"Yes...sinkhole...when's the closing date? Early June, right? In about a month, right at the start of rainy season. Say we wait for a nice storm anywhere within ten days of closing. We get some rain, and then do exactly what Tangles suggested, dig up the tanks in the middle of the night. We know the tanks are at the southwest corner of the canal by the Jet Ski rental place. We could dig up the dirt and toss it in the canal. There wouldn't be a pile to indicate anybody did any digging. There would just be a caved in hole, with a couple of rusty diesel tanks sitting in the bottom. Everybody would think a hard rain washed out the dirt...like a sinkhole. It just might work...what do you think?"

Tangles said, "I like it, and for good measure, we could dump five gallons of fresh diesel around before we left. That would make whoever discovered it nervous as hell. The EPA would be all over it in a hurry."

I reached across the table and fist bumped him. "Nice touch, but let's play it by ear and only dump fuel if absolutely necessary. What do you think, ladies?"

They were looking at each other, and Holly spoke first. "I think it just might work. It's definitely the best plan. In fact, it's the only plausible plan we have... Millie?"

Millie looked at me through squinted eyes. "That might be a lot of digging, Kit, I don't think you three could do it alone."

I thought about it while I topped everybody's wine off. *She was right, it would take several more people.* "You're right, Millie, say we have Tangles and Holly act as lookouts for the police, or anybody else who comes around. That means I would have to recruit at least two, or maybe even three people, to help dig. Three people who can keep their mouths shut. Three people who have a reason to stay quiet. That shouldn't be too hard, virtually everybody in the marina is freaking out about losing their slip once Slade takes over. Most everybody would jump at the chance to help, and knowing that if word gets out, they may lose their livelihood, they won't say spit. Just to be safe though, I'll pick only the ones I know and trust most."

"Hambone?" Millie asked.

"He's my first pick. I'll ask him who else he thinks we should use, but I already have a good idea. It won't be a problem getting a team together."

She just stared at me, and then slowly smiled. "I knew I could count on you, Kit. Now you know why I called you, instead of my lawyer. I say go for it."

We raised our glasses together, and Millie cheered. "Here's to sinkholes!"

We clinked glasses following her lead. "To sinkholes!"

Chapter 68

Mayor Vincent Mandula pulled into the Palm Beach International Airport's short-term parking lot, and nervously walked into the terminal. He quickly found a bank of pay phones that were empty and dialed the number to Rachelle's. He talked to the guy named Gino, and was given the same instructions as the day before. After hearing an array of digital noises, he finally thought he heard the phone being picked up. "Hello? It's Vince...you there?"

"Yeah I'm here," said Donny Nutz. He liked to make 'em sweat, so he didn't say anything else. He knew the mayor was eagerly waiting to hear whether he'd get involved, and was in no rush to accommodate him.

After an uncomfortable ten seconds, the mayor finally spoke. "Um...what did you find out? Are you gonna do it? Will you buy the marina and flip it to us for a tidy profit?"

"Maybe, here's the deal. Nine million's a little heavy to float myself, so I got an associate to partner up. We need another five hundred grand to make it work though. It ain't worth the trouble otherwise."

The mayor thought it over for a couple of seconds, and was ninety-nine percent sure he could get approval from the city commission to spend ten and a half million on the marina. They wouldn't be thrilled, but once they realized how critical it was to the entire waterfront redevelopment plan, they would do it. "Ten point five? Yeah, I think I can do that."

"Think? You *think* you can do it? You want me to put up nine million on something you *think*? I don't deal with people who *think*, Vince...I deal with people who *know*."

"That's not what I mean...I...I know I can do it...I gotta lock on it. The city commission's in my back pocket. I'll make it happen...*trust me*."

"I trust no one, *especially* politicians...but you and I got a little history between us...right, Vince?"

"That's right, we know how to stick to our word. It won't be any different this time, I swear."

"No need to swear, just a need to listen closely to what I say. You listening closely now, Vince?"

Was he ever. He thought he could hear the sound of the fiber optic cable humming as it carried his wavering voice over the line. "Ye...Yeah...I'm...I'm listening real good."

"That's good, 'cause I don't want no misunderstanding between us. A misunderstanding could have real unpleasant consequences. So let me explain how this is gonna work. If I agree to buy this marina for nine million bucks, and the city doesn't pay me ten and a half within ninety days...let me tell you what's gonna happen. You remember what that punk did to your sister?"

Of course he did. He could never forget how she was brutally raped and beaten into a coma, dying a few months later. The image of her the first time he saw her in the hospital after the attack still haunted his dreams. "Yeah, I remember."

"Well that's what's gonna happen to your wife and twelve-year-old daughter after we make them watch doing to *you* what we did to that piece of shit back at Giant Stadium. You get the picture? Nothing personal, Vince, just business. So you better be *real* sure you want to do this. Once I send my boys in to have a heart-to-heart with this Slade guy, there's no turning back."

The mayor almost dropped the phone. *How did he know his daughter was twelve?* Jesus, Mary, and Joseph. He briefly thought about scratching the whole plan and letting the chips fall where they may. He could go back to practicing law after he lost the upcoming election, but it would take time and a lot of hard work. On the other hand, if he pulled off the waterfront redevelopment, he would be a shoo-in to keep his job, and it might even be enough to give him a legitimate shot at the governor's office in Tallahassee. "OK, let's do it."

"You sure? It's gotta be just like before, I do my part, and you do yours, and everybody walks away happy."

"Yeah, I'm sure, you can count on it."

"Oh I am, Vince, and so's your family...don't forget that." Click.

Chapter 69

Two days later, Sonny was still on a pussy high from finally closing the deal with the fiery hellcat Kristy Kane. He was quite proud of himself for the one-Viagra, ten-minute performance he gave her. All right, so maybe it was closer to five minutes, but hey, he was back! The slump was over. She was the first piece of ass he hadn't had to pay for since moving to Boynton a few months earlier. He hated having to pay, but his reputation and legal woes made it virtually impossible for him to hook up with the waitstaff...his usual drilling field. Plus, the old man told him to leave them alone, and he didn't want to incur his wrath. Now it didn't matter. He was confident he would be tapping Kristy on a regular basis. As he bounded up the three flights of stairs to his apartment, he thought he would double down on the little purple pill for his next encounter with her. He wanted to ensure a stand-up performance.

With the marina deal in the works, and a hot new squeeze, things were really looking good as he turned the key in his apartment door. *What? That's odd.* The lock wasn't locked...*huh.* He pushed open the door, calling out, "Mr. Jenks...Daddy's home!" There was no barking though...*what the hell?* He walked in and saw Gino from Rachelle's sitting on his couch, with Mr. Jenks lying motionless, and looking dead, at his feet. Suddenly he heard the door slam behind him, and turned to see a *much* larger guy standing in front of it. He was wearing a dark blue Adidas sweat suit, with a white muscle T-shirt underneath, and his hands were crossed in front of him like a church usher. His feet were firmly planted, shoulder length apart, sporting a pair of slip-on, snow white Keds. *What the fuck?* He spun back toward Gino and bent down to the dog, speaking softly. "Mr. Jenks? Mr. Jenks, are you all right? What the hell did you do to my dog? What are you doing here?"

"Relax," said Gino. "I just gave him some doggy downers—fucking poodle wouldn't shut up. He should be fine in an hour or so, least that's what I was told."

"I told you before, he's not a poodle, he's a LABRADOODLE! AND HE BETTER BE FINE OR—"

"Or *WHAT*, Sonny? What do you think your gonna do about it? Not a *Goddamn thing* is what...so sit your ass down and shut the *fuck* up."

Sonny was rattled. *What the hell is happening?* He did what he was told and sat in the recliner across from Gino. "I...I don't get it, why are you here? The loan isn't due for almost a month. What's going on?"

"What's going on is I've got some good news for you. You don't have to pay back the loan. Well technically you do, but in reality you're gonna be getting a check for nine million dollars, so the loan can be deducted from that."

"*What?* What the hell are you talking about? Why would you be giving me a check for nine million dollars?"

"You're right. I wouldn't be giving you a check. In fact, I wouldn't give you the sweat off my balls from walking up those three flights of stairs. It's my boss that's gonna be giving you a check for nine million dollars, minus the loan of course, for buying the marina."

"WHAT?"

"Keep it down, and don't act so upset...you're still gonna clear about a million. So here's how the deal's gonna work, its real simple. You buy the marina for eight million, and sell it to my boss a week later for nine million, minus the loan. See how simple that is?"

"I don't think so. You're fucking crazy. My old man's been after that property for a long time. No way he lets it go for a measly million...no way."

"Oh, I think so. In fact, *I know so.* I also know what a sharp operator your old man's supposed to be, and the string of restaurants he owns up the coast. So here's the message you're gonna give him. He's got one week to send a contract to me at the club, with the terms I just told you. If it's not on my desk a week from today, let me tell you what I'm gonna do." He nodded toward the steroid-juiced giant standing at the door. "First, I'll have Marco here chop the paws off your poodle and take him shark fishing. Then I'll burn that salmonella-spewing rattrap you call Three Jacks down to the waterline."

Sonny went pale and started feeling sick to his stomach. Gino picked up on it. "What's the matter, Sonny? Not feeling so good? Well that's too bad, 'cause guess what? *I ain't finished.* Now listen up. If I still don't have a contract on my desk the day after Three Jacks burns down, we're gonna work our way up the coast, torching restaurants until your old man comes to his senses. Something tells me it won't come to that though, especially when you tell him who it is he's dealing with. If he's got half the smarts everybody says, he'll have the contract on my desk tomorrow morning."

Sonny's head was spinning, and he felt his whole world tumbling out of control. Holding his head in his hands, with his elbows on his knees, he asked, "Who? Who is your boss? Who's the buyer?"

Gino stood up and stepped over Mr. Jenks as he headed toward the door. "You know he's not such a bad dog when he ain't humping your leg and barking like he's got ants up his ass...Be a shame if he ended up in some hammerhead's belly."

"*Who?* Goddamn it! *Who* is it?"

Gino smiled as he stood in the doorway, the big ape Marco behind him. "Oh yeah, be sure to tell your old man he's dealing with Donny Nutz."

"Donny Nutz?"

"Yeah, that's right, Donny Nutz...from Jersey City. You be sure to tell him that and everything should go smooth. Oh, and there's one other thing you should know."

"What's that?"

"The poodle took a big dump in your bedroom. Have a nice day."

Chapter 70

I wasted no time in arranging a meeting with Hambone to discuss the plan to dig up the fuel tanks. As I sat in the cabin of the *Lucky Dog* waiting for him, Jamie gave me a call. I answered, "What up, El Jefe?" On a trip we took to Mexico, all the locals kept calling him "El Jefe," which means, "The Boss." It was probably because he paid for most everything, but may have had something to do with his intimidating size. Regardless, the name stuck, and I invoked it whenever it hit me.

El Jefe was amped up. "Dude, the show we shot with Kingfish down in Key West came out *killer*, you saw it...right?"

"Yeah, I caught it early the other morning. Kinda bloody though."

"That Tangles is worth his weight in gold, but don't tell him I said so. Blood sells, my man...blood and midgets, the ratings have never been better. I'm trying to put together a trip to Aleuthera, and wanted to check your schedule."

I thought about it for a second as I looked at the calendar hanging above the bar. *Hmmm, Blood and Midgets...has a nice ring to it...maybe a great name for a band.* "The only time I can't go is from the last weekend in May, through the first week in June, otherwise I'm golden."

"What about Tangles? Did you ask him to be part of the show?"

"I meant to last night but we got sidetracked. It shouldn't be a problem though, just let me know when you have some dates that look good, and I'll spring it on him." I saw Hambone coming down the dock so I cut it short. "I gotta run, man, anything else?"

"Yeah, the local Fox station wants to set up an interview with me, you, and Tangles. The Tangles and tuna episode got as many Internet hits as that frumpy British chick who sang on the talent show."

"You mean the face that launched a thousand quips?"

"Bingo! That's her. Anyways, the station said they would have interviewed us sooner, but they thought the show was staged too, just like the one in Key West. Call me when you get a chance, so we can set it up."

"You got it, talk to you later." I opened the cabin door and waved Hambone aboard.

He jumped on and gave me his trademark rapid fire greeting. "Whaddup? Whaddup? Whaddup?"

We shook hands, and I offered to help quench his legendary thirst. "Hambonicus, how 'bout a coldie?" It wasn't really a question though. I just reached into the fridge and pulled out a couple of Bud Lights, handing him one.

We sat down at the dinette, and he asked, "So what's going on?"

I figured no sense beating around the bush, so I just spit it out. "There may be a way to keep the marina from falling into Slade's hands. Everything would basically stay the way it is now, but I need your help. You interested?"

He was taking a big swig, but quickly set the beer on the table. "What? How? Word on the dock is he's closing in like three weeks. Everybody's scrambling to try to find someplace to go...are you *serious?*"

"Yeah, I think I figured out a way, but I need help, and it needs to be hush-hush. Hush-hush as in nobody *ever* saying a word about it, or we'll all be in a world of shit. Me especially."

"Got it. So what do you need me to do?"

"I need you to help dig up some buried diesel tanks, and we have to make it look like we didn't dig 'em up. We need a couple of other strong backs to help us too."

"What? How would we do that? Where are they?"

"They're buried over by the Jet Ski rental place at the end of the canal, next to the tiki hut they use."

"Wait...wait a second, how the hell do you know this?"

"Milfred showed me a map with their location marked. Her grandfather buried them there about eighty years ago, after a hurricane blew through. He didn't know any better at the time."

"Milfred showed you? Why? She's the one selling the place...what...she changed her mind?"

"Well...you know she's terminal, right? She's only got a few months left."

"WHAT? You're kidding me! I only heard she was sick. Holy shit, that sucks...I gotta go see her."

"Yeah, well...here's the deal. She figured she'd sell the place because she didn't have anybody to leave it to who would want to, or was capable of, running the marina. She thought she was doing her heirs a favor by liquidating. Her only family is her two nieces, Sarah and Holly. You know Sarah, she waits at Three Jacks and couldn't run water. She's actually Millie's stepniece. Holly's the one she's closest to, but she was married and living in Atlanta when she decided to sell. Turns out she just got divorced and moved back here."

"You telling me that beautiful blond who recently showed up on the docks is her niece? *That's Holly?*"

"Yeah."

"Holy mackerel...I haven't seen her since she was a teenager...since she went off to college...I think. As I recall, back in the day, she lived with Millie for a couple of years. *Wow*...she really grew up nice."

"Tell me about it, she's got brains too. Anyhow, once Millie heard that Sonny told everybody they're getting kicked out, she had a conniption. She never would have sold, knowing all the commercial guys like you would be left with nowhere to keep their boats. She asked Holly if she would take over the marina if she could back out of the deal, and she agreed. Problem is, there's no legitimate way to back out. That's when she told me about the fuel tanks, and showed me the map."

"*Holy moley.* So how is digging up the tanks gonna stop the deal?"

"Slade's got a loan lined up with the bank. If we uncover the tanks right before closing, and the EPA gets called in, which they will, the shit will hit the fan. Once the bank finds out, they'll tell Slade the site has to be cleaned up before they'll loan the money. Of course that'll take time, but Millie won't give him an extension, and the deal will die. She'll have to spend some big bucks to have the site cleaned, but the best part is she'll be using Slade's money to do it. The four hundred thousand dollar deposit he put up is nonrefundable at this point."

Hambone smiled like I haven't seen him smile in a long time. "That's great! I *hate* that weasel Slade. He was so happy telling me I was gonna be the first to go... man, this would be sweet payback."

"He can never know you had anything to do with it, Ham. Everybody needs to think it's a sinkhole."

"Huh? What do you mean?"

"That's how we pull it off. We wait for the first decent storm within ten or so days of closing, then we go out in the middle of the night and start digging. All the dirt we dig up, we throw in the canal. Once we create a big enough hole to expose the tanks, we'll pour a little diesel on top if we need to. That way, when it's discovered, everybody starts freaking. Hopefully, it'll look like the rain created a sinkhole."

"You think it'll work?"

"It's got to, it's the only plan we have. We just need a little help from Mother Nature, so brush up on your rain dancing skills. We also need a couple of other diggers who can keep their mouths shut. I was thinking Eight-Toe and Kodak—what do you think?"

"Perfect, those guys are shitting their pants right now about losing their slips. Nobody wants a commercial shark fisherman or lobster boat in their marina anymore. They all want shiny new forty-two-foot sport fishers, looking good and waiting to be chartered. Those guys will jump at the chance to help, and they know how to zip it...*Especially* given the circumstances."

"All right, will you talk to them? Everybody needs to be on call starting around the twenty-eighth or so. First big rain and we go, probably around three in the morning."

"I'm on it. I'll set up a powwow as soon as I can."

"Just remember, this is as hush-hush as it gets... right?"

"What's hush-hush? I don't know what you're talking about." He stood and stepped to the cabin door, giving me a big wink.

"Exactly."

Chapter 71

Sonny was so shaken up by the visit from Gino and the monstrous Marco that he canceled his date with Kristy Kane. For the first time in his life, he wasn't thinking with his dick. He picked up the phone several times to call his father, but each time he chickened out. After a near-sleepless night, sprinkled with dreams involving Mr. Jenks, a hatchet, and a blowtorch, he told himself he had to make the call. If he put it off another day, he might develop an ulcer...or worse. He knew his dad would freak, but what choice did he have? He picked up the phone, and with shaky fingers punched in his dad's number. Syd Slade answered on the third ring. "Hello?"

"Dad, it's me, Sonny."

"I know, what's going on? It's a little early for you to be calling."

Sonny looked at his watch and realized it was only seven thirty in the morning.

"Oh, sorry about that, you want me to call back later?"

Syd sensed the trepidation in his son's voice, and started to get a bad feeling. "No, I want you to tell me why you're calling this early, when I know damn well you usually don't roll out of bed till after ten."

He didn't really want to know though, and started to brace himself.

"Dad, I uh...I messed up...I really messed up this time. I'm sorry."

"Oh, for Christ's sake, Sonny, you didn't knock up another waitress, did you? Please, please tell me you didn't knock up another underage waitress."

"I wish."

Syd pulled the phone away from his ear like it gave him an electric shock, and just stared at it for a couple of seconds before speaking again. Now he was *really* getting a bad feeling. "You *wish?* Holy Mother of God...what did you do this time?"

"I uh, I...I..."

"What Sonny? What is it? Spit it out. What the *fuck* did you do?"

"It's ah, it's about the ah, the marina deal."

"What are you talking about? That's in the bag— we're closing in a few weeks."

"Yeah, but we can't ah, we can't keep it."

"*What?* What do you mean we can't keep it? Of *course* we're gonna keep it, I've been after it for years. What in the *hell* did you do?"

"I uh, I had to borrow some money for the rest of the deposit."

"What do you mean...*the rest of the deposit?*" Syd was getting hot.

"It was um, uh, four hundred grand, not three."

"*WHAT?* Wait a second...I read *and* signed the contract myself. It said three hundred grand, and that's what I wired them."

"Yeah, but I um, I agreed to...to four hundred... and changed the contract."

Now Syd's bad feeling gave way to confusion. "So you changed the contract and borrowed another hundred? Why didn't you just tell me it was four hundred grand?"

"I uh, I should have, I know, but it just kind of snowballed on me. I didn't think you would go for four hundred, being nonrefundable and all. I thought I would just borrow the other hundred from the Three Jacks operating account and tell you at closing, but you beat me to it."

Syd's stomach started to sink again as the obvious question dawned on him. "Who loaned you a hundred grand, Sonny? Who in their right mind would loan you a *hundred-fucking-grand?* Where did you get it?"

"I borrowed it from the manager of Rachelle's, it's just a forty-five-day loan, and everything was fine un—"

"Hold on, what's Rachelle's?"

"It's a, it's a steakhouse, with um, with entertainment."

"*Entertainment?* What do you mean *entertainment?* Don't tell me it's a strip club, *please* don't tell me it's a fucking strip club."

Sonny was sweating, and he grabbed a paper towel to mop his forehead. "Yeah, I guess some people might ah, might call it that."

"I swear to fucking God, the doctor dropped you on your head when you were born. Jesus H. Christ! *A strip club?* Who do you think owns ninety-nine point nine percent of all the strip clubs in the world? The pope? No, you dumbass, the mob, that's who. Let me guess, they gave you a nice loan at..." Syd made a few quick calculations in his head. "At what? About a grand a day in interest? Sound about right?"

Sonny was sitting on the kitchen floor with his back to the fridge now. *How in hell did he know what they were charging him?* "How...how...how did you know?"

"Because I'm not a moron like you, Sonny, that's how. I know not to borrow money from mobsters. *Un-fucking-believable.*"

"I didn't know it was the mob until last night, that's when I found out, that's when they told me we had to sell the marina to them."

"Are you *shitting me?* They told you that? Who? Why? Wait...wait a second, tell me exactly what happened...and go slow. Tell me what happened last night."

Sonny told him the whole story about the visit from Gino and the goon. He told him about the terms of the new deal, and how they had a week to get them a contract. He told him what would happen to his dog and the Three Jacks if it didn't happen, and about how they would start torching their restaurants up the coast till it did.

Syd was listening on the other end of the phone in his monogrammed bathrobe, in total disbelief. "That's it? That's everything?" He sat down on the toilet in his multimillion dollar home outside Boston, waiting for a reply. *When you gotta go you gotta go.* "Sonny, is that everything?"

"Um...no, he said to be sure and tell you who you were dealing with, that it was important for you to know."

Syd leaned forward, elbows on knees, dreading what was coming. "Who? Who is it?"

"Donny Nutz, he said be sure and tell you it's Donny Nutz...from Jersey City."

Syd dropped the phone at the exact moment his bowels evacuated in projectile fashion. Half hit the back lip of the toilet bowl, and the other half hit the top of the seat and the inside of his robe. He scrambled to pick up the phone and felt a warm squishiness as the robe stuck to his considerable rear end.

Sonny heard a clattering noise as the phone bounced on the tile floor. "Dad? Dad, you there? Is everything all right?"

Syd quickly picked the phone off the floor and spat out, "Yeah...I mean no, no, it's not all right...Shit!"

Syd heard his wife call from the bedroom. "Syd? Honey? Is everything OK?"

"I'm fine dear, the phone just slipped out of my hand, I'll be out in a minute." Syd lifted his hand off the receiver and said, "Sonny, hang on a second." He then set the phone down, took off his robe, and grabbed some toilet paper. When he was done cleaning up, he grabbed the phone again. "You there, Sonny?"

"Yeah."

"Get me this Gino guy's number. I uh, I need to talk to him."

Sonny thought his dad sounded nervous, but he wasn't sure, because he never heard him sound nervous before. "So you know who this Donny Nutz is?"

"Yeah I know who he is, so just get me the number. Think you can do that without fucking it up?"

Sonny was thinking his dad was definitely sounding shaky as he gave him the number for Rachelle's. "What are you gonna do? You gonna straighten him out? You're not gonna let them buy the marina? Right?"

Syd pulled the phone away from his ear and stared at it hard for the second time. He was shaking his head, wondering again if Sonny was truly his biological offspring. He vowed to have a heart-to-heart with his wife after he put his robe in the wash. She must have been cheating on him when she conceived Sonny. It was the only thing that made sense.

"Listen up, dip shit. The reason I'm calling this Gino character is to get some information so I can have the contract drawn up and in his hands as soon as possible. If Donny Nutz wants the marina, he can have it. I'm not sure why he wants it, but it doesn't matter. We're selling...and keeping the restaurants intact."

Sonny couldn't believe his ears, his old man was actually scared of the guy. *Holy shit!* He hadn't known him to be intimidated by anyone in his whole life, and tried to put a good spin on it. "Well, look at the bright side, we're still gonna make about a million dollars for forty-five days' work. That's not too bad, huh?"

Syd would have strangled him if he had been there, no doubt about it. He would have wrapped his hands around Sonny's weaselly neck and squeezed until his buggy little eyes popped out his head. In a voice dripping with sarcasm, he replied, "Yeah, Sonny, that's not too bad at all...*great* job. In fact, I'm gonna give you a five hundred grand bonus when we close the deal...keep up the good work."

Sonny missed his tone entirely. "*Really?* Wow, thanks, Dad, but is that before or after the loan is repaid? I have a chance to invest in this state-of-the-art emu farm, I got a customer who—" SMASH! Sonny heard the line go dead as his father smashed the phone into a million pieces on his bathroom floor.

Chapter 72

Donny Nutz was a cautious and low-key mobster, which explains how he made it to fifty-eight, in a business that routinely saw guys disappear (literally) before they were thirty-five. He wasn't too flashy, and didn't go out a whole lot. When he did, it was usually to cruise the Hudson on his forty-six-foot Grand Banks called the *JC*. On vacation, he kept an even lower profile. While other wise guys wintered in places like Miami and Ft. Lauderdale, he preferred the quiet of Stuart, where he had a nice, but unassuming condo, on the intracoastal. There he kept his other indulgence, a forty-two-foot Cruisers Express Bridge called *The Job*. He loved to drive it, but usually had Gino come up from West Palm when he wanted to cruise, so he could relax with his wife. Gino pretty much knew what he was doing on a boat. He grew up on the Jersey shore and worked the docks on Long Island, which was where he got his start with the Carpoza crime family.

The day after his meeting with Sonny Slade, Sonny's dad called Gino. Twenty-four hours later, Sonny delivered the contract to him at Rachelle's. The contract spelled out exactly what Donny Nutz said it should. Exactly one week after Slade closed on the C-LOVE Marina, he would sell it to a company controlled by Donny Nutz for nine million dollars, minus the hundred and thirty-five grand Sonny owed. As soon as Gino faxed the contract up to Donny, Donny called back and instructed Gino to take his boat down to the marina adjacent to the C-LOVE Marina and Three Jacks. He wanted either Gino or Marco to stay on the boat every night until the deal closed, which was in less than three weeks. He told Gino to keep an eye on things, and to make his presence known to Sonny at Three Jacks. He didn't want anything going wrong that might spoil his one point five million dollar payday when he flipped it to the city of Boynton Beach. A million and a half big ones was no chump change, even to a seasoned mobster like Donny Nutz. He had bluffed the mayor about partnering up with somebody to do the deal. It would be a little difficult, seeing as how his last partner was in an oil drum at the bottom of the Hudson. Donny Nutz was doing the deal all by himself. If all went well, he figured he might trade in his Florida boat, *The Job*, for something a little nicer.

Per the boss's instruction, Gino called down to the Water's Edge Marina and arranged to rent a private slip for a month. He then told Marco to be ready to drive his Hummer down to the marina when he called.

Gino liked captaining *The Job*. It sure as hell beat working at Rachelle's every day. Not that the sights and perks were bad, far from it, but being on the water brought back memories for him. As he cruised south down the intracoastal, he fondly recalled dumping his first body in New York Harbor, when he was just seventeen. *Ahhhh, yes...Those were the days.*

He became something of a "wet specialist," because he was good at driving boats and killing people. His ruthlessness and efficiency quickly earned him his stripes with the Carpozas, and his mentor, Donny Nutz.

As he reminisced about all the guys he whacked and dumped in the twenty years since, he was suddenly brought back to the present by the voice of one of the dancers he brought along for the three- to four-hour trip.

"Hey, Gino!" yelled Misty, from the cockpit. "You want me to bring you up a drink? Sunny and I want to come up for a little while. You know, maybe see the sights and keep you company."

"Yeah, bring me a Red Bull and Stoli...and bring some of your toys...it's showtime."

Misty giggled. "So you want Sunny's side up? Mmmmm, so do I, let me see if I can talk her into it."

After ten minutes of watching the girls go at it up on the bridge deck, Gino couldn't take it anymore. He radioed the bridge tender on Ocean Avenue in Lantana, who told him it would be another five minutes until the bridge opened, and he could pass. *Perfect, four more than I need.* "That's it, girls, time to take care of Little Gino. You two got me harder than a Korean karate chop. Better do it quick, or you might give the bridge tender a heart attack."

About a half hour later, Gino sidled the boat up to the fuel dock at the Water's Edge Marina. An older guy came out of the ship's store to help him tie up, and asked if he needed any fuel.

"Yeah, filler up. I'm renting a slip here for the next month. Maybe you can point out which one."

The older guy dragged the fuel hose over to the boat, and handed it to Gino once he came down from the bridge. "You called ahead?"

"Yeah, I talked to a guy named...shit, I can't remember, but he said he was the dockmaster. I take it that's not you."

"Nope, hang on a second and I'll get him, he's in the office."

As Gino continued to pump fuel into the tank, the girls came out of the cabin wearing short shorts and T-shirts over their bikinis. The one named Sunny pointed at Three Jacks. "We're gonna go over to that restaurant. You coming?"

"Yeah, I'll be over in a little while...after I get some fuel and dock the boat." The tide was kind of low, and the girls needed to climb a ladder attached to one of the pilings to get up on the dock. A scraggly young kid appeared out of nowhere, and reached out his hand to help them up. Gino slapped each girl's ass on the way up, and looked at the kid helping them. "I sure as shit know *you're* not the dockmaster." He thought the kid looked like a real greaseball, maybe twenty-five years old.

"No, I'm Ratdog. I help out around the docks. You need any help tying up, or need your boat cleaned, or just about anything else, I'm you're man."

Gino looked him over and immediately pegged him as a true dock rat. He was no different than the hundreds of thousands of young men that look for work on docks all over the world. He had done the same thing as a kid up on Long Island, where he got his start. *Hmmm...kid might be useful.* "Why don't you stick around for a few minutes, I might have some work for you."

Ratdog was checking out the girls from behind as they walked over to the bar, and turned back to face Gino. "I'll be right here, whatever you need."

Just then another guy came walking out of the ship's store and up to the boat, looking at some papers. "You the guy who called up about dockage? You Gino?"

"Yeah, yeah, that's me, I rented the slip...I take it your the dockmaster?"

Robo looked up from the paperwork with the slip rental agreement, and eyed the man fueling the boat. *Huh, that's the same guy I saw meeting with Sonny Slade a couple of weeks ago.* He had on a bathing suit and not a business suit, but no doubt about the face and body. He looked like the man who ate Baretta. "Yep, that's me, name's Robo."

"Robo, huh? Like the cop?"

"You got it, only I'm armed with a clipboard. I got you all set for slip number seventeen, on the north canal there." He pointed toward the slip and kept talking. "When you get done filling up, come on in and sign the slip rental agreement and we'll get you all squared away. Are you on vacation or something?"

Gino loved the name his boss had given the boat for just this reason. He pointed to the stern with the big letters that read, *The Job*, and replied, "No, I'm on the job." Gino hated nosy people, just like his boss. Nothing bugged him more than people who tried to pry out information that was none of their damn business. In his experience, people who snooped were up to no good and were nothing but trouble. That could be dangerous, because once they became trouble, it inevitably meant deep trouble...as in deep six kind of trouble. *His specialty.*

Robo laughed at the boat name. "Oh, that's good, that's real good. I like it."

Gino didn't laugh or say anything though, he just stared at him real hard. Robo got the message. "Just leave the hose on the dock when you're done, and I'll see you in the office." He walked away, and five minutes later Gino crowded into the tiny ship's store.

Robo didn't like the guy, or the way he filled up the place with his extra-wide body, so he said, "Let's do this outside." Gino stepped back outside and followed Robo to a table with an umbrella, where they sat down. "OK, here's the fuel bill, two hundred and twenty gallons, at three fifty a gallon, for a total of seven hundred and seventy dollars."

Gino handed him a credit card and Robo continued. "You can look over the rental agreement while I ring up the fuel. Like I told you on the phone, the rate is fourteen dollars per foot. You have a forty-two foot boat, so that's five eighty-eight plus tax. With the electric deposit, it comes to nine twenty-five for the month."

Gino didn't say anything, he just looked at the agreement while Robo ran his credit card. When Robo came back out, Gino signed the agreement, and then signed the credit card bill for the fuel. He slid the card back to Robo. "Here, put the boat slip on the card too."

"Oh crap, didn't I tell you on the phone? The dockage is privately owned and we're not set up for credit cards on that. How about a check? If you don't have one on you, just stop by tomorrow, or the next day." It wasn't normally what he would do, but Robo wanted to be done with the guy. He had a bad air about him.

"How 'bout cash? You take cash, don't you?"

"Um, cash? Sure, cash'll be fine." Gino went back in the boat and came out with a wad of bills wrapped with a rubber band. He counted out nine hundred and twenty-five dollars and handed it to Robo, who reached down from the dock. "Let me get you a receipt, I'll be right back." Ratdog was leaning against the fuel pump, watching the whole exchange.

Robo came back and gave Gino the receipt. "You're in dock number seventeen, between the Luhrs and the Viking. You need help getting tied up?"

"Nope, he's helping me." Robo looked a little pissed when he saw that he was pointing at Ratdog, who was lurking by the fuel pump. Gino picked up on Robo giving Ratdog the evil eye. "That's not a problem...*is it?*"

He said it in a way that was just begging to be challenged, but Robo didn't bite.

"No, no problem at all. I have to close up anyways, it's almost five. If you have any problems, you know where to find me." As he turned and walked back to the office, he wished he didn't.

Gino looked up at Ratdog. "Meet me over at number seventeen, and help me get tied up."

"You got it." As Ratdog headed down the dock, the *C-LOVE* passed by on its way back from the afternoon trip. After Ratdog helped Gino get properly tied up in his new slip, Gino stepped on the dock, and pulled out his still impressive wad of bills. He fingered the wad until he found a hundred-dollar bill, peeled it off, and handed it to Ratdog. Ratdog couldn't believe his good fortune. *This guy's loaded* .

A big greasy smile lit up his face. "Geez thanks, um...Mr...um..."

Gino casually looked up and down the dock, making sure nobody was listening before he answered. "Gino, just call me Gino. Now listen up, I'm here for at least a month and I want you to watch my boat when I'm not here. Got it?"

"Yeah, sure, no problem."

"I also want you to keep your eyes and ears open for anything out of the ordinary that happens on this dock, or that one over there where that big drift boat just pulled in. Think you can do that?"

"Sure, anything odd going on I'll let you know... whatever you want."

"I like your attitude, Ratdog, you do a good job and there'll be plenty more Benjamin's coming your way. Here's my number, you call it day or night, anything comes up." Gino handed him a business card from Rachelle's, with his cell number on it. "One other thing, keep your mouth shut about our arrangement. I don't like people who *talk* about my business, and I don't like people who *ask* about my business, unnerstand?"

Ratdog was a little surprised and intimidated, but managed to not let it show.

"Yeah, I got it, I'll keep my mouth shut. Anybody comes asking about you, I'll let you know."

Gino glanced up and down the dock again, and nodded. "Good, good...sounds like we have ourselves an arrangement then, right?"

"I don't have an arrangement with anybody. I just help out on the docks, I don't know what you're talking about." Ratdog winked at Gino, and Gino laughed as he pulled out his wad of bills again.

He peeled off a twenty and handed it to him. "You're a smart kid, now go get yourself a haircut and a shower. I can't be seen with you looking like that."

"You serious?"

"You bet your greasy ass I am. You hang around my boat looking like that, you're gonna scare my girls. Now go and get yourself cleaned up by the time I get back from the restaurant." Ratdog scurried away, and Gino headed for Three Jacks, hoping old Sonny boy was there.

Tangles sat back down in the *Lucky Dog*, after watching and hearing snippets of conversation between the two unlikely conspirators. He briefly wondered who in the hell the squatty guy was that parked his boat in the slip next door, then went back to napping.

Chapter 73

Over the next couple of weeks, Millie's health rapidly deteriorated, but she still managed to successfully fight every attempt by Holly to take her back to the hospital. It wasn't gonna happen, so Holly hired a nurse to come to the house daily, to administer medications that would ease her pain. I spent a little time at the house with them, but the mood was somber, and Holly was naturally upset. She was preoccupied with doting on Millie until the end, and I accepted the fact that our budding relationship was on hold for a while. I also accepted the fact that I might have feelings for her, and was willing to tough it out. Holly walked me to the door, leaving the nurse and Millie in the bedroom. As I opened it to leave, she said, "Thanks for coming, Kit, I know this isn't fun for you."

I turned around and put my hands on her shoulders. "Look, I lost a close aunt to lung cancer a couple of years ago, and I know what a difficult time this is. You need to know that you're not alone. I'm available 24-7, just call if you need a shoulder."

She pulled herself to me and hugged me tight, then buried her face in my chest and quietly sobbed. I stroked her hair and squeezed her as hard as I dared.

After a minute or so, she choked off the tears and stepped back. "Thank you so much. I don't know how I'd manage without you."

I wiped her tears away with my thumbs. "You could manage if you had to, but you don't need to do it alone, that's why I'm here."

She stepped forward and gave me a tender kiss on the lips. "I just get a little overwhelmed sometimes. I can see that I'm really going to lose Millie, and we're less than a week away from having to sell the marina too...I feel lost."

She was right about the marina, it was Wednesday, the second of June, and closing was set for Tuesday, the eighth. "Don't worry about the marina, I've been watching the weather and it looks good to finally get some rain this weekend. It might wash out the Three Jacks annual fishing tournament, but who cares, it's just what we need to pull off the plan. In fact, I'm gonna give Hambone a call right now. I need to meet up with him and make sure everybody's ready."

"You really think it'll work?"

"The weather's the key. There's a disturbance in the Caribbean that might develop into a weak tropical storm, but that's good enough for us. Hell, we just need a nice soaking downpour one of these nights and we'll be good to go."

"God, I pray we get a storm."

"That makes two of us, now go tuck in Millie and get yourself some rest. We're gonna be digging this weekend, rain or not."

She gave me another kiss, only this one was longer. In fact it was long enough to start making me hard. She must have felt it too, because she giggled a little as she pushed herself away. "My, you're an excitable boy. I hope you save some of that for when we have some alone time."

"You can count on it."

As I walked to the car, I heard her chuckle and say. "Oh I am," right before the door shut.

When I got in, I dialed Hambone's cell, and could tell from the background noise he was probably at Three Jacks. Turns out he was at the Habana Boat, because his bar privileges at Three Jacks were still suspended due to the cartwheel routine.

"Hello? Hello? Kit...that you?" he answered.

"Yeah, can you meet me on the *Lucky Dog* in ten minutes? We need to talk."

"What? Now?"

It was loud in the background, and I could tell he was having trouble hearing me, so I spoke louder. "YEAH, NOW...IT'S IMPORTANT, BE ON THE *LUCKY DOG* IN TEN MINUTES."

"OK OK, I hear you. I'll pay the tab and be right over."

* * *

Ratdog was handed a fifty-dollar bill and two bananas, and said, "No problem, just like last time, he won't find them until the damage is done." He had planted the last pair of bananas on the *Lucky Dog* in the middle of the night, when there was little chance of getting caught. That was before the new guy Tangles was sleeping on the boat though. He looked at his watch, which read nine thirty. He knew that Tangles was out on the *C-LOVE*, and that Shagball was rarely down at the boat this late, so he decided to do it right then. Although it was early, he had the advantage of Gino's boat being right next to the *Lucky Dog*. That gave him an excuse to be in the vicinity at least. The more important factor was he had spied Tangles hiding the cabin door key under one of the ladder rungs that led up to the bridge. He could jump in the cockpit, grab the key, and be inside the cabin in seconds. Once inside he would be invisible, as long as he didn't turn any lights on.

He casually strolled down the main dock, and then went out on the finger dock separating Gino's boat from the *Lucky Dog*. He acted like he was checking the lines on Gino's boat, and when he determined no one was watching, jumped into the cockpit of the *Lucky Dog*. Quickly he reached under the bottom rung of the bridge ladder and felt his way up a couple of steps until he found the key, then let himself into the cabin. He stepped down to the galley and kneeled in front of the fridge, where he shined his little LED keychain flashlight at the base plate. He figured a good spot to stash the bananas would be behind the fridge base plate, if it was accessible. He cursed under his breath when he saw that it was tightly secured by eight screws. He wanted to get off the boat as soon as possible, and started thinking of another place to put the bananas as he stood up, when—*Shit!*

He immediately dropped back down below the galley counter as a pair of Xenon headlights swept through the cabin. *Holy shit! It's Shagball's Beemer.* A feeling of dread hit him, knowing he was trapped and needed somewhere to hide. Realizing he left the cabin door unlocked, he crawled back and locked it as soon as the headlights went out. He heard the car door shut, and fast as he could, scrambled down the galley steps to the forward berth. He felt under the bed, hoping there was space enough to crawl under, but it was all storage space too small for his frame. *Shit! Think!* He groped along the wall at the foot of the bed, next to the doorway, and found a handle. He slid open a small door, and felt some shirts hanging inside, just as he heard the thump of someone hopping on board. He pushed the clothes aside and squeezed himself into the small closet, before pulling the door closed. He was thankful that it was a louvered door, which let some air in, and that he was only five foot seven and a hundred and forty pounds. He held his breath, and was quiet as a dead mouse as he heard the cabin door open.

* * *

I let myself into the boat, and as I went to grab a beer out of the fridge, there were two bananas sitting on the counter. *What the fuck?* Tangles is eating bananas on the boat? *I don't think so.* I stepped back through the cabin door and tossed them in the canal. I couldn't believe he would bring bananas on board after what I went through. I would have to have a serious talk with him. I sat down with a beer, and checked my text messages while I waited for Hambone. There were three texts from Melody saying she wanted to see me. I ran into her a week earlier at the apartment, and she said she wasn't seeing Mr. Mercedes anymore. She wanted to make me dinner, which was code for chitty-chitty-bang-bang, and looked seriously shocked when I declined. Frankly, I was surprised too. I hadn't closed the deal with Holly yet, and God knows I was horny, but the little angel on my shoulder won out for once. She had asked if she could fish the Three Jacks tournament with me, but I told her I already had a female angler. *She was pissed.*

A couple of minutes later, Hambone came aboard. He sat down with a beer, and inquired, "What's going on?"

"You been watching the weather?"

"I fish for a living, bro, I always watch the weather. It looks like we're gonna get lucky with the rain. When are you thinking we should dig?"

"If it rains Saturday and Sunday like they're predicting, I think we go Monday, three in the morning. It should be as deserted around here as it ever gets."

"You get the shovels?"

"I'm picking them up tomorrow."

"Man, I hope this works, nobody wants Slade to buy the marina...especially me."

"Believe me, when those tanks get discovered, the deal will go up in flames. The bank won't loan the money till they're removed. Slade will ask for an extension, and when Millie says no, he'll be *fucked* with a capital F."

"Man, I hope so."

"You got that right, so as of now we're going early Monday. We'll meet here late Sunday, and wait till the coast is clear."

"Sounds good, I better make the rounds."

Hambone left the boat, and headed down the dock. I finished my beer, locked up the cabin, and walked to the Beemer. As I got in, I noticed the lights were on in the cabin of the boat in the adjacent slip. Backlit behind the sliding cabin doors was a very big man, maybe six-six and two eighty. I told myself to ask Tangles what the deal was with him. The boat hadn't left the dock since it arrived, but there always seemed to be somebody on it at night. I started to think it was odd, but then realized it probably wasn't any weirder than me having a midget onboard. *Probably no biggie.* I drove back to the apartment to catch up on some much-needed rest...thinking about bananas again.

Ratdog waited a full five minutes until he was sure no one was on the boat. Ever so quietly, he eased open the closet door, then crept up to the galley. He realized when he was in the closet that he left the bananas on the counter, but now they were gone. Thankfully though, *he* hadn't been discovered. He peered through the glass next to the cabin door, and when he was sure no one was around, quickly stepped out and locked the door. He crouched, and went to put the key back under the second, or was it the third step? *Shit, which one was it?* He left it under the second step, and got off the boat. As soon as he reached the main dock, he heard a voice say, "Hey, whatta you doing?"

He turned, and was relieved when he saw it was Gino. He was standing in the cabin of *The Job*, with the sliders open.

"Gino, it's me...Ratdog." He walked over to the finger dock on the west side of the boat, wanting to get as much distance between himself and the *Lucky Dog* as possible. He was still nervous about the close call. The big guy appeared next to Gino, and Ratdog asked, "permission to come aboard?"

"Why?"

"I just heard something that you might be interested in..."

Chapter 74

The next morning, Gino called Donny Nutz from the safe phone at the club. As usual, it was routed through a few different businesses before ending up at the Rye Smile, up in Jersey City. He could hear the phone being picked up, but not answered. "Donny, it's me, Gino."

"Yeah, Gino, what's up?" It was definitely the barrel-scraping voice of his boss on the other end.

"Looks like we got a problem down on the docks. Seems there's a couple of guys bent on making sure Slade can't close on the marina next Tuesday."

"How they think they're gonna do that?"

"Something about digging up some tanks or something."

"Tanks? What kind of tanks?"

"I'm not sure...gas tanks maybe?"

"How'd you find this out?"

"I gotta kid down here working for me, and he overheard it. According to him, they sound convinced that if they dig up these tanks, it'll cause all kinds of problems, and the bank won't loan Slade the money. They're planning on doing it late Sunday night."

"Wait a second, why they trying to put the kibosh on the deal?"

"The kid told me that Sonny Slade told all the slip holders they were getting kicked out as soon as the deal closed. They're slip holders...they don't want to get kicked out."

"Yeah, but that will only buy them a little time. The owner wants to sell, it's gonna sell."

"That's the kicker. Seems the old lady who owns the place has seller's remorse. She wants the deal to die."

"That so? Sorta sounds like a double cross...and you know how much I like those."

"Not very much."

Gino heard Donny Nutz laugh, which is a disturbing thing unto itself. Half snort, half cough, half chuckle, all creepy. "Couple of fucking schmos think they're gonna get between me and a nice payday? That's a dangerous place to be...know what I mean?"

"Very dangerous."

"You got that right—so dangerous they might be standing in my way one day, and gone the next."

"You want me to take them on a one-way cruise?"

"Gino?"

"Yeah, boss."

"You complete me." Gino heard Donny Nutz gagging on his creepy laugh, right before the line went dead.

Chapter 75

The day after my late meeting with Hambone, I was down on the docks about four in the afternoon. I decided to pay Robo a visit, just to shoot the shit and see what was going on. He prided himself on knowing everything he was suppose to, and some stuff he wasn't. I found him alone in the office, his helper out on the dock, fueling up a boat.

"Hey, Robo, what's going on?"

"Hey, Kit, just doing a little paperwork. You fishing the Three Jacks tournament this weekend?"

"I'm entered, but I don't know about the weather. What's your take?"

"Well, I just looked at Weather Underground on the computer, and that low off the Dominican Republic looks like its gonna give us some rain at the very least. Most of the models show it hitting anywhere from Miami to Stuart as a tropical depression. Better pack a rain jacket."

"Wonderful." I tried to sound disappointed, but it was just what we needed...the ground getting thoroughly saturated prior to the big dig. I decided to inquire about the boat in the slip next to me. "What's the story with the boat in the slip next to mine, you know...the one with the big guy staying on it."

"Oh man, have you met those guys?"

"Guys? I've only seen the one built like that Russian guy from the Rocky movies."

"Well there's two, I'm sure Tangles has seen the other one. He's about five eight and a hundred and ninety, built like a fire hydrant. Looks like Baretta if you dropped a piano on his head. I'm supposed to tell him they're not allowed to sleep on it, but the guy looks at me like he wants to bite my head off. Hopefully, they'll be gone next week. Something's not right about those two, that's for sure."

"How do you mean?"

"A few weeks back, I see the short one, his name's Gino, meet with Sonny Slade on back-to-back days. First day, I was having a scotch at happy hour, when he comes strolling in all suited up. He asks Sonny for his ID, and they go upstairs for about five minutes before coming back down. Very next morning, I'm taking a leak, and I see this guy Gino again, coming down the dock with a briefcase. I go into the bar to get some coffee, and he and Sonny go upstairs again. Only *this* time, when they come back down, Sonny's got the briefcase."

"*What?* What's that all about?"

"You tell me...when he brought the boat in for the first time, he had what looked to be a couple of strippers on board, and paid for the slip using a big wad of cash. Ratdog's watching the boat for him when he's not here. He denies it, but he normally hangs around the fuel dock all day trying to beat me out of tips. Now he just hangs around over by *The Job*. You do the math."

"The job?"

"Yeah, that's the name of the boat. Cute...right? When I laughed about it, this Gino guy gave me the thousand-yard stare. He gives me the heebie-jeebies."

"So Ratdog's on his payroll?"

"Sure looks that way. Big shocker, huh?"

"Maybe I should have a little talk with Ratdog."

"Be careful, Shag, I'm serious. That Gino's a bad apple."

I was waiting for Tangles on the *Lucky Dog* when he came back from his afternoon trip on the *C-LOVE*. It had become a regular gig for him, and he was doing up to ten trips a week. When he came through the cabin door, I noticed the bandage was off his wrist, and the stitches were out.

He saw me sitting there. "Hey, boss, what's up?"

"Grab a beer and we'll talk."

"Sounds serious, am I in trouble?" He pulled out a Heiney Light, and sat down across from me at the dinette.

"No, but I just had a talk with Robo. There's something going on between those guys on the boat next to us, and Sonny."

"Sonny?"

"Yeah, Sonny Slade from the Three Jacks."

I filled Tangles in on what Robo told me concerning the meetings and the briefcase. "So what do you think?"

"Well, Ratdog is definitely on the guy's payroll. I heard them discussing it, and saw that guy Gino give him some money. He said he wanted to be kept up to speed on anything odd happening on this dock, or the one that the *C-LOVE* goes out of."

"Shit, when did this happen?"

"A couple of weeks back."

"Why didn't you tell me?"

"I didn't think it was a big deal, some guy asking someone to watch his boat and keep him up with dock chatter. Plus, you haven't been around much...with Holly and all." That part was true. I was still spending a lot of time at Millie's house, and had been out of town a couple of days too.

"Well shit, next time pick up the damn phone and call me when something like that happens. I don't like how these guys just happen to show up at this particular time. Robo also said the big guy spends most every night on the boat, you notice that too?"

"Yeah, he leaves most mornings about seven thirty, eight o'clock."

"Damn it!"

"Why are you so pissed?"

"Why do you fucking think? These guys got some connection to Slade, and you heard one of them tell Ratdog to keep him informed about anything strange going on. Maybe he got wind of our plan somehow, and these guys are watching us. Maybe they're here to make sure we're not successful." I looked out the window at *The Job*, but didn't see anybody. *Was I just being paranoid?*

"You think? Nah, if they knew we were up to something, they would have approached us by now. They don't look like the shy type."

"I sure hope your right—Oh, and stop eating bananas on the boat. I find one more fucking banana on the boat and you're out, got it? In fact, that goes for anything with bananas in it too...like yogurt...if you eat that shit...and—"

"Hold on a second, man, what are you talking about? I didn't bring any bananas on the boat. I don't even *like* bananas."

"Bullshit, I found two bananas sitting on the counter last night. If you didn't bring them, who did? It sure as shit wasn't the fruit fairy."

"Last night? Was the door locked?" A sinking feeling started to form in Tangles' stomach.

"Yeah...sure the door was locked. Please don't tell me you usually leave it unlocked?"

"No, no it's just that when I got back last night, my key wasn't where I thought I left it. I figured I just forgot which step I hid it under, but now I'm not so sure."

"You've been leaving your key outside? Under one of the ladder rungs? Are you kidding me? Why don't you just buy a welcome mat and put it under that? Holy Christ on a crutch...*Jesus*, Tangles!"

"I'm sorry, I uh, I've been meaning to get one of those key chains that hooks to your belt loop, but I haven't had the time. I promise I'll get one tomorrow."

"You sure the key was in the wrong spot?"

"No, but how else would a couple of bananas end up on the counter?"

"Oh man, this is bad. I need to think about this...I'm going home."

As I walked to the door, he started to apologize. "Kit, I'm sorry...I mean it...I'll walk over to ACE hardware in the morning and—"

"I hope it's not too little too late...shit!" I shut the cabin door a little harder than I should have, but I was pissed. As I fired up the Beemer, I could make out three bodies backlit in the cabin of *The Job*. The big guy, the squatty guy, and someone much smaller. *Who the hell was the third guy? Ratdog? What the hell were they up to?* I would find out soon enough.

Chapter 76

It was Friday night, and the captain's meeting at Three Jacks had just ended to a collective groan from the attendees. Everybody was bummed because they announced the tournament was likely to be canceled, but no final decision would be made until the next morning at six. Apparently, the system coming up from the Dominican Republic had gained a little steam, and was now expected to hit sometime Saturday morning. I was the captain of my team, and the only one required to be at the meeting. The rest of my team was invited, but everybody crapped out for one reason or another. My team consisted of Holly (our female angler), Jamie (my producer), my buddy Big Mike, and Tangles. Tangles originally said he'd be there, but pulled a no show. He left a note on the *Lucky Dog*, saying he had a date. I wasn't sure if that was the case, or if he was just upset with the way I laid into him about the key and the bananas. After I cooled down back at the apartment, I realized that *maybe* I had been a little tough on him. I would straighten things out the next chance I got.

I was walking out of the restroom when Ratdog appeared from around the corner. "Hey, Shagball, the boat next to yours just clipped your bow when they were docking."

"What? How bad?" I started walking across the parking lot toward the *Lucky Dog*, with Ratdog trailing me.

"Well I didn't get a good look, but the guy on board asked if I knew who the owner was. He wants to make sure you know he'll take care of it."

"You bet your ass he's gonna take care of it. Let me guess, it's the boat you've been watching, the forty-two-footer with the inflatable on the bow."

"I um, I'm not really watching it...but yeah, yeah that's the boat, it's called *The Job*. The guy's name is Gino, but don't worry...he's a stand-up guy."

"Sure he is. Apparently he can't run a boat though. Christ, just what I need."

I got to the dock, and the squatty guy named Gino was standing in the cockpit of his boat looking up at me. "Listen, I'm real sorry about the scratch, my starboard side clipped your port bow. I don't think it's too bad though—you can see it good from here." He had a flashlight and briefly shined it on my bow, then waved me down into the cockpit.

As I stepped aboard, I noticed the big guy was in the cabin, sitting on the couch. Gino handed me the flashlight, and pointed at my bow. "There, right there, shine it there."

I was shining the light on my bow from the starboard side of his cockpit, and didn't see any damage at all. I swept the beam back and forth a couple of times, but didn't see a thing. *What the hell? What's this Gibroni talking about?* I turned, saying, "Are you sure you didn't hit the piling? Because—" Wham!

He slammed his fist into my gut and I keeled over. I heard the cabin doors slide open as I tried to catch my breath. With one meaty hand he grabbed me by my belt, and with the other he pushed my head down and slung me into the cabin. The guy was strong as an ox, no doubt about it. As soon as I stumbled through the door, the big guy shut the blinds on the sliders behind me. As he turned around, I found myself staring into the wrong end of a long black gun with a silencer on it. *Holy shit! Are you kidding me?* I caught my breath, and spat out, "What the fuck are you doing?"

"Shut up and sit down, asshole. One fucking peep out of you and I duct tape your mouth after I smash it in...got it?"

I got it. Boy did I get it...I was in serious serious shit. I decided to take his advice and sat down on the couch. Then I checked my ribs to see if any were cracked.

Hambone was next to his truck in the parking lot when Ratdog came running up to him. "Hambone, quick! Shagball's getting his ass beat by a couple of guys on the boat next to him. He needs help!" Ratdog turned to lead the way, and Hambone followed, racing across the parking lot. When they got to the docks on the other side, Ratdog ran down the finger dock next to *The Job*, and pointed. "They got him in there, their beating on him!"

Hambone leapt from the finger dock into the cockpit, then threw open the sliders, yelling, "Sha—" That was all that came out of his mouth before it was smashed in by the big guy. He connected with a powerful right cross that sent him sprawling into me on the couch. Hambone was one tough dude though.

After shaking his head like a bull, he tensed and turned, preparing to go after the guy.

I grabbed him by the arm, with both hands. "Wait, wait a second...they got guns." I felt the tension dissipate as he eased himself into a sitting position next to me. He wiped some blood off his lips and checked for loose teeth. Then he said, "What the fuck."

Gino was pointing two guns with silencers at us, and he handed one back to the big guy in the sweat suit who nailed Hambone. "Nice right, Marco, but you still owe me twenty bucks, you didn't knock him out. Now shut those doors, for Christ's sake. Where's the kid?"

Gino told Ratdog to shut the doors behind Hambone when he charged in, but it didn't happen. Marco went to shut the doors, and saw Ratdog pressed up against the side of the boat, trying to hide. He flashed his gun so Ratdog saw it. "Get in here, you're not done yet."

Ratdog walked in on shaky legs, and as Marco shut the doors behind him, Gino nodded to Marco. "OK, dump out their pockets and tape their hands, I'm gonna get us going." Gino handed his gun back to Marco, and went back out through the sliders. Marco had a gun pointed at each of us. He looked at Ratdog and nodded toward the galley. "You heard him, greaseball, there's a bag and some tape on the counter there. Put everything they got in the bag, and then tape their hands up good."

Chapter 77

Tangles' date ended early and poorly, if you can call it a date, that is. He met one of the Habana Boat waitresses over at The Alley, a funky bar and restaurant on Ocean Avenue, just west of Dixie. It was a favorite local hangout due to a wide array of fine sandwiches and soups, a good beer selection, and reasonable prices. After having a nice meal, they went up to the bar. That was where his date ran into a so-called friend. The friend however, was actually some surfer dude she used to date. When it was clear she was much more interested in her friend, than Tangles, he left. He said he was going to the bathroom, but instead walked right out the front door and back to the boat. He bought dinner, so he figured the least she could do was pick up the bar tab. *Shit…another nooky-free night.*

He was still cursing his luck as he headed down the dock, and thought maybe he would go over to Three Jacks. Then he saw Hambone leap into the cockpit of the boat next to the *Lucky Dog*. What the hell? Hambone rushed into the cabin, and yelled something before his voice was cut off. Tangles started jogging down the dock, then saw the sliding doors open, and the big guy stick his head out. Instinctively, he crouched down behind a large decorative flower pot, not forty feet away. Peering out, he saw another person...*was that Ratdog?*...come out of the shadows, from the side of the boat. He watched Ratdog step inside after the big guy flashed a...*Holy shit, he flashed a gun!*

As soon as the sliders shut, Tangles dashed down the finger dock on the east side of *The Job*. He stooped behind a piling and tried to get a look inside the cabin, but all the blinds were down. Then he noticed one of the blinds closest to the bow was positioned all wrong. He scampered to the end of the finger dock and leaned up against the last piling, looking back toward the boat on a forty-five degree angle. He could plainly see the side of Shagball's head, with his ever-present visor on top. He saw a gun being handed to somebody, and heard the slider doors open again. *Shit.* He lay down on the dock in the shadows, and watched as Gino climbed the stairs to the bridge and started the engines. *What? They're heading out?* He prayed the boat didn't have one of those spotlights up on the bridge that would light up the end of the dock like the fourth of July. Mercifully, it didn't.

Once the engines were idling properly, Gino climbed back down and cast off the starboard stern lines. Unknowingly, he tossed one just a few feet from Tangles' head. When he disappeared to the other side to untie the port lines, Tangles rose to a crouch. That was when he noticed the Zodiac-type raft, beneath a cover on the bow. He briefly considered jumping from the finger dock to the bow, but thought it might make too much noise when his feet hit the side. He weighed his options, then crept down the dock toward the stern. As soon as Gino walked up the port side to untie the bow lines, Tangles took two steps, and leapt on to the starboard gunnel. Thankfully the tide was high, which made the jump easier, and what little noise he made was drowned out by the engines. As soon as Gino made his way back down the port side, Tangles slinked up the starboard side, making sure not to pass in front of the crooked blind. As quickly as he could he wriggled his way under the inflatable, managing to pull the cover back down just before the boat lurched forward.

Chapter 78

With all the activity at the bar following the captain's meeting on a busy Friday night, no one seemed to notice the forty-two foot boat as it left the canal and disappeared into the night. Gino looked up at the towering fifteen-story condos that overlooked the marina, and was glad to see almost seventy-five percent of the units had their lights off. More empty condos meant fewer potential witnesses. He steered the boat past the Boynton spillway, and turned east into the inlet. As he passed under the A1A Bridge and turned slightly south to exit the inlet, he smiled when he saw that the north jetty was closed due to construction. It was another good omen, normally the jetty was crammed full of fisherman. He set course on a slightly east-southeast bearing, and powered up to twenty knots. The conditions were perfect for some wet work. It was a balmy eighty degrees, with a gentle southeast breeze, and waves of two feet or less.

When Sonny let it slip just before the captain's meeting that the tournament was likely to be canceled, he decided to take care of business before the weather got ugly. Nothing sticks out more than a boat going out in crappy conditions. It tends to draw attention, *just ask Scott Peterson*. He looked at the console's electronic display, and saw he was in a hundred and fifty feet of water. He figured when he got past a thousand feet, in another ten miles or so, he would earn his keep. The boat seemed to meld with the night as he steered eastward into the syrupy blackness.

* * *

As soon as Marco told Ratdog to tape up our hands, I said, "Look, I don't know who you are, or what you think we did, but there's been a big misunderstanding, I—"

"Shut up," said Marco, gesturing with both guns. "You want your mouth taped? Trust me, it's no fun. Now empty out your pockets into the bag."

I complied and dropped my cell phone, wallet, and keys in the bag that Ratdog held open. *Fucking Ratdog!* The little weasel set us up. I shot him a look that said he was a dead man if I got my hands on him. He looked almost as scared as I was.

Hambone started dumping his pockets into the bag, and looked at Marco. "You got it all wrong. What the hell did we do?"

"It's not what you did, but what you were about to do. Now shut the fuck up." Marco looked at Ratdog and nodded toward the sliders. "All right, kid, put that bag over there by the doors." Ratdog walked over and set the bag on the ledge, just inside the sliders. "OK, now tape up their wrists, tape 'em up good."

As Ratdog grabbed the duct tape off the counter, I felt the boat turn east and run into a little bumpiness. *Shit!* I was pretty sure we were headed out the inlet.

Ratdog taped me first, and as I held my hands out in front of me, I couldn't believe what he was doing. I knew he was a little squirrelly, but this was crazy. Flat-out fucking crazy. *These goons wanted to kill us!* I glanced at Hambone, and he was shifting his body like he was getting ready to spring.

Marco sensed it. "Don't even think about it, fat boy or I'll fill you full of more lead than a number two pencil factory." Hambone's shoulders sagged in resignation as he leaned back in the sofa. I decided it wouldn't be prudent to inform Marco that contrary to popular belief, pencils were filled with graphite and not lead, and therefore number two pencil factories probably held little, if any lead. *Good decision.*

Ratdog had the first wrap of tape around my wrists, which didn't feel as tight as I thought it would. As he wound the second wrap he looked at me and winked. *What?* I wasn't sure if I saw it right, but then he gave me a bug-eyed stare. *Good, maybe the piece of shit was having second thoughts.* He finished wrapping me real fast, and then moved to Hambone.

When he was done, Marco asked, "You got 'em wrapped tight like I told you...right kid?"

"Yeah, tight enough they should lose feeling in their hands pretty soon."

Marco laughed. "That ain't the only place they're gonna lose feeling."

Risking having my mouth taped, I said, "You know...you're a pretty funny guy, Marco, maybe you should try stand-up, instead of hit-man."

I was starting to worry about the way Marco was staring at me as the seconds crept by, but somehow managed to maintain my best poker face. I felt like one of those wildlife photographers filming a lion feeding on a kill, when it turns toward the camera with a blood- soaked muzzle, and an expression that says, "You know, this gazelle is pretty fucking tasty, but there's always room for dessert."

Finally, Marco puffed out his chest a little, and responded. "You know you're not as stupid as you look, I finished third in an open mic night a few weeks ago...up in JC."

Hambone was still hot about getting coldcocked by Marco, and cut in. "Wow, you must be proud...how many contestants were there? Three?"

Marco's face turned crimson, and he moved with surprising speed for a big guy. Two quick steps and he crossed the cabin, smashing one of the gun butts into the side of Hambone's head. Hambone managed to deflect some of the blow by raising his taped hands, but it still left a bloody bruise.

Marco stepped back and screamed, "You want some more, porky? Just flap those meaty lips one more fucking time and I'll slice 'em off. Go ahead! Say something smart!"

I glanced sideways at Hambone who had a slightly dazed expression on his face, and his eyes said what I already knew. *This guy is nuts.*

Marco's eyes were wild, and you could see his steroid-laced neck veins pulsing against the collar of his sweat suit. "Just what I thought, you're nothing but a big fat pussy. Guess you don't want to lose your pussy lips, huh?" He started laughing. "Get it? Pussy lips?" He laughed harder and looked at Ratdog, who joined in halfheartedly, too afraid not to.

Ratdog waited for Marco to calm down a little, then asked, "Can I use the bathroom?"

Marco waved a gun toward the forward head. "Make it quick, I don't think we have far to go."

I did some mental calculations, and figured we were six or seven miles offshore. Our situation was getting worse by the minute, and my mind was scrambling to come up with an escape plan. *What the hell could I do?* My hands were taped, and some juiced-up ape had two guns pointed at me.

* * *

Ratdog closed the bathroom door behind him and was shaking like a leaf. He hadn't planned on any of this. Gino had told him they were just gonna threaten them, not take them out on the boat and kill them! He wasn't a complete idiot either; they would probably kill him too. He had decided to call for help as soon as he had the chance, and the chance was now. He reached into his pocket for his cell and...he reached around some more...*What?* His cell phone was gone! He frantically checked all his pockets, but it wasn't there. Where the hell was it? *Oh shit, oh shit.* What was he gonna do? They had to disable Marco before Gino stopped the boat and came back down. He taped up the guys as loosely as he could without it being obvious, but it would still take some effort to get free. Marco would shoot them as soon as they tried. No way could he overpower the big man by himself. *Think!*

He thought for a couple of seconds, then remembered the phones from Hambone and Shagball that were in the bag on the ledge. He would have to sneak one out of the bag, and make a call. *It was their only hope.*

* * *

I should have figured it out sooner. No way would I have been suckered onto *The Job* by Ratdog if I had. I kept thinking about the bananas left on the galley counter of the *Lucky Dog*. If somebody was trying to give me bad luck, they would have stashed them where I couldn't find them, just like before. They wouldn't leave them in plain sight on the counter. Unless... unless maybe I walked in on them in the act and they got left there by accident. Unless whoever left them there had been hiding on the boat, and heard the conversation between me and Hambone. Unless that person told Gino what was said and...Ratdog came out of the bathroom. *Fucking Ratdog.*

"You!" I yelled, staring at him as he stepped out of the bathroom. "How could you do this? Why would—"

"Shut up," said Marco, but the damage was done. Ratdog looked pale. "I...I didn't know, it wasn't supposed to—"

"You shut the fuck up too! What, you're feeling guilty? Figures. Better empty out your pockets too." Marco pointed a gun at Ratdog, and kept the other aimed toward me and Ham on the couch.

Ratdog turned out the pockets of his shorts, which held a comb, some keys, and an impressive little wad of dough, that's it. Wait a second...*a comb? No way.* Then I looked at his hair and realized he had gotten it cut, and it actually looked clean. For once, Ratdog looked presentable. Now he was up shit's creek with us. Guess that's what happens when you turn over a new leaf with dirty hands.

"Wait a second you little weasel… no phone? I'm giving you five seconds to go back in there and get it. If I go in that bathroom and come out with a phone, I'm gonna chop your *fucking* head off!"

"I don't have one…I swear…I lost it." From his tone, and the hopeless look on his face, I didn't doubt him.

Neither, apparently, did Marco. "OK, put the comb in the bag and take out all the cash. Put the cash there on the chair." He pointed a gun at the chair behind him. Ratdog emptied our wallets and laid the cash on the chair. Suddenly the boat lost acceleration, and slowed to a drifting idle.

"Your cash too…dumbass," he said to Ratdog. "Where you're going they don't take cash, they take nutsac's…one bite at a time."

Chapter 79

Gino was gazing ahead, lost in the night and the drone of the engines, when his cell phone started lighting up on the dash. He looked at the depth finder and realized he was past the one-thousand-foot mark, approaching eleven hundred feet deep. It was time to get the dirty work done. He throttled down to idle, and picked up the phone. "Hello?"

"Gino it's me." It was his boss, Donny Nutz.

"Yeah, boss."

"So when you gonna take care of the problem?"

"Right now, it's done, problem solved."

"Done?"

"Yeah, just gotta tidy a few things up, then we're heading back in."

"Where are you?"

"Let me see," he glanced at the instrumentation. "We're about fourteen miles offshore, in the Gulf Stream, about eleven hundred feet deep."

"One thing I like about you, Gino, when a problem needs taking care of, you don't waste time."

"Like they say, boss, time is money...and if you got the money...I got the time."

"That's right, and after this job you got a nice chunk of both coming. Take the rest of the weekend off, go to the Bahamas or something...Hell, you're almost halfway there already."

"You know what? I just might do that, boss, thanks."

"Fuhgedaboutit...check in on Monday." Click.

Gino set the phone down and looked around in all directions. He faintly saw the light of a boat to the north, and a cruise ship farther out, and to the south. Nobody anywhere near enough to be concerned about. *Time to lighten the load.* He cut the engines and faced the bow to descend the ladder to the cockpit. Then he took a step down, and said, "Showtime."

Tangles had been hunkered down under the life raft, doing his best not to move for over forty minutes. He was worried that Gino might notice the corner cover of the inflatable wasn't fastened, but if he did, he didn't seem to care. Even though it was pretty flat out, the ride felt bumpy because he was lying on the hard fiberglass bow, which amplified the vibrations. Finally he heard the engines wind down, and felt the boat coast to a drift. He heard snippets of a conversation Gino was having with someone on the phone, and then nothing. He was straining to hear any sound that would indicate Gino was leaving the bridge, when he heard Gino say, "Showtime." *Shit.* He waited three seconds, and then worked his way out from under the raft, astonished by the depth of dark. There was no moon to be seen, and what stars there were seemed to be shrouded in haze, or clouds. Silently, he climbed up the covered windshield to the bridge. He slid under the aluminum railing, and rose to his knees, crawling forward to give himself a view of the cockpit below. Seeing nobody, he scooched backward out of sight, and waited...trying to figure out what to do next.

Gino stepped into the cabin to find Ratdog standing next to the guys on the couch. Marco stood a couple of steps away, pointing guns at them. He looked at Marco and tilted his head slightly to the side. "So the kid got squirrely, huh?"

"Yeah, he started getting all mushy, like he wanted to help 'em." Marco turned to Ratdog and sneered. "Well good fucking luck with that...*grease bag.*"

Ratdog replied, "I wasn't doing anything, just what he—"

"Shut up, kid—too late now...you first, out the door." Gino took a gun from Marco, and waved it at Ratdog, encouraging him to move it. As Ratdog stepped outside, Gino kept talking. "Good, stand in the corner there." Gino pointed the gun at the starboard corner of the cockpit, and Ratdog complied. Then Gino turned back to face the guys. "OK you two, out the door, ass to the transom— Now!" He stepped back so he and Marco each had a weapon pointed at them.

* * *

I looked at Hambone, and he looked bad, not just from the roughing up either. I was scared shitless to the point I didn't know what to do. I had already taken a speed train around my brain trying to come up with a plan, but missed the station.

"Are you guys *fucking crazy?*" I asked, as the first tendril of panic took hold. "You working for Sonny? Look, this is a mistake, even that douche bag wouldn't want you to go this far. You'll never get away with it. Just calm down and *think* about it for a second."

Gino looked at Marco, and they both busted out laughing. Marco said, "And you think *I* should do stand-up? That's seriously funny, man...you hear that, Gino? He thinks we work for Sonny."

With his gun pointed at me and still laughing, Gino slapped his thigh. "Oh that's good...*us* working for *Sonny?* I don't think so. That stiff couldn't find his ass with both hands—now move it." He pointed at the door and I stood up, somewhat surprised my legs cooperated.

"You too" he added, gesturing to Hambone.

As we stepped out the cabin door, I asked, "wait a second, if you're not working for Sonny, who *are* you working for? Why are you doing this?" As I reached the middle of the transom, I turned to face Gino. Hambone stood next to me, to port, with Ratdog in the starboard corner.

Gino grumbled. "You ask a lot of questions, you know that? Maybe if you weren't so nosy, if you minded your own fucking business, you wouldn't be here. You think about that yet?"

No, I was actually thinking it would be a great time to be hit by another rogue wave. "No, what I'm thinking is it doesn't make a bit of difference. You're gonna kill us anyways...So why?"

"Why? 'Cause my boss said so, that's why. 'Cause he's buying the marina from Sonny's old man, and he don't want you two clowns screwing it up. Now say you're prayers...but if you get on your knees, why don't you blow me first."

Gino and Marco both chuckled, and I looked at Hambone who flicked his eyes up toward the bridge. *Huh?*

Just then Ratdog pleaded, "Gino, you said nobody would get hurt! Don't do this, let us go...nobody'll say a thing!"

Gino stood facing me, with Marco on his right facing Hambone. Both their guns were pointed directly at our chests. Gino looked me straight in the eye as he responded to Ratdog. "You know you're right, kid, and I'm gonna let you go first...straight to *hell*, that is." He swung the gun away from my chest toward Ratdog and squeezed the trigger. The silencer made a spitting sound, and Ratdog's head snapped back when the bullet smashed into his forehead. His knees buckled and he crashed backward into the gunnel, then fell face-first on the deck. Blood was pouring from his head like somebody forgot to turn off the spigot. *Holy Christ!!*

Gino complained, "Shit, I thought he'd fall overboard. Quick, Marco, toss him over the side before he bleeds out." Marco handed Gino his gun, and stepped over to pick up Ratdog. I stood stunned, as Marco bent down to pick up his very dead body. Then I felt my left foot get stepped on. I slowly turned to the culprit Hambone, who was looking up at the bridge. My eyes followed, and to my utter amazement, there stood Tangles at the top of bridge ladder. *Tangles!* He had his finger held up perpendicular to his lips. I didn't say anything, but my eyes betrayed me in the cockpit light.

Gino noticed. "You think I'm gonna fall for that? The oldest trick in the book? Wait...here...let me turn to look so you two can jump all over me. Please, you guys watch too many movies. Well, sorry, assholes, but this don't have a happy ending, except for me and—"

That was the last word out of Gino's mouth before Tangles dove off the stairs like a Flying Wallenda, crashing into him. He landed on Gino's back, and yanked his arms down in an effort to dislodge the guns. Gino stumbled forward, and Hambone swung his taped up fists into the side of his head like he was throwing a hundred-pound cast net. It sounded like Mike Tyson punching a pig. One of Gino's guns fell to the cockpit floor as I heard the splash from Marco dumping Ratdog over the side. I dropped down to try to pick up the gun, but it was like trying to toss one of those rings around the bottle at the fair, physically impossible. *At least with my hands taped it was.* While I was on my knees however, I saw the sharp stainless steel edge of a rod holder poking out below the gunnel. Having a *MacGyver* moment, I reached up and began rubbing my taped wrists across the edge as hard as I could. Tangles was latched on to Gino like a democrat to a tax hike. He had his right arm around Gino's neck, and his legs wrapped around his waist. Gino managed to point his gun at Hambone, but as he squeezed the trigger, Tangles yanked it sideways with his left hand. The bullet tore straight through Marco's right shoulder, and he screamed as he staggered to the side of the boat. *Nice.*

I almost had my hands free from the tape, when I looked up to see Hambone lower his head and charge the wounded Marco. With a low center of gravity, and some two hundred and sixty-ish pounds of adrenaline-fueled fury, he launched himself like a world-class sprinter coming out of the blocks. I heard the crunching of bone as his head rammed Marco's sternum, and they went over the side with a splash. With a final scrape against the edge of the rod holder, my hands broke free, and I snatched the gun off the deck. Gino saw me come up with the gun and took a shot at me, but Tangles yanked his arm down and the bullet went through the cockpit floor. I heard more splashing in the water, and wanted to help Hambone, but needed to take care of Gino first.

As Tangles rode Gino around the cockpit, I danced around them like I was auditioning for *DWTS*...only one of the judges had a gun. I looked for a clear shot at Gino, but couldn't find one that didn't involve Tangles. *Shit.* It was gonna be risky, but I had to take one and get to Hambone, unless...I pointed the gun down, and fired twice at Gino's feet. Somehow I missed, putting a pair of holes through the cockpit floor. *Are you kidding me? Use two hands, dummy!* I fired twice more, and put another hole in the deck, but also managed to hit his right foot. He collapsed on the deck screaming an obscenity, and I shouted, "GO FOR HIS GUN!"

The moment Tangles released him from his choke hold, and grabbed for his gun, I kicked Gino squarely in the face. I was channeling Tom Dempsey, and kicked him so hard that when his head snapped back, I thought his neck broke. He fell face forward, and Tangles came up holding his gun. Gino's nose was shattered, and he was squirming around the bloody deck in pain. Tangles and I went to the side of the boat, and called out to Hambone.

For a second we didn't hear anything, then there was a loud splash, and "help...help...my hands!" It was Hambone's voice coming from out of the darkness.

Before I could react, Tangles handed me the gun he held, and hopped up on the gunnel. I started to say, "Wait, it'll be easier for—"

"Relax," he said. He reached into his pocket and pulled out a knife, opening the blade to its four-inch length. "You watch Gino. I'll cut Hambone loose so he can swim...I wasn't about to go all *Baywatch* on him."

I called for Hambone again and we heard his voice, followed by more splashing. Tangles got a fix on the location, and dove in. I heard him swimming as he called out to Hambone, and after a few seconds, I heard a bunch of splashing, and more voices. The splashing grew nearer, and finally Hambone appeared at the swim platform, with Tangles behind him. I had a gun in each hand, and tossed one in the water so I could open the transom door. Before I stepped out to help them though, I looked back at Gino. He was lying on his side on the floor, with one hand on his foot, and the other wiping blood off his face. I kept the gun in my right hand as I unhooked the small ladder that was attached to the swim platform. The water was lapping over my feet as I helped Hambone up. Like me, he had tape stuck to both wrists.

Tangles had my left hand, and I was pulling him up...when I saw his eyes go wide. He let go, yelling, "DUCK!"

I spun down to the right, but my left arm flailed up from being unexpectedly let go of. Hambone was in the process of diving back in, when the first shot rang out. *Holy shit was it loud!* I felt a slight burning in my left forearm as I went to my knees, and kept turning as I squeezed the trigger. My first shot was high and wide, passing through the top of one of the sliding doors. I overcompensated for having to shoot over the transom from my knees. The second shot hit Gino smack in the chest, however...just as he fired at my face. *BOOM!* I felt the hair above my right ear part as I squeezed off two more shots...this time with both hands on the gun. I watched as Gino staggered and fell backward, crashing through the splintered glass door.

I dropped the gun on the swim platform, and reached for where the bullet grazed my head. My hands were shaking and my heart felt like it was going to explode. I probed around my ear and looked at my hand. No blood. *Thank God!* Then I felt for the wound on my left arm, and my right hand came away with some blood. Quite a bit of blood. *Not good.* Hambone and Tangles came swimming back up to the platform.

Hambone said, "Jesus Christ! Are you all right?"

"Yeah, got winged in the arm though...don't think it's *too* bad."

Tangles said, "Man, I thought you were a goner. Good thing you kicked the shit out of his face—had to screw up his aim."

"You ain't shittin', but that was close...*way* too friggin' close...holy crap. Come on, guys, out of the water, we gotta do something." Still shaking, I helped Hambone up, and he walked over to Gino, while I helped Tangles. Tangles saw Hambone checking out Gino, and asked if he was dead.

"If he's not, he's a very sound sleeper with three misplaced tracheotomies in his chest. Yeah, he's dead.

Holy shit, I thought we were too. That is, until *your* pretty little face appeared on the bridge...thanks, man."

"Yeah, thanks, Tangles" I said, following him into the cockpit. "We owe you big time, we were seriously fucked."

"You don't owe me anything. We're even now—you saved me once too, remember? Hambone on the other hand..."

"Saved you? C'mon...I foul-hooked you, it was a fluke."

"Forget about it, what are we gonna do now?"

Hambone dragged Gino out by his heels, answering, "First we dump *this* asshole."

"Shit!" I said. "What about Marco? Where's Marco?"

Hambone dropped Gino's legs by the transom door, and I saw the ankle holster that minutes ago held the gun he tried to kill me with. Hambone bent down and turned out his pockets, discovering a big wad of cash. He pocketed it, saying, "We'll split it up later."

"Marco," I reminded him. "What about Marco?"

"Oh yeah, old Marco and I had a little meeting of the minds, you could say. I head-butted him while he was trying to drown me, and it knocked him out. That dickhead's stand-up days are over." He dragged Gino out through the transom door, and rolled him off the swim platform into the ocean. I thought to myself, who did Robo say he looked like? Baretta? Well, bye-bye Baretta...*don't do the crime if you can't do the brine.*

Hambone reached down and held up Gino's backup gun. "We need this anymore?"

"No," I said. "Pitch it."

Hambone tossed the gun in the water, and stepped back to the cockpit. With a flourish, he snatched Tangles up in a crushing bear hug. "I love you, man, you were un-fucking believable."

Tangles' face was turning red, and he gasped, "Pu...pu...put me down. I ca...I can't breathe."

He set him down, but continued with the much-deserved praise as I headed into the galley. "Dude, I'm serious, you need to go out west and join the rodeo. You were like a rabid monkey, superglued to his back, he couldn't shake you. Where'd you come from anyway?"

Tangles wasn't about to pass up a freebie. "Well, I'm originally from Baton Rouge, but—"

"No, smartass, I mean...where were you hiding?"

"Oh...on the bow, under the raft." They both walked in the cabin, stepping over broken glass.

Hambone exclaimed, "Man I could sure go—"

"For a beer?" I asked. Then turned around from the fridge and placed three cold Kalik's on the counter, next to a first aid kit I found in the bathroom. "How 'bout one of you patch up my arm while we have a coldie and figure out what to do?"

Hambone said, "Tangles? Sit down and relax, you've done enough, let me see that wound kit."

As Hambone examined my arm, I asked Tangles how in the hell he got on the boat. He explained how he came down the dock after his aborted date, and one thing led to another.

The bullet had gouged a path straight through the side of my arm. Fortunately, it was on the outside edge, and didn't appear to be serious. Hambone doused it in peroxide, smothered some antibiotic ointment on it, and expertly wrapped it in gauze. After re-examining his work, he taped it up, declaring, "I'm pretty sure the bullet passed right through, you should be fine as long you keep it clean."

Tangles looked up from the couch, and in a deep, slow, bayou drawl, said, "You know what, Hambone? You'd make a hell of a nurse...you know...one a them... man-nurses?"

Hambone just shook his head and we all laughed.

I raised my beer to take a swig, and glanced at the back of the boat where the sliders used to be. "Oh shit," I said. "Ho-Lee-Fucking shit."

Chapter 80

It wasn't Marco appearing on the swim platform like some barnacle-encrusted monster from a pirate movie that sent a chill through me, it was the glass fragments from the slider.

"What?" said Tangles, as he looked out the back. "What is it?"

"Look at the glass on the cockpit floor, it's moving."

"Christ! We're sinking!" cried Hambone.

"We need to get the hell off this boat," I said. "Tangles, the raft you hid under on the bow, did it seem to be in decent condition?"

"Yeah, as far as I could tell, it's got a small engine, and there's a davit too."

"OK, you two drop the raft over the side and try to get the engine started. I'll grab some provisions from the fridge, and try to make sure we don't leave anything behind that can be traced to us." I went to the ledge where the slider had been, and grabbed the bag with our personal belongings. Thankfully, they hadn't been tossed overboard. "Here, Hambone, take your stuff." He pulled out his belongings and I did the same. Then he and Tangles scrambled to the bow, and I picked the cash off the chair.

I grabbed a towel from the galley, wet it, and started wiping off fingerprints...In case the boat was discovered before it sank. I worked my way to the cockpit, and wiped off the gunnels, transom, and swim platform. All the while the water kept pulsing up through the bullet holes in the deck. *Shit.* I hurried back inside to double-check my work, and wiped down the galley counters. I opened the fridge and grabbed everything that was in there: two cans of Red Bull, two bottles of water, and three more beers. I also found some pretzels, a flashlight, and a screwdriver. I put it all in a trash bag, along with the first aid kit. I heard some clanking metallic sounds coming from the bow, and hoped everything was going OK as I headed up to the bridge.

Seawater was steadily pumping up through three of the four small bullet holes, more or less located on the port side of the deck. *How can those little holes cause the boat to sink so quickly?* My fleet sloshed through the water as I stepped to the ladder and climbed up to the bridge. I found a cell phone, and tossed it overboard as I turned the key to the port engine, which was dead. I turned the key to the starboard engine, and surprisingly, it fired right up. Well, maybe not surprisingly, as I could see from the bridge we were listing to port. It seemed the starboard engine was still dry. Hambone and Tangles had the raft in the water, and Ham was feverishly pulling the starter cord on the small outboard.

The dash was lit up with an impressive array of instrumentation, and I recognized the Raymarine chart plotter as being a newer version of the one I had on the *Lucky Dog*. My *MacGyver* mojo was working overtime as I pulled up a map of West End, Bahamas, and started punching in coordinates on the autopilot.

I set the sinking vessel on a course that would take it just north of West End. That is, until the engine died and the boat foundered.

I heard the sound of the little outboard engine sputter to life, and a cry of triumph let out by Hambone. "Yes! We're in business, baby!" Tangles was standing in the cockpit, on the port side. He had water splashing over his open-toed sandals, and was holding the raft by a rope. I clambered down the ladder to join him, and handed him the bag with the supplies.

He handed the bag down to Hambone, and I pulled out my wallet and phone. "Hang on to these too."

"What? Why?"

"After I go through the cabin once more, I'm gonna go up to the bridge and throttle the engine up a little. You guys follow me in the raft, and once I have it going the right way, I'll climb down and jump on."

"All right, but hurry up," urged Hambone. "There's dead bodies floating around out here."

"You got a couple of oars, right?" I asked.

He reached under one side and held up an oar. "One on each side...let's go!"

I hurried into the cabin and wiped off the fridge, cabinets, and anything else I could think of. Then I stood in the cockpit and surveyed the scene. There was blood and glass swishing around everywhere. I climbed back up to the bridge, aimed the boat toward the Bahamas, and started wiping down the dash and steering wheel. I pushed the throttle up so the boat was going six or seven knots, engaged the autopilot, and started wiping my way down the steps.

The boat was listing about five or ten degrees to port, and it was almost ankle deep when I reached the cockpit floor. Hambone was driving the raft behind the boat, and as I sloshed my way back to the swim platform, he yelled, "COME ON...JUMP!"

I walked through the transom door to the swim platform, took one last look over my shoulder, and jumped for the raft. I landed with my arms draped over the bow, and my legs in the water, wincing from the pain in my left arm. As Ham eased off the throttle, Tangles pulled on my collar, and a few leg kicks later I was sitting in the front of the raft. Ham circled the raft around, and asked, "OK, any suggestions on a heading?" I sat up and could barely see shore lights. "I set the autopilot on a course that should take the boat just north of West End. I think we should head in the opposite direction while we can still see its lights."

"Sounds good to me, how far off do you think we are?"

"According to the last GPS reading, we're about fifteen miles east-northeast of the inlet. How fast does this thing go?"

"Shit, are you kidding me? I could barely keep up with the boat. With us in it, I'd say maybe seven or eight miles an hour tops. Plus, we're fighting the Gulf Stream, which is pushing us three or four knots to the north. This is gonna take awhile."

"Man, I can't believe those tiny holes could cause the boat to start sinking so quickly."

"Maybe one of the bullets took out a through-hull transducer, creating a bigger hole in the bottom of the hull. Hell, I don't know...doesn't matter now."

I pressed the Indiglo light on my Timex Expedition, and saw it was eleven thirty.

"How much gas we have?"

"Looks like a two, two and a half gallon tank, seems full. Should be enough, right?"

"Hell if I know. What kind of motor is it?"

"It's a little eight horsepower Yamaha, seems to be running OK."

"Let's keep our fingers crossed, I don't feel like rowing. Jesus, can you believe those guys were gonna kill us?"

"Fuck that...I can't believe we killed them instead, talk about an upset. Sure wish a little bit of that would rub off on the Dolphins this season."

"The *Dolphins?* Are you kidding me? We got three dead guys, and a blood-spattered, sinking boat nearby...and you're talking about the *Dolphins?*"

"I'm just saying, it would be nice, you know, if—"

"Enough about the Dolphins already! Let's have something to drink, and see what this little engine can do. Tangles...the bag?" Tangles reached down between his legs and came up with three beers, naturally. There was a moment of panic when we realized they weren't twist off, but Hambone had a bottle opener key chain. *Naturally.*

Everybody took a big slug of beer, and Tangles handed me the first aid kit. "You should probably take some meds before we get going. I'll shine the light while you see what's in the kit." I heeded his advice and took three Advil, sticking a couple more of the little sample size packets in my pocket.

I watched the lights on *The Job* grow fainter as it struggled into the night, and said, "OK, Ham, crank that mother up, let's get outta here."

Hambone took a final look back at the position of the listing boat, and twisted the throttle. The engine strained, but managed to push the raft along at *maybe* eight knots. Fortunately, the wind had died to a wisp, and the seas were flat. A far cry from what the conditions would be when the system moving up from the Dominican Republic reached us. Tangles and I laid low in the raft, and we finished our beers as Hambone steered toward shore. I closed my eyes and tried to get some rest, but I was too amped up from my first, and hopefully last, shootout. Sometime later, Ham slowed the raft down. I checked my watch and it was almost one in the morning. Tangles and I sat up, and looked toward shore.

"Can you make out anything?" asked Hambone.

"Well...I see lights. We're heading in the right direction, that's for sure," said Tangles.

I squinted and looked as hard as I could, but it was just a blur. "Nope, can't make out a thing, we're still too far off. How's the gas?

"Lower, maybe a gallon or so left."

"Super, anybody want some water?" Tangles pulled out a bottle of water, and we passed it around till it was gone. *It was gone quick.*

"I think I'm gonna head us a little more easterly, rather than southeast, what do you think?"

"Your call, Ham, you're the captain...right, Tangles?"

"Hell yeah, all those shore lights look the same to me. Go for it."

Hambone set a new course, and in seconds we were slapping along the ocean, hoping we would get to land before the gas ran out.

Chapter 81

About forty-five minutes later, Hambone throttled down again, pointing toward shore.

"That's the Lake Worth pier, I'm almost positive."

I strained my eyes, looking at the lights, which seemed to be about a mile away.

"I'll take your word for it, Ham, but without being able to see the water tower behind it, I can't be sure. How much gas is left?"

"We're getting low, I was really pushing it the last leg. What do you want to do? Beach the raft here?"

"Hell no, if the boat gets discovered before it sinks, the authorities will see the raft is missing, and start a search. It can probably be traced back to the boat, so we *definitely* don't want to be seen on it. In fact, we need to make it disappear altogether."

"Shit," said Tangles. "How we gonna do that?"

"Let me think a second...we certainly can't go through the inlet, even if we have enough gas to get there. It'll be close to three by then, and with the sheriff's station there, and the Coast Guard nearby, we're damn near certain to be seen and stopped. "

Hambone suggested, "What about ditching somewhere north of the inlet? There aren't many beach houses, and lots of good cover. We can make our way to the road and get someone to pick us up."

"Good call, I know the perfect spot if we can make it. Wait! Our phones...we still have our phones."

Ham pulled out his phone. "Shit...I got four missed calls from my wife. I forgot I switched to silent mode for the captain's meeting. She might actually be worried. I better call."

Tangles handed me my phone, and I looked at the display. "I was on silent too, but hang on...you can't call her without a cover story. She can't know anything about this...nothing at all...think about it. You can bet that Gino and Marco's boss, whoever that is, is gonna be pissed when he finds out they went missing along with his boat. He'll want to find who's responsible. Your wife could be in danger if she knows we had anything to do with it."

"Shit, what'll I tell her?"

Tangles jumped in. "Tell her you got drunk at the captain's meeting, and ended up passing out on the *Lucky Dog* after partying with me and Kit. Tell her you'll drive home as soon as you sober up, in an hour or two."

"*Damn,* that's good. Remind me to consult you for future alibis."

I had been checking my missed calls while Tangles laid out an alibi for Hambone. I had two missed texts, and two missed calls. The first text was from Melody, about still wanting to see me, and the second was from my buddy Big Mike, wanting to know if the tournament was still on. The two missed calls were from Holly. With the engine idling in the background, I listened to her last message. "Kit, it's me again, is everything OK?

You said you would call after the captain's meeting. Call me whenever you get this message. Millie's not doing well, I'm up with the nurse...taking care of her. I hope everything's OK, bye." I looked at the time the message was left and it read 1:15 a.m. She sounded worried. *I know I was.* "Ham, do you think we can risk shutting down the engine while we make a couple of calls?"

"Yeah, I think so...it's plenty warm. Besides, I have to call Mo before she goes looking for me. Who are you gonna call?"

"Our ride home...Holly. She just left me a message saying she's up taking care of Millie. She's worried too. I was supposed to call her after the captain's meeting. She's at Millie's, right around the corner from the inlet...so I'm gonna ask her to pick us up. She's already involved anyways...It's our plan to dig up the tanks that got us in this mess. Let's keep the calls short though, with the engine off we'll be drifting the wrong way. In fact, Tangles and I will paddle while you talk, and you can paddle while I talk."

Tangles handed me an oar, and we both started paddling toward shore as soon as Hambone killed the engine. His wife, Maureen, finally seemed to calm down after a little shouting could be heard from his phone. Less than a minute later, he hung up. "She bought it...she's pissed...but she bought it. OK, Kit, your turn."

I handed Ham my oar, and dialed Holly. Even though my watch said it was almost two in the morning, she picked up on the second ring. "Kit? Is everything OK? I've been worried."

"Yeah, well...not exactly. I could really use a ride."

"Now? Why? Where are you?"

"Not now, in about a half hour or so. I'll call you when we get to shore."

"What? We? Your fishing? What's going on?"

"I'll explain everything later. I'm with Hambone and Tangles. Can you do it?"

"Of course, where am I picking you up?"

"Fourth driveway north of the inlet, pull over on the shoulder. We'll be in the bushes on the beach side."

"What about the people who live there?"

"There's nobody living there, the estate's in probate...that's why I picked it. You still need to watch for the Manalapan cops though, don't pull over unless the coast is clear."

"Kit, what happened? Is everybody all right?"

"We're fine, as long as you meet us there. Don't leave the house till I call."

"OK, be careful."

"We will, see you in a bit...and thanks." I hung up and pointed to shore. "You were right, Hambone. That's the pier, look...there's the Ritz. Let's get going."

"Just north of the inlet? That's where you wanna go?"

"Yeah, but run us in closer to shore, and then head south, just in case we run out of gas."

"Here we go." Hambone pulled the starter cord and the little engine fired right up. He ran us in to about a quarter mile from shore, and then headed south, past the Ritz, and the mansions of Manalapan. After we passed Chillingsworth curve, the mansions went from being east of A1A to west of A1A. Halfway between the curve and the inlet, the engine started to sputter.

"Shit," said Hambone.

"Point us toward shore," I urged. "Tangles, come on, let's paddle." Tangles and I paddled as the engine continued to sputter, and we were about two or three hundred yards from shore when it quit altogether.

"Any way to dump the engine?" I asked.

"I dunno, can't see shit, it's too dark...gimme that flashlight." We kept paddling while Hambone shined the flashlight on the raised engine.

Less than a minute later, he gave his prognosis. "Looks like there's six screws holding the engine mounting plate to the bracket. If I can get them out, it should be bombs away."

Tangles reached in the trash bag and handed the screwdriver to him. "Here you go."

I said, "Have at it. It'll be way easier to get rid of the raft if we can drop it. Tangles and I will paddle us south, parallel to shore, and we'll head in once you lose the engine. For the record, if we weren't in such serious shit, I would never consider dumping the engine. I know you guys feel the same way."

"It goes without saying," said Tangles. "Dumping bodies is one thing, but dumping pollutants is crossing the line."

"Exactly. The only oil leaking out of those goons is from hair gel, and the rest is fish food."

Hambone laughed. "Amen to that, but Tangles needs to hold the flashlight for me. You're gonna have to paddle by yourself...how's the arm?"

"Guess we'll find out, at least it'll be good practice for digging, here goes." I kneeled in the bow and alternately rowed left, right, left, right...finally finding a rhythm.

In five minutes Hambone had four of the screws out. "We're lucky, somebody sprayed this with some WD40 or something not too long ago, they're coming out easy."

"Hurry up then, my arm's not too bad, but my back's killing me." Truth was, my arm hurt a little more than I let on. It was bleeding through the bandage, and dripping down on my hand as I rowed.

The last couple of screws took him a little longer to remove. He let out a few "son- of- a- bitches," but finally got them all out. "That's it, soon as I tilt the engine back down, it should slide right off. What do you think?"

I looked around in the dark and saw a couple of fishing boats straight out the inlet, but they were a good mile away. "I say drop that sucker, then we hightail it to shore."

Hambone tilted the engine back down, but it didn't fall off. "Oh, come on!" He smacked the engine twice with his open palm, and it made a brief scraping sound before disappearing with a splash. The rear of the raft popped up a little after losing the weight of the engine, and he said, "That's more like it...now hand me an oar. You ready, Kit?"

"Ready, willing, and semi-able...just *try* to hang with el gimpo."

I knew I could never keep up with him, especially with a bum arm. I was just using a little reverse psychology to get him to row like hell so I didn't have to...and it worked. Thanks to Hambone's furious stroke, we were at the shoreline in a flash. I was first out of the raft, and jumped into knee-deep water.

"What do you wanna do?" asked Tangles. "Drag this into the sea grass and hide it?"

"Something like that," I replied. "But not here. Let's keep the raft in the water and tow it up the beach a little farther. I know the perfect place to stash it."

Hambone said, "Give me the bow line. I'll walk it down the shore, you go find the hiding spot."

"Good idea. Come on, Tangles, let's go." I grabbed the flashlight and we jogged down the beach about three hundred yards, before slowing to a walk.

I was tired, and apparently so was Tangles. "Please... tell me we're...tell me we're there," he panted, between breaths.

I bent over to catch my breath too. "Yeah, we're close...come on...this way." I struggled up the slope of sand to the high-water mark, and walked into the sea grass. Then I shined the flashlight toward the ground and swept it back and forth, before switching it off.

"What are we looking for?" whispered Tangles.

"A path...but we're too far north I think, come on." We walked back to the sand and jogged a little farther toward the inlet. After making sure the coast was clear, I stepped back into the tall wispy grass, Tangles following. I turned the light on and held it low to the ground again, swinging it back and forth a few times before seeing it. "There, there it is, there's the path. Quick, find a stick or something that we can use to mark it."

Tangles ran back to the beach and came back with a couple of sticks about three feet long. I stuck one in the ground at the start of the path, then walked east through the sea grass till I hit the beach, and stuck in the other one. "OK, let's go help Hambone."

We ran down to the water and Hambone was about seventy-five yards away. He was slogging through knee-to-waist high water, the raft in tow. I noticed the waves had kicked up a little, and were slowing his progress. When we reached him, I asked Tangles if he had his knife handy.

"Yeah, right here." He pulled the knife out of his pocket and opened the blade, handing it to me handle first.

"Thanks, I think we should let a little air out of the raft, it'll be easier to carry."

Hambone asked, "Is this far enough? Man...I'm pooped."

"Yeah, this is good...let's drag it up on the beach." We hauled the raft out, and I slashed the sides with Tangles' knife. It wasn't nearly as heavy, minus the engine.

As the air hissed out, Hambone plopped down in the sand, saying, "I need a minute." I looked in the deflating raft, and saw two Red Bulls and a bottle of water lying in the corner. I grabbed the water, and offered it to Ham. "Here, drink some water."

Hambone started gulping it down, just as it started to drizzle. I opened a Red Bull and washed down a couple more Advil.

"Shit, it's starting to rain," said Tangles.

I jumped on the raft to try to push the air out faster, and he joined me as Hambone finished off the water.

A little thunder rumbled in the distance as Hambone rose from the sand. He plopped back down on the bow of the raft, effectively forcing the remaining air out of the knife holes with the thrust of a NASA rocket. He said, "We better get moving before it gets ugly. Which way, Kit?"

"It's just a little ways up, I'll take the bow, and you guys follow." I grabbed the front of the raft with my good arm, while Tangles and Hambone grabbed the rear. We marched down the beach, and then up the dune to the sea grass. I turned on the flashlight and shined it around quickly, flicking it off after I spied the piece of wood stuck in the sand. We carried the raft over to it, and I said, "OK, we just walk straight through the grass for about thirty yards, then we'll pick up the trail. Follow me." After going what I estimated to be about thirty yards, I stopped and turned the light on again, locating the second piece of wood about ten feet to the left of us. "There's the start of the path, come on." The rain was coming down harder now, and we were about to be totally soaked when it suddenly got drier with every step.

"What the hell?" said Hambone.

"What? What is it?" Tangles apparently hadn't noticed, because he was walking under the raft, while Hambone and I carried it.

"It stopped raining on us, that's what, only I can still hear it coming down. Where the hell *are* we, Kit?"

I stopped walking, and announced, "This is good, we can stash it here."

When I flicked on the light, and shined it around, Tangles and Hambone simultaneously said, "*What the?...*"

"It's a tunnel, cut out of a stand of sea grape trees. It leads up to a little beach house near A1A, where Holly's gonna pick us up. See that little space between the trunks there?" I shined the light to a gap in the path. "Let's shove the raft in there and cover it up, just in case anybody comes down here before we get rid of it."

"How do you even *know* about this place?" Hambone asked.

"I'll tell you about it when we're up by the street waiting for Holly...Come on, let's get this thing hid."

Tangles scrounged around for some branches and dead leaves, while Ham and I tucked the crumpled raft off to the side of the tunnel. Once we thought we had it adequately covered, I led us to the end of the path. We stood in silence for a moment, looking at the darkened beach house.

"How do you know nobody's home?" whispered Tangles.

"An old Hollywood movie actress lived here for years, and she passed away a few months ago. The property is in probate, and it's vacant...at least it should be."

"How do you know?" said Hambone.

"A friend of mine is one of her heirs, and is trying to buy the place. The main house is across the street on the intracoastal, and there's a guest cottage too. I used to spend a lot of time here. You guys stay put, while I go check to make sure no one's home."

I left the shelter of the tunnel, and got soaked as I ran the twenty feet to the side of the beach house. I inched my way around to the kitchen and looked in...it looked empty. I walked around the other side and peered into the only bedroom, which was faintly illuminated by a yellow bug light on the corner of the house. As expected, it was empty too. *Good, nobody home.* I ran back to the tunnel. "No one's there, I'm calling Holly." I pulled out my phone, which was a little wet, and wiped it on Tangles' shirt. "You mind? I'm soaked."

"My shirt is your shirt."

"Actually, that is one of my shirts...isn't it?"

"Fuck you, I bought this at the mall— call Holly."

I looked at my watch, and it was five minutes to three. Holly picked up on the first ring this time. "Kit, are you there?"

"Yeah, you ready to come get us?"

"I told the nurse I would relieve her at four. That's when she goes home, she thinks I'm sleeping. The day nurse won't be here until nine, I'll slip out as soon as I hang up."

"OK, listen...as soon as you cross over the inlet, go slow and flash your headlights if there's no cars around. We'll run into the street and wave you down."

"I'm on my way."

"See you in a few, thanks." We waited under the dryness of the sea grape canopy for about four or five minutes before heading up to the street. As we ran around the side of the house, headlights swept through the rain, heading north on A1A. I stopped in my tracks, and the guys bumped into me as the speeding car passed, not twenty feet away. It was a Manalapan Police car. Thank God it was heading north instead of south, the direction Holly would be coming from.

"That was a cop." whispered Hambone.

"I know. He's headed away from us, that's good." We crept up the stone path that led to the street, and ducked down behind the chest-high gate, which was bordered by a hedge on each side. Not a minute later, I saw headlights coming from the south, and suddenly they flashed on and off. I went to open the gate and it was locked, so I swung my legs over the top and stepped into the street, waving my hands. Holly pulled off to the side in her Jeep Grand Cherokee Laredo 4x4, and I jumped in the passenger seat.

Holly asked, "Kit, what's going on? Are you all right?"

"Yeah, we need to get out of here though." A few moments later, Hambone and Tangles piled into the backseat.

"What took you so long?" I asked. Holly turned the Jeep around in the street and headed back over the inlet.

"I had to lift Tangles over the gate—little fucker's heavy," replied Hambone.

"I was doing just fine without you, until my shorts got snagged on something."

"That's what she said."

"Enough already," said Holly. "Will *somebody* please tell me what the heck's going on?"

"I'll fill you in at the marina," I answered.

"You want me to go to the marina?"

"Yeah, our vehicles are there." The street was deserted as we drove past the Ocean Ridge Police Department, and then over the Ocean Avenue Bridge that overlooked the marina. As we crossed the bridge in the pouring rain, a flash of lightning lit up the night, and a loud thunderclap followed.

"Man, that was close," said Tangles.

"This kind of rain is exactly what we need for our plan to work," I said. "And in light of tonight's events, we better push up the dig by twenty-four hours. Hambone, before you zonk out, you need to tell the other guys we're digging early Sunday, and not early Monday." I looked at my watch and it was three fifteen. "That's just less than twenty-four hours from now. Everybody should be on the *Lucky Dog* by midnight tonight."

"That shouldn't be a problem, why do you want to move it up though?"

Holly turned into the marina and interrupted. "In light of what events? What happened to you guys tonight? Hambone, where's your truck?"

Ham pointed out his truck, which was hard to miss because there were only a couple of other cars in the lot, and his truck had "Ham it Up Charters," written on the side.

"We need to move it up, because by Sunday afternoon there could be some people down here asking questions."

Holly pulled in front of Ham's truck, and he said, "Good idea, I'll tell the guys. We'll be at the boat by midnight."

"You should probably carpool it too—the fewer cars the better...and get plenty of rest."

"I'm gonna sleep like a rock, no doubt about it." He opened the door, and as he stepped into the rain, he turned, saying, "Tangles? I owe you, I owe you big time. Thanks, man." He reached his big paw inside and squeezed Tangles' shoulder, before shutting the door.

Just before it closed, Holly caught sight of my arm in the dome light. "Oh my God, Kit! What happened to your arm? It's bleeding. Will you please tell me what the heck happened?"

"Drive over to my boat, and I'll start filling you in. It has to do with our plan to stop the marina sale." She crossed the parking lot and pulled up next to the Beemer.

I asked, "You still got the boat key, right Tangles?"

"Yeah, boss."

"Like I told Ham, rest up good, tonight's the night. If you get a chance, sniff around the ship's store in the afternoon. Let me know if you hear anything...and thanks...thanks for sticking your neck out like you did. I owe you too, just like Ham."

Tangles opened the door, and as he stepped out in the rain, said, "If I had known you guys were gonna get all mushy on me, I woulda let 'em shoot you." He shut the door, and we watched through the headlights as he jumped on the boat, and went in the cabin.

I turned to Holly, and she had a horrified look on her face. "*Shoot* you? Did he say *shoot* you? Kit, my God, is that what happened to your arm? Did you get shot? "

"Yep, my first and hopefully last bullet wound, but trust me, it could have been a whole lot worse. You should see the other guys." She put her hand over her mouth, and then dropped it to the steering wheel and started backing up.

"Where are you going? My car is—"

"Forget about your car. I'm taking you to the hospital, you've been shot!"

"It's not that bad, really it isn't, it just looks that way with all the blood. Besides, you can't take me to the hospital, the police will be called...and that would be bad."

"All right, then, I'm taking you back to the house. Thanks to Millie, we've got more meds and bandages than a small pharmacy. I can clean the wound and change the dressing myself. Oh my God, Kit...what happened?"

Chapter 82

We made it back to Millie's, but not without some drama. As we headed back up A1A, an Ocean Ridge cop was sitting in the park parking lot, and followed us. It was three thirty in the morning, and he was probably licking his chops until we turned in to Sabal Island. He followed us to the end of the little island, where we turned into Millie's driveway. The cop flashed his headlights and drove off, as if saying, "Just making sure you belong." *Phew*. We had just experienced the upside to a little demographic profiling at its finest.

I filled Holly in up to the point where we were led out to the cockpit of *The Job*, and Ratdog was killed. I wasn't entirely comfortable with telling her the rest, and was glad for the chance to collect myself as we ran to the house through the rain. I followed Holly around to the side, where we discreetly entered through the kitchen door.

When she turned on the light, she said, "your arm looks even worse in the light, hold it over the sink while I round up some bandages." I did, but not before going in the fridge and pulling out a bottle of water and a beer.

I finished the water, and was drinking a Heiney Light when she came back with a handful of bandages and ointments. "I need to get you fixed up before the nurse gets off, so bear with me."

"Bear with you? Does that include hibernation? I'd like that right now, a few months alone with you in a cave. Do they have caves in the Caribbean?"

She smiled, "Are you sure you didn't injure your head? That was incredibly lame, cute...but lame."

"As lame as this?" I waved my injured arm over the sink like Rodney Dangerfield in *Caddyshack*, and did my best impression of him. "My arm...I think it's broke!"

"Oh my God." She laughed. "You *did* take a header. Now stop it...let me take that bandage off and get you fixed up." I decided to can the cornball routine, and let her do her thing. She cut away Hambone's gauze job, and started rinsing my arm off in the sink.

When she got the blood scrubbed off, she peered at the wound closely. "You're right...I think...maybe it's not as bad as it looked." She took a Q-Tip and dunked it in peroxide. "I need to clean out the inside, just to be safe...this might hurt a little."

"That's what most doctors say right before they inflict blinding pain. Be gentle."

"Suck it up, big boy, it's just a little peroxide. Here we go..." She pushed the Q-Tip into the small hole in the side of my arm, and kept on pushing and twisting until it came out the other side, some two inches away. You could say it hurt. You could also say I could barely stifle an eardrum-shattering scream.

"You OK?" she asked, noting the lack of color in my face. "Sorry about that. Let me do it once more from the other direction, and then I'll get you bandaged up."

"*Again?* You want to do that *again?* I should have asked if you have the same last name as Millie, or if it's actually Mengele, as I now suspect."

"Very funny. Come on, one more time, and then no more ouchy...I promise."

"No more ouchy? Easy for you to say...*Jesus.*"

She repeated the procedure, and I actually broke out in a cold sweat, steadying myself with my good arm by clutching the countertop. She dabbed the wound dry with a paper towel, put some Neosporin on it, and bandaged it up like before. "There you go, that wasn't so bad now? Was it?"

"I guess it depends on how you define the word 'so'...but thanks anyways."

"It's almost four. Let me check on Millie and let the nurse go, then you can finish telling me what happened." I watched her walk through the living room to Millie's bedroom, then grabbed another beer and went for the couch. I sent texts to Jamie and Big Mike, to say the tournament was cancelled. I didn't know for sure at that point, but the way the rain was coming down, it seemed more than likely. Regardless, the *Lucky Dog* was not leaving the dock, tournament or not.

I clicked on the tube, making sure it was muted, and found my way to the Weather Channel. I stretched out on the couch and set my beer down after a few long pulls, pleased to see my boy Dave Schwartz doing his late night shtick. "Yes, my sunny southern friends, it's time to break out those galoshes from Key Largo to Palm Beach...and some parts of the Bahamas. Do they even *have* galoshes in the Bahamas? Good question...I don't know...but I do know my Hungarian grandmother made a TREMENDOUS galosh. We'll be right back with the full Tropical Update at ten till the hour. See you then, friends." *God I love Dave Schwartz.* I was exhausted, but wanted to see the Tropical Update, so I decided to just rest my eyes for a minute.

* * *

Five minutes later, after walking the night nurse to the door, Holly came around the kitchen and saw Kit's bare feet sticking out from the couch. She started saying "OK, so you were all in the back—" then stopped talking when she realized Kit was fast asleep... and snoring, on the couch. *No!* It was killing her that she still didn't know what happened, and she briefly considered shaking him awake, but she just couldn't.

She leaned over and propped his bandaged arm up across his chest, then picked up his half-empty beer bottle, and went in the kitchen. After getting a spare sheet from the hall closet, she turned off the Weather Channel and knelt next to him, draping the sheet from his toes to his chin. With the touch of an entomologist handling an injured butterfly, she brushed back his thick brown hair and kissed him on the forehead.

Suddenly, a flash of lightning lit up the darkened room. She soaked up his presence, shuddering when the thunder rumbled a few seconds later. She kissed him tenderly on the lips, and laid her head down under his chin, feeling the gentle heave of his chest. As she reached her arm across his body to hug him, she whispered, "Oh, Kit...what have I gotten us into?"

Chapter 83

I woke up from a dead sleep to the intoxicating smell of bacon. My watch read 10:00 a.m., and when I used my left arm for support to roll of the couch, I winced. Looking at the bandage on my arm, I reacted the same way you do when a complete stranger mistakes you for someone else. Basically like, "What? Who? Me? *Who are you?*" I stared at it for another second, and then the surreal night before came crashing into today's reality. Some guy really tried to kill me last night, and I ended up killing him instead. *Holy shit! I killed a man!* I shot him dead...and dumped him in the ocean along with a couple of other dead guys. *Oh man, oh man, this is bad.*

Just then, Holly came around the corner. "I thought I heard you get up, I have some break—" She stopped in midsentence when she saw my face with its *what have I done?* look, written all over it.

"Kit? What is it? Come on, have something to eat and tell me what happened last night."

"Where's the nurse?"

"She's with Millie in her room. She normally doesn't come in the kitchen until lunchtime."

"How's Millie?"

415

"Not so great. Now come on, I made some scrambled eggs and toast to go with the bacon. You want a cup of coffee?"

"Yes, thanks." I followed Holly in to the kitchen and grabbed a bottle of water from the fridge, gulping it down while she heaped a pile of eggs and bacon on a plate for me. Then I used the restroom, and re-joined her at the kitchen table. I was starving, having only eaten some finger food at the captain's meeting the previous night. "Holly, I'm famished. Let me get a little food in my stomach and then I'll tell you everything. Thanks for helping out last night."

"You don't have to thank me. Now eat before it gets cold."

She didn't have to tell me twice. I annihilated the entire serving in about three minutes. At her suggestion, I plated up a second time, then sat back down.

"Wow, you weren't kidding you're hungry. Think you can fill me in between bites?"

I poured some more ketchup over my eggs, smushed it around, and continued the debriefing. "OK, where were we?" She didn't say a peep as I recounted how Tangles saved us by suddenly appearing on the bridge, and then jumping on Gino's back after he shot Ratdog. Nor did she say anything when I described the crushing hit that Hambone laid on the wounded Marco, landing them in the drink. Then I told her how Gino suddenly pulled a gun from an ankle holster and shot at me from about six feet away, hitting my arm, and grazing my head. She had her hand over her mouth as I described firing back, and watching him crash through the sliding cabin doors.

That was as far as I got before she jumped up from her seat. "My God! You were almost killed!..All of you!...I'm so sorry for getting you into this."

Tears welled up in her eyes, and I tried to downplay it. "*Almost*, is the key word. Everybody's OK...everybody but the bad guys, that is."

She looked a little panicky, and as I got up from the table, she rushed into my arms and buried her head in my chest.

I stroked her back, and she pulled away. "We... we have to go to the police, right? It was self-defense, that's what it was. You'll be all right...right?"

"Yeah I'll be all right, but we can't go to the police, at least not now, maybe not ever."

"What do you mean?" She looked at me like I was crazy. "You think nobody will miss these people? You think you can just act like it never happened and go about your business?"

"I didn't say that. In fact, I'm extremely worried about who might miss these people. They were a couple of thugs, mobster types, who didn't think twice about killing us to make sure the marina deal closes. But they were hired hands. It's their boss I'm worried about, the one who's suppose to buy the marina from Slade. When he discovers his boat and his boys are missing, you can bet he'll want answers...and payback. If we go to the police now, there'll be no way to stop the sale of the marina. Plus, me, Ham, and Tangles will have targets on our backs. No...we can't go to the cops. We need to play it by ear, and see if any of the bodies...or the boat...gets discovered first."

"The boat? Of course they'll find the boat...won't they?"

"Maybe, maybe not." I finished telling her how the boat was sinking when I sent it toward the Bahamas on autopilot. "If it didn't sink before getting into Bahamian waters, there's no telling what might happen to it. If the engine died soon after we abandoned it, it could be half sunk and drifting in the Gulf Stream right now, somewhere north of the Bahamas. Who knows? Maybe some Bahamian fisherman finds it and calls his cousin, who tows it in and strips it for parts. There's no telling, we just have to wait and see."

"I can't believe all this happened over the C-LOVE Marina."

"Me neither."

"Why would a mobster want to buy the marina? Why would Slade sell it so fast when he's wanted it forever, and has all these big plans for it?"

"Excellent questions, and ones I'd like to have the answers to, but first we dig up those tanks and queer the deal."

"I can't believe you still want to go through with this. You're *crazy*."

"I'm pissed too. No way I'm gonna sit by and let some mobster who tried to have me whacked take over the marina, no way."

"Kit, you said it yourself, he's gonna be wanting answers once he finds out his boat and his guys are gone. If our plan works, and we stop the marina sale, it will make him even madder. He'll be out for blood."

"Yeah, but whose? First he has to realize they're missing, and then he has to figure out what happened. He won't know that we didn't get whacked until he finds out the tanks got dug up. If we do that tonight, he may not know there's a problem until it's too late.

There's no guarantee he knows who we are either. Ratdog can't tell him. Unless his thugs identified us to him by name, he won't have a clue. Ratdog...the poor bastard, tried to help after realizing what he got us into. Even *he* didn't deserve what he got."

"What about me? If we dig up the tanks, and I end up as the new owner of the marina, won't he come after me? He'll think I was involved, and he'll be right."

"That's the part I haven't quite figured out yet, but there's no reason to think he knows about you. Millie's still the owner, and you won't officially own the marina until..."

"Don't remind me...oh my God, this is crazy...what are we gonna do?"

"Stick to the plan."

Chapter 84

The rain was steady until about four in the afternoon, when it eased to a drizzle, but the tournament was still postponed because more rain was coming. The Mother Nature part of our plan was falling nicely into place, now we had to do our part and make the rest happen. Hambone, Eight-Toe, and Kodak showed up at the *Lucky Dog* right at midnight. Holly, Tangles, and I were already there. I wanted them at the boat early, because it wouldn't look as suspicious as them showing up at two or two thirty. The plan was pretty simple. Holly and Tangles would be posted as lookouts, and the rest of us would dig. I had picked up another pair of walkie-talkies, to go with the four shovels and large tarp, sitting in the trunk of the Beemer.

The six of us sat and watched Carl "The Nose" Parker, on the Weather Channel. He said that our area had received almost three inches of rain already. "Yes, folks, it's a wet one down in South Florida thanks to this tropical depression that originated in the Dominican Republic." He pointed to a blob of green on the TV screen, and traced his finger down to the Caribbean. "Surface radar shows a break in the heavy rain over the last several hours, but don't put those

421

umbrellas away just yet, this systems got plenty more precipitation in store." Thanks, Nose.

Due to the shitty weather, the Three Jacks and Habana Boat both closed, and were lights out, by one thirty. At two thirty, I sent Tangles out to his spot on the east side of the Ocean Avenue Bridge. I gave him a fishing rod for cover, just in case. At quarter to three, the rest of us left the boat. I transferred the gear from my trunk to the back of Hambone's pickup, and noticed the five-gallon can of diesel in the back, briefly wondering if we would be using it. The guys piled into Hambone's pickup, and they crept across the parking lot. He parked on the side of the road at the end of the canal, near the *C-LOVE*. He had one of his charter signs there, and occasionally left his truck parked under it all night after drinking too much. Nobody would think twice, seeing his truck there, no matter what the time.

Holly and I drove over in her car, and she jumped out and unlocked the office. She hurried back, and said, "OK, if Tangles or I spot anybody coming, you can hide in the office if you need to. Good luck...and be careful." She gave me a quick kiss and I got out. Then she drove around the corner to her position, behind a paint store near the corner of Ocean Avenue and U.S.1. I walked over to Hambone's truck, and looked around. It was dark and drizzling, and only a couple of lights were turned on in the condos overlooking the marina...*good*. The guys were leaning on the side of the truck, in the shadows. As I approached, my walkie-talkie beeped, indicating a transmission was incoming.

It was Tangles. "Kit, there's a car coming over the bridge heading west, but it's not a cop." Click.

"OK, you're loud and clear, thanks. Holly, you hear that?"

"Yes, clear on my end too."

"Alrighy then, it looks as good as it's gonna get, so let's do this."

They both radioed back, "Good luck."

I said to the guys, "Let's do some digging and then get the hell out of here, what do you say?"

"I can dig it," deadpanned Kodak. *Everybody thinks they're a freaking comedian lately...Jesus.* After a collective groan at the lame joke, we all grabbed shovels and walked over to the tiki hut, where the Jet Ski rental place was.

I also grabbed the tarp, and said, "If we have to run to the office, drop the shovels on the tarp so I can cover them up, got it?" I pointed to the tarp that I spread out on the ground next to the tiki hut.

Everybody said, "OK," and Hambone asked, "Where do we start?"

"Let's start at the corner of the canal, and work our way toward the tiki hut, It's gotta be right there somewhere. Remember to throw all the dirt in the canal."

The four of us began digging...and it was a *bitch*. Although the ground appeared to be dirt, it was actually loaded with gravel, and hard to get through. After ten minutes, my injured arm was aching, and I hadn't made a whole lot of progress. "How's it going?" I whispered.

Eight-Toe replied, "If this don't get easier, we're in trouble."

"Shut up and keep digging, I just hit sand," grumbled Kodak. Encouraged by the news that Kodak broke through to a layer of sand, we all started digging harder. Sure enough, within a few minutes everybody was having an easier go of it, as the gravel and rock gave way to sand.

After ten more minutes, Eight-Toe asked, "How deep are these tanks supposed to be? I'm almost four feet down, and it's just more and more sand."

"The map didn't indicate how deep they were, just where they were."

"If they're more than five feet down, it's gonna get dicey."

My radio sounded and Holly came on. "Kit, a car just turned onto Ocean, watch out." I had everybody drop their shovels on the tarp, and duck down behind the tiki hut. We watched as the car passed over the bridge to Ocean Ridge, then got back to work. It was almost three thirty, and we had a decent trench dug up from the corner of the canal, halfway to the tiki hut.

"OK, let's start digging closer to the hut. We must be just missing it," I said. Everybody bitched at having to dig through more rock. Fifteen minutes later though, we had lengthened the trench from the canal, right up to the corner of the tiki hut.

"Where the hell are these things?" complained Kodak. "I thought you said they were right here."

"They're supposed to be, Goddamn it...they're probably just a little deeper...I hope."

"Come on, guys," pleaded Hambone in a loud whisper. "We gotta find these tanks or we're screwed, now keep digging!" Hambone climbed down into the ditch, and started furiously shoveling sand over his shoulder into the canal behind him. Kodak and Eight-Toe joined him, and it was agreed I should stay topside to dispose of the sand as they tossed it on the tarp.

They were about five feet deep when my walkie-talkie crackled to life with an urgent message from Holly. "Kit! There's a police car coming in the back entrance to the marina, hide quick!"

I saw the lights of the slow-moving cop car as soon as she stopped transmitting. It was already coming across the parking lot from where the *Lucky Dog* was. *Shit.*

Hambone got out of the ditch, but the other guys were still scrambling to get out when I saw it was too late.

"Stay where you are and duck down. There's no time to run," I urged, as I ducked behind the tiki hut with Ham. The rain started to come down a little harder, and I heard one of the guys say, "Shit, this sucks!"

"Shut up and stay down, here he comes." We watched as the police car crawled by the marina office, then stop by Hambone's truck, before recognizing it, and continuing on. We worked our way around the corner of the hut as the car passed, and peered out as it turned east, and went over the bridge. *Please, no more close calls.*

My walkie-talkie went off again, and Tangles asked, "I take it he didn't see you. Still no luck with the tanks?"

"No, but we have to be getting warm, keep your eyes peeled."

The guys were already digging again, as Ham and I stepped out from behind the hut. Ham helped me dump the tarp full of wet sand in the canal, then asked Kodak to pick up his shovel, so he wouldn't land on it when he hopped back in the trench.

Eight-Toe obliged, and commented, "We go any deeper, and we'll never get out. The walls look like they could collapse any minute."

Hambone was crouched down by the ditch, and hopped in, saying, "Stop your bitch—Aaaaaghh! " He had crashed through the floor of the ditch up to his waist. "Holy shit!" he cried. "I think I'm in one of the tanks, help me out of here!"

Kodak took a step over to grab his arms, and he crashed through the muck bottom too. "Fuck! Oh shit! Do you smell it? That's some kinda gas...We're standing in gas. Come on, help us get the hell out of here!"

"Quiet!" said Eight-Toe. "Somebody's gonna hear you."

"Help me out and then I'll gladly shut the fuck up," he hissed. "I'm getting some serious fumes down here. Shit! Do something."

"Don't move Eight-Toe," I yelled down. "We don't need you stuck too. Everybody stay calm for a second." I radioed Holly and told her we found the tanks, but we may have a problem getting the guys out.

"Is there a ladder in the office?" I asked.

"I think so...in the back, by the bathroom...in the corner. Hurry, Kit."

I ran through the rain to the office and slipped inside, working my way to the back. I pulled out my Surefire flashlight and clicked it on low, then cupped a hand around the beam to diffuse it. I knocked over a mop bucket with my foot, and stopped dead in my tracks as it clanged across the floor. *Shit, that was loud.* I finally made it to the back of the office, and found a six-foot ladder propped up in the corner. *Yes!* I turned off the flashlight, and carefully made my way back to the door. I gave a quick look around, and then carried the ladder over to the trench with my good arm.

As soon as I appeared, Kodak nervously urged me on. "Hurry up, man, this fucking hole's starting to fill up with water."

He was right, it sure as shit was, and the rain was coming down even harder. I had Eight-Toe lie on his stomach to help distribute his weight, and he was able to slowly pull Kodak up until he was back on the floor of the trench. I dropped the ladder into the hole at the end of the trench closest to the tiki hut, and they both climbed out, bringing the shovels with them.

"Don't forget about me, guys," said a concerned Hambone. "I'm just stuck here in a gas tank at the bottom of a trench, in the mud and rain, having a good old time...Now get me out of here!"

Since Kodak crashed through the floor right next to Hambone, there was no way to extract him from inside the trench.

"Shit," said Eight-Toe. "I'm tired of lying down in the mud, but if you guys hold me by the legs, I might be able to lean over the edge and haul him up." Only Eight-Toe Earl, the shark fisherman, had the upper body strength to even consider lifting a two-hundred-and-sixty-pound man from a prone position. He was a little over six feet tall, but had the chest and arms of an NFL linebacker. Eight-Toe laid back down, with his head and arms hanging over the trench, and said, "Somebody hand me the ladder, I'll try to get it wedged into the hole next to Ham. I think I can lift him up enough so that he can get on it."

I grabbed the ladder, and walked it down the trench to him. "Here you go, Earl."

He said, "OK...Kodak, you got me by the feet good, right?"

"Yeah I got you, let's get going before this trench collapses and takes us with it."

"Here we go, then." I was holding Kodak, and he was holding Eight-Toe, who leaned into the trench so that his entire torso was dangling over the side. He maneuvered the ladder in the hole next to Ham, while Ham reached over and helped wedge it in place. He got it so the top of the ladder was about three feet above the trench floor.

"The ladder seems stable," said Hambone. We pulled Eight-Toe back up, got him repositioned over Hambone, and eased him back down. The rain kept coming and the ground turned to mud, making it difficult to get any traction.

"All right, guys," strained Eight-Toe. "I got Ham by the hands and I'm about to lift, don't let me go." Kodak was lying down behind Eight-Toe and holding his feet. I sat in the mud with my feet dug in, holding onto Kodak's feet.

"We're ready, let's go," I urged. With a mighty heave that caused my feet to burrow even farther in the mud, Eight-Toe let out a cry of exertion as he hoisted Hambone out of the buried tank, and onto the ladder.

I saw Hambone's head appear just below the edge of the trench. "That's it, now help me out, the fumes are getting to me."

Hambone reached his arms up just over the edge, and as we pulled Eight-Toe backward, some of the side collapsed around him. "Shit!" he cried. "The ground's starting to give way. We gotta get him out quick!"

The rain was relentlessly steady and hard, coming straight down on us. We were covered in mud as we reset our human chain to extract Hambone. As Hambone scrabbled his legs against the side of the trench, Eight-Toe pulled him out, using Kodak and me as his anchor.

We were on our knees, and breathing heavy, when my walkie-talkie alerted again. I crawled over and lifted the corner of the tarp where I hid it from the rain, just as the transmission came from Tangles. "Police car coming over the bridge toward you."

Everybody heard it, and I said, "Stay on your knees, follow me behind the tiki hut." I scrambled the ten feet or so to the hut, hearing the slapping and sloshing sounds of three grown men doing the same thing behind me. We crowded behind the tiki hut and watched the headlights pass the entrance to the marina. I lit up the dial on my watch, and saw that it was four fifteen in the morning.

I looked at the guys with a smile. "Boys...we did it, now we just have to get the ladder out, and skedaddle. Anybody got a gaff or something we can pull that ladder out with?"

"I have one in the back of the truck," responded Hambone. "While I get it, why don't you guys hose off so you don't trash my truck? You can use the one by the cleaning table." He pointed at the cleaning table about twenty feet away, and then ran over to his truck, while Kodak and Eight-Toe ran to the cleaning table.

I picked up the walkie-talkie and spoke. "Tangles, head back to the boat, we're done here, mission accomplished."

My next transmission was to Holly. "Holly, you heard that, right? We did it, meet you at the boat, take the back way."

Hambone was back with his gaff, and bellied up to the side of the trench, before reaching down and hooking the ladder. As he pulled it up, I grabbed the top of the ladder and hauled it out. "Nice work, Ham. Now hose yourself off and get out of here. I'm throwing the shovels, tarp, and ladder in the back of your truck. You can keep them as souvenirs."

"Like I'm gonna have trouble remembering the last couple of nights? Please, I just wanna go home and take a hot shower."

Kodak and Eight-Toe were piled into the cab of Hambone's F-150, and I quickly loaded the bed with the gear, and covered it with the tarp. Hambone had hosed off, and as he opened the driver's door and got in, I whispered, "Great work, guys. See you later."

They drove away, and I dashed to the cleaning table and quickly hosed myself off. I locked the door to the marina office, and when I turned to go, there was Tangles, startling me. "Christ, you almost gave me a heart attack, sneaking up like that."

"I'm fucking soaked, I had get out of the rain."

"Well, come on, let's get back to the boat."

"Did you dump some diesel in the hole?"

"Didn't need to, it already reeks." We jogged across the empty parking lot, and found Holly's Jeep parked next to my Beemer.

I told Tangles, "I'll see you on the boat after I talk to Holly." He scampered into the cockpit and disappeared into the cabin, as I climbed into the passenger side of the Jeep. Before I could do or say anything, Holly leaned over and hugged me tight.

"I can't believe you did it, I was getting worried after I didn't hear from you." She kissed me hard on the lips, and I reciprocated, until my left arm got pressed against the seat. I pulled away with an "Ow!" massaging it with my right hand.

"Oh, your arm, I forgot...how is it?"

"It's not too bad, the other guys did most of the heavy work." I filled her in on how Hambone and Kodak fell through the floor of the ditch, into the rusted-out diesel tanks, and then how we got them out.

"I never thought about that happening. Thank God nobody got hurt."

"Me neither, plus with all this rain, the sides started to cave in. We got lucky on a number of fronts."

"What do we do now?"

Even though I was exhausted, soaked, and muddy, I briefly thought about how nice she smelled and... and then I looked at my watch, and saw it was four thirty in the morning.

"Now? Now you go home and take care of Millie, while I crash on the boat. I need to get up in a few hours and make sure someone calls in the authorities. Otherwise, all our efforts could go to waste."

The rain was still beating down on the windshield, and a parking lot light faintly illuminated her face. She quietly said," Thank you, thank you for everything, I never thought you'd be in harm's way, or have to go to the lengths you have to help us save the marina. I owe you so much, I can't even begin to think how I can repay you."

"You can start by driving yourself home and resting up, you'll need all your strength come repayment time. You have no idea what lengths I still have left." I leaned over and kissed her, before opening the door and getting out.

She laughed. "Is that a promise or a threat?"

"It's a plan, plan C."

"Plan C?"

I ducked my head back in the car. "Yeah, just you wait and see." I winked and shut the door, stepping back onto the dock. As she backed out, I could see her teeth sparkle when the streetlight briefly shone on her face...she was smiling.

Chapter 85

The rain slowed to a drizzle about six thirty Sunday morning, after coming down hard all night. It was still overcast and generally crappy, but that wouldn't stop the *C-LOVE* from going out, unless there weren't enough customers. The first of the *C-LOVE* team to show up was Regina, Captain Bart's girlfriend, who handled ticket sales. She parked in the new public parking garage, and ran through the rain up to the C-LOVE Marina building that housed the ticket office. As she stood under the canopy, fishing through her purse for the office key, she glanced up and noticed something different. *What is that by the Jet Ski rental hut?*

She opened the office door, and set her purse on a chair, then stepped back outside to investigate. With the hood on her rain jacket still draped over her head, she walked toward the tiki hut, and stopped about five feet away. "Holy Toledo," she mumbled to herself. She was looking at a large hole in the earth. It ran from the seawall, to the tiki hut. It was at least eight feet wide in places, and maybe fifteen feet long. She baby-stepped forward with trepidation, trying to peer down into the hole to gauge its depth. When she got about two feet away, she could see that the sides gently sloped toward the middle, where there was a more pronounced ledge. From the ledge it looked like it was about a five- or six-foot drop to the bottom, which was filled with water. *What the heck happened here?* Unsure of what to do, or who to call, she started walking back to the office, and spotted Robo coming out the garage.

"Robo! Come take a look at this." She waved him over, and he joined her under the office canopy.

"What's going on, Regina?" he asked.

"Look at this over here." She walked back toward the hole, pointing with her finger as Robo followed. "Don't step too close to the edge—the ground's soft, and it looks like it's collapsing with all the rain."

As Robo got his first good look of the gaping hole, in what little early morning light there was, he let out a low whistle. "Holy Matrimony," he commented, as he sized it up. "This just happened?"

"Well I can tell you it wasn't here yesterday. I noticed it as I was opening up the office. What should I do?"

Robo inched a little closer, and leaned his head forward, taking a big sniff. "Do you smell that? It smells like gas." He took another deep breath, and said, "Diesel fumes...I think." He crouched a little, and looked hard at the water in the bottom of the hole. He was eyeing what appeared to be a little slick on the surface.

Regina followed his lead, and took a big sniff as well. "Oh yeah, I smell it now, that's not good...is it?"

Robo's mind was racing. This was the kind of thing he studied about, and trained for, in order to obtain his dockmaster's certification. "No it's not good at all. You should call the fire department right now. This is dangerous. Somebody could fall in, or inadvertently toss a cigarette in, and KABOOM!"

He threw his hands in the air for dramatic effect, and Regina said, "I'm on it."

As Regina ran to the office and called the fire department, Robo walked around on the Habana Boat side of the canal. He saw that a couple of Jet Skis had some mud on the handlebars. *That's odd.* Then he looked at the water outside the sea wall where the mysterious hole had formed, and noticed the water had a filmy layer of oil, or fuel on top. It wasn't unusual to see a little fuel slick in a marina, but new environmental regulations required even the smallest of spills be reported. Was it just a little spillage from the drift boat? Or maybe one of the Jet Skis? Or was it fuel from the mysterious hole that was leaking into the canal?

He mulled it over as he walked to the fuel dock, unlocked the door to the small office, and sat down at his desk. He picked up the phone, and briefly wondered whether he should make the call or not. Technically, the C-LOVE Marina wasn't his responsibility, but technically, he was also a certified dockmaster, and shouldn't look the other way. He looked at the list of emergency numbers he had posted on the side of the computer, and dialed the Coast Guard. *Better safe than sorry.* After hanging up, he spun through his Rolodex until he found the other number he wanted, and dialed the EPA.

Chapter 86

I didn't wake up until a little after nine. I thought I had set the alarm on my Timex to wake me at seven, but I either forgot to set it, or fell back asleep after turning it off. Tangles was still sleeping on the couch when I stepped up to the galley, and pulled a bottle of water out of the fridge. *Man, what a night...what a couple of nights, in fact.* I brushed my teeth and put some clothes on, throwing everything I wore the night before in a garbage bag. Tangles stirred to life, and I said, "I'm gonna go see if anything's happened yet."

"Hang on." He yawned. "I'll join you." I looked out the window as Tangles got dressed, and noticed it had stopped raining. Granted, the sky still looked like Cleveland in February, but this was South Florida—it wouldn't stay that way for long.

"You ready yet?" I asked.

"Yep, let's go see if anybody noticed anything."

"If they didn't, we need to make damn sure they do. Come on."

We left the boat, and as soon as we came in view of the C-LOVE Marina, we saw the aftermath of our digathon. I slowed my walk down, and stuck my arm in front of Tangles, saying, "Ho-Lee-Christ-On-A-Crutch."

Coast Guard and Marine Patrol boats were blocking the end of the canal, with their lights flashing. Parked in the road by the Jet Ski place, we could see fire trucks and police cars.

"I think they noticed," said Tangles.

We casually walked over, milling our way through all the onlookers. I asked a stranger what happened. "Looks like the ground just opened up. The fire department says there's some kind of fuel tanks buried at the bottom, that's what all that foam is about."

"Fuel tanks? No kidding? That's serious."

Tangles punched me in the thigh, as the stranger pointed his finger toward some type of government car with a flasher on the dash. "No kidding its serious, there's a Homeland Security vehicle over there too. Guess they're making sure it isn't some kind of al-Qaeda plot."

"Wow, thanks." We made our way to a point where we could see better, and when I got my first good look at the trench, I whispered to Tangles. "Jesus! Look how big it is!"

He poked his head between a couple of gawkers, and whispered back, "Man, you guys really went to town."

I held my forefinger perpendicular to my lips, the universal sign for *shut the fuck up*. With my other hand I grabbed his shoulder, and escorted him away from the hole. When we were out of earshot of the crowd, I released my grip. "Dude, watch what you say."

"Sorry, I guess I was just surprised how much you dug up."

"Are you kidding me? So am I. I mean...we didn't dig up *that* much. The trench we left was only about three feet wide, five feet deep, and maybe ten to twelve feet long. That hole's at least twice as big. I guess we got out of there just in time, looks like the sides collapsed."

"Yeah, but it looks like it worked, looks like they think the rain caused it."

"So far so good, but did you notice the Jet Skis?"

"The Jet Skis? No, why?"

"Two of them had some mud on the handlebars, we must have accidentally shoveled some dirt on them."

"You think anybody will notice?"

"I did. The question is will anybody else? Hopefully not."

Chapter 87

Tangles and I went back to the *Lucky Dog*. Once we were in the cabin, I said, "Hambone and I are gonna go pick up the raft and get rid of it. Then I'm gonna go over to Milfred's and fill them in, even though somebody's probably called by now. Why don't you mosey on down to the fuel dock, and keep your ears open for any news about our missing neighbors. If anybody asks, tell them their boat was gone when you got back from your date. I'll corroborate it by saying that when I came back from the captain's meeting, it was gone. That's the story."

"OK, boss."

"If you have anything that needs washing, throw it in that garbage bag." I pointed to the bag that had all my muddy clothes in it. "I'm gonna try to squeeze in some laundry time if I can." He stuffed his Kid Rock T-shirt and a couple of pairs of shorts in the bag, and I headed to Millie's.

Twelve stories above the *Lucky Dog*, Kristy Kane untangled herself from Sonny's grasp, and padded across the bedroom floor in her bare feet. She put on her robe, and opened the door to the living room to be greeted by Mr. Jenks, his tail wagging. She couldn't believe she actually let Sonny spend the night at her place. *With his dog no less.* In a moment of weakness, she had relented, realizing he was too drunk to drive. He seemed to take the postponement of the fishing tournament hard, too hard, for some unknown reason. Why was he so upset about not having a stupid fishing tournament, when in a couple of days he was going to own the C-LOVE Marina? Something wasn't right, and she planned to find out what. After pouring herself a glass of orange juice, she walked over to the floor-to-ceiling window to take in the spectacular view. She looked out at the ocean, and then down toward the Three Jacks and the C-LOVE Marina. *What the hell's going on down there?*

Sonny came out of the bedroom in his leopard print bikini underwear. "What's up, toots?"

He walked up behind her, and reached his arms around to give her a hug, but she swatted them away. "Not now. Look down there, look at all the fire trucks and police. The canal is even blocked by the Coast Guard. I wonder what's going on."

Sonny stepped out from behind her, and looked down. "What the hell? What's that big pile of foam there at the end of the canal by the Jet Ski place?"

"How would I know? Let's go find out."

They got dressed, and ten minutes later walked up to where the police had taped off a restricted area. Kristy recognized one of the young cops posted there. "Hi, Joey, what's going on here?"

"Oh, hi, Miss Kane. It looks like a sinkhole opened up, and there's a couple of old diesel tanks buried at the bottom."

"Diesel tanks?"

"Yes, ma'am, chief says they've probably been down there a long time. It's going to be a bear of a cleanup, that's for sure."

"Cleanup?" asked Sonny.

"You bet, chief says it's gonna cost the owner a pretty penny to get them dug out...you know...with all the EPA regulations and stuff."

"EPA?" Sonny started feeling uneasy.

"Oh yeah, they'll be out here tomorrow morning. There's some worry the tanks are leaking into the canal, if that's the case the canal might be closed for a while."

Sonny looked at Kristy. "I um, I gotta go, I gotta make a call...I'll talk to you later...come on, Mr. Jenks."

Kristy just stood there, watching him walk down the dock toward Three Jacks with his dog in tow. She was trying to calculate the ramifications of the buried tanks. It would likely mean the marina closing would be delayed, but it wouldn't kill the deal. *Would it?* The young cop noticed her standing there, lost in thought. "You all right, Miss Kane?"

"Huh? What? Yes...yes of course, I'm fine. Thanks for filling us in, Joey, I'll see you around City Hall." He tipped his hat, and smiled as he watched her walk toward the tall condo building. *Baby got back.*

Sonny was halfway down the dock when he pulled out his cell and called his dad, only to find out from his mom that he was golfing. He tried his dad's cell number, but was kicked to voice mail. "Dad, it's Sonny, listen, call me as soon as you get this message. There's a problem with the C-LOVE Marina...call me."

* * *

I called Holly's cell number on my way over to Millie's, and she answered with a sleepy, "hell-hello? Kit? Is that you?"

"I'm glad I'm not the only one who's tired today."

"I'm just waking up. What time is it?"

"Almost quarter to ten, it's not too early for me to come over and bring you up to speed, is it?"

"What? No, what happened?"

"I'll be there in about five minutes, can you wait?"

"Sure, I'll leave the kitchen door unlocked. I'm jumping in the shower, give me ten minutes."

"Need some help scrubbing your back?"

"Hah, hah, hah...I'll see you in ten minutes." Click.

A few minutes later I let myself into the kitchen, and opened the fridge. It's not something I would normally do, but neither is getting into a shootout with a gangster or digging large holes in the middle of the night. I discovered those types of activities can make you very hungry.

I sized up some bacon and eggs, and briefly thought about throwing them in a skillet, but decided to wait for Holly.

A few minutes later she came walking in, wearing a pair of jeans shorts, and a tank top, toweling her hair dry. *Man she looked good...per usual.*

"I thought you would have some breakfast cooking already. What...you're not hungry?" she asked.

"You know maybe I *could* go for a little something, if you were planning on whipping up some vittles anyways."

She shot me a *gimme a break* kind of look. "Vittles? I bet you'd like that. How 'bout you talk, while I cook."

"Deal. Is Millie up? She needs to know what's going on."

"Let me check." She kept towel drying her hair as she went to Millie's bedroom, and returned a minute later working a comb through it. "She just woke up a little while ago. The nurse is going to bring her out in a few minutes, I'll get breakfast started." As she opened the fridge and placed some bacon and eggs on the counter, she noticed the light blinking on Millie's landline phone.

She pressed the message button, and we heard Regina's voice calling from the C-LOVE Marina office. "Holly? Milfred? It's Regina, I'm at the office. There's a big sinkhole with gas in it by the Jet Ski rentals, and there's police, and fire trucks, and Coast Guard all over the place. Call me, thanks. Oh, and Milfred? I hope you're feeling better, bye."

Holly looked at me. "Is that what you wanted to fill us in on?"

"Pretty much. She forgot to mention the Marine Patrol and Homeland Security though."

"Are you serious?"

"Yep, the entire end of the canal is covered in some type of foam, it's unbelievable."

"That's good though, right? It sounds like they think it's a sinkhole."

"Yeah, so far so—"

"Kit, your arm! It looks like it's bleeding again." She stepped in front of me and gently lifted my left arm, which was still semi-muddy. It did indeed look like it was bleeding through the bandage. "We've got to get you cleaned up and re-bandaged. Why don't you take a shower while I make breakfast?"

"I'm sorry, I should have showered before coming over, I got caught up in all the excitement at the marina. I must really look skeevy."

"You're definitely not ready for a GQ shoot, but considering what you did last night, you're forgiven. Come on, I'll show you where the spare towels are."

Fifteen minutes later I was freshly showered, and Holly was putting the final touches on my new bandage while the eggs cooked.

"Ta-da," she said. "That looks so much better...so do you, by the way."

"Thanks...I guess...you're not so bad yourself."

"Wow, you're a real charmer."

I couldn't take it anymore, and pulled her to me with my good arm, kissing her on the lips. She was kissing me back, with one hand on my chest, and the other wrapped around my neck, when—"Ahem, ahem." Millie coughed. *Millie? Oh shit.* We pulled apart, and Holly turned beet red as we turned to face Millie and her nurse, standing in the hallway.

Millie shook her head and giggled. "You'd think with two of you in the kitchen, one might notice the eggs burning. If you hadn't cooked the bacon first, the house would be on fire. Wow! That was some kiss."

Holly quickly took the eggs off the burner. "Millie, stop it! I um, I'm sorry, I—"

"Oh hush, sweetie, it's OK. It's nothing I haven't seen or done myself. I was your age *once* you know." Millie's nurse had her by one arm, and with her other arm she used a cane to hobble to the kitchen table, and sit down. "I was wondering how long it would take for you two to—"

"MILLIE!"

"OK, OK, I'll zip it."

"How many strips of bacon do you want?"

"Two, it takes two to tango, you know...now what happened at the marina?"

Chapter 88

Mayor Vincent Mandula and his wife were on their way home from nine o'clock mass, when they saw all the flashing lights at the marina entrance. He pulled out his cell and called police dispatch. The dispatcher filled him in on the sinkhole, and the discovery of the buried fuel tanks.

"Whose property are they on?" he asked.

"According to the fire chief, they're on the C-LOVE Marina's property. They're buried by the Jet Ski rental place, at the southwest corner of the canal."

"Thanks, Dee Dee." Click.

"What's going on, honey?" inquired the mayor's wife.

"A sinkhole opened up at the end of the canal, next to the *C-LOVE*, and there's some buried fuel tanks at the bottom."

"Didn't you tell me that place just got sold?"

"Yes, but it hasn't closed yet. I think it's supposed to happen this week. You know, I should find out for sure." He pulled into his drive in Boynton Isles, and after letting his wife in the front door, he scrolled his cell phone for Kristy Kane's number. He found it and dialed.

After a few moments, Kristy answered. "Hello?"

"Miss Kane, it's me, Vince. You see what's happening down at the C-LOVE Marina?"

"Couldn't miss it if I tried. It spoiled my view this morning, what a mess."

"I guess so. Isn't Slade supposed to close on it this week?"

"On Tuesday."

"Tuesday? Shit. That could be a problem, don't you think?"

"I imagine they'll just extend the closing, but who knows? I thought you wanted to kill the deal though. Why are you worried about it closing?

"Oh, um, I'm not worried about the closing," he lied. "I'm um, just concerned about the environmental impact."

Kristy pulled the phone away from her ear, and looked at it like she had never seen one before. *What bullshit!* "Yes, well, somebody's gonna be stuck with a big cleanup bill, that's for sure."

"No doubt. I'll talk to you later, thanks." Click.

Kristy stood in front of her condo window, looking down at all the activity around the marina, and wondered what the mayor was up to. He should have been ecstatic there was an unexpected glitch in the marina sale. It might be an opportunity for the city to step in...but he was just the opposite...hmmm.

Tangles moseyed down to the fuel docks per Kit's suggestion, and was greeted by Robo. "Good morning, did all the sirens wake you up?" Robo knew that Tangles was staying on the *Lucky Dog*, but looked the other way. He liked Kit, and had to admit the little guy was growing on him too.

"Yeah, it's quite a mess. You checked it out, I'm sure."

"Why do you think the Coast Guard's there?"

"Seems like everyone with a flashing light is there."

"Wait till tomorrow, it'll be worse."

"Tomorrow? Why?"

"Tomorrow the EPA will be here. They love this stuff."

"Thank God the *Lucky Dog* isn't on that canal, we'd be screwed."

"You better believe it. By the way, I noticed the boat that was in the slip next to you is gone. They weren't here yesterday either. Did you happen to see them leave?"

"No, they were gone Friday night when I got back from a date. Why? They skip out on some dock rent or something?"

"No, just the opposite, they're paid for another week. It's just odd they left without letting me know."

"Maybe they went somewhere for the weekend, and they'll be back."

"Yeah, maybe, but I don't know. Slip renters usually let me know if they're going somewhere. To be truthful though, it wouldn't bother me if I never saw those two again. There was definitely something shady going on with them. Did you notice anything suspicious?"

"Huh? Me? No, no, they kept to themselves."

"That's what I mean, they were hiding something. I just know it."

Skeeter came walking around the corner. "Who's hiding something?"

Robo wasn't a big fan of Skeeter's, and even less so of his roommate, Ratdog. He reminded him, by replying, "Nobody was talking to you, what do you want?"

"I was wondering if anybody's seen Ratdog. He didn't come home Friday night, and I haven't seen him since."

"Lucky you." Robo *really* didn't like Ratdog.

"I'm serious, he's gone...didn't take anything with him either. What about you, shorty? You seen him?"

Tangles didn't take kindly to scrawny punks calling him shorty, and he let it be known. "No, I haven't seen him, but what I do see is me kicking your ass up and down these docks if you call me shorty again... got it?"

Skeeter had him by a foot and a half, but was only about twenty pounds heavier...*maybe.* One thing was for certain, he didn't want to test him, and apologized.

"Sorry about that, I'm just worried something happened to him."

Robo jumped back in. "When did you say he didn't come home? Friday night? That's when the boat that's been staying here for the last few weeks left without notice. You know...the one that Ratdog was getting paid to keep an eye on? The one named, *The Job?*"

"What, you think he went with them?"

"Your guess is as good as mine, but neither one's been seen since Friday."

"Nah, he wouldn't go away for a couple of days without letting me know, I'm his roommate."

"You sure?"

"Yeah I'm sure. We been living together for six months."

"No, dumbass. You sure he wouldn't leave without telling you? Maybe they hired him to mate for the weekend, and they'll be back today...or tomorrow."

"You think? Without saying anything? He's not answering his cell either. I've left him a couple of messages."

"Maybe they're out of cell range down in the Keys or something. What can I tell you?"

"I don't get it. Something's not right."

"You can file a missing person's report with the police, if that's what you think."

"If I don't hear from him by tomorrow morning, I will. If you happen to see or hear from him, let me know, OK?"

"OK."

Skeeter went walking down the dock, and Robo turned back to face Tangles. "So Ratdog's gone too... what do you make of *that*, Tangles?"

Tangles looked down at a dead fiddler crab next to his foot on the dock, and instinctively kicked it in the intracoastal. As he watched the crab slowly sink into the murky current, he nodded. "Like you said, they're probably out on the water somewhere. That'd be my guess too."

Per Kit's suggestion, Millie called her attorney and told him what happened. He said, "So *that's* what all those fire trucks were doing at the marina. I saw them on my way home from church."

"I guess it's quite a mess, but we're still closing on Tuesday...right?"

"Seriously? I doubt it. Tomorrow morning I've got to notify the buyer's attorney, as well as their lender, about the fuel tank issue. No way is the bank going to close without knowing the extent of the environmental impact, not to mention the cost."

"What about the deposit? They guaranteed me they would close on Tuesday." "I know, but that was before this environmental problem came up. I'm sure they still want to close, but they'll need more time."

"Too bad, I'm not giving them any more time. They don't close Tuesday, they don't close at all, that's the deal."

"What?"

"You heard me, Bob. A deal's a deal. Besides, I gave them plenty of time to conduct all their high-falutin' tests."

"True, but they obviously missed a spot."

"That's their tough luck. You let them know if they don't close Tuesday, the deal's dead and the deposit's mine...end of story."

"You sure? It might not be easy to find another buyer with eight million dollars, and you'll be stuck with the cleanup costs too."

"That's my problem, but at least I'll be using their money to clean it up...right?"

Bob Boone had been Milfred's attorney for a long time, and it struck him as odd that she was jumping at a chance to kill the deal. Her health was deteriorating, and she told him she wanted to get her estate in order. Had something changed? "Yes, you'll be using their money *when* you get it, but they'll probably fight it in court. It may be tied up for a while."

"But in the end, I'll get it, right? The contract is very clear."

"Yes, you'll get it, unless..."

"Unless what?"

"Don't take this wrong way, Milfred, but as your attorney, I have to ask, because it will be sure to come up. You didn't know these tanks were buried there, *did you?*"

"I had no idea. Why I'm as surprised as anybody... *who knew?*"

"For the record, I'll take that as a no. I'll let you know what happens."

"Thanks, Bob."

"Hope you're feeling better, Milfred, bye." Click. He just sat there for a few moments and looked at his phone suspiciously. *Who knew?* Something about the way she said it made it very clear...*she knew*. Was it just coincidence a sinkhole opened up and exposed some fuel tanks two days before closing? Doubtful. He knew her to be a shrewd operator, but this? One thing was for sure, the buyer was gonna go ape shit when he found out there would be no extension. *God, he loved being a lawyer.*

Chapter 89

There was a big party on the dock Tuesday evening, when word spread that Slade's deal to buy the C-LOVE Marina was dead. There were a lot of people saying, "God works in mysterious ways," when referring to the sinkhole. So far, nobody suspected it was the work of some desperate slip holders and an old lady with seller's remorse. The next night, Holly invited all the conspirators over to Millie's for a celebratory dinner.

Tangles and I arrived on the *Lucky Dog*, and Hambone brought Eight-Toe and Kodak over on the *Ham it Up*. Hambone announced on arrival that Sonny Slade had been shipped off somewhere to work at another of his dad's restaurants. Word on the dock was Sonny owed somebody a lot of money, and old Syd had to bail him out again. I remembered Robo telling me about the briefcase exchange between Gino and Sonny. *Was it full of money?* Why would Sonny be borrowing money from Gino though? Did it matter? Not to Gino anymore, that was for sure.

For dinner, Kodak supplied freshly caught lobster, and Holly offered up steaks with all the trimmings. It was quite a feast. Millie wasn't feeling well, but appeared long enough to tell the guys that their slip fees for the rest of the year were comped. The guys were ecstatic, and Hambone did a cartwheel across the deck, to everyone's delight. That was the signal that it was time for Ham and company to get back to the marina. Since I had plans to take Holly out on the *Lucky Dog* the next day, Tangles went back with Hambone too.

After they left, Holly said, "Millie wanted me to tell you that she wants to do something special for you and Tangles. She didn't want you to think she forgot."

"She doesn't have to do anything, not having Slade own the marina is reward enough."

Holly had a hand on her delectable hip, and sounding coyly disappointed, asked, "So you don't want anything? *Anything at all?*"

I didn't need any encouragement after weeks of near-misses, and grabbed her hand, pulling her into a passionate kiss. She reached her hands up around my neck, and pressed her firmness against me, causing my blood pressure, and shorts, to spike. She pulled away long enough to whisper in my ear, "Let's go on the boat."

I realized we were standing on the deck in the moonlight, probably giving the neighbors across the canal a show. *Sorry folks, show's over.*

I took her hand, and led her on to the *Lucky Dog*. We ended up in the forward berth, somehow managing to remove our clothes without taking our lips off one another. Our lovemaking was beyond intense. There were more sparks than a shuttle launch, and the finish was like reentering the atmosphere at mach fifty. It was like nothing I had experienced before, and as I lay beside Holly with her head on my chest, my heart felt like it was fibrillating. I was the first to break the post-lovemaking silence with a romantic, "Holy shit."

I think Holly felt my ventricular palpitations too, and asked, "Are you all right?"

I took several deep breaths before answering. "All right?" (Breath)..."Are you kidding me?" (Double breath)..."Never been better...you?" (Triple breath).

"That was fantastic, I'm glad we waited."

"Not intentionally, at least on my end. You've been driving me crazy."

"It's not a very long drive, is it?" She laughed and started kissing me again. The only sounds were her beautiful wet lips tasting mine, and the gentle slap of water against the hull. That's when I heard the faint sound of an odd ringtone.

I gently pushed her away. "Do you hear that?"

She scrunched her facial muscles together, and pointed at the closet. "I think it's coming from there."

I scooched to the foot of the bed, and opened the closet door, just as the last ringtone sound faded away. I flicked on the light, and there on the closet floor was a cell phone. I knew it wasn't mine or Tangles', and held it up for her to see. "This isn't yours...*is it?*"

"No...it's not mine, and besides, what would it be doing on your closet floor?"

"Good point." I flipped the phone open and noticed it was very low on battery power. I scrolled through the recent calls list, and saw several calls from the same number. A number I recognized as being Melody's. *What the fuck?* Holly noticed the look on my face.

"What? What is it?"

"I...I'm not sure...wait." I saw the phone had some messages on it, and pressed the voice mail button.

After a few seconds, the last message that was left on it started playing. "Ratdog? How come you're not returning my calls? Just let me know if you got the bananas planted, call me." The hair on my arms stood up, as Melody's voice cut off. *Melody? Are you shitting me?* Melody had Ratdog plant the bananas on my boat? *You think you know somebody...* "Son of a bitch!"

Chapter 90

The next morning ushered in the start of another beautiful day. Holly and I were on our third drift, in a hundred feet of water, when the *C-LOVE* set up about a hundred and fifty yards off our port side. I grabbed my binoculars, just for shits and grins, to see if Tangles was working. I scanned the deck, and sure enough, there was Tangles, baiting some guy's hook. *Huh?* I adjusted the focus and was shocked to see it was Rudy, the bartender from the chikee hut at the Ole House. He and Tangles seemed to be laughing and talking to each other. *Since when did Rudy fish? Since when did they start getting friendly? Was Rudy planning on telling Tangles he might be his father?*

I had all kinds of questions swirling in my mind, when Holly asked, "Are you gonna fish or bird-watch all day?"

"Depends—if you were a bird, I'd definitely be watching."

I put the binoculars down and kissed her for longer than I should...until the *C-LOVE*'s horn tooted. We waved at the big drift boat, and then Holly took on a serious tone. "Kit, I'm so happy...for the first time in forever...I don't want this to end. I'm worried about Millie too...and what happened out there." She was pointing out to sea.

461

"Me too. I'm wondering what happened to the boat, but if it hasn't been found by now, it probably sunk."

"You think?"

"I hope so, just like this..." I pulled Ratdog's phone out of my pocket, and casually dropped it over the side. Holly and I watched it flash in the sunlight, before it disappeared into the blue. After a few moments, she looked at me. "Well...it looks like the fish stopped biting. What do you want to do?" I looked around, and out of the corner of my eye spotted a frigate bird, circling high in the sky.

I pointed up. "Look...up there...it's a frigate." It was headed out to sea, effortlessly meandering with an occasional flap of the wing, tracking the unsuspecting fish that would unwittingly provide it's next meal. The frigate bird (also known as a man-o'-war bird) is a fisherman's best friend, and always considered a good omen. *Find the frigate and you find the fish.* I thought about everything that had happened over the last few months... Almost losing my fishing show, almost getting killed, losing a girlfriend, finding a midget...and then Holly.

"Why don't we follow that frigate offshore?" she suggested. "Maybe he'll change our luck."

I said, "Good idea," as I stepped to the lower helm and steered us toward the bird, "but my luck's already changed."

She came up behind me and stuck both her hands in the pockets of my shorts, pressing into me as she breathed in my ear. "It has? Well maybe you better put us on autopilot, then come in the cabin and prove it."

I just smiled and did as I was told. *God, I love fishing.*

THE END

Epilogue

The very next day, Robo was in the fuel dock office, talking on the phone. "OK...let me be sure I got this right. You got a forty-six-foot Grand Banks, called the *JC*, coming down from Jersey City in a couple of weeks. How long do you need it for? Indefinitely? That shouldn't be a problem, we just had a slip open up unexpectedly. You only need to send me the first month's dock rent. What? OK...I'll call when I get the check, see you when you get here, thanks." Robo hung up, thinking the guy sounded like Jabba the Hut with pneumonia...on a ventilator.

Over a thousand miles away, in his back room office at the Rye Smile, Donatello DeNutzio, aka Donny Nutz, leaned forward in his chair, and hung up the phone. *Yeah, you'll see me when I get there all right.* He was missing a hit man, a heavy, and a quarter-million dollar boat. There was also the minor matter of the million and a half bucks he wouldn't be making on the marina deal. He slammed his considerable fist and forearm down on his desk, spilling a little coffee. Somebody cost him dearly, and somebody was gonna pay. *Somebody was definitely gonna pay.*

Made in the USA
Charleston, SC
14 April 2013